About the Authors

Andrea Laurence i author who has been since she learned to transplanted into t trying to develop a caring for her boyfriend and her old bulldog. contact Andrea at her website: andrealaurence.com

USA TODAY bestselling author **Jules Bennett** has penned more than fifty novels during her short career. She's married to her high school sweetheart, has two active girls, and is a former salon owner. Jules can be found on Twitter, Facebook (Fan Page), and her website julesbennett.com. She holds contests via these three outlets with each release and loves to hear from readers!

Michelle Smart is a *Publishers Weekly* bestselling author with a slight-to-severe coffee addiction. A book worm since birth, Michelle can usually be found hiding behind a paperback, or if it's an author she really loves, a hardback. Michelle lives in rural Northamptonshire in England with her husband and two young Smarties. When not reading or pretending to do the housework she loves nothing more than creating worlds of her own. Preferably with lots of coffee on tap. michelle-smart.com

Enemies to Lovers

April 2022
Trusting the Enemy

May 2022
It's Only Business

June 2022
Love, Honour and Betray

July 2022
Business to Pleasure

August 2022
Challenging her Enemy

September 2022
Consequence of their Mistrust

Enemies to Lovers:
Consequence of their Mistrust

ANDREA LAURENCE

JULES BENNETT

MICHELLE SMART

MILLS & BOON

First Published in Great Britain 2022
By Mills & Boon, an imprint of HarperCollins*Publishers,* Ltd
1 London Bridge Street, London, SE1 9GF

www.harpercollins.co.uk

HarperCollins*Publishers*
1st Floor, Watermarque Building,
Ringsend Road, Dublin 4, Ireland

ENEMIES TO LOVERS: CONSEQUENCE OF THEIR MISTRUST
© 2022 Harlequin Enterprises ULC.

Rags to Riches Baby © 2018 Andrea Laurence
Twin Secrets © 2017 Jules Bennett
Claiming His One-Night Baby © 2017 Michelle Smart

ISBN: 978-0-263-30578-4

RAGS TO RICHES BABY

ANDREA LAURENCE

To Dr Shelley—

Thanks for dusting off your MoMA catalogue and helping me navigate the modern art references for this book. I never would've found those pieces on my own. I also never expected to find myself watching a YouTube video of naked women in blue paint pressing against a canvas while a string quartet played. Your suggestions were perfect for the book! Thank you!

One

"And to Lucy Campbell, my assistant and companion, I bequeath the remainder of my estate, including the balances of my accounts and financial holdings and the whole of my personal effects, which entails my art collection and my apartment on Fifth Avenue."

When the attorney stopped reading the will of Alice Drake aloud, the room was suddenly so quiet Lucy wondered if the rest of the Drake family had dropped dead as well at the unexpected news. She kept waiting for the lawyer to crack a smile and tell the crowd of people around the conference room table that he was just kidding. It seemed highly inappropriate to do to a grieving family, though.

Surely, he had to be kidding. Lucy was no real estate expert, but Alice's apartment alone had to be worth over twenty million dollars. It overlooked the Metropolitan Museum of Art. It had four bedrooms and a gallery with a dozen important works, including an original Monet, hanging in it. Lucy couldn't afford the monthly association fees for the co-op, much less own an apartment like that in Manhattan.

"Are you serious?" a sharp voice cut through the silence at last.

Finally, someone was asking the question that was on the tip of her own tongue. Lucy turned toward the voice and realized it was her best friend Harper Drake's brother, Oliver. Harper had helped Lucy get this job working for her great-aunt, but she'd never met Harper's brother before today. Which was odd, considering she'd cared for their aunt for over five years.

It was a shame. He was one of the most handsome men she'd ever seen in real life and since he was across the conference table from her, she had a great view. Harper was a pretty woman, but the same aristocratic features on Oliver were striking in a different way. They both had the same wavy brown hair, sharp cheekbones and pointed chins, but he had the blue-gray eyes and permanently furrowed brow of their father. His lips were thinner than Harper's, but she wasn't sure if they were always like that or if they were just pressed together in irritation at the moment.

His gaze flicked over Lucy, and she felt an unexpected surge of desire run down her spine. The tingle it left in its wake made a flush rise to her cheeks and she squirmed uncomfortably in her seat. She didn't know if it was the surprising news or his heavy appraisal of her, but it was suddenly warm in the small conference room. Lucy reached for the button at the collar of her blouse and undid it as quickly as she could, drawing in a deep breath.

Unfortunately, that breath was scented with the sharp cologne of the man across from her. It teased at her nose, making the heat in her belly worsen.

It was painfully apparent that she'd spent far too many years in the company of a ninety-plus-year-old woman. One handsome man looked at her, and she got all flustered. Lucy needed to pull herself together. This was not the time to get distracted, especially when the man in question was anything but an ally. She closed her eyes for a moment and was relieved to find when she'd reopened them that Oliver had returned his focus to the attorney.

Yes, Lucy definitely would've remembered if he'd stopped by to visit. Actually, she hadn't met any of these people before Alice died and they all started showing up to the apartment. She recognized a few of them from pictures on the mantel, but they hadn't visited Alice when she was alive that Lucy was aware of. And Alice certainly hadn't gone to see them. She was ninety-three when she died and still an eccentric free spirit despite confining herself to her apartment for decades. Lucy had been drawn to her radically different beat, but not everyone would be. She'd thought perhaps Alice's family just didn't "get" her.

Judging by the stunned and angry looks on their faces, they all seemed to think they were much closer to Aunt Alice than they truly were.

"Really, Phillip. Is this some sort of a joke?" This time it was Thomas Drake, Harper and Oliver's father and Alice's nephew, who spoke. He was an older version of Oliver, with gray streaks in his hair and a distinguished-looking beard. It didn't hide his frown, however.

Phillip Glass, Alice's attorney and executor of her estate, shook his head with a grim expression on his face. He didn't look like the joking kind. "I'm sorry, but I'm very serious. I discussed this with Alice at length when she decided to make the change to her will earlier this year. I had hoped she spoke with all of you about her wishes, but apparently, that is not the case. All of you were to receive a monetary gift of fifty thousand dollars each, but she was very clear that everything else was to go to Lucy."

"She must've been suffering from dementia," a sour-looking woman Lucy didn't recognize said from the far end of the table.

"She was not!" Lucy retorted, suddenly feeling defensive where Alice was concerned. She'd had a bad heart and a fondness for good wines and cheeses, but she wasn't at all impaired mentally. Actually, for her age, she was in amazing shape up until her death.

"Of course *you* would say that!" the woman retorted with a red flush to her face. "She was obviously losing her senses when she made these changes."

"And how would you know?" Lucy snapped. "Not a one of you set foot in her apartment for the five years I've cared for her. You have no idea how she was doing. You only came sniffing around when it was time to claim your part of her estate."

The older woman clutched her pearls, apparently aghast that Lucy would speak to her that way. Lucy didn't care. She wouldn't have these people besmirching Alice after her death when they didn't know anything about how wonderful she was.

Harper reached out and gripped Lucy's forearm. "It's okay, Lucy. They're just surprised and upset at the news. They'll get over it."

"I will not get over it!" the woman continued. "I can't believe you're taking the help's side in this, Harper. She's basically stealing your inheritance right out from under you!"

"The *help*?" Harper's voice shot up an octave before Lucy could respond. The time for calm had instantly passed. "Wanda, you need to apologize right now. I will not have you speaking about my friend that way. Aunt Alice obviously felt Lucy was more than just an employee as well, so you should treat her with the same respect."

Lucy started to shut down as Alice's relatives fought amongst themselves. The last few days of her life had been hard. Finding Alice's body, dealing with the funeral and having her life upended all at once had been too much on its own. That was the risk of being a live-in employee. Losing her client meant losing her friend, her job and her home.

And now she found herself in the middle of the Drake family money battle. Lucy wasn't one for conflict to begin with, and this was the last thing she'd anticipated when she'd been asked to come today. At best, she thought perhaps Alice had left her a little money as a severance package until she could find a new job and a place to live. She had no real idea how much Alice was worth, but from the reactions of the family, she'd been left more than a little money. Like millions.

For a girl who'd grown up poor and gone to college on a scholarship and a prayer, it was all too much to take in at once. Especially when Oliver's steely blue eyes returned to watching her from across the table. He seemed to look right through her skin and into her soul. She felt the prickle of goose bumps rise across her flesh at the thought of being so exposed to him, but she immediately tried to shelve the sense of self-awareness he brought out in her. If he was studying her, it was only to seek out a weakness to exploit or an angle to work. He might be Harper's brother, but he was obviously no friend to Lucy.

The spell was finally broken as he casually turned away to look at his sister. "I know she's your friend, Harper, but you have to admit there's something fishy about this whole thing." Oliver's rich baritone voice drew Lucy back into the conversation.

"Fishy, how?" Lucy asked.

"I wouldn't blame you for influencing her to leave you something. You're alone with her day after day. It would be easy to drop hints and convince her it was her idea to leave you everything." Oliver's blue eyes narrowed at her again, nearly pinning Lucy to the back of her leather chair with his casual accusation.

"Are you serious?" She repeated his earlier question. "I had no idea about any of this. We never discussed her will or her money. Not once in five years. I didn't even know why Phillip called me in here today. I'm just as surprised as you are."

"I highly doubt that," Wanda muttered.

"Please, folks," Phillip interjected. "I realize this is a shock to all of you. I wish I could say something to make things better, but the bottom line is that this is what Alice wanted. Feel free to retain a lawyer if you're interested in challenging the will in court, but as it stands, Lucy gets everything."

Wanda pushed up from her seat and slung her Hermès purse dramatically over her arm. "You bet I'm calling my attorney," she said as she headed for the door. "What a waste of a fortune!"

The rest of the family shuffled out behind her until it was only Harper, Lucy and Phillip sitting at the table.

"I'm sorry about all that, Lucy," the attorney said. "Alice should've prepared the family so this wasn't such a shock to them. She probably avoided it because they'd have pressured her to change it back. With this crowd, I'd anticipate a fight. That means you won't be able to sell the apartment and most of the accounts will likely be frozen until it's resolved in court. Alice put a stipulation into the will that authorizes me to maintain all the expenses for the apartment and continue paying you and the housekeeper in the event the will is contested, so you won't have to worry about any of that. I'll do my best to get some cash available for you before her family files, but don't go spending a bunch of it right away."

Lucy couldn't imagine that was possible. She'd made a lot of wealthy friends while at Yale, but she'd always been the thrifty one in the group by necessity. Thankfully, her sorority sisters Violet, Emma and Harper had never treated her any differently.

Having her penniless circumstances change so suddenly seemed impossible. Nearly every dime she made from working for Alice went into savings for her to finish school. She wouldn't even know what she'd do with money in her accounts that wasn't earmarked for something else.

"Wanda is full of hot air," Harper said. "She'll complain but she won't lay out a penny of her own money to contest the will. More than likely, they'll all sit back and let Oliver handle it."

Lucy frowned. "Your brother seemed really angry. Is he going to take it out on you?"

Harper snorted. "No. He knows better. Oliver will leave the battle to the courtroom. But don't be surprised if he shows up at the apartment ready to give you the third degree. He's a seasoned businessman, so he'll be on the hunt for any loophole he can exploit."

Lucy's first thought was that she wouldn't mind Harper's brother visiting, but his handsome face wouldn't make up for his ill intentions. He intended to overturn Alice's wishes and was probably going to be successful. Lucy didn't have the means to fight him. She could blow every penny she'd saved on attorneys and still wouldn't have enough to beat a man with his means. It was a waste of money anyway. Things like this just didn't happen to women like her. The rich got richer, after all.

That did beg the question she was afraid to ask while the others were still around. "Phillip, Alice and I never really discussed her finances. How much money are we talking about here?"

Phillip flipped through a few papers and swallowed hard. "Well, it looks like between the apartment, her investments, cash accounts and personal property, you're set to inherit about five hundred million dollars, Lucy."

Lucy frowned and leaned toward the attorney in confusion. "I—I'm sorry, I think I heard you wrong, Phillip. Could you repeat that?"

Harper took Lucy's hand and squeezed it tight. "You heard him correctly, Lucy. Aunt Alice was worth half a billion dollars and she's left most of it to you. I know it's hard for you to believe, but congratulations. It couldn't happen to a better person."

Lucy's breath caught in her throat, the words stolen from her lips. That wasn't possible. It just wasn't possible. It was like her numbers were just called in the lotto. The odds were stacked against a woman like her—someone who came from nothing and was expected to achieve even less. Half a *billion*? No wonder Alice's family was upset.

The help had just become a multimillionaire.

So that was the infamous Lucy Campbell.

Oliver had heard plenty about her over the years from his sister and in emails from his aunt. For some reason, he'd expected her to be more attractive. Instead, her hair was a dark, mousy shade of dishwater blond, her nails were in need of a manicure and her eyes were too big for her face. He was pretty sure she was wearing a hand-me-down suit of Harper's.

All in all, she seemed incredibly ordinary for someone with her reputation. Aunt Alice was notoriously difficult to impress and she'd written at length about her fondness for Lucy. He'd almost been intrigued enough to pay a visit and learn more about her. Maybe then he wouldn't have been as disappointed.

She had freckles. Actual *freckles*. He'd never known anyone with freckles before. He'd only remained calm in the lawyer's office by trying to count the sprinkle of them across her nose and cheeks. He wondered how many more there were. Were they only on her face, or did they continue across her shoulders and chest?

He'd lost count at thirty-two.

After that, he'd decided to focus on the conversation. He'd found himself responding to her in a way he hadn't anticipated when he first laid eyes on her. The harder he looked, the more he saw. But then she turned her gaze back on him and he found the reciprocal scrutiny uncomfortable. Those large, doe eyes seemed so innocent and looked at him with a pleading expression he didn't care for. It made him feel things that would muddy the situation.

Instead, Oliver decided he was paying far too much attention to her and she didn't deserve it. She was a sneaky, greedy liar just like his stepmother and he had no doubt of it. Harper didn't see it and maybe Alice didn't either, but Oliver had his eyes wide open. Just like when his father had fallen for Candace with her pouty lips and fake breasts, Oliver could see through the pretty facade.

Okay, so maybe Lucy was pretty. But that was it. Just pretty. Nothing spectacular. Certainly nothing like the elegant, graceful women that usually hung on his arm at society events around Manhattan. She was more like the cute barista at the corner coffee shop that he tipped extra just because she always remembered he liked extra foam.

Yeah, that. Lucy was pretty like that.

He couldn't imagine her rubbing elbows with the wealthy and esteemed elite of New York City. There was new money, and then there was the kind of person who never should've had it. Like a lottery winner. That was a fluke of luck and mathematics, but it didn't change who the person really was or where they belonged. He had a hard time thinking Manhattan high society would accept Lucy even with millions at her disposal.

His stepmother, Candace, had been different. She was young and beautiful, graceful with a dancer's build. She could hold her own with the rich crowd as though she'd always belonged there. Her smile lit up the room and despite the fact that she was more than twenty years younger, Oliver's father had been drawn to her like a fly to honey.

Oliver looked up and noticed his driver had arrived back at his offices. It was bad enough he had to leave in the middle of the day to deal with his aunt's estate. Returning with fifty thousand in his pocket was hardly worth the time he'd lost.

"Thank you, Harrison." Oliver got out of the black sedan and stepped onto the curb outside of Orion headquarters. He looked at the brass plaque on the wall declaring the name of the company his father had started in the eighties. Tom Drake had been at the forefront of the home computer boom. By the turn of the new millennium, one out of every five home computers purchased was an Orion.

Then Candace happened and it all fell apart.

Oliver pushed through the revolving doors and headed to his private elevator in the far corner of the marble-and-brass-filled lobby. Orion's corporate offices occupied the three top floors of the forty-floor high-rise he'd purchased six years earlier. As he slipped his badge into the slot, it started rocketing him past the other thirty-nine floors to take him directly to the area outside the Orion executive offices.

Production and shipping took place in a facility about fifteen miles away in New Jersey. There, the latest and greatest laptops, tablets and smartphones produced by his company were assembled and shipped to stores around the country.

Everyone had told Oliver that producing their products in the US instead of Asia or Mexico was crazy. That they'd improve their stock prices by going overseas and increase their profit margins. They said he should move their call centers to India like his competitors.

He hadn't listened to any of them, and thankfully, he'd had a board that backed his crazy ideas. It was succeed or go home by the time his father handed over the reins of the company. He'd rebuilt his father's business through ingenuity, hard work and more than a little luck.

When the elevator doors opened, Oliver made his way to the corner suite he took over six years ago. That was when Candace disappeared and his father decided to retire from Orion to care for their two-year-old son she'd left behind.

Oliver hated to see his father's heart broken, and he didn't dare say that he'd told him so the minute Candace showed up. But Oliver had known what she was about from the beginning.

Lucy was obviously made from the same cloth, although instead of romancing an older widower, she'd befriended an elderly shut-in without any direct heirs.

His aunt Alice had always been different and he'd appreciated that about her, even as a child. After she decided to lock herself away in her fancy apartment, Oliver gifted her with a state-of-the-art laptop and set her up with an email address so they could stay in touch. He'd opted to respect her need to be alone.

Now he regretted it. He'd let his sister's endorsement

of Lucy cloud his judgment. Maybe if he'd stopped by, maybe if he'd seen Lucy and Alice interact, he could've stopped this before it went too far.

Oliver threw open the door to his office in irritation, startling his assistant.

"Are you okay, Mr. Drake?" Monica asked with wide eyes.

Oliver frowned. He didn't need to lose his cool at work. Letting emotions affect him would be his father's mistake, and look what that had done. "I am. I'm sorry, Monica."

"I'm sorry about your aunt. I saw an article about her in the paper that said she'd locked herself in her apartment for almost twenty years. Was that true?"

Oliver sighed. His aunt had drawn plenty of interest alive and dead. "No. Only seventeen years," he said with a smile.

Monica seemed stunned by the very idea. "I can't imagine not leaving my apartment for that long."

"Well," Oliver pointed out, "she had a very nice apartment. She wasn't exactly suffering there."

"Will you inherit her place? I know you two were close and the article said she didn't have any children."

The possibility had been out there until this afternoon when everything changed. Aunt Alice had never married or had children of her own. A lot of people assumed that he and Harper would be the ones to inherit the bulk of her estate. Oliver didn't need his aunt's money or her apartment; it wasn't really his style. But he resented a woman wiggling her way into the family and stealing it out from under them.

Especially a woman with wide eyes and irritatingly

fascinating freckles that had haunted his thoughts for the last hour.

"I doubt it, but you never know. Hold my calls, will you, Monica?"

She nodded as he slipped into his office and shut the door. He was in no mood to talk to anyone. He'd cleared his calendar for the afternoon, figuring he would be in discussions with his family about Alice's estate for some time. Instead, everyone had rushed out in a panic and he'd followed them.

It was best that he left when he did. The longer he found himself in the company of the alluring Miss Campbell, the more intrigued he became. It was ridiculous, really. She was the kind of woman he wouldn't give a second glance to on the street. But seated across from him at that conference room table, looking at him like her fate was in his hands…he needed some breathing room before he did something stupid.

He pulled his phone out of his pocket and glanced at the screen before tossing it onto his desk. Harper had called him twice in the last half hour, but he'd turned the ringer off. His sister was likely on a mission to convince him to let the whole issue with the will drop. They'd have to agree to disagree where Lucy and her inheritance was concerned.

Oliver settled into his executive chair with a shake of his head and turned to look out the wall of windows to his view of the city. His office faced the west on one side and north on the other. In an hour or so, he'd have a great view of the sun setting over the Hudson. He rarely looked at it. His face was always buried in spreadsheets or he was doodling madly on the marker board. Something always needed his attention and he liked it that way. If he was busy, that meant the company was successful.

Free time…he didn't have much of it, and when he did, he hardly knew what to do with it. He kept a garden, but that was just a stress reliever. He dated from time to time, usually at Harper's prodding, but never anything very serious.

He couldn't help but see shades of Candace in every woman that gave a coy smile and batted her thick lashes at him. He knew that wasn't the right attitude to have—there were plenty of women with money of their own who were interested in him for more than just his fortune and prestige. He just wasn't certain how to tell them apart.

One thing he did notice today was that Lucy Campbell neither smiled or batted her lashes at him. At first, her big brown eyes had looked him over with a touch of disgust wrinkling her pert, freckled nose. A woman had never grazed over him with her eyes the way she had. It was almost as though he smelled like something other than the expensive cologne he'd splashed on that morning.

He'd been amused by her reaction to him initially. At least until they started reading the will. Once he realized who she was and what she'd done, it wasn't funny any longer.

Harper believed one hundred percent in Lucy's innocence. They'd been friends since college. She probably knew Lucy better than anyone else and normally, he would take his sister's opinion as gospel. But was she too close? Harper could be blinded to the truth by her friendship, just as their father had been blinded to the truth by his love for Candace. In both instances, hundreds of millions were at stake.

Even the most honest, honorable person could be tempted to get a tiny piece of that pie. Alice had been ninety-three. Perhaps Lucy looked at her with those big, sad eyes and told Alice a sob story about needing the money. Perhaps she'd charmed his aunt into thinking of her as the child she never had. Maybe Lucy only expected a couple million and her scheme worked out even better than she planned.

Either way, it didn't matter how it came about. The bottom line was that Lucy had manipulated his aunt and he wasn't going to sit by and let her profit from it. This was a half-billion-dollar estate—they weren't quibbling over their grandmother's Chippendale dresser or Wedgwood China. He couldn't—wouldn't—let this go without a fight. His aunt deserved that much.

With a sigh, he reached for his phone and dialed his attorney. Freckles be damned, Lucy Campbell and her charms would be no match for Oliver and his team of bloodthirsty lawyers.

Two

Lucy awoke the next morning with the same odd sense of pressure on her chest. It had been like that since the day she'd discovered Alice had died in her sleep and her world had turned upside down. Discovering she could potentially be a millionaire and Alice's entire family hated her had done little to ease that pressure. It may actually be worse since they met with Phillip.

Someone would undoubtedly contest the will, which would put Alice's estate in limbo until it was resolved. When she asked Phillip how long that would take, he said it could be weeks to months. The family's attorneys would search for any way they could to nullify the latest will. That meant dragging their "dear aunt's" reputation through the mud along with Lucy's. Either Alice wasn't in her right mind—and many would argue she never had been—or Lucy had manipulated her.

It made Lucy wonder if she could decline the inheritance. Was that an option? While the idea of all that money and stuff seemed nice, she didn't want to be ripped to shreds to get it. She hadn't manipulated Alice, and Alice hadn't been crazy. She'd obviously just decided that her family either didn't deserve or need the money. Since she never discussed it with anyone but Phillip and hadn't been forthcoming about her reasoning even to him, they would never know.

Alice had been quirky that way. She never left her apartment, but she had plenty of stories from her youth about how she enjoyed going against the flow, especially where her family was involved. If it was possible for her to listen in on her will reading from heaven, Lucy was pretty sure she was cracking up. Alice would've found the look on Wanda's face in particular to be priceless.

While the decision was being made, Lucy found herself at a loss. What, exactly, was she supposed to be doing with her time? Her client was dead, but she was still receiving her salary, room and board. After the funeral, Lucy had started putting together plans to pick up her life where she'd been forced to drop it. She had a year left in her art history program at Yale. Her scholarship hadn't covered all four years and without it, there was no way she had been able to continue.

Working and living with Alice had allowed her to save almost all of her salary and she had a tidy little nest egg now that she could use to move back to Connecticut and finish school. Then, hopefully, she could use the connections she'd established the last few years in the art world to land a job at a prestigious museum.

Alice and Lucy had bonded over art. Honestly,

Lucy'd had no experience as a home health nurse or caregiver of any kind, but that wasn't really what Alice needed. She needed a companion, a helper around the apartment. She also needed someone who would go out into the world for her. Part of that had included attending gallery openings and art auctions in Alice's place. Lucy had met quite a few people there and with Alice Drake's reputation behind her, hopefully those connections would carry forward once she entered the art community herself.

Today, Lucy found herself sitting in the library staring at the computer screen and her readmission forms for Yale, but she couldn't focus on them. Her gaze kept drifting around the apartment to all the things she'd never imagined would be hers. Certainly not the apartment itself, with its prewar moldings, handcrafted built-ins and polished, inlaid hardwood floors. Not the gallery of art pieces that looked like a wing of the Met or MoMA. It was all lovely, but nothing she would ever need to worry about personally.

Except now, she had to worry about it all, including the college forms. It was September. If this court hearing dragged through the fall, it would mess with her returning to school for the spring semester. Phillip had recommended she not move out, even if she didn't want to keep the apartment. He was worried members of the family would squat in it and make it difficult for her to take ownership or sell it even if the judge ruled in her favor. That meant the pile of boxes in the corner she'd started to fill up would stay put for now and Yale in January might not happen.

All because Alice decided Lucy should be a millionaire and everyone else disagreed.

The sound of the doorbell echoed through the apartment, distracting Lucy from her worries. She saved her work and shut the laptop before heading out to the front door. Whoever was here must be on the visitor list or the doorman wouldn't have let them up. She hoped it was Harper, but one glance out the peephole dashed those hopes.

It was Oliver Drake.

Lucy smoothed her hands over her hair and opened the door to greet her guest. He was wearing one of a hundred suits he likely owned, this one being navy instead of the black he'd worn to the lawyer's office the day before. Navy looked better on him. It brought out the blue in his eyes and for some reason, highlighted the gold strands in his brown, wavy hair.

She tore her gaze away from her inspection and instead focused on his mildly sour expression. Not a pleasure visit, she could tell, so she decided to set the tone before he could. "Oliver, so glad to see you were able to find the place. Do come in."

She took a step back and Oliver entered the apartment with his gaze never leaving hers. "I have been here before, you know. Dozens of times."

"But so much has changed since the nineties. Please, feel free to take a look around and reacquaint yourself with the apartment." Lucy closed the door and when she turned around, found that Oliver was still standing in the same spot, studying her.

"You know, I can't tell if you're always this cheeky or if you're doing it because you've got something to hide. Are you nervous, Lucy?" His voice was low and even, seemingly unbothered by her cutting quips.

Lucy crossed her arms over her chest and took a step

back from him, as though doing so would somehow shield her from the blue eyes that threatened to see too much. "I don't have anything to be nervous about."

He took two slow strides toward her, moving into her personal space and forcing her back until the doorknob pressed into her spine. He was over six foot, lurking over her and making Lucy feel extremely petite at her five-foot-four-inch height. He leaned down close, studying her face with such intensity she couldn't breathe.

Oliver paused at her lips for a moment, sending confusing signals to Lucy's brain. She didn't think Harper's arrogant older brother would kiss her, but stranger things had already happened this week. Instead, his gaze shifted to her eyes, pinning her against the door of the apartment without even touching her. By this point, Lucy's heart was pounding so loudly in her ears, it was nearly deafening her during his silent appraisal.

"We'll see about that," he said at last.

When he finally took a step back, Lucy felt like she could breathe again. There was something intense about Oliver that made her uncomfortable, especially when he looked at her that way.

As though nothing had just happened between them, Oliver stuffed his hands into his pockets and started strolling casually through the gallery and into the great room. Lucy followed him with a frown lining her face. She didn't understand what he wanted. Was this just some psychological game he was playing with her? Was he looking to see if she'd sold anything of Alice's? How could he even tell after all these years?

"So, I stopped by today to let you know that my attorney filed a dispute over the will this morning. I'm sure Phillip explained to you that all of Aunt Alice's assets would be frozen until the dispute is resolved."

Lucy stopped in the entry to the great room, her arms still crossed over her chest. Harper was right when she said that her brother would likely be the one to start trouble for her. "He did."

Oliver looked around at the art and expensive tapestries draping the windows before he turned and nodded at her. "Good, good. I wouldn't want there to be any awkward misunderstandings if you tried to sell something from the apartment. I'm fairly certain you've never inherited anything before and wouldn't know how it all worked."

"Yes, it's a shame. I was just itching to dump that gaudy Léger painting in the hallway. I always thought it clashed with the Cézanne beside it, but Alice would never listen to reason," she replied sarcastically. Calling a Léger gaudy would get her kicked out of the Yale art history program.

Oliver narrowed his gaze at her. "Which painting is the Léger?"

Lucy shelved a smirk. He thought he was so smart and superior to her, but art was obviously something he didn't know anything about. "It's the colorful cubist piece with the bicycles. But that aside, I was just kidding. Even if I win in court—and I doubt I will—I wouldn't sell any of Alice's art."

He glanced over her shoulder at the Léger and shrugged before moving to the collection of cream striped sofas. He sat down, manspreading across the loveseat in a cocky manner that she found both infuriating and oddly intriguing. He wore his confidence well, but he seemed too comfortable here, as though he were already planning on moving in to the place Lucy had called home for years.

"And why is that?" he asked. "I would think most people in your position would be itching to liquidate the millions in art she hoarded here."

She sighed, not really in the mood to explain herself to him, but finding she apparently had nothing better to do today. "Because it meant too much to her. You may have been too busy building your computer empire to know this, but these pieces were her lover and her children. She carefully selected each piece in her collection, gathering the paintings and sculptures that spoke to her because she couldn't go out to see them in the museums. She spent hours talking to me about them. If she saw it in her heart to leave them to me, selling them at any price would be a slap in the face."

"What would you do with them, then?"

Lucy leaned against the column that separated the living room from the gallery space. "I suppose that I would loan most of them out to museums. The Guggenheim had been after Alice for months to borrow her Richter piece. She always turned them down because she couldn't bear to look at the blank spot on the wall where it belonged."

"So you'd loan all of them out?" His heavy brow raised for the first time in genuine curiosity.

Lucy shook her head. "No, not all of them. I would keep the Monet."

"Which one is that?"

She swallowed her frustration and pointed through the doorway to the piece hanging in the library. *"Irises *in Monet's Garden,"* she said. "You did go to college, didn't you? Didn't you take any kind of liberal studies classes? Maybe visit a museum in your life?"

At that, Oliver laughed, a low, throaty rumble that unnerved her even as it made her extremely aware of her whole body. Once again, her pulse sped up and her mouth went so dry she couldn't have managed another smart remark.

She'd never had a reaction to a man like that before. Certainly not in the last five years where she'd basically lived like her ninety-year-old client. Her body was in sore need of a man to remind her she was still in her twenties, but Oliver was *not* the one. She was happy to have distance between them and hoped to keep it that way.

"You'd be surprised," Oliver said, pushing himself up from the couch. He felt like he was a piece on display with her standing there, watching him from the doorway. "I've been to several museums in my years, and not just on those painful school field trips. Mostly with Aunt Alice, actually, in the days when she still left her gilded prison. I never really cared much about the art, but you're right, she really did love it. I liked listening to her talk about it."

He turned away from Lucy and strolled over to the doorway to the library. There, hanging directly in front of the desk so it could be admired, was a blurry painting, about two and a half feet by three feet. He took a few steps back from it and squinted, finally being able to make out the shapes of flowers from a distance. He supposed to some people it was a masterpiece, but to him it was just a big mess on a canvas that was only important to a small group of rich people.

Even then, he *did* know who Monet was. And Van Gogh and Picasso. There was even a Jackson Pollock hanging in the lobby of his corporate offices, but that was his father's purchase. Probably Aunt Alice's suggestion. He didn't recognize the others she'd mentioned, but he wasn't entirely without culture. Aunt Alice had taken him to the museums more times than he could count. It was just more fun to let Lucy think he didn't know what she was talking about.

When she blushed, the freckles seemed to fade away against the crimson marring her pale skin. And the more irritated she got, the edges of her ears and her chest would flush pink as well.

With her arms crossed so defensively over her chest, it drew her rosy cleavage to his attention. In that area, she had the cute barista beat. Lucy wasn't a particularly curvy woman—she was on the slim side. Almost boyish through the hips. But the way she was standing put the assets she did have on full display with her clingy V-neck sweater.

"Irises are my mother's favorite flower," Lucy said as she followed him into the library, oblivious to the direction of his thoughts.

Or perhaps not. She kept a few feet away from him, which made him smile. She was so easy to fluster. It made him want to seek out other ways to throw her off guard. He wondered how she would react when she was at the mercy of his hands and mouth on her body.

"I've always appreciated this piece for its sentimental value."

When Oliver turned to look at her, he found Lucy

was completely immersed in her admiration of the painting. He almost felt guilty for thinking about ravishing her while she spoke about her mother. Almost.

It wasn't like he would act on the compulsion, anyway. His lawyer would have a fit if he immediately seduced the woman he'd decided to sue the day before. He did want to get to know her better, though. Not because he was curious about her, but because he wanted to uncover her secrets. He knew what Harper and Aunt Alice had thought of her, but he was after the truth.

This sweet-looking woman with the blushing cheeks and deep appreciation of art was a scam artist and he was going to expose her, just like he should've exposed Candace before his father was left in ruins with a toddler. He was too late to protect Aunt Alice, but that didn't mean he couldn't put things right.

Turning to look at Lucy, he realized she was no longer admiring the painting, but looking at him with a curious expression on her face. "What?" he asked.

"I asked what you thought of it."

He turned back to the painting and shrugged. "It's a little sloppy. How much is it worth?"

"Your aunt bought it many years ago at a lower price, but if it went to auction today…probably as much as this apartment."

That caught his attention. Oliver turned back to the wall, looking for a reason why this little painting would be worth so much. "That's ridiculous." And he meant it. "No wonder my cousin Wanda was so upset about you getting all of Aunt Alice's personal belongings as well as the cash. She's got a fortune's worth of art in here."

Lucy didn't bother arguing with him. "It was her passion. And it was mine. That's why we got along so well. Perhaps why she decided to leave it to me. I would appreciate it instead of liquidating it all for the cash."

Oliver twisted his lips in thought. It sounded good, but it was one thing to leave a friend with common interests a token. A half-a-billion-dollar estate was something completely different. "Do you really think that's all it was?"

She turned to him with a frown. "What is that supposed to mean?"

"I mean, do you honestly expect everyone to believe that she just up and changed her will to leave her employee everything instead of her family, and you had nothing to do with it? You just had *common interests*?"

Lucy's dark eyes narrowed at him, and her expression hardened. "Yes, that's what I expect everyone to believe because that is what happened. I'm not sure why you're such a cynical person, but not everyone in the world is out there to manipulate someone else. I'm certainly not."

This time, Lucy's sharp barb hit close to home. Perhaps he was pessimistic and became that way because life had taught him to be, but that didn't mean he was wrong about her. "I'm not cynical, Lucy, I simply have my eyes open. I'm not blinded by whatever charms you've worked on my sister and my aunt. I see a woman with nothing walking away from this situation with half a billion dollars. You had to have done something. She didn't leave the housekeeper anything. You're telling me you're just that special?"

The hard expression on Lucy's face started to crumble at his harsh words, making him feel a pang of guilt for half a second. Of course, she could just be trying to manipulate him like she did everyone else.

"Not at all," she said with a sad shake of her head. "I don't think I'm special. I'm as ordinary as people come. I wish Alice had explained to me and everyone else why she was doing what she did, but she left that as a mystery for us all. There's nothing I can do about it. You can take me to court and try to overturn her last wishes. Maybe you will be successful. I can't control that. But know that no matter what the judge decides, I had nothing to do with it. Just because you don't believe it, doesn't make it any less true."

Boy, she was good. The more she talked, the more he wanted to believe her. There was a sincerity in her large doe eyes and unassuming presence. It was no wonder everyone seemed to fall prey to her charms. He'd thought at first she wasn't as skilled and cunning as Candace, but he was wrong. She'd simply chosen to target an older, vulnerable woman instead of a lonely, vulnerable man. A smarter choice, if you asked his opinion. She didn't have to pretend to be in love with a man twice her age.

"You're very good." He spoke his thoughts aloud and took a step closer to her. "When I first saw you at Phillip's office with your big eyes and your innocent and indignant expression, I thought perhaps you were an amateur that I could easily trip up, but now I see I'm going up against a professional con artist." He took another step, leaving only inches between them. "But that doesn't mean you're going to win."

Lucy didn't pull back this time; she held her ground. "The mistake you're making is thinking that I care, Oliver."

"You're honestly going to stand there and tell me that you don't care whether you get the apartment, the Monet and everything else?"

"I am," she said with a defiant lift of her chin. Her dark eyes focused on him, drawing him into their brown depths. "See, the difference between you and me is that I've never had anything worth losing. If I walk out this door with nothing more than I came in with, my life goes on as usual. And that's what I expect to happen. To be honest, I can't even imagine having that kind of money. This whole thing seems like a dream I'm going to wake up from and I'll go back to being Lucy, the broke friend that can never afford the girls trips and expensive clothes her friends wear. Things like this don't happen to people like me, and the people in the world with all the money and power—people like you—are happy to keep it that way."

"You're saying it's my fault if you don't get your way?"

"Not my way. Alice's way. And yes. You're the only one in the family that lawyered up."

That was because he was the only one in the family with nerve. "Someone had to."

"Well, then, you've made your choices, Oliver, and so have I. That said, I'm not sure there's much else for us to say to one another. I think it's time for you to go."

Oliver raked his gaze over her stern expression and smirked. He didn't have to leave. She had no more claim on the apartment than he did at this point. But it was too soon to push his luck. Besides, the more time he spent with her, the softer his resolve to crush her became. The closer he got, the more interested he was in breathing in the scent of her shampoo and touching her hand to see if her skin was as soft as it appeared. He would have to tread very carefully where Lucy was concerned or he'd get lured into her web just like the others.

Three

"I don't know why you insisted on me wearing this dress, Harper. It's a baby shower, not a cocktail party."

As Lucy and Harper walked up the driveway of the sprawling Dempsey estate, she looked down at the white strapless frock her friend had practically pushed on her. It had taken nearly two hours to drive out to the property where Emma had grown up, and Lucy had doubted her clothing decision the whole way. Why they couldn't have the party at the Dempseys' apartment in Manhattan, she didn't know.

Harper shook her head and dismissed Lucy's concerns, as usual. "That J. Mendel dress is perfect for you. You look great. It's always a good time to look great."

"You need to print that on your business cards," Lucy quipped.

Even then, she felt incredibly overdressed for a baby

shower, but Harper insisted they dress up. It was a couples shower for their friend Emma and her new husband, Jonah. Since they were both single and the event was coed, Harper had got it in her head that they should look even cuter than usual, in case there were some single friends of Jonah's there as well. At least that was what she'd said.

"You need to remember you're not just the poor friend from Yale anymore, Lucy. You have to start acting like someone important because you are someone important. You were before the money, but now you have no excuse but to show the world how fabulous you are."

Lucy sighed and shifted the wrapped gift in her arms. "I'm still the poor friend from Yale and I refuse to believe otherwise until there's cash in my hand and in my bank accounts. Thanks to your brother, I may not get a dime."

"We'll see about that," Harper said with a smirk curling her peach lips.

Oliver had made that same face when he visited the apartment the other day. The brief encounter had left her rattled to her core. Thankfully, no one else had decided to drop in unannounced. But seeing that expression on her friend brought an anxious ache back to her stomach. She intended to get some cake in her belly as soon as possible to smother it.

"Who does a couples baby shower anyway?" Lucy asked. "Any guy I know would hate this kind of thing."

"Knowing Emma and her mother, this will be anything but the usual baby shower. It's more of an event."

Lucy paused at the steps leading up to the Dempsey

mansion and caught the distant sounds of string music playing. Live music for a baby shower? They'd passed dozens of cars parked along the drive up to the house from the gate. "I think you may be right."

They stepped inside the house together, taking the butler's directions through the ornately decorated house to the ballroom. Lucy bit her tongue at the mention of a ballroom. Who, other than the house in the board game *Clue*, had an actual ballroom?

Apparently, the Dempseys.

They rounded a corner and were bombarded by the sound of a huge party in progress. Lucy was instantly aware that this was not the punch-and-cake gathering with cheesy baby shower games she was expecting. A string quartet was stationed in the corner on a riser. Round tables were scattered throughout the room with sterling gray linens and centerpieces filled with flowers in various shades of pink.

A serpentine table of food curved around the far corner of the space, flanked by a silver, three-tiered punch fountain on one end and an even taller cake on the other end. A mountain of gifts were piled onto tables in the opposite corner. There were easily a hundred people in the room milling around, and thankfully, most of them were dressed as nicely as she and Harper were.

Lucy breathed a sigh of relief for Harper's fashion advice. At least for some of it. Harper had tried to get her to wear a piece of Alice's jewelry—a large diamond cocktail ring that would've matched her dress splendidly, she said—but Lucy had refused. It wasn't hers yet. She wasn't touching a thing of Alice's until the deal was done.

"I think Emma's mother went a little overboard for this, don't you?" Harper leaned in to whisper. "I guess since Emma and Jonah eloped in Hawaii, Pauline had to get her over-the-top party somehow."

Lucy could only nod absently as she took in the crowd. Being friends with Emma, Harper and Violet in college had been easy because they'd all lived in their sorority house and their economic differences were less pronounced. After their years at Yale, they all returned to New York, struggling to start their careers and make names for themselves. It leveled the playing field for the friends. This was one of the few times she'd been painfully reminded that she came from a very different world than them. She tried to avoid those scenarios, but this was one party she couldn't skip. Even with Alice's fortune, she'd still be a nobody from a small town in Ohio that no one had ever heard of.

"I see someone I need to talk to. Are you okay by yourself for a while?" Harper asked. She was always good, as were all the girls, about making sure Lucy was comfortable in new settings that were second nature to them.

"Absolutely, go," Lucy said with a smile.

As Harper melted into the crowd, Lucy decided to take her gift to the table flanked with security guards. There were apparently nicer gifts there than the pink onesies with matching hats she had picked out from the registry. One of them had a sterling silver Tiffany rattle tied to the package like a bow.

Without immediately spying anyone she knew, she decided to get a glass of punch. At least she would look like she was participating in the event.

"Lucy!" A woman's voice shouted at her as she finished filling up her crystal punch glass. She turned around to see a very pregnant Emma with a less-pregnant Violet.

"You two are a pair," Lucy said.

"I know," Emma agreed with a groan as she stroked her belly. "Four weeks to go."

"I wish I only had four weeks." Violet sighed. "Instead I have four months."

Just after Emma and Jonah announced their engagement and pregnancy to the world, Violet had piped up with a similar announcement. It had come as a surprise to everyone, including Violet, that she was expecting. She and her boyfriend had been on and off for a while, but finding out she was pregnant a few weeks after she'd been in a serious taxi accident had sealed the deal. Her boyfriend, Beau, insisted he wasn't losing her again and they got engaged. The difference was that Violet wanted to set a date after the baby was born. She, unlike Emma, wanted the big wedding with the fancy dress and wasn't about to do it with a less-than-perfect figure.

"Speaking of how far along you are," Lucy said, "how did the ultrasound go?"

Violet's cheeks blushed as she turned to Emma. "I'm not announcing anything because it's Emma and Jonah's night, but I'll tell you both, and Harper when I see her. We're having a boy."

"Oh!" Emma squealed and wrapped her arms around Violet. "Our kids are going to get married," she insisted.

Lucy suffered through a round of giggly hugs and baby talk. Since Violet discovered she was pregnant, it had been all the two of them could talk about. Lucy understood. It was a big deal for both of them. She just felt miserably behind the curve when it came to her friends, in more ways than one. She hadn't even dated since college. Marriage and children were a far-off fantasy she hardly had time to consider.

"Darling." An older woman with Emma's coloring interrupted their chat. It was her mother, Pauline Dempsey. "I want to introduce you to a couple business acquaintances of your father, and then I'd like you and Jonah to join us up front for a toast."

Emma smiled apologetically and let her mother drag her away. Violet turned to Lucy with a conspiratorial look on her face. "So... Harper said you have some news."

Lucy twisted her lips in concern. A part of her didn't want to talk about Alice's estate until she knew what was going to happen. She didn't want to get her hopes—or anyone else's—up for nothing. Then again, keeping a secret in her circle of friends was almost impossible. "It's not news," she insisted. "At least not yet."

"I don't know," Violet teased. "Harper said it was huge. Are you pregnant?"

Her eyes went wide. "No, of course I'm not pregnant. You have to have sex to get pregnant."

Violet shrugged. "Not necessarily. I mean, I don't remember getting pregnant. I assume sex was involved."

"Yes, well, you were in a car accident and forgot a week of your life. I'm pretty sure that missing week included you and Beau making that little boy." Lucy was suddenly desperate to change the subject. "Any names picked out yet?"

"Beau wants a more traditional Greek name, but I'm

not sold. I was thinking something a little more modern, like Lennox or Colton."

"Where is Beau, anyway?" Lucy asked. "This is a couples shower, right?"

"Yes, well, he's been working a lot lately. Finding out we were pregnant put him in a tailspin. He's been empire-building ever since. This isn't his cup of tea, anyway."

Lucy nodded, but didn't say anything. As a friend, she tried to be supportive, but she didn't like Beau. He and Violet argued too much and their relationship was so up and down. It was hard on Violet. He seemed to rededicate himself after her accident, and later, when he found out she was having a baby, but Lucy still worried about her friend. She wanted it to work out like the fairy tales claimed. But fortunately, with or without Beau, Violet would be fine. She was the sole heir to her family's Greek shipping fortune and could easily handle raising her son on her own if she had to.

"I'm going to sit down for a bit. My feet are swelling something fierce and I'm only halfway through this pregnancy," Violet complained. "Come find me in a bit. I still want to hear about this big news of yours."

Lucy waved Violet off and took a sip of her punch.

"Big news of yours?" A familiar baritone voice reached her ears just as her mouth filled with punch. "Do tell."

Lucy turned around and felt that anxiety from earlier hit her full force. She swallowed the gulp of punch before she could spit it everywhere and ruin her white dress. She wished it were spiked; it would help steel her nerves for round two of this fight.

Oliver Drake was standing right behind her with a ridiculously pleased grin on his face.

Oliver was willing to admit when he was wrong, and his prior opinions of Lucy's attractiveness were way off base.

Where had this version of Lucy been hiding? He had no doubt that Harper, his fashion-conscious sister, had gotten ahold of her tonight.

Lucy's dark blond hair was swirled up into a French twist with a rhinestone comb holding it in place. Her dress was white and cream—a color combination that on most women, brides included, made them look ill. For some reason, Lucy seemed to glow. It was off the shoulder, and with her hair up, it showcased her swan-like neck and the delicate line of her collarbones.

It was hard to focus on that with the expression on her face, however. The rosy shade of her lipstick highlighted the drop of her jaw as she looked at him in panic. She hadn't been expecting him here tonight and he quite liked that. Catching her off guard was proving to be the highlight of his week lately.

"This big news," he repeated. "I hope it's something exciting to help you get over the shock of inheriting, then losing, all that money."

At his smart words, her lips clamped shut and her dark brow knitted together. When she wrinkled her nose, he noticed that only a few of her more prominent freckles were visible with her makeup on. He found he quite missed them.

"You've got a lot of nerve, Oliver Drake! How dare you come to the party for one of my best friends, just so you can harass me! Is nothing sacred to you? Tonight is about Emma and Jonah, not about your ridiculous vendetta against me."

Oliver looked around at the dozen or so people who turned and took notice of her loud, sharp words. Apparently their banter was about to escalate to fighting tonight. He had no plans to cause a scene here, despite what she seemed to think. Reaching out, he snatched up her wrist and tugged her behind him. There were French doors not far from where they were standing, so he made a beeline through them and out onto the large balcony that overlooked the east grounds of the Dempsey estate.

"You let go of me!" Lucy squealed as he hauled her outside, the end of her tirade cut off from the guests inside by the slamming of the door. Thankfully, the weather was a touch too chilly for anyone to be out there to overhear the rest of their argument.

"Is nothing sacred to *you*?" He turned her question on her. "Stop causing a scene in front of my friends and colleagues."

"Me?" Lucy yanked her wrist from his clutch. "You started this. And they're *my* friends and colleagues, not yours."

Oliver noticed the palm of his hand tingled for a moment at the separation of his skin from hers. He ached to reach out and touch her again, but that was the last thing he needed to do. Especially right now when she was yelling at him. "Yes, you. And you don't get to lay claim on everyone inside just like you laid claim to my aunt's fortune. They're my friends, too."

"I didn't lay claim to your aunt's fortune. I would never presume to do that, even if I had the slightest reason to think I should get it. Despite what you seem to think, it was a gift, Oliver. It's a kind thing some people do, not that you would know what that's like."

"I am kind," he insisted. The collar of his shirt was suddenly feeling too tight. Oliver didn't understand why she was able to get under his skin so easily. He'd felt his blood pressure start to rise the moment he'd seen her in that little dress. And then, after he touched her… "You don't know anything about me."

"And you don't know anything about me!"

"I know that yelling is very unbecoming of a lady."

"And so is manhandling someone."

"You're correct," Oliver conceded and crossed his arms over his chest to bury his tingling hand. "I'm not a lady."

Lucy's pink lips scrunched together in irritation, although there was the slightest glimmer of amusement in her eyes. Could she actually have a sense of humor? "You're not a gentleman either. You're a pain in my a—"

"Hey, now!" Oliver interrupted. Ixnay that thought on the sense of humor. "I didn't come here to start a fight with you, Lucy."

She took a deep breath and looked him over in his favorite charcoal suit. He'd paired a pink tie with it tonight in a nod to Jonah's baby, but he doubted Lucy would be impressed by the gesture. At the moment, he wanted to tug it off and give himself some room to breathe, but he wouldn't give her the satisfaction of seeing him react to her, good or bad.

"So why are you here?" she asked.

"I'm here because I was invited. Jonah and I are friends from back in prep school. Did Harper not tell you that?"

"No, she didn't." Lucy looked through the window with a frown lining her face, then down at her dress. It was short, ending a few inches above her knee with a band of iridescent white beads that caught the light as she moved. "Although a lot of other things make sense now."

Oliver couldn't help the chuckle that burst out of him in the moment. "You actually thought I'd driven two hours out of my way just to come here and stalk you tonight?"

Lucy pouted her bottom lip at his laughter and turned toward the stone railing of the balcony. "Well… it's not like we've ever run into each other before this. You have to admit it seems suspicious that you keep showing up where I am."

He stifled the last of his snickering and stood beside her at the railing, their bodies almost touching. He could feel the heat of her bare skin less than an inch away. "Maybe you're right," he admitted.

Oliver turned to look down at her. She was wearing white and silver heels tonight, but even then, she was quite a bit shorter than he was. Outside, the flicker of the decorative candles stationed across the patio made the golden glow dance around her face, a game of shadow and light that flattered her features even more.

She met his gaze with her wide brown eyes, surprised by his sudden agreement with her. "I'm *right*? Did I actually hear you say that?"

"I said you *may* be right. Maybe I got all dressed up, dropped a ton of cash on a registry gift and came to this baby shower in the middle of nowhere just in the hopes I would see you here."

Lucy turned away and stared off into the distance. "I don't appreciate your sarcasm. I also don't appreciate you accosting me at a party. I'm missing one of my best friend's baby showers to be out here with you."

Oliver turned toward her and leaned one elbow onto the railing. "You're free to go at any time."

She turned to face him with disbelief narrowing her gaze. "Oh yeah, so you can start something else inside? Or throw me over your shoulder and carry me off next time? No. We're finishing this discussion right now. When I go back inside, I don't want to speak to or even lay eyes on you again."

He looked at her and noticed a slight tremble of her lips as she spoke. Was she on the verge of tears? He wasn't sure why, but the idea of that suddenly bothered him. "Are you okay?"

"Yes, why?"

"You're trembling. Are you really that upset with me?"

Lucy rolled her eyes and shook her head. "No, I'm shivering. It's freezing out here. I'm not dressed for an alfresco discussion this time of year."

Without hesitation, Oliver slipped off his suit coat and held it out to her. She looked at it with suspicion for a moment before turning her back and letting him drape it over her bare shoulders.

"Thank you," Lucy said as reluctantly as she could manage.

"I'm not all bad."

"That's good to know. I was starting to feel sorry for Harper having to grow up with you."

"Oh, you can still feel sorry for her. I was a horrible big brother. I made her life hell for years." Oliver laughed again, thinking of some of the wicked things he'd done to his sister. "One time, when she was about eight, I convinced her that my father's new Ming vase was made of Silly Putty and would bounce if she dropped it onto the floor. She got in so much trouble. Dad wouldn't believe her when she said I'd told her that. He grounded her for an extra week for lying."

Lucy covered her mouth with her hand to hide a reluctant smile. "Why are you being nice to me all of a sudden?" she asked. "You're not here to fight with me, and yet you're out here making small talk with me instead of inside with Jonah and your friends. What's your angle?"

That was a good question. He hadn't exactly planned any of this. He'd just wanted to get her away from the crowd before they made a scene. Once they stopped arguing, he was surprised to find he enjoyed talking with Lucy. There was an understated charm to her. The longer he spent with her, the more he wanted to spend. It was an intriguing and dangerous proposition, but one that explained his aunt's bold decision. If he felt swayed by her, his elderly aunt hadn't stood a chance.

"I don't have an angle, Lucy." Or if he did, he wasn't going to tell her so. "I guess I'm just trying to figure out what my aunt saw in you."

Lucy opened her mouth to argue, but he held up his hands to silence her. "I don't mean it like that, so don't get defensive. I've just been thinking that if my aunt really did want to leave you half a billion dollars, you had to be a pretty special person." Oliver leaned closer, unconsciously closing the gap between them. "I guess I'm curious to get to know you better and learn more about you."

Lucy's nose wrinkled, but for the first time, it didn't appear to be because she was annoyed with him. "What do you think so far?" she asked.

"So far…" He sought out the smart answer, but just decided to be honest. "…I like you. More than I should, given the circumstances. So far, you've proven to be an exciting, intelligent and beautiful adversary."

Lucy's lips parted softly at his words. "Did you say beautiful?"

Oliver nodded. Before he could respond aloud, Lucy launched herself into his arms. Her pink lips collided with his own just as her body pressed into him. He was stunned stiff for only a moment before he wrapped his arms around her waist and tugged her tighter against him.

Kissing Lucy wasn't at all what he expected. Nothing about her was what he expected. She didn't back down from what she'd started. She was bold, opening up to him and seeking his tongue out with her own. Oliver couldn't help but respond to her. She was more enthusiastic and demanding than any woman he may have ever kissed before.

This wasn't the smart thing. Or the proper thing. But he couldn't make himself pull away from her. She tasted like sweet, baby-shower punch, and she smelled like lavender. He wanted to draw her scent into his lungs and hold it there.

But then it was over.

As she pulled away, Oliver felt a surge of unwanted desire wash over him. It was the last thing he needed right now—with Lucy of all women—but he couldn't deny what he felt. It took everything he had not to reach for her and pull her back into his arms again. He was glad he didn't, though, as his need for her was stunted by a sudden blow to the face as Lucy punched him in the nose.

Four

"What the hell do you think you're doing?" Lucy asked with outrage in her voice as she backed away from him.

Oliver didn't immediately reply. First, he had to figure out what the hell had just happened. He was being kissed one second, hit the next and now he was being yelled at.

"Me?" He brought his hand up to his throbbing nose and winced. It wasn't broken, but there was blood running over his fingers. He'd never actually had a woman hit him before. One for the bucket list, he supposed. "*You're* the one that kissed *me*!"

"I did not," she insisted.

Oliver frowned and sighed, reaching into his coat for his pocket square to soak up the blood. Harper had never mentioned Lucy being impulsive, but he was learning new things about her all the time. It had been ten seconds since their lips had touched and it hadn't been his doing. Surely she recalled that. "Yeah, you did kiss me. I said you were beautiful and you threw yourself at me."

Lucy must have been caught up in the moment, because she seemed very much embarrassed by the truth of his blunt description. Her skin was suddenly crimson against her white dress and she wasn't even the one who got punched. "Yes…well…you kissed me back," she managed.

What was he supposed to do? Just stand there? Oliver was not a passive man, especially when the physical was involved. "My apologies, Miss Campbell. Next time a woman kisses me, I'll politely wait until she's finished with me and hit *her* instead."

Lucy took a cautious step back at his words, making him grin even though he shouldn't.

"I'm not going to hit you," Oliver said, dabbing at his nose one last time and stuffing the handkerchief into his pocket. "I've never hit a woman and I'm not going to start now. Although it would be nice if you would extend me the same courtesy. What ever happened to an old-fashioned slap of outrage? You straight-up punched me in the face. You hit hard, too."

She twisted her pink lips for a moment before nodding softly. "I take kickboxing classes twice a week. I'm sorry I hit you. It was almost a reflex. I was… startled."

"You were startled?" Oliver snorted in derision at her Pollyanna act and immediately regretted it as his nose throbbed with renewed irritation. "How could you be caught off guard when the whole thing was your doing?"

"Was it?" Lucy asked. "You weren't compliment-ing me and moving closer to me with that in mind?"

Oliver didn't remember doing that, but it was en-tirely possible. Lucy had a power over him that he hadn't quite come to terms with yet. Despite his best in-tentions, he found himself wanting to be nearer to her. To engage her in conversation, especially if it might fluster her and bring color to her pale cheeks. He'd wondered several times, in fact, how it would feel to have her lips against his and her body pressed into his own. Unfortunately, it had all happened so suddenly just now that he'd hardly been able to enjoy it.

He wasn't about to tell her that, though. She might be a pretty, nice-smelling con artist, but she was still a con artist. She'd worked her magic on his sister and his aunt. He'd had no doubt she would eventually turn her charms on him to get him to drop the contest of Aunt Alice's will, and she'd tried it at her first real opportu-nity. Letting her know she'd gotten to him would give her leverage. No. Let her stew instead, thinking her plan hadn't worked and she'd flung herself at a com-pletely disinterested man. She'd have to find a differ-ent way to get what she wanted.

"I didn't come to this party to see you and I most certainly didn't come to this party to try and seduce you. I can't help it if I'm a charming man, Lucy, but that's all it is. I'm sorry if you confused that with me being attracted to you."

Her mouth dropped open for a moment before she clapped it shut and pressed her lips into a tight frown.

"That wasn't exactly the kiss of a man that wasn't interested," she pointed out.

Oliver could only shrug it off. "Well, I don't want to be rude, now, do I?"

Lucy balled her hands into fists and planted them on her narrow hips. "So you're saying you faked the whole thing just to be polite?"

"Yes. Of course." The arrogance of his response nearly made him cringe as the words slipped from his lips. Normally, he wouldn't speak to anyone this way, but Lucy was a special case. He wasn't handling her with kid gloves. She needed to know she wouldn't get her way where he was concerned.

Her brown gaze studied his face for a moment before she shook her head. "No. I don't believe you. I think you're just too arrogant to admit that you're attracted to me, of all people. That you could actually want the help. The trash that robbed you of your inheritance."

Oliver narrowed his gaze at her. She was good. Not only was she able to get under his skin, she was able to get into his head as well. That was disconcerting. He was the one who was supposed to be finding out all her secrets so he could expose her as a fraud, and there she was, calling him elitist in the hopes that his knee-jerk reaction would be to deny it and somehow fall prey to her charms to prove her wrong.

"We've established that we hardly know each other, Lucy. I'm not sure why you're so confident about who I am and what I do or don't think of you. But here... I'll prove to you that you're wrong."

He took two steps forward, closing the gap between them. Lucy stiffened as he got closer, but she held her ground. He had to admit, it impressed him that she didn't turn tail and run.

She wanted to, though. He could tell by her board-straight posture and tense jaw. "What are you doing?" She looked up at him with big brown eyes that were full of uncertainty.

She thought she could just call his bluff and he'd back down. No way. He was going all in and winning the hand even with losing cards.

Oliver eased forward until they were almost touching. He dipped his head down to her and cupped her face in his hands. Tilting her mouth up to him, he pressed his lips against hers. He wanted this kiss to be gentle, sweet and meaningless, so he could prove his point and move on with his night. He'd kissed a lot of women in his time. This would be like any other.

Or so he thought.

The second her lips touched his, it was immediately apparent that wasn't going to be the case. It was like a surge of electricity shot through his body when they touched. Every nerve lit up as his pulse started racing. The pounding of his heart in his rib-cage urged him to move closer, to deepen the kiss, to taste her fully. In the moment, he couldn't deny himself what he wanted, even knowing his reaction played into her hands.

Lucy didn't deny him either. She melted into him, just as he'd expected. She wrapped her arms around his neck, her soft whimpers of need vibrating against his lips. Her mouth and her body were soft, molding to his hard angles. When she arched her back, pressing her belly against his rapidly hardening desire, she forced him to swallow a groan.

With her every breath, he could feel her breasts pushing against his chest, making him ache to touch them and hating himself for the mere thought. He wanted to press her back against the wall of the Dempseys' mansion and feel them beneath his hands. He was certain his father had felt the same way when he was swept up in Hurricane Candace.

This was getting *way* out of hand.

Oliver pulled away from Lucy at last, nearly pushing himself back although it was almost physically painful for him to do it. That simple kiss was supposed to prove to both of them that the other kiss had meant nothing. Instead, it had changed everything. Now he wasn't just curious about her as the woman who'd charmed his aunt out of a fortune. He wasn't just playing a cat-and-mouse seduction game. He wanted her. More than he'd wanted a woman in a very long time. His plan had clearly backfired in spectacular fashion, but he could still recover.

"See?" he said, taking another large step back to separate himself further and regain a semblance of control. He struggled to keep as neutral and unfazed an expression as he could, as though she hadn't just rocked his world in the midst of a stuffy baby shower.

"See what?" Lucy asked with a dreamy, flushed look on her face. She'd obviously enjoyed the kiss just as much as he had. On any other woman at any other time, that expression would've convinced him to swoop in again and push the kiss even further. Instead, he had to retreat before she caught him in her web for good.

"Do you see that you were wrong? That kiss was all an act, just like the first one. Honestly, it didn't do a thing for me." The truth was anything but, however he couldn't let her know that and think she had any chance of winning him over with feminine wiles.

Lucy's expression hardened as she came to realize that he was just messing with her and her plans had failed. Her jaw tightened and her hand curled into a fist again. Thankfully, he was out of her reach if she tried to take a swing at him a second time. "Are you kidding me?" she asked.

Oliver smiled wide and prayed his erection was hidden by his buttoned suit coat. "Not at all. I told you I wasn't attracted and then I proved it. That was skill, not attraction. Nothing more. Anyway, I'm glad we were able to clear that up. I wouldn't want there to be any other confused encounters between us. Now, if you'll excuse me, I'd like to get back in to the party. It appears as though they're about to do a toast for the new parents."

Lucy stood motionless as he nodded goodbye, brushed past her and headed back inside the ballroom.

What a pompous, arrogant jerk-face.

Lucy stood alone on the patio for a few minutes just to get her composure. The last twenty minutes of her life had thrown her for a loop and she just couldn't go back inside and act like nothing had happened.

First, she was too angry to return to the party. She knew she was flustered and red, and the minute one of the girls saw her like that, they would swarm her with questions she wasn't ready to answer. In addition, her hand was still aching from when she'd popped him in the face. She'd probably bruised her knuckles, but her only regret in hitting him was that it was premature.

He'd certainly earned a pop in the nose with the nasty things he'd said later.

Second, she wasn't ready to run into him again so soon. It was a big room filled with a lot of people, but she knew that fate would push them together repeatedly until one of them surrendered and went home. The alternative was another fight, this one more public, ruining the party. She didn't need that. It was bad enough that whispers would follow about them being alone on the balcony together for so long. Or if they came back inside together. Or came back in separately.

There was no winning in this scenario, really. Tongues would wag and there had already been enough tongue wagging on the patio tonight. At best, she could make sure she was presentable before she went back inside.

Reaching into her small purse, Lucy pulled out her compact. Her hair and makeup were fine, save for her lipstick that was long gone. She wasn't surprised. That kiss had blown her socks off. Oliver could yawn and say it was as much fun as getting an oil change, but she knew better. She could feel his reaction to it in the moment. Men lied. Words lied. Erections…those were a little more honest. And his had been hard to ignore.

What was his angle, anyway? Yes, she'd kissed him. It was possible she'd read the signs from him wrong, but she really didn't think so. He responded to her. He held her like a man who wanted to hold her. But then he'd turned around and laughed the whole thing off like it was nothing and made her feel stupid for thinking it was anything else.

She felt the heat in her cheeks again as her irritation grew. Why would he toy with her like that? Was it because he was determined to think she was some sort of crook? Why couldn't he just get to know her and make up his mind that way instead of jumping to hurtful conclusions? Didn't he trust Harper's judgment at all?

Lucy finished putting on her lipstick and returned it to her bag. She might as well go back inside. If she waited until she wasn't angry any longer, she'd sleep out on the patio. Instead, she took a deep breath, pasted on her best smile and headed back into the house.

Apparently, she'd missed the toast. The string quartet was playing music again and the crowd had returned to mingling. Her trio of girlfriends were together and looked her direction when she came in the door.

Lucy stopped short in front of them. "What?"

Emma arched a brow at her. "Seriously?"

"I'm sorry I missed the toast. I had to get some air," she said, making a lame excuse so she wouldn't hurt Emma's feelings.

"Air out of my brother's lungs," Harper quipped.

Lucy froze. "What? How did you—"

"That's a wall of windows, Lucy." Violet pointed over her shoulder. "Anyone who looked that direction could see the two of you playing tonsil hockey on the veranda."

Lucy turned and realized that she and Oliver had been far more visible on the patio than she'd anticipated. She'd thought for certain that the dim lights of the patio and the bright lights of the ballroom would've given them a little privacy. "Uh, we were having a discussion."

Emma snorted. "Quit it. Just tell us what's really going on."

"Yes, is this your big news? That you're dating Harper's brother?"

"Heavens, no!" Lucy blurted out. "That…" She gestured back to the patio. "What you guys saw was just…"

"Amazing?" Emma suggested.

"A CPR lesson?" Harper joked.

"A trial run?" Violet tossed out.

"A *mistake*," Lucy interjected into their rapid-fire suggestions. "And when I tell you the big news Harper alluded to, you'll understand why."

"Let's sit," Emma suggested. "I'm worn out and I want to hear every detail."

They selected a table in a far corner that wasn't quite so loud and gathered around it. The girls waited expectantly for Lucy to start her story as she tried to decide where to begin.

"Alice made me a beneficiary of her will."

"That's great," Emma said. "I mean, it makes sense. You two were so close."

"Yeah," Lucy agreed. "There's just one problem."

"How could an inheritance be a problem?" Violet asked.

"Because she left me damn near all of it. About half a billion dollars in cash, investments and property."

The words hung in the air for a few moments. Emma and Violet looked stunned. Harper sat with a smug smile on her face. She was confident that all of this would work out. Perhaps because that was the kind of life she led. Things were different for Lucy.

"You said billion. With a *b*?" Emma asked.

Lucy could only nod. What else did you say to something like that?

"And why aren't you more excited? You didn't even seem like you wanted to tell us." Violet's brow furrowed in confusion. "You'd think you'd be shouting it from the rooftops and lighting cigars with hundred dollar bills."

That would be a sight to see. "I'm not excited because I don't believe for one second that it's going to really happen the way Alice wanted."

"And why not?" Emma asked.

"Because of Oliver," Harper interjected. "He's all spun up about the whole thing. The family is convinced that Lucy is some kind of swindler that tricked Alice into giving her everything."

"I swear I didn't even know she did it," Lucy said.

"You don't have to defend yourself to us, honey." Violet shook her head. "We know you better than that. If Alice left you that money, it's because she thought you deserved it. Who are they to decide what she could and couldn't do with her own money?"

"I think they're trying to prove that she wasn't mentally competent to make the change. She only did it a few months ago. It doesn't look good for me, so that's why I didn't say anything. I didn't want to get anyone's hopes up and have it all fall through. Oliver has a team of fancy attorneys just ready to crush me. Honestly, I don't think I stand a chance."

"So why, exactly, were you kissing Oliver on the patio if he's the bad guy?" Emma asked, bringing the conversation back around to the part Lucy had wanted to avoid.

Once again, the other three women looked at her and she was at a loss for words. "When I saw him, I thought he'd followed me here. He showed up at the apartment the other day and we argued. When we started to argue again, he pulled me outside so we wouldn't cause a scene at the party. Somehow… I don't really know how…we kissed. Then he kissed me a second time to prove that kissing me was meaningless."

"What happened to his face?" Harper asked. "He was all red when he came back inside."

"It might have been because I punched him in the nose."

Violet covered her mouth to smother a giggle. Emma didn't bother, laughing loudly at Oliver's expense. It didn't take long before all four friends were laughing at the table together.

"You seriously punched him?"

Lucy nodded, wiping tears of laughter from her eyes. "I did. And he didn't deserve it. At least not yet."

"Oh, I'm sure he deserved it," Harper added. "He's done something to warrant a good pop, I assure you. Taking Alice's will to the judge is cause enough."

"Do you really think he'll get it overturned?" Emma asked. "He doesn't even need the money. Jonah says he's loaded."

"He is," Harper said. "He's done very well with Daddy's business the last few years. But it isn't about the money, I'm pretty sure."

"Then what is it about?" Lucy asked. "Because this has been the most confusing week of my life. I'm rich, but I'm not. I'm unemployed, but I may not need to work ever again. I'm homeless, and yet I may own a Fifth Avenue apartment. I'm applying to go back to Yale and finish school, but I may not even need to bother when I have an art gallery in my own living room. I've barely had time to grieve for Alice. Your whole family has a vendetta against me and I didn't do anything. I just woke up one day and my entire life was turned upside down."

Harper reached out and took Lucy's hand. "I know, and I'm sorry. If I'd thought for a moment that Aunt Alice was going to toss you into this viper pit, I would've warned you. But know it's not personal. They'd go after anyone. They all wanted their piece and they've been waiting decades for her to die so they can get their hands on it."

"What a warm family you have," Lucy noted. "I bet Thanksgiving was really special at your house."

"It's not as bad as I make it sound. Everyone had their own money, it's just that most of them were mentally decorating their new vacation homes and planning what they'd do with the money when the time came. Then nothing. In their minds, you yanked it out from under them, whether you meant to or not."

"Can't you talk some sense to Oliver?" Emma asked.

"I've tried. He's avoiding my calls. I think we just have to let the case run its course in court and hope the judge sees in Lucy what we all see. Once the judge rules in her favor, there's nothing any of them can do about it. But I didn't know he was bothering you, Lucy. If he shows up at the apartment again, you call me."

Lucy nodded. "I will." Looking around the crowded room, she was relieved not to see him loitering around the party. "But enough about all this. We're here to celebrate Emma and Jonah's baby, not to rehash all my drama. We can do that any day."

"I'm actually starving," Emma admitted. "Every time I think I should make a plate, someone starts talking to me or wants to rub my belly or something."

"Well, I'm pretty sure it's almost time for you to cut that beautiful cake. We can at least get you some of that to eat without interruption."

Lucy smiled as Emma's eyes lit up with excitement. "It's a vanilla pound cake with fresh berries and cream inside. At the tasting, Jonah had to take the plate from me so he could try a bite."

"Ooh…" Violet chimed in. "That sounds amazing. I've been nothing but hungry the last month. Beau keeps chastising me for eating too much. He says I'm going to overdo it, but I say pregnancy is my only chance to enjoy eating without feeling guilty. The baby and I are ready for some cake, too."

"Well, it's settled then," Lucy said. "Let's get these pregnant ladies some cake."

Five

"What are you doing here?"

Oliver could only grin at his sister's irritated expression as she opened the door to the apartment. A large portion of his life had been dedicated to goading that very face out of her. It was an unexpected bonus to the day. He hadn't actually been certain she was at Aunt Alice's apartment; he hadn't seen her since the baby shower the week before. But when he saw the Saks Fifth Avenue commuter van unloading downstairs, he knew that Harper was involved somehow. Where expensive clothes went, his sister was sure to follow.

"I saw the people from Saks unloading downstairs and I thought I would pop in to say hello. Personal shoppers coming to the house. It's as though someone has come into some money. Is that for you or for Lucy?" he asked, knowing full well that Harper was far too particular to let someone else shop for her.

"It's for Lucy."

Harper made no move to step back and let him into the apartment. Fortunately, the elevator chimed behind him and a well-dressed woman stepped out with a rack of plastic-wrapped clothing pushed by two gentlemen.

Harper's entire expression changed as she turned from her brother. "Hello, come in!" she said, moving aside to allow the crew in.

Oliver took advantage of the situation by going in after them. He happily took a seat on the sofa in the living room, waiting for what would likely be an interesting fashion show. After seeing what she'd worn the few times they were together, he knew Lucy needed a new wardrobe. Anything she wore that was remotely high quality was a hand-me-down from his sister. Honestly, he was surprised it took them this long to start shopping.

What would she buy first with her pilfered millions?

The two men from Saks left the apartment, leaving the rolling clothing hanger near the fireplace. He watched as the woman moved quickly to unwrap the clothes and present them to what she presumed was her wealthy client.

Lucy spied him the minute she entered the room, despite thousands of dollars' worth of clothes on display beside her. "What is he doing here?" she asked, echoing Harper's question.

Harper turned to where he was sitting and sighed. "I don't know, but it doesn't matter. We've got to find you an outfit for the gala. Perhaps a man's perspective will be helpful."

Lucy wrinkled her nose as she studied him and turned back to the clothing. "Harper," she complained, "these outfits are all way, way out of my price range." She picked up one sleeve and gasped. "Seriously. I can just wear something I already have in the closet."

"Absolutely not. You're a millionaire now and you have to look the part, especially at this gallery event. You want to work in the art world, don't you? This is your chance to make an entrance as Miss Lucille Campbell, not as Lucy, the assistant sent by Alice Drake. The invitation had your name on it this time, Lucy. Not Alice's."

Oliver watched curiously as Lucy shook her head and looked at the clothes. "How did they even know to invite me? I haven't told anyone about the money."

"Things like that leak out whether you want them to or not. I'm sure Wanda couldn't wait to share her outrage with her circle of friends and it spreads from there. The art world is small and people were probably eager to find out who would get Alice's estate. Honestly, I don't know how you've managed to keep it a secret."

Lucy pointed over to where Oliver was sitting on the couch. "That's why. He's why. You act like I already have this massive fortune, but I don't. All I have is what I saved to go back to school. I'm willing to spend some of that to get a dress for the gala, but not much. I have no guarantee that I'm ever going to see a dime of that money to replace what I spend."

"Will you at least try some of it on? You never know what you might end up liking."

"Yes, fine."

The saleswoman pulled out what was probably the most expensive designer dress on the rack. "Let's start with this one. Where would you like to change?"

She and Lucy disappeared down the hallway and Harper started sorting through the clothing on the rack.

This was an unexpected development. He thought for certain that Lucy would jump at the chance to buy some expensive designer clothes and start flaunting herself around Manhattan. Yes, he was responsible for putting a hold on the flow of cash from his aunt's estate, but there were ways around that. He was certain she could probably get a loan from a bank to front her lifestyle until the money came in. At the very least, charge up a credit card or two.

But she didn't. It was curious. She didn't seem to enjoy the position she was in at all, much to Harper's supreme disappointment. That woman loved to shop. Of course, so had Candace. She was full speed ahead the moment she'd gotten her hands on one of his father's credit cards. Candace had insisted that she just wanted to look as beautiful as possible at all times for his father. It was amazing how much money it took to make that happen.

Perhaps Lucy had a different angle. Her wide-eyed innocent bit was pretty convincing. Perhaps not spending money was part of it. Or maybe he was overthinking all of this.

He'd run through that night on the patio in his head dozens of times in the last week. Was she sincere? Did it matter? His body certainly didn't care. It wanted Lucy regardless of her innocence or guilt. Of course, his father had proved that following the advice of one's arousal was not always the best course of action. His dad had followed his right into near bankruptcy.

Speaking of what his groin wanted…

Lucy stepped back into the room wearing a gown.

It was a sheer, tan fabric that looked almost as though she was wearing nothing at all but some floating tiers of beaded lace. It looped around her neck and when she turned to show Harper, it was completely backless.

"This one is Giorgio Armani," the saleswoman said proudly. "It looks lovely with your coloring."

The women talked amongst themselves for a moment before Harper turned to him. "What do you think, Oliver? If you're going to sit on the couch and gawk at her, you should at least make yourself useful."

It did look nice. He felt almost like a Peeping Tom, getting a look at her that he shouldn't have, but he'd rather see her in some color. "She looks naked. She could go naked for free. If she's going to pay that much money, she should at least look like she has an actual dress on."

Lucy laughed, clapping her hand over her mouth when she saw the saleswoman's horrified expression. Oliver was pleased that he'd gotten her to laugh, although he wasn't entirely sure why. She did have a beautiful smile. He hadn't really gotten to see it before. She spent all her time frowning at him, although he probably deserved that.

Harper just shook her head. "Okay, it's not my favorite either. Let's try this one," she said, pulling another gown from the rack.

"What are you dressing her up for?" he asked once Lucy disappeared again.

"The charity gala they're holding at the Museum of Modern Art Saturday night."

"Ah," Oliver said. "I got invited to that. Champagne, weird sculptures and people pressuring you to write checks. I bet the only reason they invited her was to get their hands on some of that money she's inheriting."

Harper put her hands on her hips. "And why did they invite you, hmm? The same reason. It's a charity event. That's the whole point. At least she knows what she's looking at when she walks around the museum."

Oliver shrugged off his sister's insult. It wasn't ignorance on his part when it came to art. He'd taken all the required art appreciation classes in college, as many class field trips as any well-educated child in New York, and followed Aunt Alice around museums on the occasional Saturday. He just didn't get it. Especially modern art. And if he didn't like it, why should he waste his brain cells remembering who this artist was or what that piece symbolized? He just didn't care. He could name maybe six famous painters off the top of his head, and four of them just happened to also be Teenage Mutant Ninja Turtles.

The saleswoman returned to the room looking very pleased with herself, but when Lucy came in behind her, she looked anything but. To be honest, this time Oliver had to hold in a chuckle. The dress was black with sheer fabric that highlighted the black structure of the dress like lingerie of some sort. On its own that would've been fine, but it also had red and pink cutouts all over it, looking like some kind of couture craft project.

"What on earth is that?" he asked.

"Christian Dior!" the saleswoman said with an insulted tone.

"No, just no," Lucy said, turning immediately to take it off. Apparently, she agreed with him.

"Is there anything on that rack that isn't a neutral

or see-through?" Oliver asked. "I don't know what's wrong with color these days. The women are always wearing black or gray. Lucy should stand out."

The saleswoman clucked her tongue at him before turning to the rack again. "So no black, nude or white…" She flipped until she got to the last dress on the rack. "I guess we'll try this one, although it's not my favorite. The designer is relatively new and not very well-known."

"Give it a try," Harper said encouragingly. "You're not really helping us," she said to Oliver when they were alone again.

"It's not my fault her personal shopper picked out ridiculous outfits. I mean, you saw that last one, right? I know it's for a modern art event, but she doesn't want to be confused for an exhibit."

Harper's lips pressed together as she tried to hide a smirk. "Yes, well, this one is nice and I like it. You'd better like it, too, or go home so we can do this without your help. Don't you have a business to run, anyway?"

Oliver shrugged. It was a well-oiled machine and at the moment, he was far more concerned with what was going on with Lucy. For multiple, confusing reasons.

When Lucy returned a moment later, Oliver struggled to catch his breath. The dress was a bright shade of red with cap sleeves and an oval neckline that dipped low enough to showcase her breasts. It fit Lucy beautifully, highlighting her figure and flattering her coloring with its bright hue. It had a sash that wrapped around Lucy's tiny waist, but other than that, wasn't particularly flashy. No beading. No lace. No sheer panels. No wonder the saleswoman hated it. If Lucy picked this gown, her commission would hardly be worth the trip.

"I really like this one," Lucy said. "Especially this part." She turned around and surprised everyone. The dress was completely open in the back, almost like a reversed robe that was held in place with the sash. It was paired with a pair of black satin capris.

Oliver wasn't even entirely sure if that qualified as a dress or a pantsuit, but he liked it. It was different and for some reason, he thought that suited Lucy. He liked the flash of skin along the whole length of her back. Any man who asked her to dance at the gala would get to run his palms over her smooth, bare skin. While he might enjoy that, he felt an unexpected surge of jealousy at the thought of her dancing with anyone else. Plus, the capri pants accented the high, round curve of her ass. He hadn't noticed before, but it was quite the sight.

When Lucy stopped preening, she sought out the price tag and sighed in relief. "This is the one," she said at last.

Oliver watched the women discuss the dress, tuning out the noise and noting nothing but the stunning vision in red. He hadn't intended on going to the museum gala on Saturday, but if Lucy would be there, in that dress, he might just have to amend his plans.

Lucy was fairly certain the woman from Saks Fifth Avenue was never coming back. There weren't nearly enough digits in the price of the dress she selected for the woman's taste. She just didn't see the point in spending thousands of dollars on a dress. A wedding dress, maybe, but not just some pretty outfit to wear to a party.

As it was, the price still seemed pretty steep—nearly a week's worth of her usual salary. But Harper was right; she needed to make a good impression on her first event out. Hopefully the inheritance would come through and she wouldn't have to worry about blowing that much on a single dress, but if not, she would be wearing that red outfit to every damn thing she could think of.

The apartment seemed to clear out all at once. The men returned and hauled the clothes out with a grumpy-looking saleswoman in their wake. Harper had an appointment and left soon after. That just left Oliver mysteriously perched on the couch when she went to change. She hoped by the time she got back, he would be gone, too.

Back in her own clothing—a nice pair of jeans and her favorite sweater—she returned to the room and found him sitting right where she'd left him.

"I still don't understand why you're here. Or still here, for that matter."

Oliver smiled and stood up. "I had some business on this side of town and when I saw the Saks truck, thought I'd pop in. Where Saks goes, Harper follows."

"And now she's gone," Lucy noted. "And you're still here. Want to ask me more questions? Hook me up to a lie detector this time?"

He strolled across the large Moroccan rug with his hands in his pockets. She tried not to notice how gracefully he moved or how he looked at her as he came closer. "Are you hungry?"

"What?" He'd completely ignored everything she

asked him. How was she supposed to have a conversation with him when he did that?

"It's lunchtime. I'm starving. I'd like to take you to lunch if you're hungry."

She stood awkwardly, considering his offer for far too long. "Okay," she blurted out at last. If his sole purpose of coming by here was to uncover her dark secrets, he wouldn't find much. She might as well let him buy her lunch in the meantime. "Let me just grab my coat."

They walked silently out of the building together and downstairs to the street. Although they didn't speak, touch or even make eye contact as they strolled down the street together, she found herself keenly aware of his physical presence. Her body had somehow become attuned to Oliver, and the closer they stood, the harder it was for her to ignore even the tiniest of his movements or gestures.

Lucy was almost relieved when they encountered a more congested area and she had to drop back and follow his lead through crowds of people. The distance helped her nerves, at least until Oliver noticed she'd fallen behind. Without hesitation, he reached out and took her hand, pulling her back to his side. The skin of her palm buzzed with the sensation of his touch, making her whole body hum with awareness as though he intended to do more than just keep from losing her in the crowd.

Lucy expected him to let go once she'd caught up to him, but his grip on her held tight as they walked a few more blocks to a restaurant she'd never been to before.

"Do you like Korean barbecue?" Oliver asked as he finally released her hand.

Lucy peered in the window and shrugged before self-consciously stuffing that hand into her pocket. "I don't know, but it sounds like an experience."

Oliver smiled and held open the door for them to head inside. They were taken to a quiet table in the back with a grill set into the center. The host turned on the table and handed them both menus. It didn't take her long to realize that Korean barbecue involved cooking the meat at their individual table. When the waiter arrived, they selected their drinks and meats. Oliver opted for a glass of red wine and Lucy decided to stick with a soda. After their last encounter at the baby shower, she wasn't sure what to expect when she was alone with Oliver. There was no need to add alcohol to that mix.

Especially with her hand still tingling. Beneath the table, she rubbed it over her jean-clad thigh and wished the feeling away. She needed to keep her wits about her when she was alone with Oliver. She couldn't let her guard down no matter how much she tingled or how he smiled at her. This might all be part of his plan to undermine her claim on Alice's estate. She didn't know how, exactly, but she refused to believe he just wanted to take her to lunch to be nice.

The waiter arrived with their drinks, then placed half a dozen bowls on the table. There were different vegetables, rice and a few foods she didn't recognize. One had tentacles.

"Can I ask you something?" Lucy said once the waiter disappeared from their table. Her bravery where food was concerned was starting to wane, so she opted for a distracting discussion instead.

"Sure." Oliver picked up his glass of wine and awaited her question.

"I lived in that apartment with Alice for over five years. Harper was the only family member I ever saw visit, and in part, she was there to see me. I don't understand it. Why didn't you ever visit your aunt?"

Oliver nodded and focused for a moment on the wood grain of their table. There was an intensity about his expression when he was thinking that Lucy found intriguing, even when he was antagonizing her. He had the same look on his face when he was studying her. She didn't know what he saw or what he expected to see when he looked at her so closely. It made her uncomfortable, especially after those kisses on the patio, but she still liked watching the wheels turn in his mind.

"Aunt Alice didn't like having guests. You wouldn't know it if you went by, she'd treat you like royalty, but inside, she hated it. I missed her, and I wanted to see her, but I knew that it made her anxious, just like leaving her apartment made her anxious. So I gave her a computer, got her all set up and we emailed every day."

Lucy perked up at the last part. "You spoke to her every day?" How could she not know that? And why didn't she realize company made Alice uncomfortable? She'd never said a word about it to her.

Oliver nodded. "Aunt Alice was a complicated woman, although few knew it. Since you asked me a question, I'll ask you one. How much do you really know about my aunt?"

Lucy opened her mouth to answer, but when she thought about it, she realized she didn't have that much to say. "We shared a common love of art. She liked

Chinese takeout from the place a few blocks away. She only drank hot tea with cream and one lump of sugar." There, she stopped. Most of the things she could think of were inconsequential, like being an early riser and watching *Jeopardy!* every weeknight.

"Now that I'm thinking of it, I guess she never really shared that much about herself. Not really. She never talked about her family or her childhood. I don't know if she ever worked or married or anything else. When I told you I didn't know anything about her will or how much money she had, it was true. We never talked about things like that."

"Aunt Alice never married," he began. "My father told me once, a long time ago, that she'd been in love with a young man in the forties. Unfortunately, he got shipped off to World War II right after they got engaged and never came home. She never dated anyone else, to my great-grandfather's dismay. He constantly thrust well-to-do men in front of her, hoping to secure business deals or strengthen ties, but you know her. She had none of it. I guess she never got over losing her first love."

Lucy sat back in her seat and frowned. "That's horrible. There's an old black-and-white photograph of a soldier in a frame beside her bed. That must be his picture."

Oliver nodded. "She got used to being alone, I think, and when everything else happened, she just decided it was better to be alone."

"What do you mean by 'when everything else happened'?"

"The terrorist attacks of September 11, 2001. It affected every New Yorker differently, but the whole thing really shook her up. She was supposed to go downtown to meet with a financial advisor later that morning. Then she turned on the news and realized what was happening. If her appointment had been an hour or two earlier, she would've been in the North Tower of the World Trade Center when the first plane hit. It scared the hell out of her. She never set foot out of her apartment again."

Lucy's jaw dropped as Oliver spoke. All this time, she'd been pointing fingers at him and his family for not visiting or even knowing Alice at all, when in truth, Lucy didn't know her either. Of course, she'd wondered why Alice never left the apartment, but it seemed rude to ask, so she never did. Some people developed agoraphobia without any particular incident at onset.

"What was she like before that?" she asked, suddenly curious about the friend and employer she knew so little about.

Oliver smiled, the sharp features of his face softening. "She was fun. After my mother died, sometimes my father would leave Harper and me with her for an afternoon while he worked. She would take us to the park or the zoo. The art museums, of course. She never worried about getting dirty or eating too much junk. As kids, we thought she was the greatest aunt in the world. It wasn't until we got older that we realized she was going out less and less. She was getting older, too, but I think she was feeling less comfortable out in the city. The attacks were the last nail in the coffin for her, I think. She decided it was safer to stay inside. And in time, she wanted less and less company, until she was almost completely closed off from the world."

"Why?"

"Fear, I guess. It's odd considering she seemed like the most fearless and exciting person I'd ever known. I sometimes wonder what she would've been like if her fiancé hadn't died. If she'd had a family. Would she still have closed herself off the way she did? I don't know. I hated it, though. I hated seeing that light in her extinguish."

The waiter appeared with their tray of meat and started to cook the first portion on the grill, effectively ending that line of conversation. Lucy was glad. Learning about Alice was enlightening, but also sad. There was a good reason why her employer hadn't talked about her past. She'd lost her chance at love and chosen to spend the rest of her life alone rather than be with someone else. Whether it was incredibly romantic or just sad, Lucy didn't know. But at the rate her love life was going, she might end up alone, too.

The server expertly flipped the meat, putting the finished pieces on their plates and explaining the different sides she'd been eyeing earlier. Once he was gone, they started eating and Oliver tossed a few raw pieces of Korean short ribs onto the grill to eat next.

Lucy watched him as he ate, thinking about their interactions since Alice died. She was a little ashamed of herself after everything she'd said and done. Yes, he was determined to prove she was a scam artist, but what did he know of her? Nothing. And she knew nothing of him. Or Alice, apparently. But she could tell that he had genuinely cared for his aunt. He couldn't fake the affection that reflected in his blue eyes when he spoke about her.

"Oliver, I want to apologize."

He paused, his food hanging midair on the end of his fork. "Apologize for what?"

"For judging you so harshly. For judging your whole family. All these years, I had this burning resentment for all of you. Sometimes I'd see Alice sitting in her chair looking at family photos and it ate me up inside that no one ever came to visit. She seemed so lonely and I felt like everyone had abandoned her for some reason."

Lucy shook her head and felt her cheeks start to flush with embarrassment. When she tilted her head up and looked him in the eye, the softness of his expression took away the last of her worries. She wasn't sure what she'd expected from Oliver, but it wasn't patience and understanding.

"That's why I lashed out at the reading of the will. When all these people showed up after her death, it felt like circling sharks drawn by chum in the water. Now I realize that it was how Alice wanted it. Or at least, how she needed it to be. So I'm sorry for anything ugly I said to you about all that."

Oliver held her gaze for a moment before smiling and popping a bite of food into his mouth. "It was an easy assumption to make," he said after swallowing. "I think we're all guilty of doing that to some extent, don't you?"

His gaze was fixed on her, with almost a pleading expression on his face. He wasn't going to apologize for the things he'd accused her of, but maybe this was his way of acknowledging that perhaps he'd judged her too harshly as well. It didn't mean he was going to call off his lawyers, but maybe he wouldn't show up at the apartment to give her the third degree any longer.

"A truce, then?" Lucy asked, lifting her soda and holding her breath. While she would be glad to put an end to the fighting, she worried what could happen between the two of them without it keeping them apart. It was a dangerous proposition, but a part of her was anxious for him to say yes.

Oliver smiled and lifted his wine to clink her glass. "A truce."

Six

"Welcome, Mr. Drake. So good of you to join us this evening."

Oliver strolled into the Museum of Modern Art and stopped as he was greeted by a table of committee members organizing the charity event. The older woman who stood to welcome him looked familiar, but he couldn't place her.

"I am so sorry to hear about your aunt," she said. "She was a valued patron to the museum and the art world as a whole."

He nodded politely. "Thank you." Turning to the table where a young male volunteer was checking off guests on the attendee list, he leaned in. "Can you tell me if Miss Campbell has already arrived?"

"She has." The young man beamed. Apparently he was a fan of her new outfit, too.

"Thank you."

They directed him up the short staircase to the second-floor atrium where the main portion of the event was taking place. At the top of the stairs, a waiter with a large silver tray offered him a flute of champagne, and he accepted. This type of event was not his idea of a good time, but at least there was alcohol involved. It helped to open people's pocketbooks, he was fairly certain.

The wide-open room with white walls that reached for the sky was dominated by a large pyramidal sculpture in the center. He was ashamed to admit he hadn't been to the museum since it had been redone years ago. A couple hundred or so people milled around the space, chatting and sipping their drinks. A band was playing in a corner of the room, but no one was dancing yet. The far wall was peppered with special pieces that his invitation said were being offered on silent auction to raise funds for the nearby LaGuardia High School of Music & Art and Performing Arts.

It didn't take long for Oliver to locate Lucy in the crowd. His eyes were immediately drawn to the crimson red of her dress that stood out amongst the sedate blacks, tans and whites of the people who accepted what the saleswoman pushed on them without question. The outfit looked equally stunning tonight, although now it was paired with elegantly styled hair, glittering jewelry and flawless makeup.

Altogether, it made for a woman he simply couldn't ignore. His body was drawn to her, urging him to cross the room and join her immediately. The only thing that held him in place was his desire to prolong the anticipation.

He enjoyed watching her chat with a couple about

the large Monet that dominated an entire wall of the museum. Oliver could tell she hadn't spied him at the gala yet. When she knew he was nearby, there was something about her that changed. A stiffness, almost as though she were holding her breath when he was around. He wasn't sure if she was just more guarded, he made her nervous or if the palpable attraction between them simply caused her to be uncomfortable in his presence.

At the moment, she was sipping her champagne, smiling and speaking animatedly with a couple he recognized from other events around town. He liked watching her with her guard down. It was a side of her he'd never gotten to see, not even in the past when they'd called a truce or shared a kiss. That was his own fault, he supposed, but it made him want to know more about this side of Lucy. Perhaps it was the last piece of the puzzle he was missing.

Oliver watched as the couple finally dismissed themselves to say hello to someone else, leaving Lucy standing awkwardly alone. She bit at her lip, the confident facade crumbling without the distraction of conversation. Now was his chance. He moved through the crowd of people to join her.

When their eyes met, Oliver felt a jolt of electricity run through him. Lucy smiled wide as he came closer, possibly relieved to see someone she knew. He could imagine that being in this situation and knowing almost no one must be quite intimidating. When she attended for Alice, she could fade into the background, but with that dress, she couldn't hide from anyone. A familiar face, even his, would be cause for excitement. Or maybe, just maybe, she was happy to see *him*.

"Good evening, Miss Campbell," he said with a wide smile of his own. Lately just the thought of her brought a grin to his face. As his gaze flicked over her beauty up close, he wished he hadn't waited so long to approach her. "You're looking lovely tonight."

Lucy blushed almost as red as her dress. "Thank you. I didn't expect to see you here this evening. I don't recall running into you at any of the events I attended for your aunt. I thought you weren't much of a fan of art."

Oliver shrugged. He wasn't about to say he'd only come because her might see her. "I'm always invited, but I usually have other engagements. Tonight was for a good cause and I had time, so I dusted off my tuxedo and came down."

Her gaze ran over his Armani tux for a moment with appreciation before she awkwardly turned away to glance at the art display across the room. "Have you looked at the pieces they have for sale tonight? There's some really lovely ones if you're looking to add to your personal collection."

"I haven't." The moment he'd seen her, the rest of the museum had faded into the background.

Oliver politely offered his arm and escorted Lucy to the other side of the atrium where maybe twenty-five paintings and sculptures were set up with silent auction sheets posted at each.

"Some of these were done by students at the school and others are donated by local artists. These kids show so much promise for their age. It's amazing."

He knew at this point he could let her arm go, but he didn't. He liked the feel of her against his side. A lot. "Did you ever have a desire to be an artist yourself?"

"Oh no," Lucy said with a nervous chuckle. "I love to look at it, to study it, but I can't draw a stick figure. I mean look at this one." She gestured toward a large painting of the Manhattan skyline with the Brooklyn Bridge stretching across the foreground. "This piece gets more amazing the longer you study it."

Oliver stepped closer to try to figure out what distinguished the piece from every other one they sold on street corners around the city. It was only when he got a foot or so away that he could see the image wasn't painted, but actually made up of millions of tiny hearts. Only from far away did the colored hearts make up the image of the city.

"The artist loves New York," Lucy continued. "The painting practically screams it. The color palette she chose, the light in the sky…it's a very well-balanced piece."

"It sounds like you really like this one. You should buy it," Oliver suggested. Part of him was waiting for her to start spending his aunt's money. Where was the joy in achieving one's goal when they couldn't enjoy it? He leaned in to look at the current bid. It was well within her means if the windfall went through. "It's only up to ten thousand dollars right now. If this artist is half as talented as you think she is at seventeen, this painting will be worth triple that one day. It's a great investment."

Lucy laughed off his suggestion and he realized how much he liked that sound. Arguing with her was fun, but he much preferred this version of his aunt's companion.

"You're just as bad as Harper," she said. "Counting chickens that may never hatch, no thanks to you. As far as I'm concerned, I have no money. Just some savings that have taken me the past five years to accumulate. I'm certainly not spending it on art when I may have no place to live in a few weeks' time."

Oliver felt a momentary pang of guilt. He'd taken the fun out of this moment for her. How different would it be tonight if he hadn't contested the will? Would he be the one there for her when she made her first big purchase? "But what if you did? What if you had all those millions at your disposal right now?"

Lucy's crimson-painted lips twisted in thought. "I haven't given it much thought. But in this case, since it was for charity, I would consider buying it. I would at least bid. But otherwise I would just feel too guilty spending that much money on something like that."

Oliver couldn't help a confused frown. He turned to look at her with a furrowed brow. "My aunt spent a hundred times that on a single piece. Why would you feel guilty doing the same? It's your money to spend however you want to."

Lucy pulled away from him and the painting and started toward the staircase that led up to other exhibits. Oliver caught up and took her arm again, in part to be a gentleman and in part because he liked the feel of her so near to him. The moment she moved from his side, it felt like a cold emptiness sidled up against him. He was eager to feel the warmth of her skin and smell the scent of her perfume again. It was a soft fragrance, like a garden after the rain, that made him want to draw it deep into his lungs.

"It's not my money," she said after quite a few steps. "It's Alice's money. And if by some stroke of luck it does become mine, I couldn't just blow it on whatever suits me. It was a gift and I need to cherish it. Do something good with it. Help people."

Curious. He'd never once spoken to someone who felt like money was a kind of burden of responsibility. Especially someone who'd schemed to get the money in the first place. "You could give it all to charity, I suppose. But Alice could've done that herself. She gave it to you for a reason. I wish I knew what that reason was."

Lucy stopped on the landing and turned to him with an understanding expression softening her features. "So do I. It would make things easier for everyone if she'd let us in on her little secret, don't you think?"

Her words rang true in Oliver's ears, making his stomach start to ache. Had he made the wrong call with her? He'd started spending time around Lucy with the intention of finding out what she was really about and all he'd uncovered was a woman who seemed kind, thoughtful, caring and intelligent. She was attractive as well, but didn't seem too concerned with that.

Either she was one of the greatest con artists he'd ever met or he was way off base with this whole thing.

"This is my favorite part of the museum," she said, letting their prior discussion drop.

They had stopped on the surrealism floor. They started wandering through bizarre sculptures and even more bizarre paintings. "Your favorite, eh? Myself, I just don't get it," Oliver said, gesturing to the large painting hanging on the wall just ahead of them. "This one, for example."

Lucy sighed and stepped beside him. She studied the painting, but all he could focus on was the intriguing scent of her perfume and the glittering rubies at her ears. The sparkle drew his gaze to the long line of her neck. It was hard for him not to ogle, knowing the bare skin traveled down to the small of her back, exposed by the red dress she'd chosen from the personal shopper.

"This looks like something a child would doodle with crayons," he said.

"This is a popular piece by Joan Miró."

"Never heard of her."

"Him," she corrected. "This is part of his *Constellation* series from the early 1940s, and one of my favorites, actually. It's called *The Beautiful Bird Revealing the Unknown to a Pair of Lovers*."

Oliver forced his attention back to the painting and searched for whatever Lucy saw in it. He could find no bird, beautiful or otherwise, nor a pair of lovers. There was just a bunch of black circles and triangles scattered around a brown background with a couple random eyeballs. He turned his head sideways but it didn't help. It didn't make any sense to him. "Okay, Miss Art Connoisseur, show off your expertise and explain this piece to me."

"Okay," Lucy said with a confident nod. "This painting is well-known for its simplified color palette and line work designed to simulate a constellation in the night sky. What I've always appreciated about the piece is the sense of joy despite the chaos, which is a reflection of the artist's life at the time, in war-torn Europe. He worked on the pieces during the Spanish Civil War and actually fled the German advance into France with little more than this collection of paintings. He said that working on this collection liberated him from focusing on the tragedy of war. They were a joyful escape and

I see that in his works. You have the calm of night, the jubilant dance of the stars…"

Lucy continued to talk about the work, but Oliver was far more interested in watching her. It was as though she was finally comfortable in her own skin, but it had nothing to do with him. She was no longer the fish out of water amongst the rich, mingling crowds of the charity event. She was the contemporary art expert, finally solid in her footing. Her dark eyes twinkled and her face lit up with excitement for the beauty of what she was looking at.

It was transformative. The dress was pretty, the makeup and the hair were well done, but it was this moment that Lucy truly became stunningly beautiful in his eyes. His breath caught in his throat as she gestured toward the painting and the overhead lights cast a shadow across the interesting angles and curves of her face. Her full, red lips moved quickly as she spoke, teasing him to come closer and capture them with his mouth.

"Oliver?"

His gaze darted from her lips to her eyes, which had a twinkle of amusement in them. "Yes?"

"You're not listening to a word I'm saying, are you? I've bored you to tears. You did ask me to tell you about it."

"Yes, I did. And I was listening," he lied. "I just got distracted by the beauty."

Lucy smirked and turned back toward the painting. "It is lovely, isn't it?"

"I was talking about you."

Lucy's head snapped to look in his direction as she gasped audibly. Her ruby lips parted softly as she looked at him without finding any words.

"You know, the last time I said you were beautiful, you kissed me. And hit me. But first, you kissed me."

Lucy's mouth closed into a smile. "Yes, well, I don't intend to do either of those things here, no matter what you say." She took a sip of her champagne and continued to stroll through the exhibit.

Oliver grinned and hurried to catch up with her. They'd just see about that.

"This section of the museum is dedicated to works of the sixties," Lucy said as they rounded the corner. She didn't want to keep talking about how beautiful he thought she looked tonight or about the kisses they'd shared at Emma's baby shower. Nothing good could come of the way he was looking at her, especially on the mostly deserted upper floors of the museum where anything could happen without witnesses.

She hadn't dated a lot, especially since she dropped out of Yale, so understanding men was not her strong suit. She got the feeling that even if it were, she would still be confused where Oliver was concerned. He didn't seem outwardly to like her, and yet he was always around. He was insulting her integrity one moment and complimenting her so-called beauty the next.

His mood swings were giving her whiplash. There was one thing she was certain of, however—those kisses on the Dempseys' patio had been passionate, tingle-inducing and toe-curling. Maybe the best kisses of her life. And yet his calm dismissal of the whole thing had left her uncertain of him and what he wanted from her.

Since Lucy couldn't be sure where she stood with Oliver, she knew her best course of action would be to keep her distance physically. Truce or no truce, it would only lead to trouble. She might not be able to avoid him when he seemed determined to seek her out, but she didn't need to encourage him. At least until the court case was decided either way, she needed to stay away from Oliver Drake.

She just didn't want to.

On the wall ahead of them was the famous collection of Yves Klein. She'd studied his work extensively in college as his artistic techniques were quite the scandalous production back then, and even now, although for somewhat different reasons. She was relieved to have art to talk about instead of focusing on the unmistakable connection between the two of them.

"I think you'll like this collection by Yves Klein. It's called *Anthropométrie de L'époque Bleue*."

Oliver stopped to study the first piece with a confused expression furrowing his brow. "I didn't understand the other one we discussed, but at least I could tell it was an actual painting that took skill of some kind. This is a giant white canvas with blue smears all over it."

Lucy smiled. "That's the final outcome, yes. But Klein was more of a performance artist in his day than just a painter. He created all these works with live audiences and an orchestra playing music in the background. He was quite famous for the events he put on. His most well-known piece, *Fire-Color FC 1*, sold at auction for over 36 million dollars in 2012."

His jaw dropped as he turned to look at her in disbelief. "I can't imagine why anyone would want to sit and watch a man paint for hours, much less pay that much for the sloppy outcome."

If that was all he'd done, it wouldn't have been interesting, that was true. She couldn't help leaning in and sharing the critical tidbit about Klein's methods into his ear. She pressed her palm on his shoulder and climbed to her toes to brush her lips against the outer shell. "He painted with nude women."

The lines in Oliver's brow deepened as he turned to her. "So he painted with nude women standing around? A little distracting and gimmicky, don't you think?"

"No. He didn't use paintbrushes. He didn't even touch the canvas, actually. He used what he called 'living brushes.' He literally used the bodies of beautiful nude women smeared in paint. Or he traced their naked bodies onto the canvas and burned the image into the fabric with a torch."

"Seriously?"

Lucy nodded. "I've watched video recordings of his exhibitions and they were quite the spectacle. Just imagine all these well-to-do art lovers coming to a museum, and when they get there, they're greeted by a man in a tuxedo and maybe six young, attractive and very naked women. They sat there and watched as the women smeared the paint all over their skin, then pressed their bodies into the canvas, just as the artist guided them. He was more of a director, really, coaching the women into creating the shapes and images he wanted to portray. With the music and the lighting… it was such a sensual experience. To capture that kind of feeling in a work of art is amazing, really."

He squinted at the canvas, but Lucy could tell he needed help envisioning it in the peculiar shapes left behind.

She stepped between him and the closest painting.

"So picture me naked," she said with a smile. "There's buckets of blue paint and plastic tarps all over the floor. Even some canvases on the floor. I rub the paint all over my skin, covering everything as Yves directs, then position my body just so and press into the canvas." Lucy stood in front of the painting and tried to situate her body to mimic the imprint. "Can you see it now?"

He didn't answer. Finally, she dropped her arms and turned back to where he was standing. He was looking at her, but the expression in his eyes was not one of a casual appreciation for art. It looked as though he'd taken her far too literally when she'd told him to imagine her naked. A desire blazed in his blue-gray eyes as he watched her. So much for a distraction.

"I see it now," Oliver said, but he still wasn't looking at the painting. Instead, he took a step closer to her, closing the gap between them.

Lucy was suddenly very aware of her body. Despite the pleasant temperature of the museum, a blanket of goose bumps settled across her skin and made the hairs prickle at the back of her neck. She could feel the heat of Oliver as he hovered ever nearer, yet not touching her. The scent of his cologne made her long to press against him and bury her nose in his throat. All that talk about Klein's work had been the last thing they'd needed.

His hand reached out and his fingertips brushed across hers, sending jolts of electricity through her whole body. A warm rush of desire settled in her belly, urging her not to pull away from him this time. They'd both danced around this moment and she found she was desperate to see what would come next if they let things just happen.

Oliver leaned in, his face close enough to kiss her if either of them turned just right. "Lucy...?" he whispered.

She might be on a long celibate streak, but she knew what it meant when a man said her name like that. She wanted to say yes and throw her arms around his neck, but she wouldn't. This simmering passion just beneath the surface was dangerous, and she knew it. Did she dare give in to it? Could she trust the man who had previously been determined to call her out as a manipulative crook?

He certainly didn't seem interested in talking about his aunt's estate right now.

"Yes?" she replied, her voice trembling as her body ached to reach for him.

"Would you mind if we left the party a little early?" His breath was hot against her skin, sending a shiver down her spine.

"It just started," Lucy argued half-heartedly. It was a charity event and neither of them had been very charitable so far. "What about the school?"

Oliver leaned back and pierced her with his blue-gray gaze. "How about we go back downstairs, I write a check to make everyone happy and then you and I go back to my place. To talk about art," he added.

"A big check," Lucy suggested. He could afford it, even if she couldn't.

"Of course. You'll learn that with me, it's go big or go home," he said with a sly grin and a wink that promised more big things to come.

Seven

"Nice place," Lucy said as they stepped into his penthouse apartment.

Oliver just shrugged off the compliment. "It works for me. It's not a Fifth Avenue apartment overlooking the park or anything."

"Most people don't have that. Just because your aunt did doesn't make your place any less fantastic. If I hadn't been living with her all these years, I'd be renting a place the size of your entryway."

Lucy looked around in curiosity, taking in every detail of the place he'd paid to have professionally decorated. Oliver didn't really care about things like that. This was just a place to sleep at night. He did what was expected of him in this case because his apartment needed furniture and things on the wall. Thanks to all the money he'd spent, he now had expensive glass bowls that appeared to serve no real purpose and tiny statues that gathered dust. Thankfully he also had a cleaning service that came in to deal with that.

Oliver slipped out of his suit coat and threw it over the arm of the leather sofa. In his pocket, he found the receipt for the painting he'd just purchased at the charity event. He folded it neatly and tucked it away before Lucy could see it. She thought he'd simply made a donation to the high school before they left, but he'd actually gone in and placed a ridiculously high bid on the student painting she'd admired earlier. It ensured he would win the auction. Once the piece was assessed by the art department for the senior's final grade, it would be delivered anonymously to Lucy's apartment.

He wasn't entirely sure why he'd done it. Oliver wasn't exactly known for making flashy donations to charities or giving extravagant gifts. Most of the people in his life didn't need anything, so he quietly supported a few causes. In this case, however, he just knew he wanted to do something nice and unexpected for Lucy. She would appreciate it in a way few women he knew would. He hoped he'd be there when it was delivered so he could see the smile on her face when she saw it. That was enough for him.

"I see now why it's so easy for you to show up at the apartment unannounced," she said, pulling him from his thoughts. "You're only a few blocks away."

He approached her from behind as she stood in his living room and reached up to help her slip out of her coat. The night had grown chilly, but his apartment was very warm. He sighed as his eyes took in one inch after the next of her exposed back as the coat slipped down her arms and into his. The movement brought the scent of her skin to his nose, urging him to lean in closer. He longed to run his fingertip along the curve of her spine and follow the path with his mouth. Every time he looked at that outfit, he liked it more.

With the coat in his arms, Lucy turned to look at him expectantly. What had she asked about? Where he lived. "Yes," he responded. Oliver took a deep breath to push aside the building desire for a little while longer. He had no intention of attacking Lucy the moment he got her alone, as much as he might like to. "It's convenient to my offices and such. It's nice to live close to my father and sister as well. Dropping in on you so easily was just a bonus." He laid her coat across his own on the sofa. "Would you like a drink?"

"I would," she said with a polite smile. "Do you have a patio or a balcony where we could step out and enjoy it?"

He hesitated for a moment, not sure if he wanted to share that part of his life with her. At least not yet. It was one thing to want to seduce Lucy, another entirely to open up his most private place. His apartment didn't have a traditional balcony; it had something much nicer that was very personal to him. He'd actually never showed it to a woman he was dating before, and he wasn't even sure he'd call this situation with Lucy *dating.* "Not exactly," he replied as he disappeared into the kitchen to stall his response.

"What does that mean?" Lucy asked as she turned the corner to join him.

He wasn't entirely sure why, but he'd always kept that part of his life very private. Maybe it was watching his father give over everything to Candace, only to have her ruin it. Maybe it was just keeping something for himself that he didn't have to explain to anyone else. Harper had only seen his garden once.

And yet, he wanted to show it off to Lucy.

He'd never felt that compulsion before, and it unnerved him that he wanted to show her, of all people. "I have a large rooftop patio," he explained. "It's more of a garden, really. That's where I go when I want to…get dirty and unplug." From life, from stress, from all the drama of his family. He found his center when he was up to his elbows in potting soil. It was hard to explain that to the other rich CEOs who preferred racquetball, cigars and fine scotch to unwind.

"That sounds wonderful," Lucy said. "I'd love to see it."

Oliver worked on opening a bottle of wine and pouring two healthy glasses of chardonnay. He tried not to appear nervous about taking Lucy to see his handiwork. Surely he could manage to show it to her without letting her know how significant it was to him. "Sure. There's some great views from up there."

He handed her a glass and she followed him to a door in the hallway that looked like a closet, but actually hid a staircase up to the roof. Oliver took a soothing breath as he stepped out onto the patio with Lucy in his wake. "This is my retreat from the concrete jungle," he said.

Lucy's reply didn't come right away. Instead, when he turned to see what was wrong, he found her slack-jawed and wide-eyed. She looked around his garden as though she'd never seen anything like it in her life. And maybe she hadn't. He knew immediately that there was no way to hide how important this place was to him. It was obvious just by looking at it.

"I don't know what I was expecting," Lucy said at last. "Maybe some clay pots with petunias in them or something. But nothing like this."

That's probably because there were few rooftop gardens like this in the city. He had trees and shrubs in huge planters along the edges of the roofline that made the garden feel private and secluded. There were twinkle lights wrapped through the branches and strung overhead, mixing with the stars. Pea-gravel pathways made a complicated pattern around raised flowerbeds where he was growing all manner of flowers and a few vegetables he donated to the food bank. Many of the plants would soon die back for the winter, but most were still showing off their foliage and brightly colored blooms.

"I had no idea you were a gardener. Harper never mentioned it. How did the CEO of a computer company get into something like this?"

"Few people know about it. Harper knows, she just doesn't mention it very often because she's afraid I'm going to make her come up and pull weeds or something." Oliver stuffed his free hand into his pants pocket and slowly strolled along the gravel path.

"It's funny you should ask how I got into it… When I was very young, my mother had a garden like this on their rooftop, and I helped her from time to time. I guess I got my green thumb from her. After she died, my father basically let her garden run wild. He didn't want anyone up there messing with her things. Years later as a teenager, I got the stupid idea to go up there and grow some weed. It was such a mess that I didn't figure anyone would notice, but my dad saw me sneaking out there once or twice and eventually busted me."

"As my punishment, I had to clean up my mother's garden and maintain it flawlessly for six months. By the time my sentence ended, I'd found I really enjoyed it. I chose this apartment in part because of the roof access. It's all mine and since it's taller than most of the nearby buildings, it's incredibly private despite being surrounded by millions of other people. The previous owners had just put some patio furniture out here, but I transformed it over the last few years into a place that I think my mother would've loved."

Oliver had no idea why he kept rambling on about the garden and his love for it. He'd never told this story to anyone, and yet Lucy's simple question had prompted a flow of words that even he hadn't expected. He didn't understand why she had this effect on him. There wasn't just an attraction between them, there was more. A real connection that he wanted to build and maintain beyond this nonsense about the will. That was the scariest part of all.

"Are there still places to sit up here?" Lucy asked as she leaned in to smell a large, dark red rose.

That was one of his favorites—the Mister Lincoln rose. It gave off an amazing perfume in addition to being a beautiful, classic, crimson rose. "Yes. If we follow the path around, we'll see the pergola where I've put up some furniture."

They walked along the trail lined with rosebushes, gardenias and zinnias, to the trumpet vine-wrapped pergola on the south side of the building. It framed the best view from the roof, showcasing the ever-changing colors of the top of the Empire State Building. Under the pergola was a double chaise lounge that was perfect for sunbathing, naps or working evenings on the laptop with a glass of wine or scotch and ice.

"Wow," Lucy said. With the giddy grin of a child, she kicked off her heels and lay against the raised back of the chaise. She tugged up her dress to expose the cropped pants underneath and wiggled her pink painted toes in their newfound freedom. "This is amazing. I would spend every minute I had out here if I could."

Oliver smiled and settled onto the seat beside her. She'd jumped into the chaise without giving a second thought to getting her designer dress dirty and he appreciated that. "I don't spend much time just sitting here, actually. Maintaining the garden takes up most of my free time since I do it all myself. If I'm out here, I'm pulling weeds and repotting plants. Trimming back bushes and watering. It's a lot of work but it helps me keep my mind off of my worries."

Lucy sighed and snuggled against his shoulder as she took a sip of her wine. Oliver felt the heat of her body sink through the fabric of his tuxedo shirt and warm his skin. The feel of her so close made his pulse speed up. Suddenly, he had the urge to rip off his bowtie and tug her into his lap. He wasn't going to rush things tonight, though. There was no need to not take their time and enjoy it.

"And to think," Lucy said, "I assumed you were just some heartless workaholic with nothing better to do with your limited free time than screw with me."

That made him laugh out loud, chasing away his heated thoughts for a moment. Lucy just said whatever came to her mind and he loved that about her. There wasn't anything practiced or polished about her words. It was authentic and refreshing, even when it was mildly insulting.

"Well, I am a heartless workaholic, but I have plenty of things I could do with my limited free time. I simply chose to spend the time screwing with you because I…" Oliver turned his head toward her with his lips nearly pressing against her temple. "I like you, Lucy. More than I ever thought I would. Probably more than I should, if I were smart. But I can't help it. And I can't help wanting you."

Lucy was stunned to silence. It was one thing to say that they'd called a truce on their war over Alice's estate. It was another thing entirely for him to declare he wanted her while they were alone on a romantic rooftop patio. That was serious. That was the kind of statement that led to action.

So action is the course she took.

She set her glass of wine and small beaded black clutch on the table beside them and shifted onto her side to face him. His expression was different as he looked down at her in the glow of the garden's lights. The hard edge of his jaw seemed softer, the sharp glare of his blue eyes warm instead. Welcoming. And not just with need, although she could sense the tension of desire in the press of his lips into one another. There was something about being here, in this place that was so special to him, that had changed him or at least shown her a side of him she didn't know existed. She liked that part of Oliver. Liked him enough to throw the last of her reservations out the window where he was concerned.

"Sometimes the things we want aren't the smartest choices," she said softly. "But they're the chances you're the most likely to regret not taking. I hate having regrets."

Lucy followed her words by leaning in and kissing him. This was no desperate assault like their first kiss on the Dempsey balcony, but a sultry warm-up to something more. She melted into him as she felt his hands seek out her waist and pull her closer. His mouth parted and his tongue slid past her own. The caress sent a surge down her spine, making her skin prickle with goose bumps and her core throb with need.

She never expected to be here, in a place like this, with a man like Oliver. Despite her desire to make more of herself one day, she never wanted it to be because she dated up on the social ladder. Even though being friends with women like Emma and Violet exposed her to plenty of sexy, successful men, she didn't think for a moment they would be interested in her.

But Oliver was definitely interested.

His hands moved over her body, exploring and caressing each curve and hollow like he was trying to commit it to memory. When his fingertips brushed over the bare curve of her back and waist, she shivered from the sizzling heat of his hand against her skin.

"Are you cold?" He whispered the question against her lips. "Your skin is freezing. We can go back inside."

"I'm not cold. You're just hot." *In more ways than one*, she thought silently. "And I like it."

"Oh really?" He smiled and gripped firmly at her hip. "Then I think you'll like this, too."

Lucy let out a soft squeal of surprise as Oliver pulled her into his lap with a firm tug, guiding her to straddle him on the chaise. The position was much more comfortable than lying side by side and allowed her free access to his body with her hands. She ran her palms over his chest with a naughty grin, feeling the hard muscles beneath the starched fabric of his shirt. "You're right. I like this as well. I'd like it better with some of this fabric out of the way."

She moved quickly to his tie and the buttons of his shirt. He didn't resist, he just closed his eyes and tensed his jaw as her hips slowly moved back and forth, teasing at his rock-hard arousal.

"Damn," he muttered under his breath.

His response to her made Lucy bolder. Once his shirt was unbuttoned, she pushed it open and ran her hands across the golden bronze ridges of his chest. He wasn't a soft, pale businessman who spent all his time indoors in front of a computer. Apparently gardening was hard work that he did without his shirt on and she appreciated that.

He lay mostly motionless with his eyes still closed as she admired the gift she'd just unwrapped. Her fingers traced the edges of his muscles, grazing over his sprinkle of dark chest hair and trailing the path it made down his belly to his belt. She could feel his stomach quiver beneath her touch as she moved lower.

Oliver could only tolerate that for so long, it seemed; as his eyes flew open, he reached out to cup Lucy's face and pulled her mouth to his own. There was an edge of frenzy when he kissed her this time, the slow, sensual kiss from earlier harder to maintain as the tension built between them. She didn't mind. She gave as good as she got, touching him and pressing into his caresses to intensify the pleasurable feelings that they sent through her body.

Lucy only felt a moment of nerves as Oliver's fingers unfastened the strip of red fabric that held on her dress. There was nothing beneath it but the black cropped pants that paired with the open-backed gown, so she would be fully exposed. She didn't want to act nervous, however. She didn't want Oliver to know how long it had been since she'd been with a man or how badly she didn't want to screw tonight up. So instead, she pasted on her most seductive expression—at least that was what she was going for—and let the gown slip down her arms to pool with the rest of it bunched up at his waist.

She bit at her lip as Oliver studied her bare chest with appreciation. She held her breath until he brought his hands up to cover her breasts and knead them gently. He groaned aloud with approval as she leaned into his touch.

Oliver let go of her only long enough to tug the fabric of her discarded dress into a ball and cast it to the vacant side of the chaise. That allowed them to get closer, and he took advantage of that by sitting up, wrapping his arms around her waist and capturing one of her hard, pink nipples in his mouth.

Lucy's head went back with a soft cry she couldn't hold in. For a moment, she looked around, expecting to feel exposed somehow, but the garden was incredibly private. She could shout, cry and remove every stitch of clothing she had on without anyone being the wiser. It was an unexpected turn-on, titillating the inner exhibitionist she didn't know she had.

She clutched the back of his head with her hands, burying her fingers in the thick waves of his chestnut hair and holding him close. She was so caught up in the moment, the feel of his lips on her skin, that she didn't realize she was moving backward until her skin made contact with the chaise.

Now Oliver was on top with Lucy's legs clamped around his narrow hips. He held himself up with his arms planted to each side of her as he looked down with a satisfied smirk. Pressing forward, he rubbed his firm desire between her thighs. The sensation shot through her like a fiery arrow despite the pesky pants they both still had on. Not for long.

Oliver placed a gentle kiss on her lips, then continued down her body. One on her chin, each collarbone, her sternum, each breast, her stomach…stopping when he reached her capris. Those were quickly unzipped and pulled down her hips along with the lace hipster panties she was wearing beneath them. For every few inches of skin he uncovered, he placed another kiss on her skin. Each hipbone, her lower belly, the tops and inside of her thighs, knees, calves, ankles.

And then she was naked. Totally and completely exposed, panting and trembling with the overwhelming sensations he was stirring inside of her. She ached for him to touch her center, to fill her with the hard heat he'd teased her with so far. But instead, he stopped moving altogether.

Lucy opened her eyes to see him kneeling between her legs with an almost painful expression lining his face. "What's wrong?" No woman wanted to finally take off all her clothes and have the guy freeze up like that.

"I don't have anything," he explained with a sheepish look. "Protection, I mean. To be honest, I wasn't expecting this to happen. Especially not up here. It's not an excuse not to wear anything. I wouldn't do that.

I don't know why I didn't think of this sooner. I was just wrapped up in you…and now you're naked and so beautiful and I…"

Lucy smiled and leaned over to reach for her purse sitting on the table. There, she pulled out the duo of condoms she carried for emergencies. She'd never had an emergency in all the years leading up to now, but she knew better than to not be prepared. That was when bad decisions happened. "Here," she said, holding up the foil packets and saving him from the torture he was leveraging on himself.

Oliver took them from her, clutched them in his fist and grinned. "You're amazing. Thank God."

He leaned down and kissed her with a renewed surge of energy. Oliver pulled away for a few moments and when he returned to her, the pants were gone, the latex was in place and he was poised between her thighs. "Now," he said with a grin as he looked down at her. "Where were we?"

Lucy reached between them and wrapped her fingers around his length. He groaned as she rubbed the tip of him against her moist flesh, teasing them both to the point of madness, then positioning him just at her opening. "Right about here is a good place to pick up, I think."

"You're right," he agreed before pushing forward into her warmth. He moved at an agonizingly slow pace, savoring every inch until he was buried deep inside of her.

Lucy gasped at the sensation of being so completely filled after all the years she'd gone without it. She suddenly wondered why she'd allowed herself to become so much like her agoraphobic older client while only in her twenties, but at the same time, she wouldn't have traded this moment for anything. If five years of celibacy earned her a payoff like this, it was worth it.

It was as though he was the perfect key for her lock. Everything from the way he touched her, to how he kissed her, the taste of his skin, to the scent of his cologne, couldn't have been more right. And when he started to move, the floodgates opened deep inside of her.

She clung to his back, gasping and crying out to the inky black sky overhead as Oliver thrust into her. They rocked together on the chaise, their movements more frantic and their muscles growing more tense as the pleasure started to build up between them.

"You feel so amazing," he growled into her ear. "I don't ever want this to end."

Lucy couldn't respond. She was past the point of rational thought with her climax barreling closer with every surge. All she could manage was a steady chorus of encouraging yeses. *Yes, keep doing that. Yes, I don't want it to end. Yes, this is what I've been waiting for. Yes, yes, yes.*

That's when it finally happened. Like a tightly wound coil inside her body giving way, her orgasm exploded through her. It pulsated through her core, radiating to every limb and making her head swim with pleasure. Her hips bucked against his, forcing him in deeper as her muscles tightened around him. The combination sent Oliver over the edge a moment later. He thrust hard, finishing with a low groan of satisfaction.

They lay together that way—weak muscles, throbbing parts and harsh, panting breaths—for what seemed like an hour, but it was only minutes. Too exhausted to move far but content in each other's arms, they finally untangled and righted themselves on the chaise to snuggle up together. Lucy nuzzled into the crook of his arm and molded to his side. Oliver tugged her voluminous red gown over them to shield their bare bodies from the night air and they fell asleep there under the ever-glowing Manhattan sky.

Eight

Making love to Lucy was amazing, but Oliver found he quite liked just talking to her as well. After a short nap on the rooftop, they got chilly, gathered their clothes and moved downstairs to his bed. There, he made love to her again, but instead of being sleepy, they were energized with conversation. They'd managed to lie in bed talking to the wee hours of the morning. He could tell she was getting tired, but like a stubborn toddler, not willing to give in to sleep quite yet.

"Harper and I are taking the train up to Connecticut next weekend," Lucy said.

"A fun girls trip?" Oliver asked.

"Something like that. Do you have any plans? Maybe we can do something when I get back."

Oliver picked up his phone from the nightstand to check his calendar. He would be lost without it. "Yep.

I'm taking Danny to Coney Island. He's finally tall enough to ride the roller coaster and he's been pestering me for weeks."

"Who's Danny?"

Oliver frowned. Not at Lucy, but at the fact that he hadn't mentioned his brother to her in all this time. He supposed the focus of their discussions hadn't really been on his family aside from Aunt Alice. "Hasn't Harper ever mentioned our little brother?"

"Oh," Lucy said, the pieces almost visibly coming together in her mind. "Yes, she has, she just never uses his real name. She calls him Noodle for some reason. I honestly had no idea his real name was Danny."

At that, Oliver had to laugh. "His name is Daniel Royce Drake after my grandfather and my stepmother's favorite car, respectively. Harper has called him Noodle almost since the day he was born but has never told me why. Do you know?"

Lucy shook her head. "She's never said, and I guess I didn't ask. She just mentions doing things with Noodle or posts pictures with him on Snapchat every now and then. I have to admit, that's quite a nickname to grow up with."

Oliver shrugged it off. "I'm sure he'll be in therapy for far more serious things than a cutesy nickname his older sister gave him."

"Why would you say something like that? That's awful." Lucy frowned at him, wrinkling her freckled nose.

"It's true." Oliver's brow furrowed as he studied Lucy. Was it possible she didn't know the strange and sad tale of Thomas and Candace Drake? Surely Harper had mentioned it. She had just started at Yale when their father began dating Candace. Or perhaps Alice said something. Just because she didn't leave her apartment didn't mean she didn't know exactly what was going on in the family at all times. Or maybe Alice didn't know. At least to the full extent. Their father may not have wanted to admit he'd squandered his fortune on a beautiful woman.

"What could a little rich boy possibly have go wrong in his life to necessitate counseling?"

Only people without money would think that life was easy if you had it. Yes, the necessities of life were no longer a worry, but it came with a whole new set of troubles. Women like Candace being one of them.

"Nothing, now," Oliver admitted. "He was so young. I mean, I'm sure he misses his mother as a concept, but at the same time, she left when he was still a toddler. He may not remember much about her, only what's told to him. But eventually he's going to get old enough to realize that his mother used him as a pawn to get her hands on my father's fortune, and then dumped him when he wasn't useful to her any longer. When that dawns on him, it's going to hurt. And it doesn't matter how much Dad loves him, or Harper and I love him. It's going to make him question why he wasn't good enough for his mother to want him."

Lucy's big, brown eyes widened in concern, getting larger the more he said. "What kind of woman would leave her baby behind like that? That's horrible."

Her response and disgust seemed genuine. "A woman like my stepmother. Does Harper just not talk about our family at all?" he asked.

She shook her head. "Not really. I always got the feeling that talking about herself made her uncomfortable. I don't know why. Violet and Emma grew up with wealth and privilege like she did. I'm the broke outsider in the group."

"Not even when the stuff came up with the will? She didn't mention Candace?"

"No, she didn't."

Oliver sighed. He wrapped his arm around her shoulder and she snuggled in against his chest. "Candace is Danny's mother. My father remained single for over ten years after our mother died of cervical cancer. Mom's illness was hard on everyone, and when it was all over, he wanted to focus on raising us and running his company. There just wasn't any room left for a relationship, even if he had been ready to date again. After Harper went off to college, he met Candace and got all wrapped up in her. It all happened so fast. The whole situation was a nightmare from start to finish."

"Why was it a nightmare?"

"Because, for a start, she was three years older than *me*. Dad didn't seem to care about cradle robbing. She was beautiful and she fawned over him like he was the most amazing man she'd ever met. I guess he needed that after all those years alone. It was obvious to everyone but him that she was just after his money. He was blinded by her beauty and was so desperate to find someone to love him that he fell right into her trap. They got married within a year and she got pregnant with Danny pretty quickly. Before his second birthday, Candace had spent all my father's liquid assets and charged up all his credit accounts into the millions. When he finally put his foot down over her spending, it was only because he had no choice. She had wiped him out. He cut her off financially and she split almost immediately, leaving Danny behind. I guess he wasn't worth taking just for the child support checks when she could do better on her own. Last I heard, she married another tech billionaire from Silicon Valley. One of our competitors, if you can believe her nerve."

Oliver didn't want to drone on and on about Candace, so he got to the point as quickly as he could and waited to see what Lucy had to say about it. Very little, it turned out. Instead, they sat together in an awkward silence that seemed to stretch on forever.

Finally, Lucy spoke in a small voice. "So that's why."

"What do you mean?"

"That's why you automatically presumed that I'm an awful person. Because of her."

Now that he'd gotten to know Lucy better, he was ashamed to tell her as much, but he knew it was true. That's what experience had taught him. "I'll admit it colored my opinion, yes."

Lucy pushed herself up in bed and tugged the sheets to her chest defensively. She had a pained expression lining her brow and the corners of her mouth were turned down just slightly. "Colored your opinion, my foot," she snapped. "You didn't know me from Adam and you lashed out at me as though you'd seen a sketch of my face on a Wanted poster or something. You thought I'd conned your aunt just like your stepmother conned your father. Admit it."

"It's not—"

"Admit it," Lucy pressed. "You thought I was such a horrible person that I was willing to steal all your aunt's belongings out from under you all. Do you think I killed her, too?"

"Of course not!" Oliver replied. "Don't be ridiculous. Do you think I'd be lying in bed with you if I thought you were capable of something like that?"

"Okay, so not a murderer, but certainly a swindler."

Oliver twisted his lips in thought for a moment before he turned away from Lucy's accusatory gaze and sighed. "Okay, I guess I did. But you have to understand that the situation with Candace left me suspicious of *everyone's* motives, not just yours. On a date, the moment a woman asked what business I was in or what area of town I lived in, I could feel this anxiety start to creep in."

"Those are pretty common first date questions."

"I know," he said, feeling foolish about the whole thing but unable to suppress it. "But it felt like women were just trying to figure out how much money I had. Or if they knew my family and showed an interest, I convinced myself that it couldn't be because they were genuinely interested in me. Watching Candace work my dad over was hard. Especially since we couldn't say a bad word about her to him. Trust me when I say we tried, but he wouldn't listen. In the end, he looked like a fool and I never wanted to make that same mistake."

"So a woman couldn't possibly be interested in you because you're smart or handsome? Well dressed? Did you ever think that maybe one of those women was just interested in seeing if you had a big...garden?"

"I do have a larger than average garden." Oliver started to laugh, and then he clapped his right hand over his eyes in dismay. "Oh, you're right. I know you're right. I erred on the side of caution."

"And what good did it do you?"

Oliver looked down at Lucy, her naked body warm and curved against him. "It got you here, for a start. If

I hadn't been so suspicious of you, I might not have followed you around and therefore, might not have fallen for your many charms."

Lucy smirked at him, unimpressed by his flattery. "And now that you've fallen for my charms…do you still think I conned your aunt?"

He knew this was a critical moment in the relationship he'd never expected to have with Lucy. After spending this time together, he should know, one way or another, if she was guilty of everything he'd accused her of. If he thought she was innocent, he'd say so right now without hesitation. And yet the seconds ticked by without his answer as he struggled with his prejudices.

Finally, he found the right combination of words. They might not be the ones she wanted to hear, but it was an honest response. "I really like you, Lucy. More than I ever expected to. I don't want to believe you could do something like that. I'm not sure if that makes me idealistic or just plain stupid."

Lucy watched his face for a moment. He could tell by the dimmed light in her eyes that he'd still hurt her even though she was trying to act as though he hadn't. "Thank you for answering that honestly," she said at last. She sat in deep thought for a few seconds before a yawn overtook her and he could tell she was losing the fight to sleep. "I don't know how to prove to you that I'm not like your stepmother, but I'm not going to figure that out tonight. I guess all I can do is keep trying. Good night, Oliver."

She leaned in to give him a kiss, then she lay back down, cuddling against him with another contagious yawn. After a few moments in the dark silence, he could tell she'd drifted off to sleep. He wished he could fall asleep that easily. But not tonight.

Tonight, he was left with questions he couldn't answer. Not with enough certainty to make him feel better. When Lucy called him out for putting his hang-ups over Candace on her and painting them with the same guilty brush, he felt foolish about the whole thing.

Oliver had decided Lucy was guilty without a stitch of evidence to prove it. And his big plan to uncover her secrets hadn't resulted in a single incriminating thing about her since that day at the lawyer's office. Honestly, he hadn't really tried. A background check hadn't revealed anything insidious. She was the only child of two blue-collar parents from central Ohio who split up when she was only a few years old. No criminal record, no negative remarks on her credit report...even her transcript from Yale proved her to be an above-average student.

By all accounts, she was delightful to be around, thoughtful, smart and sexy as hell. He couldn't imagine her being a crook like Candace was.

Even then, he had a hard time turning off his suspicious thoughts.

He'd like to think that if he truly suspected she was guilty of tricking Alice into changing her will, he wouldn't be in bed with her at the moment. That had to be worth something. And yet he hadn't called off his lawyers either. It was entirely possible that his aunt had simply left her estate to someone she thought deserved it.

As far as she knew, no one in the family was truly hurting for money. He was fine. Harper seemed to be getting along okay. And despite his father's claims of being broke, he was far from it. He still brought in more income in a single month from his investment portfolio than most people earned in a year. It didn't last as long in Manhattan as it would other places, but he wasn't about to be out on the street. He also had his retirement from the company. Real estate holdings. It just wasn't enough to maintain the lifestyle Candace wanted.

His father may have been blinded by love, but Aunt Alice was no one's fool. If she could see all the quibbling going on over her will, she'd come back from the grave and tell them all to quit it because she knew full well what she was doing when she changed it. Lucy would have to be a very skilled scam artist to pull one over on her.

He didn't see that level of cunning in her. So why didn't he drop the protest? He was the only one keeping Lucy from getting everything she was due.

Maybe he would.

Oliver sighed and closed his eyes to try to sleep.

Maybe he wouldn't.

Lucy woke up in Oliver's bed the next morning. She wasn't sure if it was nerves or regret about last night, but she found herself wide awake at dawn with her mind racing over the night before. She didn't want to disturb Oliver, so she put on her capris, stole a T-shirt from his dresser and slipped out of the room.

She made herself a cup of coffee using the Keurig on his Carrara marble countertop, doctored it with half-and-half from his refrigerator and settled at the kitchen table. There was no reason she would be awake at this hour after staying up half the night, but there was an anxiety swirling in her stomach and in her head. It demanded she wake up, so here she was. There would no doubt be a nap in her future once she was back at her apartment.

For the time being, Lucy sipped her coffee. It felt strange sitting idly in Oliver's kitchen, but she felt equally weird about doing anything else in his home while he was still asleep. That left her the option of leaving, and she knew that wasn't the right path to take. Last night, while unexpected, had been amazing and romantic. This morning might prove awkward, and they might never share a moment like that again, but it wouldn't be because she chickened out and ran before he woke up.

Taking another sip of her coffee, she felt her stomach start to rumble. Unlike her friend Violet, who could charge through the day on a steady diet of coffee and the occasional protein bar before she got pregnant, Lucy liked to eat, and she especially liked to eat breakfast. Eggs, pancakes, waffles, sugary cereal, oatmeal, toast, bacon…you name it. She was a fan of the meal in general. She wasn't the kind who could make it to lunch without eating anything.

How long could she last today? She looked at the clock in the hallway. It was just after six thirty. There was a deli up the block where she could get a bagel or order delivery, but she didn't need to be seen by the general public. Especially not wearing silk capris, a hole-ridden old T-shirt, no bra, last night's makeup and morning-after hair. Lucy didn't need a mirror to know that she'd announce "walk of shame" to anyone she passed.

Including Oliver.

On that note, Lucy pushed aside the idea of food for

a moment and sought out the hall powder room to see how bad it really was. She winced in the mirror when she switched on the light. It was a rough look.

The clothes were what they were unless she wanted to wear her gown around the house, but she could clean up the rest. She splashed warm water on her face and used a disposable towel to wipe away the remnants of last night's smoky eye. Then she finger-combed her hair into a messy knot on the top of her head. It was still a far cry from her polished look at the museum the night before, but it was a casual, carefree messy instead of a hot-mess messy. The best she could do on an unplanned overnight stay.

The apartment was still silent when she stepped back out into the hall. Silent enough for her loud tummy rumbling to nearly echo. She couldn't put off breakfast for too much longer.

Lucy started rummaging through his cabinets for an easy option but found nothing she could grab like a pastry or a granola bar. That left real food. Oliver didn't strike her as the kind of man who did a lot of cooking, but she hadn't thought he was a gardener either. While the selection wasn't outstanding, she did find just enough between the contents of the pantry and the refrigerator to cobble together a decent breakfast for the two of them.

It was actually a dish that Alice had taught her to make in the years she'd lived with her. She'd called it Trash Casserole, but it was basically a crustless quiche filled with an assortment of breakfast foods. The idea was to make it with whatever was on hand, hence the trash, but Alice always made it following a strict recipe, which Lucy appreciated.

Her mother was an excellent cook after working at the local diner for twenty years, but it never rubbed off on Lucy. She wasn't a natural at it the way her mom was. Her mother could never explain how or why she did certain things, she just cooked it until it looked right and never followed a recipe. Eventually, Lucy just got frustrated with trying to learn and gave up.

Alice had been a lot easier to follow. She kept all her recipes on neatly handwritten cards in a brass box that sat in the cupboard. Those cards were gospel as far as Alice was concerned and she never strayed. Lucy had thought she would copy them all down for herself so she could make those dishes in her own home one day. Now, she realized, those painstakingly scripted cards were hers, along with everything else.

Maybe.

Lucy doubted that Oliver would begrudge her some recipe cards if she really wanted them, but at the moment, they were tied up with about half a billion in other assets of the estate. She'd tried not to think about Oliver as her adversary, but his aunt's will was definitely the elephant in the room with them. Lucy didn't expect him to drop the protest just because they'd had sex, but a part of her hoped that maybe he knew her well enough now not to confuse her with his greedy stepmother. Or perhaps not. Sex somehow could change everything and yet nothing all at once.

"Something smells good."

Lucy looked up to see Oliver standing near the Keurig. He was looking deliciously messy himself, wearing nothing but a pair of jeans and some heavy stubble. The hard, tan stomach she'd explored the night before was on full display with his jeans hanging low on his hips. He ran his fingers through his hair and smiled sheepishly. The combination sent her pulse through the roof. It was nearly enough of a distraction to make her burn their breakfast if the timer hadn't gone off that very second.

"Good morning," she said, anxiously turning away from him and focusing on pulling the casserole out of the oven. "Are you hungry?"

"Mmm-hmm," he muttered as he came in closer and snuggled up behind her. He planted a kiss on her neck that sent a chill down her spine and a warmth of awareness across her skin. She turned to give him a proper good-morning kiss but realized his attention had shifted to what she was cooking.

"Is that Trash Casserole?" he asked with a look of astonishment on his face.

Lucy nodded. "It is. Have you had it before?"

"Have I had it before?" He took a step back and shook his head. "It's only the best thing Aunt Alice ever made. She cooked it every morning for Harper and me after we stayed the night with her."

She turned off the oven. "Well, good. She's the one that taught me how to make it, so hopefully it's at least half as good as hers."

Oliver eyeballed the dish with a wide grin. "It looks exactly like I remember it. I don't think I've eaten that in twenty years."

Lucy looked at him with a confused frown. "How is that possible? You had all the stuff to make it in the house. It's not a particularly complicated recipe. You mean you've never tried to do it yourself in all this time?"

He shook his head and took a step toward the coffee maker. "No. I don't cook. Not even a little. I pay a lady to come in twice a week to clean and stock the fridge with a few things I can eat. I found if I didn't do that, I'd just eat takeout until I needed bigger pants. Anything you found in the house, she left here, I can assure you."

Lucy wasn't surprised. "Well you'll have to apologize to her for me when she comes by again and finds I've used up her supplies."

Oliver chuckled as he popped a pod into the coffee machine and turned it on. "She won't mind. I'm sure Patty would be happy to come here and find evidence of cooking instead of candy wrappers and take-out containers in my trash can."

Lucy made them both plates and they settled together at the kitchen table. It was a nice moment to share, diffusing any of the morning-after awkwardness. They were nearly finished when Oliver's cell phone rang.

She sat silently as he answered, giving one-word replies and frowning at the table. "Okay. I'll be there shortly. I just got up."

He hit the button to hang up and looked at her with an apologetic expression on his face. "That was my dad. They're taking Danny to the hospital in an ambulance. He had an accident at his riding lesson this morning. I'm sorry to cut our breakfast short, but I need to go meet Dad in the emergency room."

Lucy's soft heart ached at the thought of his little brother at the hospital without his mother there to comfort him. She was hardly a suitable substitute—she'd never even met the little boy Harper called Noodle— but she couldn't go home in good conscience. She had to do something to help. "I'll go with you," she offered, getting up from the table with her dish in her hand.

He flinched at the suggestion, making her wonder if she was crossing a line by imposing on his family even after the night they'd shared. Was it too soon? Perhaps his father wouldn't want her there. He hadn't seemed any more pleased with her at the will reading than the rest of the family.

"You don't need to do that, Lucy. I'm sure he'll be fine."

She wasn't about to let him push her away that easily. "I know I don't need to do it, but I want to. If we can just stop by my place on the way, I'll do a quick change of clothes and I'll be happy to keep you company. It sounds like it's going to be a long day for everyone. I can fetch coffee or something. Let me help."

Oliver's thin lips twisted in thought for a moment, then he nodded with an expression of relief. "Okay." He stepped forward and pulled Lucy into his arms, dropping his forehead down to gently meet her own as he held her.

"Thank you."

Nine

Danny was a trooper. Oliver had to give him credit for that. He wasn't sure he'd have handled all of this as well when he was his age. He'd broken his wrist riding his scooter when he was nine and had been convinced at the time that no one had experienced his level of pain, ever.

Danny had four broken ribs, the doctor had said. X-rays showed the breaks were clean and would come together on their own. There was no risk for the bones puncturing the lungs. It sounded bad and it was quite painful, but it could've been much worse. During his riding lesson, the horse had gotten spooked by something. It bucked Danny out of the saddle, then stomped on his chest while he was lying on his back in the riding ring. He could've been killed in about four or five different ways, so some bruises and a few cracked ribs were a best-case scenario, really.

Dad had gone back to the apartment to get a few things. The doctors were going to keep Danny overnight. The first twenty-four hours were the most painful and where his breaks were located, he couldn't do much of anything for himself, even raise a juice box to his mouth.

That just left Oliver and Lucy with him for the time being, as Harper was out of town. Although Oliver had initially been thrown off by Lucy's request to come with him to the hospital, she'd been a lifesaver today. She'd brought them food from the cafeteria, magazines from the gift shop, and she even had a phone charger in her purse when their phones started to die from the constant calls and texts. Having her here had been nice. Nicer than he wanted to admit to himself.

Waking up with her, sharing breakfast together, even weathering a crisis together…every moment he spent with Lucy made him want to spend more and more. This was going to be a problem.

"Can I have a popsicle?" Danny asked. He was sitting up in his hospital bed with pillows propped up under his arms and a thin blanket thrown over his legs. He looked so small in that bed, even smaller than the seven-year-old usually looked.

Oliver got up from the chair, relieved to have a quest to occupy his mind. "I'll go see what I can do. Are you okay to stay with him?" he asked Lucy.

She nodded from her perch at the end of his bed. "We'll be fine."

Oliver went down the hallway in search of a popsicle. The pain medicine was making Danny queasy, so he wasn't much interested in the food they were bringing him. If his baby brother wanted a popsicle, Oliver would find him one. The nurses didn't have any, just pudding and gelatin cups, so he headed downstairs in the hopes of finding something in the cafeteria or gift shop that would make Danny smile. He'd hit a street cart if he had to.

He scored a Bomb Pop, finally, and carried it back upstairs after about twenty minutes of hunting. As he neared the doorway to Danny's hospital room, the sound of voices made him pause. Danny wasn't normally much of a talker, but the pain medications had him chatting up a storm. He and Lucy were talking and Oliver was curious about what the two of them would discuss without anyone else around.

"The nurses cut off my favorite shirt when we got to the hospital," Danny complained. "It hurt too much to pull it over my head."

"I bet your daddy can get you another shirt just like that one."

"Yeah, but it won't be the same. My mother sent me that shirt for my last birthday."

Oliver froze in place. He'd never heard Danny mention his mother. He hadn't even known she was in contact with her son until now. Dad hadn't said anything about it. For a moment, Oliver wasn't sure if he should be happy she was involved or mad for stringing his brother along.

"Did she?" Lucy asked in a polite voice that didn't betray what she knew about Danny's mother. "That was nice of her."

Oliver leaned forward until he could see around the corner of the door frame. Danny was still sitting up in bed. Lucy was sitting at the end of the bed, turned toward Danny with interest.

Danny shrugged on reflex and winced with the movement. "Not really. She sends a package on my birthday and at Christmas, but that's it. A *good* mom would do more than that. A good mom would've stayed around or taken me with her. Or at least visit every once in a while. That's what people say when they think I'm not listening."

He could see Lucy stiffen awkwardly in her seat. What did you say to something like that, knowing it was absolutely true but not being able to fix it?

"I'm sorry to hear that. Not having both parents around can be hard. You know, my daddy left when I was young, too."

Danny perked up. "Why did yours leave?"

Lucy sighed. "Well, I was small, so I don't know all the details, but my mom said he met someone else and started a new family. I never saw or heard from him again."

"Do you have more brothers or sisters?"

"Yes. Someone told me that I have two little sisters somewhere. I don't know their names."

Oliver couldn't believe how little he actually knew about Lucy's past and her family. What little he did know had come from the file on her the private investigator gave him. She never really talked about her life before she went to Yale and met his sister. Now he knew why. Being a single parent was hard. His father had enough money to get help when he needed it, never having to worry about bills or childcare, but the average mother on her own had no one to depend on but herself.

He imagined that drove Lucy to work even harder at everything she did. Getting into Yale was no easy feat, and getting a scholarship to cover most of the sky-high tuition was near impossible. He knew that having to drop out when she couldn't afford the tuition had to hurt. Being the companion of a wealthy old woman probably hadn't been her goal in life, but then again, that detour could very well make her richer than any Yale degree ever could.

"I just have Oliver and Harper," Danny said. "I've heard people say that's because my mom learned her lesson with me. I was a lot of work and I ruined her body, she said. She got her shoes tied after I was born."

"Do you mean she got her tubes tied?" Lucy asked, stifling a chuckle at the seven-year-old's interpretation of the story he'd heard.

"That's it. I think." Danny sat thoughtfully for a minute, gazing down at the IV in his hand. "I'm sorry about your dad, Lucy. I guess my mom could be a lot worse. At least she sends nice gifts. She can afford to though, since she's married to a super-rich guy in California. I heard the housekeeper say that the guy invented a thing that's in every smartphone in the world. She wasted all of Daddy's money in just a few years, but I think it will take her a lot longer to spend all of the new guy's money."

Oliver was surprised to listen to how much his brother knew about Candace. He was young, but perhaps he wasn't as sheltered as Oliver thought. It sounded as though the grown-ups around him had the habit of talking about Candace as though Danny were too young to understand what they were saying. The knowledge seemed to steal a touch of his innocence too soon, but perhaps the truth wouldn't be as crushing as if he'd learned it all later. He was a smart, savvy little boy. Much more than Oliver gave him credit for.

He was also amazed at how deftly Lucy handled Danny. She was such a caring person, so unlike Candace. In a moment, she'd shifted the discussion away from bad parents and had Danny chatting animatedly about his favorite video game. Any bad emotions roused by their talk faded away as he prattled on about trolls and secret passages. Danny loved playing on any kind of gadget and would happily sit and get lost in a game for hours on end. Considering his family owned one of the largest computer companies in the world, it was probably in his blood.

Dad had actually forced Danny to take the riding lessons to get him out of the house. That had backfired a little, considering it had landed him in the hospital, but at least it had given him something to do that didn't entail cheat codes and warlocks. The next week of his recovery would be spent playing his game the moment he could hold up his own controller.

Lucy listened to him speak as though it were the most interesting conversation she'd ever had. She had that ability, that way of making you feel like you were the only person in the room. The most important thing in her life. No wonder Alice had been so taken with her. And Harper. And now, Danny, too. She was like a planet swirling around in space and pulling everyone else into her orbit.

He realized he was tired of fighting to escape her pull. The conversation they'd had in the late hours the night before had been enlightening for him. Danny's accident had occupied his mind for most of the day, but when he had a quiet moment, his thoughts always returned to Lucy. He had judged her unfairly. If he set all his prejudgments aside, he had no reason not to let himself fall head over heels for this woman. It was a leap he'd never risked taking before and he wasn't sure he was ready to do it yet.

But he could feel it coming. Before too long, the solid ground beneath him would crumble and he would have no choice but to fall hard for Lucy Campbell.

Oliver was startled from his thoughts by the drip of the popsicle onto his hand through a hole in the wrapper. He couldn't stand out in the hallway forever. Instead, he rounded the corner as though he'd just returned and presented the prize to the grinning little boy waiting for it.

After closing out the weekend at the hospital, the following workweek seemed to fly by. Lucy spent almost every evening with Oliver, returning to the apartment on Fifth Avenue when he left for work in the morning. During the day, she looked at apartments near Yale online and plotted out an itinerary for the trip she and Harper were taking up there the following weekend.

In all the time Oliver and Lucy spent together, they existed in a protective bubble—neither of them mentioning the fact that Alice's will was still pending a decision from the judge. They simply didn't talk about it, like an elephant in the room that they kept their backs to.

At this point, Lucy thought for sure that he should trust her enough to know she had nothing to do with the change in the will. And yet she didn't ask him to withdraw the protest and he didn't offer. They just carried on with their relationship as though the explosive events that brought them together initially never happened.

It lingered in the back of Lucy's mind, but at the same time, she was happy to ignore that aspect of their association. Things were so much better without that topic creeping into their conversations. She also tended to ignore the fact that she was planning on leaving Manhattan after the New Year to finish school regardless of what the judge decided. She hadn't mentioned that to Oliver either, and she didn't know why. Perhaps it seemed too early in the relationship to worry about the future.

If they were still together when the holidays rolled around, then it would be an important discussion. Now it would just be like putting a ticking time bomb out ahead of them, ready to blow their fragile relationship apart at its mere mention.

But would there be a better time, she thought, looking through the layouts of another apartment complex. Maybe.

Maybe not.

About six that evening, the doorbell rang and Lucy found Oliver standing in the foyer with sacks of takeout in his hands.

"What are you doing here?" she asked. "I was just getting dressed to come over to your place."

"I thought we could use a change of scenery," he said, stepping past her into the apartment. "I've also always wanted to eat in the formal dining room."

Lucy followed him curiously. "That's fine by me. What's so great about the dining room?"

Oliver set the bags down on the table, revealing

some Italian dishes from a place close to his office. "When we were kids, we weren't allowed to eat in the formal dining room because we might spill on the priceless Moroccan rug. We had to eat in the kitchen where there was tile. When I was an adult, we didn't come over any longer, so I've never gotten to eat in here."

Lucy laughed. She'd honestly never eaten in this room either, but it was more out of convenience than anything else. When it was just Alice and her, it was easier to eat in the kitchen or to take a dish into her room and eat in bed by herself. "It's a first for us both then."

They settled at the table, eyeing the cream silk tablecloth, the infamous Moroccan rug and the large containers of pasta with red and white sauces sitting in front of them.

"Let's eat in the kitchen," they both said in unison, getting up and carrying everything out of the intimidating space as they laughed together.

When they were finished, Oliver grabbed the small container of tiramisu and two forks, and took Lucy's hand to lure her into the bedroom. "It's time for dessert," he said.

Lucy groaned as she followed him into her bedroom. She had eaten so much. She loved tiramisu, but she wasn't sure if she could stomach another bite of food. "I'm not sure I'm ready for dessert yet."

Oliver looked over his shoulder and gave her a coy wink. "That's okay. I think some physical activity first might make some room for more."

"Oh yeah? What do you have in mind?" she teased.

Oliver entered her room and set the container on

the nightstand. Lucy came up behind him and ran her hands over his broad shoulders. She loved seeing him in his suits every day after work. She loved the contrast of the soft, expensive fabrics draped over the hard steel of his body.

He shrugged out of the jacket, letting it fall into her hands. She draped it over the nearby chair and they continued their familiar dance of undressing. It had felt strange at first to expose herself so easily to someone, and now her fingers couldn't move fast enough for her bare skin to touch his.

Oliver flung back her comforter and they crawled into bed together. He immediately pulled her body against his and captured her mouth in a kiss. It was amazing how quickly this had become like coming home to Lucy. It didn't matter where they were, being in his arms was what was important. The rest of the world and its problems just melted away and all that mattered was the two of them.

"I think I might eat some of the tiramisu now," he murmured against her lips, "if you don't mind."

Lucy did mind. They were in the middle of something and he wanted to stop and eat. But she kept her mouth shut and was rewarded for her patience.

He grabbed the container from the bedside table and carried it with him as he positioned himself between her thighs. Oliver kissed the inside of each knee before opening the container and filling the room with the scent of chocolate and espresso. He swiped his index finger through the cream on top and painted each of her nipples with it. Swirling more across her belly, he stopped at the satin edge of her neatly trimmed curls.

Oliver set the box aside and smiled widely at her as he prepared to enjoy his dessert. He licked a leisurely trail across her belly, circling her navel and climbing higher. Lucy squirmed with a mix of need and impatience, clutching at the sheets as he teased her. Finally reaching her breasts, his tongue teased at one tight nipple and then the next, sucking in the mocha-dusted mascarpone and swirling it around her skin with his tongue.

Lucy had never been someone's dessert course before and she found she quite liked it. The only downside to this arrangement was that she didn't have any for herself. When he picked up the box for more, she caught his wrist to stop him. "I want some, too," she requested sweetly and reached for it.

"I thought you were full," Oliver teased, holding the box out of her grasp.

She stuck out her bottom lip in a pout. "I just want a little taste. Please?"

"Well, since you said please…" Oliver dipped his finger in the dessert and offered it to her. She grasped his hand with her own, holding it steady as she drew it into her mouth and sucked every bit from his skin. When it was long gone, she continued to suck at him in a suggestive way that made him groan her name aloud with a hint of desperation in his voice.

"Okay. That's enough tiramisu for now," she said, finally releasing her hold on him. "I'm ready for the rest of my dessert."

"Very well," he said, tossing the carton to the far side of the bed. He lay down beside her. "Come here."

Gripping her waist, he pulled Lucy into his lap. She straddled him, feeling unexpectedly powerful as he looked up at her with a light of appreciation in his eyes. Lucy had never thought of herself as particularly pretty or having a good body—average at best—but Oliver looked at her like she was his fantasy come to life. It made her feel like maybe that could be true.

He brought his hand up to her face. His fingertips traced the curve of her cheek, then trailed across her swollen bottom lip. "You are so beautiful. I never want to close my eyes when you're near me."

How did this amazing man come into her life? Things had been so surreal since Alice died. The estate, the future…that was hard enough to believe. But Oliver—being with a man like him was beyond her wildest imagination. He was handsome, smart and successful. He was everything she'd dreamt of but never believed she would have. And yet here she was, straddling his bare hips and feeling his desire for her pressing against her thigh.

She sheathed him with a nearby condom, and shifting her weight, Lucy captured Oliver's firm heat and eased him inside of her. She closed her eyes and bit her lip as her body expanded and enveloped him. His palms cupped her hips and held her still. They both took a moment to savor the sensation of their bodies joining. Then at last, she moved her hips forward and back again, settling into a slow, steady rhythm.

They'd come a long way since that first day at the attorney's offices. It was hard to believe it had only been a few weeks since they'd met for the first time. Now she could hardly imagine her life without him. Just the thought was enough to make her chest ache in a way she could hardly describe. She'd never felt anything like that before. Lucy had spent more than one night lying in bed beside him, wondering what it could mean.

But now as she looked down at Oliver, she knew the truth of it—she was in love with him.

Did that mean she was making love to him for the first time? The realization intensified the sensations already building inside of her. She'd had a few partners in her life, but nothing she would call serious. Nothing that created the kind of emotional bond to the other person the way this did. This knowledge changed everything and she could feel it down to her core.

The pleasure started rippling through her, radiating from deep inside. She could feel her muscles tighten around him as her body tensed and prepared for her much-needed release.

"Yes," Oliver coaxed, his fingertips pressing into the flesh of her hips. "Give in to it."

It was a demand she couldn't help but follow. Her orgasm exploded through her like a shockwave. She gasped and cried out to the ceiling as the sensations pulsated through her like never before. Even as the pleasure filled her, it was the warmth in her chest that truly gripped her. That feeling of peace and happiness being here with Oliver seemed to envelop her. She bit her lip and savored it, even as Oliver's hoarse groans began to mingle with her panting breaths.

She collapsed beside him in exhaustion and contentment. After a moment, Oliver gave her a soft kiss. "I'm going to go get a drink from the kitchen. Do you want anything?"

Lucy shook her head. She had everything she wanted in this moment. It couldn't be more perfect. As she watched Oliver and his perfectly round tush saunter out of the bedroom, all she could think of, all she could feel, was this overwhelming sense of love. She loved him. Really, truly.

She hoped that wasn't a huge mistake.

Ten

"I don't understand why we're back in Connecticut looking at apartments," Harper complained.

"I'm too old to live in a dorm or a sorority house," Lucy explained. "If I'm going back to school, I'm getting my own place near campus."

It was a cool, crisp day in New Haven. Summer had lingered longer than expected this year and the first signs of fall were finally arriving even though it was late September. Soon it would be time for changing leaves, oversize sweaters and boots. And when she started in the spring term this January, she would've moved on to heavy coats, hats, scarves and gloves.

"I really don't know why you're bothering with any of this. I mean, once the inheritance goes through, do you really need to worry about going back to school? You don't have to work another day in your life if you don't want to, much less move into a cheap off-campus apartment with loud jocks living upstairs."

Lucy could only shake her head and look at the map of nearby apartments she'd been given by the campus housing office. No, moving from a Fifth Avenue apartment to one of these places wasn't ideal, but it was reality. No one else seemed to be functioning in reality except her.

"This has got nothing to do with my inheritance. Whether I get it or not, I want to finish my art history degree. That's been my plan all along. When I dropped out, it was so disappointing. I've saved up all these years to pay for school, and with Alice gone, now is my chance. If that means an old apartment with shag carpeting and a run-down laundromat I have to share with a hundred other residents, so be it."

Harper halted her complaints as they approached the closest of the rental complexes near campus. "This doesn't look too bad," Lucy said. "Since it's so close, it's probably the most sought after and expensive place, too."

They found the front office and the manager walked them to an empty one-bedroom apartment they could tour.

"I've got a one-bedroom just like this one coming up after the fall term," the manager explained. "They're graduating and moving out before the holidays. I have a couple two-bedroom apartments coming up, too. Any chance you would be interested in one of those?"

"No thanks," Lucy replied. She'd basically lived in a bedroom the last five years and a shared sorority bedroom the years before that. Spreading out into her own apartment would be luxurious. "It's just me. I'm not interested in roommates."

"Okay. Go ahead and look around. I'll be here if you have any questions."

Lucy and Harper stepped inside and she breathed a sigh of relief. It wasn't that bad at all. To the left, there was a spacious living room with a patio. To the right, a dining room and the kitchen. Down a short hallway was the bedroom and bathroom. The fixtures weren't the newest and fanciest, but it looked clean and well maintained.

"I could make this work."

Harper wrinkled her nose. "Have you considered buying a condo or a townhouse instead?"

"With what money?" Lucy asked. "I swear you rich people can't quite come to terms with what it's like to be broke. After I pay for classes, books and fees, I'll have just enough for this apartment and food. That's it. I can't pull a down payment out of my rear end." She held up her finger to silence her friend. "And don't you dare bring up the inheritance again. I haven't heard two words from the attorney since Oliver filed a dispute. I can't plan my life around money that may never arrive."

Harper sighed and crossed her arms over her chest. "Okay, fine. What about Oliver then?"

Lucy frowned. "What about Oliver?"

"You two are...together. Dating? Whatever you want to call it. Things seem to be pretty good between the two of you. Are you really going to want to leave him behind in the city come January?"

That was something Lucy had tried to ignore. Not even her recent emotional revelation had changed that.

Her plan before Oliver was to go to school and her plan remained the same. "We're hardly in what you would call 'a relationship.' Certainly not a serious enough relationship for me to give up my dream in order to be with him."

"I don't know. It hasn't been long, but you two seem pretty serious. It might not be love yet, but at the very least you're twitterpated."

"Twitter-what?"

"Twitterpated," Harper explained. "It's from the movie *Bambi*. It means you're infatuated. Maybe not 'in love' yet, but excited and optimistic and definitely 'in like.'"

Lucy ignored her observation and turned to study the appliances in the kitchen.

"You could transfer to another school that's in the city. Columbia? NYU? You don't have to go back to Yale."

Lucy turned to Harper with her hands planted on her hips. "I worked hard to get accepted to Yale and I want that degree framed on my wall with Yale University emblazoned across the top of it."

Harper didn't seem convinced. "It's not as though the schools I mentioned are community colleges, you know."

"Yeah, I know. But before Oliver or money came into the picture, I made plans to come back here. I'm already registered for the spring. It's happening. So are you going to help me find a place to live or complain the whole time?"

She rolled her eyes and pasted on a smile. "I'm going to help you find an apartment in New Haven because I'm a supportive friend who loves you."

"Good. Let's go."

They walked out of the apartment together with a brochure from the manager and her card to call when Lucy made a decision. They toured two more apartment complexes before they went to Vito's Deli, one of their former college haunts, for lunch.

"I'm starving," Harper declared as they lined up at the counter to place their order.

Lucy had loved this shop when they were in school, but suddenly, the idea of it wasn't as exciting as it used to be. The smell of meat and pickles hit her like a blast of unwelcome air when they walked inside. She hadn't been feeling great the last couple of days, but she figured it was something she'd eaten. Now she wasn't so sure.

"Lucy, are you okay?"

She turned her head to her friend. "Why?"

Harper cocked her head to the side with concern lining her eyes. "You look a little green around the gills. Do we need to go somewhere else?"

Lucy hated to do it, but she really needed some air. "Maybe if we just step out a second. The smell of dill pickles is really getting to me for some reason."

They stepped out onto the street, where Lucy sucked in a big lungful of fresh air and felt a million times better. The queasiness was still there, but she didn't feel like she was about to make a mess in the deli during the lunch rush. "Thanks. I don't know what's gotten into me lately. I felt puny yesterday, too. I thought maybe it was the chicken sandwich I'd had for lunch, but I should be over that by now. I had a bagel and coffee for breakfast. Pickles have never bothered me before. I love pickles."

"My dad told me that when my mom was pregnant with Oliver, she couldn't abide the smell, taste or sight of pickles. I always thought that was funny, considering it's the stereotypical pregnancy thing. Oliver has always hated pickles, too. When she was pregnant with me, she couldn't get enough of them and I love pickles."

Lucy chuckled nervously at Harper's story. "Well, that's weird, but of course, I'm not pregnant."

"I'm not saying you are. It would be a funny coincidence if you were repelled by pickles, though, since it would be Oliver's baby." Harper paused for a moment, then turned and continued to eye her critically. "Lucy, are you pregnant with my brother's baby?"

Lucy lowered herself down onto a nearby bench as she mentally ran through her biological calendar. How many days had it been? It was before Alice died. She counted on her fingers and shook her head. "No," she declared at last. "I couldn't be. I mean, we used protection. I am certain that I am not pregnant."

Harper sat down on the bench beside her. "Well, what if we popped over to the drugstore and you took a pregnancy test just so we know for sure whether you need an antacid for a stomachache or a baby registry? You haven't been feeling well. I'm sure it's just the stress of everything going on, but if you take the test, then you'll know. If it's negative, then no worries, right?"

No worries? That wasn't exactly the state of mind Lucy was in at the moment. The truth was she'd lied just now. She was anything but certain. If her math was right, her period was over two weeks late. She was never late. Her uterus was made in Switzerland.

With everything else going on, she hadn't even thought about it. But she *was* late. And they *had* used protection. It was just her luck that she'd fall into the three percent failure rate.

She couldn't be pregnant. Pregnant! And with Oliver's baby. How was she going to tell him? How was she going to handle all of these changes? Just as she was about to go back to college and start her life new. This was a major complication. One she simply wasn't prepared to think through on a bench in downtown New Haven.

"Come on," Harper said. She reached out for Lucy's hand and tugged her up from her chair. "We're going to the pharmacy, you're taking that test, and then we're going someplace less smelly to eat and celebrate the fact that you aren't about to give birth to my niece or nephew."

Lucy stood up and followed Harper down the block, but in her heart, she already knew the answer. Like it or not, she was going to be Oliver Drake's baby mama.

Oliver was surprised to get a message from Lucy, asking if he would meet her for dinner. He thought she'd gone away for the weekend with Harper, but apparently they'd cut their trip short. That was fine by him. He didn't want to admit it, but he didn't like not seeing her, even if it was just for a day or two. Since she left, it seemed like she was constantly on his mind and he couldn't focus on anything else.

The place she'd chosen for dinner was busy and on the louder side. Not exactly what he would've selected for a romantic dinner for two, but he wouldn't complain about it. Traffic wasn't the greatest, so he arrived to the restaurant a few minutes later than planned and Lucy was already seated at their table.

He smiled when he came around the corner and spied her sitting there. He couldn't help it. It had only been a few weeks and yet just the sight of Lucy made his whole body respond. The smile on his face, the increase in his pulse, the bizarre feeling in his stomach when she looked at him…he'd never reacted to a woman like this before. Could it be that this was what all the poets and musicians wrote about?

Then she looked up at him. When her gaze met his, he instantly knew there was something wrong. She wasn't beaming at the sight of him the way he was at her. He tried not to frown and take it personally. It was possible she was tired. Or maybe something had happened. He didn't know much about her family, but perhaps an emergency had brought her back from her trip early.

"Hello, beautiful," he said as he leaned down to give her a soft, welcome kiss.

She smiled and kissed him back, but he could sense some hesitation there. "Thank you for coming tonight."

"Of course," Oliver said as he unbuttoned his suit coat and sat down. "I was surprised to hear from you. I didn't think you were coming back until tomorrow."

Lucy nodded, her expression unusually stoic. "We decided to cut the trip short. Something…uh…came up."

Oliver stiffened in his seat. He was right. He didn't like the sound of that. "Is everything okay?"

The waiter arrived with imperfect timing to get their drink orders. Oliver was forced to drop the subject for a moment and scanned the menu. "Would you be interested in sharing a bottle of cabernet with me?"

"No, thank you. I think I'm just going to have a Perrier, please."

Oliver opted for a single glass of wine instead and the waiter disappeared. "What happened? Is it something serious?"

"Everything is okay. I'm fine. Harper is fine. Serious? I would say so. Whether or not it's good or bad news depends on how you take it. I just…" her voice trailed off for a moment.

Oliver had never seen Lucy so distraught. Not even at Aunt Alice's funeral. She seemed to be tied in knots over something. "Whatever it is, you can tell me. Let me help."

"I'm sorry, Oliver. I'm just going to have to come out and say this because I don't know how to do it any other way. I spent the whole train ride back from Connecticut trying to find a good way, and there just isn't one." She took a deep breath and let it out. "I'm pregnant."

Oliver's breath froze in his lungs and his heart stuttered in his chest with shock. He sat for a moment, not breathing, not thinking, just stunned. This wasn't possible. The restaurant was loud; maybe he just hadn't heard her correctly. He grasped at that straw in desperation. "I don't think I heard you right. Could you say it again?" He leaned in this time, praying to hear anything other than Lucy telling him she was having his child.

Lucy winced slightly and move closer to him across the table as well. "You heard me just fine, Oliver. I'm pregnant. With your baby," she added, presumably to ensure he was clear on that part of the news.

He was crystal clear on that point. She wouldn't be telling him like this otherwise. The pit of his stomach wouldn't ache with dread. No, it was obvious she was having his baby. *His baby.* He didn't even know what to say to that. Formerly stunned, his brain finally kicked into overdrive with a million thoughts running through his mind all at once. He couldn't settle on one, couldn't say a word until he'd come to terms with what she'd just said.

"I don't know what happened," Lucy continued, apparently uncomfortable with his silence. "We used protection every time. It didn't even occur to me that it was the cause of why I wasn't feeling well until Harper brought it up. I bought a pregnancy test at a drugstore and took it in the bathroom thinking it would come up negative and I could stop worrying, but it was positive. I have a doctor's appointment on Wednesday, but I don't think it will change anything. The test was pretty clear. We came back early so I could tell you right away."

He tried to listen as she spoke, but it was hard to focus on anything but the punchline. When the wheel of emotions stopped spinning in his mind, it landed on anger and betrayal, which burst out of him all at once.

"Of course you wanted to tell me right away," he said in an unmistakably bitter tone. "Who wouldn't want to inform their rich boyfriend that they got knocked up the first time they had sex? It's exciting news. Worst case scenario, you've locked down eighteen years of child support payments. If you're going to get pregnant, you might as well make sure the daddy is a millionaire, right?"

"What?" She flinched as though he'd reached out and slapped her.

This obviously wasn't the reaction she was expecting. He didn't know why. Did she think he would be excited over the prospect of the potential scammer having his child? Believe that fate had intercepted and brought them together to be one big, happy family? No. Life didn't work that way without someone like her pulling all the strings. She'd been manipulating him from the very beginning—perhaps angling for this outcome since the day they met.

"You certainly didn't waste any time," he continued. "You must have sabotaged that first condom you handed me in the garden. Pretty bold. And to think I was relieved you had one ready to go. Of course you did. My stepmother at least married my father and moved into the penthouse before she locked him down with a child and spent all his money. I guess you're in a hurry, though."

"A hurry for what?" she asked.

"Well, I mean, the judge will rule on my aunt's will soon. This really was the best way for you to ensure that you'll get a chunk of cash from the Drake family, win or lose."

A shimmer of tears flooded Lucy's big, brown eyes. Crocodile tears, he had no doubt. "Is that what you think I've done? Do you really believe I'm capable of getting pregnant on purpose? Derailing my whole life just for money?"

"Not just money, Lucy. A shit-ton of money." The flood of angry words rushed from his mouth and he was incapable of stopping them. "I had you pegged as shady from that first day. That Pollyanna ignorance when the attorney announced you were getting everything... I knew you were playing us all. Playing my aunt. Even playing Harper, unless she's in on it for a cut. I thought that if I got to know you better, I could figure out your game, but I was wrong. You're better at this than I ever expected. I was on the verge of dropping my contest of the will, you had me so convinced. I mean, well played, Lucy. Cover all your bases."

He clapped slowly with a wide smile that probably looked more like a grimace. The bitter words were the only thing keeping him from being sick. "You've set yourself up for a win-win situation. You could walk away from this with my aunt's fortune, half of mine and then that kid will be set to inherit more from my family someday. I thought Candace was crafty and cunning going after my father, but you've got her beat, hands down. You didn't have to sleep with a lonely old man to get what you wanted."

The tears in her eyes never spilled over, but the longer he talked, the redder her face got and the tighter her jaw clenched. "Yeah," she agreed in the coldest voice he'd ever heard pass from her lips. "I just had to sleep with a lonely, bitter young man instead."

Oliver laughed at her cruel retort. "Maybe I am lonely and bitter, but I never had to screw anyone to make my way in the world."

"I thought you were a better man than this, Oliver." Lucy threw her napkin on the table and got up from her seat. "Don't point fingers at me and act so self-righteous. You may not do it now or tonight or even in a year, but one night, when you're lying alone in bed, you'll realize the mistake you've made and it will be too late." She picked up her purse and slung it over her shoulder.

"Leaving so soon?" he asked as casually as he could muster. Of course she would act upset and insulted.

That was part of the charade. He wouldn't let her words get to him even if every arrow painfully struck the bull's-eye in his chest. He would keep up the facade of the bored businessman unfazed by her until she was long gone. He wouldn't give her the satisfaction of knowing she'd gotten to him.

Lucy just shook her head with sadness pulling down at the corners of her mouth. "You know, I am just as surprised by this whole situation as you are. I'm actually terrified and knowing now that I'll be doing it on my own makes it that much scarier. The difference is it's going to uproot my entire life, destroy my body and take over the next twenty years of my life, and you're just going to sit back and cut a damn check. If you don't want to be a part of your child's life, then don't bother sending money. That's an insult to me and the baby. Let's just skip the paternity test game with the attorneys and pretend we never met, okay?"

"Sounds fine. At this point, I wish we hadn't."

"Me, too. Goodbye, Oliver." Turning on her heel, Lucy barely missed a collision with the waiter as she nearly ran from the restaurant.

Oliver made a point of not watching her go. Instead, he calmly accepted his wine from the waiter and sipped it, ignoring the stares of the nearby restaurant patrons. After all that, he needed a glass of wine. Or some scotch. Anything he could get his hands on, really, to dull the pain in his chest and chase away the angry tears that were threatening to expose themselves in the restaurant.

The first large sip seemed to settle him. The blood stopped rushing in his ears and he was able to take his first deep breath since he arrived at the restaurant.

That was a start. Wine couldn't undo the mess he'd just found himself in, but it would get him through this painfully uncomfortable moment.

"Sir." The waiter hovered awkwardly nearby. "Will the lady be returning?"

Oliver shook his head. "She will not."

"Very well. Will you be staying to dine with us tonight?"

He might be known for being cool under pressure, but even Oliver couldn't sit here and eat as though his world hadn't just disintegrated in his hands. "No. I think I'll finish my drink and free up the table if you'd like to run the bill."

"Yes, sir." The waiter disappeared, as visibly uncomfortable on the outside as Oliver was on the inside.

Oliver went through the motions to wrap up, finished his cabernet and stuffed his wallet back in his suit pocket. Pushing up from the table, he made his way out of the restaurant and onto the noisy street. Once there, he felt his anger start to crumble into disappointment.

Why? Why had he let himself get involved with Lucy when he knew she was just playing him, and everyone else? Instead, he'd let himself get wrapped up in her smile and her freckles. He'd lost himself in the warmth of her body and the softness of her touch. And now she was going to have his child.

His child.

Oliver sighed and forced his feet down the sidewalk toward his building. It was a long walk, and he'd normally take a taxi, but he needed the time to think. It pained him to realize that as much grief and blame as he'd heaped on his father, he'd made the same mistake. He'd fallen for a woman and let himself be used. And he'd enjoyed it. Every single second. He supposed it was karma's way of teaching him that he wasn't any smarter than his father when it came to love.

Love? He didn't dare even think that word. It wasn't love. He didn't know what to call it, but it wasn't love.

One thing he did know, however, was that if Lucy was carrying his child, Oliver would be in his or her life whether Lucy liked it or not. It wasn't about money or child support or anything else but being a good father. Oliver knew what it was like to grow up without one of his parents. Cancer had stolen his mother away, greed had taken Danny's mother from his life, but Oliver had no excuse not to be there for his child.

So whether Lucy liked it or not, he would be.

Eleven

Sitting at Alice's desk, Lucy picked up the sonogram photo again, staring at the fuzzy black-and-gray image and wondering why the Fates got so much amusement by messing with her life. This tiny photo, these blurry little blobs, no bigger than a sesame seed, were about to change her life forever.

Twins, the doctor said. Not just pregnant. Pregnant with twins. She'd laughed hysterically as she looked at the two fat little circles side by side on the monitor. It was that or cry until she ran out of tears. Fraternal twins. Because a single baby wouldn't be enough of a challenge for her to raise on her own.

The doctor was concerned by her response, not entirely sure if she was happy or sad or freaking out. Honestly, it was a combination of all three spinning in her head so fast she could hardly keep up. It was early in the pregnancy, he'd warned. Things could change. One or both could fail. Both could last to term. Be in "wait and see" mode, he'd said. Perhaps wait until her twelve-week ultrasound to confirm the twins before announcing it to everyone.

That wouldn't be a problem. Lucy doubted she could say the words aloud. She'd hardly known what to say to him and the nurse anxiously watching her in the exam room. All she could do was lay there in her crinkly paper dress and watch her world start to crumble around her.

Putting the picture aside, Lucy focused on sorting through the apartment brochures she'd brought home from Yale. It was hard to believe how much her life had changed since she'd gotten on a train and toured that first apartment with Harper. Now, she was not just going back to college, she was doing it while pregnant. Hugely pregnant. She was having twins by herself. And even that was hard to focus on while she was also completely heartsick.

Somehow, the idea of Oliver thinking she was scamming his aunt hadn't hurt her that much. He didn't really know her, and given his past experience with his stepmother, she understood his suspicions. It was a lot of money to give someone who wasn't family. If she had been in his shoes, she might've had the same concerns, even if she didn't need a penny of Alice's money.

But when he accused her of getting pregnant on purpose—to hedge her bets, so to speak—that stung.

She wasn't just some woman he hardly knew anymore. How many hours had they spent together over the last month? How many times had they made love and held each other? Enough to know she wouldn't do something like that.

And yet there wasn't a single moment, a flicker of expression across his face at that restaurant, where the news of her pregnancy stirred anything but anger in him. He'd probably think that her having twins would be karmic retribution for her scheming.

Lucy looked down at the apartment brochure for the place she'd liked the best. The price for the two-bedroom was pretty steep. Add tuition and books, furniture, baby *everything times two*…she wasn't even certain she could afford it all. Not on what she had saved, and that was all she could count on getting. Oliver certainly wasn't going to back down on his protest of the will. The news of her "deliberately trapping" him with a pregnancy would likely hurt her case, so odds were she wouldn't see a dime of Alice's estate.

In truth, that was fine by her. That was more money than she could fathom, much less handle properly. She was much better at barely getting by. Her mother had taught her well. But getting by with babies meant a job with medical insurance for all of them. Day care expenses times two. Diapers times two. Chaos times two. She'd always admired her mother's ability to make it work, but could she do the same?

She let the brochure fall from her fingers down to the desk as tears began to well in her eyes. Could she even do this? Was going back to school a pipe dream now? Was it smarter to put her savings into a place to live and things for the babies instead? Hell, maybe she needed to spend it on a plane ticket back home to Ohio. At least there, she would have her mother to help her with the twins. And she wouldn't run the risk of seeing Oliver again.

"Yes, this was absolutely deliberate, you ass," she said aloud to Alice's large, empty office. "I ruined all of my plans of going back to school and building my future so I could trap you with a child. Because that's the best way to keep a man you love in your life forever. But you get the last laugh, don't you? Twins!"

Lucy dropped her face into her hands and let the tears fall in earnest. She hadn't really let herself cry yet. It had been almost a week since the trip to New Haven and her breakup with Oliver, but she hadn't really let herself wallow in it. It seemed like a misuse of valuable time. Instead, she'd tried to keep herself busy with other things. After her earth-shattering doctor's appointment, she spent hours in different stores, studying everything from prenatal vitamins and stretch-panel jeans to onesies and twin strollers.

It was a tough realization to find she was completely unprepared for any of this. Before Oliver came around, she'd almost forgotten she had a uterus, much less spent time anticipating it to have not just one but two nine-month occupants. Kids were a far-off idea. One that came after love and marriage and the decision that it was time to start a family with someone she could count on.

At least she'd found the love part. Lucy did love Oliver. He didn't love or trust her one iota, but she had done her part and fallen for him. She knew now why they called it falling in love. It had been that easy, like tripping and smacking her face against the rough, hard sidewalk. Like a fall, she wasn't expecting it, but all of a sudden there she was, in love with Oliver. She could only hope that falling out of love with him was just as easy.

Easing back in the desk chair and resting her hand on her flat tummy, she knew that wouldn't be the case. Getting over him would be hard. Especially with two tiny, blue-eyed reminders of him staring at her from their cribs each morning.

It was easier than she expected to picture two wide-eyed toddlers standing in their crib in matching footie pajamas. Wild brown curls. Devious smiles. Pink cheeks. One sucking his thumb with a furrowed brow of concern while his sister clutched her favorite stuffed bunny and tried climbing over the side. In her mind, they looked like tiny clones of Oliver, although the boy had her freckles across his nose.

It was just a daydream, not a reality, but it made Lucy's heart ache. Life didn't always go to plan, but that didn't mean that she couldn't come up with a new plan. She needed to find a way to be happy about this, no matter what happened with Oliver or the will or with school. Things would work out and she had to keep that in mind. One of the pregnancy books she'd picked up had mentioned how her emotions could impact the babies. She didn't want that. No matter what happened, they would be just as loved and cared for as if they'd been planned.

A ring of the apartment's phone pulled her out of her thoughts. No one really called that line except for the doorman, so Lucy reached out and picked it up off the desk. "Hello?"

"Good morning, Miss Campbell. I have a large delivery for you."

Lucy frowned. A large delivery? She hadn't bought

anything. "Are you sure it's for me? Where is it from?" she asked.

"I'm sure. It's from the Museum of Modern Art. It's another painting for the collection, ma'am."

The staff at the building was used to priceless paintings and sculptures being delivered to Alice's apartment. Every few months, something would catch her eye on an auction website and a new piece would arrive. The difference this time being that Alice was deceased and Lucy hadn't bought any art. There had to be a mistake.

"Send them up," she said. She wouldn't know for sure until she saw what it was. Perhaps Alice had a piece on loan to MoMA that Lucy had forgotten about and was being returned.

About ten minutes later, two men came out of the freight elevator with a painting in a wooden crate. Lucy stood holding the service entrance door open as they brought it inside. "Where would you like it?" the older of the two men asked.

"The gallery," she said. That's where most of the paintings went, so it was a knee-jerk response. "I'd like to see what's inside before you leave, however. I didn't buy anything. This may be a mistake and if so, I'll want you to take it back with you."

After they set down the box, the second man pulled a sheet of paper out of his pocket. "You're Miss Lucille Campbell, right?"

"That's me," she replied, even more confused. If it was a piece on loan, it would've had Alice's name on it, not hers.

"Then this is for you."

The older man pulled out a crowbar to pry open the

side and expose the painting. They carefully pulled it out of the straw and paper bedding that protected it and held it up for Lucy to inspect.

She remembered the painting now. It was one of the items available at the silent auction. The painting of the New York skyline made entirely out of hearts. She'd loved it, but she hadn't bought it.

In an instant, that whole amazing night came flooding back to mind. Touring the museum with Oliver, leaving early after getting overheated, making love—and conceiving the twins—on the rooftop garden. There was only one painful answer to where this had come from—Oliver bought it for her that night before they left and it was just now arriving.

The timing was agonizing.

"You can leave it there," she said, indicating the wall where it was leaning.

The men nodded, gathered up the box and packing materials and made their way back out the door. Lucy watched them leave, then stood looking puzzled at the painting in front of her.

What was she supposed to do with it?

Part of her wanted to set it on fire, just to spite him. She didn't need a reminder of that night hanging on the wall, taunting her about everything she'd lost. But destroying it was an insult to the artist and the painting. It didn't have anything to do with the situation with Oliver, and she loved art too much to consider it for long. Besides, she wasn't sure how much he'd paid for it, but since she'd turned down child support in her anger, she might need to sell the piece to support the twins. Unlike everything else in the apartment, that belonged only to her. His romantic gesture come too late.

The thought made her knees quiver beneath her. Better safe than sorry, she lowered herself down to the cold, marble floor of the gallery. There, she had a better view of the painting. She really did love it. Under any other circumstances, she'd be thrilled to own it. It was just a painful reminder of Oliver that she didn't need.

Staring at it for a moment, she reached out and ran her finger along the edge of the painting. Lucy knew then that she would keep it. If nothing else, it might be the only thing the twins would have from their father.

With a sigh, she stood up and went in search of a place to hang it.

Oliver was miserable.

There just wasn't any other way to describe how he felt. He wasn't even entirely sure how long it had been since he spoke with Lucy and found out about the baby. The days had all started to blur together. He hadn't been in the office. Hadn't left his apartment. He hadn't even gone up to the roof to start trimming back for the fall because being up there reminded him too much of Lucy and the night they'd spent together there. Somehow, even his sanctuary was tainted by the situation.

He wouldn't go so far as to say Lucy had ruined it. He wasn't that ignorant. It had taken a few days for his temper to cool down so he could come to that conclusion, but he knew it was true. Start to finish, this was a mess of his own making. Nothing Lucy had done since the day he met her had warranted the horrible things he'd said to her at dinner that night. She had immediately come to him to do the right thing and tell him about the baby, and he'd thrown it in her face. And yet, after hours spent racking his brain for a way to undo the things he'd done, he'd come up with nothing.

Was that even possible?

Oliver Drake: CEO and savior of Orion Technology, eligible bachelor, millionaire and complete asshat.

He was stewing on his sofa when there was a knock at the door. That in itself was unusual since the doorman hadn't called. At the same time, it was concerning. He'd dodged calls from his family for days and they were the only ones who could get up here without his permission. He hoped Harper hadn't arrived to chew him out. He hadn't even bothered to listen to the fifteen voice-mail messages she'd left him.

With a frown, he turned off the television and crossed the room to the front door. Peering through the peephole, he was relieved to find his father and brother there instead of his sister. "Dad?" he asked as he opened the door.

Tom Drake looked at his son and shook his head. "You look like hell," he said, pushing past Oliver into the house with Danny in his wake.

His little brother had recovered remarkably well from his accident. You'd hardly even know he'd been in the hospital as he took off for the living room and changed the channel to pull up his favorite show. Oliver knew that when he was bored with that, he'd whip his latest gaming device out of his back pocket and play until Dad made him stop. Technology ran deep in the veins of this family.

With a sigh, Oliver shut the door behind his dad and followed him to the kitchen where he was making himself some coffee.

"I didn't think you drank coffee anymore, Dad."

Tom looked up at him with a dismayed frown. "It's not for me, it's for you."

"I don't need any coffee, Dad. I'm not hungover."

His father narrowed his eyes at Oliver, taking in the robe and pajama pants he had on, the week-old scruff that had grown on his face and his bedhead. "Even if you're not hungover, you're drinking this," he said at last. "You need something to wake you up."

"I'm not sleepy."

"I'm not saying you are. Sometimes in a man's life, he needs to wake up and take a look at what's going on around him. He gets too set in his ways, gets lost in a routine and doesn't notice things right in front of his face. I was like that once. I don't want you to end up like me."

Oliver scratched his head in confusion but accepted the coffee his father handed him.

"Sit down, son."

Oliver sat down at the kitchen table, trying not to think about the breakfast he'd shared here with Lucy. "I just needed a break, Dad."

Tom reached into the refrigerator and pulled out a bottle of water before sitting across from his son. "The hell you did. This is about that woman. Lucy."

Oliver hadn't said two words to his father about what had happened with Lucy, so his sister must've narc'd on him. "She's pregnant, Dad." It was the first time the words had passed his lips. Even days later, it felt alien on his tongue.

His father shrugged off his bombshell announcement. "It happens. What are you doing to do about it?"

"I don't know. I'm worried I'm going to make the same mistakes you did. I don't know that I can trust her. The whole family thinks she's some kind of crook."

"What do you think?"

"I…" Oliver stopped. He'd wrestled with this question since the day he'd met her. Now, he tried to answer honestly just as he knew her, not letting his fears answer for him. "I don't think she had anything to do with Aunt Alice changing her will. These last few weeks, I've found that Lucy is naturally charming. I think Alice would've wanted to help her out and do something nice for Lucy by leaving her the estate. At least that's my guess. But what if I'm wrong? What if she's just like Candace? How do I know the child isn't just another ploy to get her hands not only on Aunt Alice's money but mine, too?"

"You don't," his father said simply. With a sigh, Tom ran his hand through his mostly gray hair. "I think this is all my fault."

Oliver perked up in his chair. "What?"

"I thought you were old enough when all this happened with Candace, but I think I still managed to give you some trust issues. Listen, I was an idiot, Oliver. I got all wrapped up in your stepmother and made some choices that were pretty foolish in retrospect. But I was lonely so I took that chance. And now, years later, I would probably do everything exactly the same if I were given the chance to go back in time."

That surprised Oliver. He thought for sure that his father regretted what happened with his second wife. "Really?"

Tom chuckled at his son's surprise and sipped his water thoughtfully. "Yes. Despite our outward appearances, Candace and I really did have chemistry. She certainly put a dent in my finances, but it was a fine price to pay for a couple fun years and that little boy in the living room. If changing the past with Candace means that I wouldn't have Danny, then I want no part of it."

Both men turned toward the living room to watch Danny as he sat cross-legged on the floor and grinned at the television.

"Things don't always happen the way you plan, but that doesn't mean they didn't work out the way they were supposed to. If you believe Lucy didn't scheme her way into Alice's will, why would you think she's trying to trap you by getting pregnant? Maybe it was an honest mistake."

Oliver turned back to the table and studied the mug in his hands. The look on Lucy's face in the restaurant came to his mind. With a little time and perspective, he was able to see how scared she was to tell him. How hard she struggled to hide how nervous and confused she was over the pregnancy. She'd needed him in that moment and he'd failed her by turning on her and accusing her of such horrible things.

"Here's a better question," his father continued. "Does it really matter? Will it make you love your child any less?"

"No." That question was easier for Oliver to answer. If he'd figured anything out over the last few days, it was that he would love that child more than anyone on the planet had ever loved their child. The harder question was whether he was willing to love the mother just as much.

"And how did you feel about Lucy before you found out about the baby?"

"I thought that maybe I was falling in love. I guess that scared me. I've never felt that way about a woman before. It all happened so fast."

"It was that way with your mother, you know? We went from our first date to married in two months. It was intense and scary and wonderful all at once, but I couldn't stand the idea of being apart from her."

Oliver had never heard that about his parents before. He supposed that he hadn't asked, thinking it would be a sore spot for his father after his mother died. "Why did you decide to get married so quickly?"

Tom smiled and reached out to pat Oliver's shoulder. "You. Like I said before, it happens." He got up from the table and called out to Danny. "Daniel, we're getting ready to go." Then he turned back to Oliver and handed him a small box that had been stuffed into his coat pocket. "When you make up your mind, this might come in handy. It was your mother's. Talk to you later, son."

Before Oliver could really respond to everything his father had just said to him, his brother was gingerly giving him a hug and the two of them were out the door.

Alone in his apartment again, Oliver reached for the box on the table and opened the hinged lid. Inside, he found what could only be his mother's engagement ring. It was marquise-shaped with a single baguette on each side, set in platinum. It wasn't at all fashionable at the moment; it was more a throwback to another time. But it was simple, elegant and classic—the perfect ring for his mother, and he realized, perfect for Lucy as well. His mother had been one in a million and Lucy didn't fit into the mold either. It was just the ring he would choose for the mother of his child and his future wife.

If she would accept it.

In that moment, he wanted her to accept it more than he ever expected. Not just because of the baby, but because he was in love with her. Despite his suspicious nature and cautious approach, Lucy had slipped past all his defenses and reached a part of him that he'd managed to keep locked away from all the women before her. He didn't want to lock away that part of himself any longer. Like his garden, he wanted to share it with her. Share it with their child.

There was another knock at the door, startling him. Oliver got up, presuming Danny left something behind, but when he opened the door, he found a fuming Harper standing there instead. It was time to get the earful he'd avoided all week.

"You are a jerk! How could you possibly accuse Lucy of getting pregnant on purpose? That's absolutely absurd! She had plans, you know? That's why we were in Connecticut. She was planning on going back to college. How is she supposed to do that raising your baby on her own, huh? Especially with you holding all of Aunt Alice's money hostage for no good reason!"

With a sigh, Oliver stepped back to let his seething sister inside. He could tell she was just getting warmed up. Once she was done yelling at him, perhaps she could help him figure out how exactly he could clean up the mess he'd made with Lucy so everyone could be happy again.

Twelve

"Lucy, this is Phillip Glass. How are you?"

Lucy nervously clutched the phone. She hadn't heard from Alice's estate attorney in quite a while. Had the judge made a ruling yet? "Good," she answered and held her breath.

"Excellent. Well, I'm calling because I have some good news for you. Amazing news, actually. Mr. Drake has dropped his dispute over Alice's will."

Lucy slumped down into a nearby chair as her knees gave out from under her. Surely she hadn't heard him correctly. "What?"

"It's all yours now, Lucy. The money, the apartment, the art, all of it. Congratulations."

She knew she should say something, but she didn't have any words. This was not the call she was expecting to get. She'd prepared herself for the consoling discussion about how the judge felt Alice's state of mind may have been compromised at her age and given the change was so close to her death... Instead, she found she really truly had the winning lotto ticket in her hand.

An initial wave of relief washed over her. Not excitement, but relief. She'd been twisting her stomach into knots the last few days trying to figure out how she was going to support the twins on her own. Now, that question was answered and it didn't require her to go crawling to the twins' father. Although it did raise a curious question.

"Did Mr. Drake say why he dropped the protest?"

"He didn't. Honestly, I wish I knew what changed his mind, as well. Listen, I'm going to work on getting everything transitioned over to you and I'll be in touch in a week or two. There's some paperwork and hoops still to jump through, a huge chunk of estate taxes to pull out, but you can finally celebrate, Lucy."

"Thanks, Phillip."

Lucy hung up the phone and found herself still too stunned to move from her seat. She was more surprised by Oliver changing his mind than anything else. There had always been the possibility that the judge would rule in her favor, but she never thought he would back down, even when they'd gotten so close. That seemed too much like mixing business and pleasure where he was concerned.

What had changed?

Oliver had been so angry with her that night. He told her he didn't even want anything to do with his child and now, he was just handing over his aunt's estate after weeks of fighting over it? Was this his roundabout way of providing child support without paying a dime of his own money? She didn't dare to dream that

it was an olive branch or first step on their way to rec-
onciliation. Two miracles wouldn't happen in one day.

Lucy wasn't quite sure what to do. She felt like she
should tell someone, and yet she was hesitant to even
now. It didn't feel real. It never had. Just like looking
at that sonogram.

An hour before, she'd been wondering if she could
fit a bed and two cribs in the one-bedroom apartment
near campus and now she could buy a house and a
car, hire a full-time nanny and not have to work. Her
life was undergoing a major upheaval every couple of
days and she wasn't sure how many more big changes
she could take.

She knew she should be excited. She was an instant millionaire hundreds of times over. Rich beyond
her wildest dreams. Her children would never want
for anything the way she had. Their college was paid
for. Her college was paid for. Life should be easier, at
least on that front. While she felt a bit of the pressure
lifting from her shoulders, she still wouldn't call herself excited.

How could she be excited or happy with the way
things ended with Oliver? It was impossible. All the
money in the world wouldn't bring the man she loved
and the father of her children back into her life. Honestly, she'd trade every penny in a heartbeat if he would
knock on the door right now and tell her that he was
sorry—that he loved her and their babies more than
anything else. But that wouldn't happen. Not after all
the horrible things he'd said. Oliver wouldn't change
his mind and Lucy couldn't forget it.

The doorbell rang the moment after the thought
crossed her mind, startling her from the sad path her

thoughts had taken. She stood up from her seat, the phone still clutched in her hand from Phillip's call. Could it be?

Her heart started pounding in her chest, even as she tried to convince herself that it was probably the cleaning lady or Harper checking on her. Lucy stood at the door a moment, willing herself not to be disappointed if she opened it and found someone else.

Taking a deep breath, she opened it. And there, against all odds, was Oliver.

He was standing in the marble-tiled foyer looking like a tall glass of water to a woman lost in the desert. He was wearing her favorite gray suit with a blue shirt that made his eyes an even brighter shade than usual. His lips were pressed together anxiously, even as he clutched a bouquet of bright pink roses and blue delphinium in his hands.

"Hi," he said after a few long seconds of staring silently at one another.

Lucy wasn't quite sure what to think. She'd hardly recovered from the shock of her call with Phillip. "Hello." That was a start.

She took a step back to let him into the apartment. She was curious about what he had to say, but wouldn't allow herself to mentally leap ahead. Just because he was here didn't mean he was begging for her back. She didn't know what he wanted, or if she was even willing to give it to him if he did. She loved him, but she loved herself and her babies, too, and she knew she had to be smart about this. He'd been unnecessarily cruel to her and it would take more than a "sorry" and some flowers for her to forget the things he'd said.

"These are for you," he said, holding out the flowers

and smiling sheepishly at her. "I picked out the pink and blue flowers for the baby."

"Thank you." Lucy accepted the flowers and turned her back on Oliver to put them in water. She needed a moment without his soulful eyes staring into her own.

When she returned from the kitchen, he was still standing in the same spot in the gallery, only now he was looking at the painting he'd bought her. She'd finally hung it on the wall.

"Thank you for the painting," she said, stopping alongside him to admire the piece. "You didn't have to do that."

"I know I didn't. That was the point of the gift."

Lucy set the vase of flowers onto the table in the entryway and turned to him. "You also didn't have to drop your contest of Alice's will. We could've seen it through to the judge and let him rule on it."

Oliver turned to her and shook his head. "No, we couldn't. I couldn't risk the judge's ruling. I dropped the suit because I changed my mind."

Lucy crossed her arms defensively over her chest. Standing this close to Oliver again after these horrible few days, she felt like she needed the buffer to protect herself. From herself.

"You changed your mind about what?" she snapped. "That I was a seasoned con artist that manipulated your elderly, agoraphobic aunt into leaving me all her money? Or that I deliberately got pregnant to trap you into financially supporting me and your child for life?"

Oliver swallowed hard, the muscles in his throat moving with strain and difficulty. She'd never seen him so tense. Not in the lawyer's office that first day, not even in the restaurant when she saw him last. He appeared outwardly calm, but she was keenly aware of how tightly strung he seemed.

"I'm sorry, Lucy," he said at last. "I'm sorry for all of that. I never should've given a voice to the doubts in my head, because that's all they were—my own demons twisting reality. You never did anything to deserve the way I treated you. You're nothing like my stepmother and I knew that, I was just afraid because I had feelings for you that I didn't know how to handle. I was scared to make a mistake like my father and instead, I made an even bigger mess by ruining the best thing I had in my life. I can only hope that one day you can see it in your heart to forgive me for that. I intend to try every day for the next fifty years until you do."

Lucy stood quietly listening to his words. They seemed painfully sincere, making her heart ache in her chest for him. But he wasn't the only one who was scared. She was scared of trusting him again too soon and having her heart trampled on. "Thank you," she said. "I know it wasn't easy for you to say all of that."

"I'll admit when I'm wrong, Lucy, and I have been in the wrong since the day we met. I wish we could start all over again, but I can't change what I've done. Can you forgive me, Lucy?" he pressed with hopeful eyes gazing into hers.

She could feel the pain and regret in every word he spoke. She'd never heard a sincerer apology. "I do forgive you for the things you said and did." She sensed that wasn't quite enough for him, but she wasn't betraying her heart too quickly.

Oliver reached out and wrapped his fingers around her hand. "Thank you. I'm so happy to hear you say that because to be honest, I'm head over heels in love with you and I thought I might never get the chance to tell you." He stopped, looking at her with an obvious question on his mind. "Do you think you might be able to love me someday?"

The warmth of his skin against hers made it hard for her to focus on his words. She could feel her body start to betray her. It longed to lean in and press against the hard muscle of his chest. She wanted to breathe in the warm scent of his cologne at his throat and feel his arms wrapped around her. She fought the urge, knowing this conversation was too important. It needed to happen and it couldn't if she started rubbing against him like a contented kitten.

She forced herself to look up at him. His eyes were pleading with her. But she had to tell the truth about how she felt.

"No," she said.

Oliver did his best not to react. He knew there was a risk in coming here—that she couldn't forgive him for how he'd treated her. He'd told himself that no matter what her answer, he would accept it, even supporting his child without being in its mother's life if that's the way Lucy wanted it. And sadly, it appeared that was how she wanted it.

"Okay," he said, dropping her hand even though it was the last thing he wanted to do.

"I can't love you *someday*, Oliver. That would mean I didn't love you now. And I do." She placed a gentle hand against his cheek and smiled warmly. "Even when I was angry and hurt, I still loved you. Of course I do."

Relief washed over him all at once and he scooped her up into his arms for a huge hug. "Oh, thank goodness!" he breathed into her ear. "I haven't blown it." Pushing back to put some distance between them again, he looked her in the eyes. "So you're telling me I haven't ruined everything for us? For our new family?"

A sheen of tears appeared in Lucy's dark brown eyes. "We're going to be a family?" she asked.

"If you'll have me." Oliver scooped her hands into his and dropped down onto his knee. He'd practiced this speech twenty times since his father had given him that ring, and in the moment, with adrenaline pumping through his veins, he couldn't remember a word of it. All he could do was speak from his heart and hope that it was romantic and wonderful enough for her to accept him.

"Lucy, I have spent the last few years of my life living under a cloud of pessimism. I never believed that a woman would love me just for who I am. I saw what happened to my father and let it color my outlook of the world. A part of me had given up on the kind of love others seemed to find. And then I met you. And you challenged me at every step. You made me question everything and I'm so thankful that you did. It forced me to realize that I was hiding from my life. And it forced me to realize that I am very much in love with you.

"Unfortunately," he continued with a sheepish grin, "I didn't know how much I loved you until I'd nearly ruined everything for us. It was there, alone and miserable in my apartment, that I decided that I was willing to do anything to make it up to you, if I even could. First, I had my lawyer withdraw the protest because I wanted you to know that I believed you. Aunt Alice wanted you to have that money, and I want you to have it, too, whether or not you wanted me in your life again. There's no strings attached."

"You really, truly believe me? You have no reservations at all about the will or the baby?"

He'd failed to answer this question properly the first time because he was plagued with doubts even as she lay in his arms. Now, he was confident in his decision. "You don't have a malicious bone in your body, Lucy. I can't believe I ever thought otherwise. And if I did, I wouldn't have taken this to the jeweler to be cleaned and sized just for you."

Oliver reached into his pocket and pulled out the jewelry box his father had brought him a few days before. He opened the lid to show her the ring inside. "This ring belonged to my mother," he said as she gasped audibly. "My father gave it to me in the hopes that I would stop moping around my place and start living my life with you in it. And not just you, but with our child, too."

Lucy looked at the ring expectantly, but she didn't say anything. At first, he thought that maybe she was just dazzled by the sight of it, but Oliver quickly realized that he was so nervous, he forgot to ask the critical question.

"Lucille Campbell, will you please do me the honor of being my wife, accepting all the love I have to give and standing by my side for the rest of our lives?"

At that, Lucy smiled through her tears. "Yes," she said. "There's nothing more I want than to be your lover and partner in life."

Oliver's hands were shaking as he pulled the ring from its velvet bed and slipped it onto her finger. "It's a little large on you right now, but the jeweler suggested sizing up so you could wear it well into your second and third trimesters."

"It's perfect," she said as she admired it on her hand. "I'm honored to wear the ring your mother once wore. I know she was important to you."

He clutched her hands in his as he stood up. With his eyes pinned on hers, he leaned in and planted a kiss on the ridge of her knuckles—one hand, then the other— before seeking out her lips. When his mouth pressed to hers, it was like a promise was made between them. The engagement was official—sealed with a kiss.

He wrapped his arms around her and pulled her close. Oliver didn't want to let go. Not after almost losing her for good. She felt so right here, how could he ever have said or done something to drive her away? He was a fool once, but never again. She would be his—and he, hers—forever.

When their lips finally parted, he leaned his forehead against hers. "I want us to be a real family. Like my parents had. These last few days thinking about you raising our child without me... I couldn't bear the thought of it despite what I said that night at the restaurant. I was upset and confused about the news. It may not have been planned, but this child will always know that he or she was wanted. I'll do everything in my power to see to that. But most of all I want to make you happy, Lucy. Anything you want, we can make it happen."

"I don't know what I could possibly ask for, Oliver. Today alone, you've proposed with your mother's engagement ring and given me a half a billion dollar estate. It seems greedy to ask for anything else."

"Harper told me that you were trying to go back to school. You never mentioned it to me before."

"Yes," Lucy hesitated. "That was my plan, but…"

"No buts. If you want to go back to Yale, you absolutely should do it."

"It's so far away, Oliver. From you and your job. I don't want to be alone in Connecticut while you're here running your computer company."

Oliver just shrugged off her concerns. "If you want to be in Manhattan every night, I'll have you flown to class and back on Orion's private jet each day. If you want to stay there during the week, we'll buy a nice place and I'll come spend every weekend I can with you until you graduate."

"I don't know," Lucy said. "That seems like it would make things far more complicated than they need to be. If I was moving up there by myself as I'd planned originally, that's one thing, but I'm not leaving you behind. Maybe I can look at some of the local programs. I'm sure Columbia or NYU has something that will allow me to stay in the city. And when the babies— er, *baby*—comes," she stuttered, "we'll all be together. That's the most important thing."

Oliver grinned. Of course, he preferred having her as close as possible, but that was completely up to her. "Are you sure? Like I said, whatever makes you happy, Lucy."

"Being with you makes me happy." Leaning in, she rested her head on his shoulder and sighed in contentment. "After everything that has happened, I may even defer school for another year or two. I'm not sure I can manage a wedding, a pregnancy and caring for an infant on top of the senior-level classes I need to graduate. The art will always be there when I'm ready. I want to focus on remembering every moment of these early months with you."

"If that's what you want." Oliver smiled. They certainly did have a lot coming up in their lives over the next year. "And don't forget, we have to decide where we want to live. We have two amazing Manhattan apartments to choose from."

"I want to move to your place," Lucy said without hesitation. "For one thing, I couldn't ask you to leave your beautiful garden. And for another, Alice's place is stunning, but way too formal and stuffy for children running around all wild."

Oliver smiled at her decision. "Children, huh? Are we already planning on having more than one?"

A curious expression came across Lucy's face. She wrinkled her nose and bit at her lip. "There's something I need to tell you," Lucy admitted.

"Yes? Anything, love."

"The doctor says we're having twins."

Twins? The room began to spin and close in on him.

Oliver was about to experience a lot of new firsts. His first time in love, his first time to be engaged, his first children were on the way... And this was the first time he'd ever fainted.

He was out cold before he hit the floor.

Epilogue

Lucy eyeballed the three paint swatches on the walls of what would soon be the twins' nursery. Three months later, they were both growing and thriving, pressing Lucy's belly out to a larger bulge than she anticipated this far along. She and Oliver had decided not to find out the sex of the twins, so she was comparing different shades of gray paints for the neutral design they had planned.

With her hands planted on her hips, she frowned at the wall and continued to after Oliver came up behind her. "The one in the middle," he said without hesitation. "And Emma is on the phone for you."

Emma's baby girl, Georgette, had been born right after Lucy announced her pregnancy. Little Georgie, named after her maternal grandfather, George Dempsey, had occupied most of Emma's time the last three months. Lucy accepted the phone from Oliver, curious as to what prompted the call from her friend.

"Hey, Emma," Lucy said. "I'm trying to pick out a color for the nursery. What's going on with you?"

"It's not me I'm calling about, it's Violet."

Lucy didn't like the way her friend said that. "What's wrong? Are she and the baby okay?" Violet was due any day now.

"They're both fine. She delivered a healthy baby boy this morning."

"That's wonderful!" Lucy gushed. "I'm glad you called, I hadn't heard anything yet. Stupid Beau. He was supposed to let us know when she went into labor."

"Yeah, well…" Emma said. "There's a reason he didn't call."

The feeling of anxiety returned to Lucy's stomach. "What's that?"

"It turns out the baby isn't his."

Lucy's jaw dropped. "What? How do they know that? Did he demand a paternity test so soon after she delivered?"

"No," Emma replied. "They didn't need one. Beau and Violet are both dark haired, dark skinned and dark eyed. Mediterranean lineage through and through."

"And the baby?"

"The baby is a fair-skinned, blue-eyed redhead."

A redhead? Violet had never once mentioned anything about a dating a ginger. She'd been on again, off again with Beau for the last few years, but even then, Violet hadn't dated anyone else. At least that Lucy knew about. "Then who *is* the father?"

"That's just it. No one knows. Not even Violet. Ap-

TWIN SECRETS

JULES BENNETT

This goes to Stacy Boyd, who said she loves cowboys and baby stories...so I delivered an entire series of both! Thanks for the ideas!

One

How the hell could her father have gambled away all of his savings? As in, every last penny to his name. His reckless way of living finally caught up with him…with them. He'd lost major things before: his car, his retirement funds, all of her mother's jewelry—save for the one piece Annabelle had hidden away. But he'd gone too far this time.

As if Annabelle Carter didn't have enough on her plate. She'd come home to Stone River, Texas, to start over. She'd brought her sweet twins, six-month-old Emily and Lucy, and planned to offer them a new life and begin building her dream…a vision of her late mother's.

But, no. Now Annabelle was driving to the ranch next door to do damage control. As she turned onto the long drive, flanked by a pristine white fence, she pulled in a breath. The arched, metal sign over the entrance was a good indicator of the amount of money these people had. The stone columns suspending the sign were nothing short of remarkable. The beauty started from the street and she could only imagine what she was about to see at the end of this drive.

Pebblebrook Ranch was one place she'd never ventured into. It was owned by the hoity-toity Elliott family, and they didn't necessarily run in the same circles. The five–thousand-acre spread boasted several massive homes. Just one of their mansions was worth more than Annabelle's entire farm.

And that was when they'd actually had livestock. Her father, however, had gambled animals away, too. She'd been gone two years, living in Houston, and in that time he'd completely lost everything.

Rage ripped through her. What would he have done had she not come back home to nurse her own wounds? A fresh wave of anger surged through Annabelle as she remembered her sister and fiancé's betrayal. And the crippling effects of her sister's recent death. So much pain, Annabelle wasn't sure how to log it all inside her heart.

Now she had to deal with Colt Elliott on top of everything else. She'd never met the man, but she knew of the Elliott brothers. Sexy ladies' men, all much older than her. If she recalled correctly, Colt was a twin. Were the twins the youngest of the siblings?

None of that mattered. What mattered was that her father had borrowed money to pay off the farm loan before it could go into foreclosure, without informing her. Of all people to go to, her father had gone to Colt Elliott. Not that there were many people who could've helped, but Neil Carter could have come to Annabelle first. She didn't have that chunk of cash, but she would've gone through hell before borrowing from the Elliotts.

Now her father owed Colt instead of the bank. Perfect. Just perfect. The loan had been so close to being paid off, but her father just couldn't hang on any longer. He'd gone through all the money he'd put aside. Thankfully, Annabelle had set aside money for her sister's funeral expenses, or her father would've gone through that, as well.

According to her father, he and Colt had come to an agreement that he had to pay off the debt within three months. The bimonthly payments couldn't be a day late or a penny short or the farm would permanently belong to Colt.

Fine. Annabelle had no problem taking over her dad's end of the bargain. She refused to lose the only thing she had left. Her childhood home would not go to the family whose hobby was probably sitting around counting their wad of cash.

Annabelle's father claimed Colt was helping, but she didn't believe that for a second. People like the Elliotts didn't just do things out of the kindness of their hearts. In terms of wealth and influence, they were a giant leap above all other people in this town. With their mansions on the sprawling estate, the billions of dollars that passed through the farm from all their livestock…the rest of the businesses in the area didn't even compare. They were Stone River's answer to a cattle monopoly…if that was a thing. Random people didn't just go to Pebblebrook. It was like some sacred ground that mere peons didn't dare trespass on.

Well, too bad because she wanted to know what Colt's agenda truly was. She suspected he wanted her land for himself and she was going to have no part of that. She had her own dreams: marriage, siblings for her twins, opening her bed-and-breakfast. She'd already lost so much—she wasn't about to lose her home or her future.

Annabelle approached the sprawling three-story log and stone home. Sturdy wooden porches stretched across the first and second floors and two balconies extended from double glass doors off the third floor. Probably bedrooms. She imagined Colt on a balcony overlooking his massive estate, as if he were a king overlooking his kingdom. Annabelle swallowed. She couldn't even fathom the money these people had.

When a horse came from around the side of the two-story stable, Annabelle immediately forgot about the house. And it wasn't even the striking black stallion that had her attention.

Hellllo, Shirtless Stable Boy.

She may be nursing a shattered heart but she wasn't dead, and this hottie with excellent, tanned muscle tone was a perfect temporary distraction. How much work did it take to get ripped like that? Ranching certainly produced some fine—

Annabelle jerked as her car hit something and came to an abrupt stop. Gripping the wheel, eyes squeezed shut, she had no clue what had just happened, but she'd been distracted and obviously ran into...*oh, please don't be a person or an animal.*

Opening one eye at a time, she saw nothing but the barn and grassy fields...and the shattered post where the fence had been. Mercy, she'd been so caught up in the hunk on horseback, she'd run into the fence. Way to make an entrance.

As if she needed another problem in her life.

Mortified and shaken up, Annabelle shut off her car, thankful the babies weren't in the backseat. Her door jerked open, startling a squeal out of her.

"Are you all right, ma'am?"

That perfect Southern drawl combined with the bare chest she now stared at was enough to render her speechless. But even that couldn't override the reason she came. Just because she'd wrecked her sporty car, her only material possession worth any money, didn't mean she could deviate from her plan. What was one more setback at this point?

"I'm fine," she stated, trembling more from the sight of the sexy stranger than the actual accident.

Annabelle swung her legs out and came to stand, but the cowboy didn't back up. With one hand on her open car door and the other on the hood, he had her trapped. On any other day, she would've welcomed this stranger getting in her space and making her forget her cheating fiancé, but today there was no time for lustful thoughts. She shivered again as his eyes swept over her.

"Sorry about the fence," she stated, shoving her hair away from her face. "I'll pay to have it repaired."

With the savings that were supposed to go toward realizing my mother's dream.

"The sun was in my eyes," she went on. No way was she about to admit she'd been staring at his perfect…riding form.

"Don't worry about the fence."

Now he stepped back, but just enough for her to take in his well-worn cowboy boots, fitted jeans over a narrow waist…that glistening chest and his tipped cowboy hat. Black, of course.

"What brings you to Pebblebrook?" he asked, propping his hands on his hips.

Annabelle pulled in a breath. "I'm here to see Mr. Elliott. My name is Annabelle Carter and I live next door. Well, I used to a few years ago, but I'm back now."

Despite the chiseled jaw and the heavy-lidded gaze, the man's mouth tipped into a slight grin. "Well, ma'am, Mr. Elliott is busy right now. Is there something I can help you with? A glass of sweet tea? You look like you could use a break."

Sharing a sweet tea, or anything else with this hunky stranger, was tempting, but not on her agenda.

Annabelle blew out a breath. Mr. Elliott was busy. Of course. Probably at the bank purchasing more properties to add to his collection. A man like Colt didn't work outside in the heat tending to his own animals and land. That would be too far beneath him.

"You work here?" she asked, crossing her arms.

His mouth twitched again. "Yes, ma'am."

"Then give your boss a message." She may not be able to talk to the man himself, but she would leave her mark—and she didn't mean the broken fence. "I'd like to talk to him about my ranch next door and the agreement he made with my father. Please tell Mr. Elliott, when he's done getting his manicure or finished stealing puppies from children, he will be dealing with me from now on. I'll be waiting at my house for his visit."

Because she certainly wouldn't be showing her face here again.

The stable hand simply tapped the brim of his black hat and tipped his head. "I'll be sure to let him know."

His eyes raked over her once more, sending shivers through her despite the Texas heat. "Are you sure you don't want something to drink? Have a seat on the porch. You look like you could use a break."

Oh, she could use a break. Like a monthlong vacation somewhere exotic with a fruity umbrella drink full of alcohol and unlimited refills. But she'd just settle for a break from all the pain life kept dishing out.

"No, I don't have the time." Not to mention, she couldn't stay in his presence too much longer. It was difficult keeping her eyes off that broad chest sprinkled with dark hair and the tattoo on his right bicep.

"Is there anything else I should pass on?" he asked.

Since she was in a mood, she nodded. "I'm not a pushover like my father. Make sure you tell him he has twenty-four hours to contact me."

The "or else" hung in the air, but she had no idea what her "or else" threat would be so she left it at that. She hoped she sounded badass, but it was kind of hard with her bright red car mounting the fence.

The cowboy stepped toward the front of her vehicle,

assessing the damage. She didn't even want to know how this would affect her insurance. *One crisis at a time.*

"Your little car has quite a bit of damage, ma'am."

With a flick of his fingertip, he adjusted his hat, bringing that cobalt blue gaze up to hers. The striking color of his eyes only added to his appeal. Did all the stable hands at this ranch have the qualifications to do calendars? Because she wouldn't mind buying one of those.

"I'm pretty sure this would fit in the bed of my truck," he muttered around a grin. "Should I haul it next door for you?"

Annabelle ignored his snarky jab. It was only because of his sex appeal that she let the question slide. Besides, she wasn't here to impress people or make friends.

"I can drive. Thank you."

She turned to get back into her car. As she started it up again, the cowboy closed her door, then leaned inside the window. "I'll be sure Mr. Elliott gets in touch with you today."

Annabelle nodded and shifted into gear. He stepped back, giving her one last glimpse of the fine body she didn't have time to fully appreciate.

Disappointed that she hadn't gotten face time with Colt Elliott, Annabelle headed back down the drive and prepared the speech she'd deliver when she did see him. She was done letting life—and men—rob her of her dreams.

He watched her tiny red car until it disappeared at the end of the drive. Annabelle Carter was one fired-up woman. The vibrant red hair and flashing green eyes had him more intrigued than he should be.

When he'd come around the side of the barn to put Lightning away after his morning ride, he'd caught a glimpse of the car just before it missed the turn in the drive and slammed into the fence.

"Colt?"

He turned to see Josh, one of his best stable hands, heading his way.

"Everything all right?" he asked. At nearly forty, Josh was probably Colt's hardest worker.

Colt nodded toward the fence. "This is top priority. Tell Ryan to assist you. I'll put Lightning in her stall."

Colt almost wished he hadn't fired a worker last week, but the guy had it coming and Colt didn't put up with lazy. He worked too damn hard. Just because his bank account had more zeroes than this town had ever seen, didn't mean he wasn't a hands-on type of guy—in business and in pleasure.

Josh nodded. "Is the lady okay?"

Speaking of hands-on...

Was she? Colt thought of the way she'd demanded to see "Mr. Elliott." He nearly lost it when she mentioned a manicure and puppy stealing. She truly didn't have a high opinion of him, but that was fine. He'd seen the sexual interest when he'd gotten close. She was pretty damn sexy herself.

But Colt hadn't been ready to tell her who he was until he knew what she wanted. Being mistaken for a worker was just one of the advantages of loving the ranch life. He may be the owner, well, he and his three brothers, but Colt was by far the most active. He took pride in what he had. There was no question of authority around here and his staff respected him. He wouldn't have it any other way.

Keeping in control of every situation is what led him to the success he had today. So, letting Annabelle believe he was just a ranch hand had definitely worked to his advantage. Now he had time to plot, to think of exactly how he wanted to play this situation out.

She said she was back in town, and he hadn't missed the way she'd looked at his chest. Maybe a little flirting, even a little seduction, would be in order.

Colt mounted Lightning and trotted back to the stable while Josh went to get supplies to fix the broken fence. Annabelle may be more financially savvy than her old man, but that wouldn't change the outcome.

The documents Neil Carter had signed without taking the time to read were completely legal and binding.

Colt had been wanting to get that land for years. The Carter's five-hundred-acre farm wasn't vast in comparison to his, but he and his brothers had shared a vision of owning it. Their main goal was to turn the property into an adjoining dude ranch. The Carter home was perfect for additional housing for guests.

Colt's father had always been a dreamer, not a doer. He'd discussed owning a dude ranch, having people come to stay on their property and learn the ways of their life, but he'd never gotten beyond the talking stage. Dementia had stolen Grant Elliott's mind, leaving Colt to carry on and bring his father's legacy to life.

From the time Colt was a young boy, he'd itched to see this property grow, to see people from all over flock in and see what they'd created. He refused to let anything stand in the way of his goal, even the sassy, beautiful Ms. Carter.

After putting the saddle and blanket away, he grabbed the brush to groom the dust from Lightning. While stroking the stallion, an epiphany struck him. Colt was a smarter businessman than Neil, clearly. Hell, Colt knew Neil had no idea what he'd agreed to when he'd accepted the money to pay off the loan—the man had been too desperate. But Colt would give Annabelle a chance to pay that debt. There were six installments left. Three months was all that stood between him and everything he'd ever wanted.

Suddenly being one stable hand short wasn't such a hardship. Perhaps Annabelle would be interested in a little work to help pay off the debt. She no doubt wanted to discuss the arrangement. She'd controlled her anger with him, thinking she'd just been talking to a stable hand, but there had been fury in those deep green eyes. Well, he'd use that fury to his advantage and make her an offer she couldn't refuse.

Colt patted the side of the stallion and finished brushing him as his brilliant plan took shape. He had no intention of ever handing that land over again. It finally belonged to him, but her father had to learn a lesson. He owed more than just this debt, but Annabelle didn't need to know that.

Having such a beautiful woman on his property sure would perk things up around here. She had drive and determination. He couldn't help but admire her spirit.

Colt whistled as he headed back toward the main house. His limp from the accident wasn't even bothering him today. Sometimes it ached, but right now, he had his mind on other things…like the sexy redhead he needed to properly introduce himself to.

He made his way to his third-floor master suite to get ready for a very important meeting. He owned the land, now he wanted to own the woman. And Colt Elliott always got what he wanted.

Two

Infuriating man.

Annabelle found herself on Colt Elliott's property for the second time today. She'd wanted to have the meeting in her house, where she could have some level of control. But when Colt's assistant or minion, or whatever, had called, he'd made it clear that Colt would meet with her, and only her, at precisely 7:00 p.m. at Pebblebrook. Otherwise, the meeting was off.

Damn infuriating man. She'd never met him and she already despised the air he breathed.

Whatever. She just wanted this to be over with. The sooner she could get Colt to agree to her terms, the better. Hopefully he'd see that this new arrangement would be beneficial to both of them. No matter what he threw at her, Annabelle wasn't leaving until she had something to cling to, some hope that she wasn't doomed to a life of failure when she was only twenty-four years old.

She was a mother to two beautiful twin girls now. Her father was doting all over them at the moment and would have to be her babysitter when she found a job. He was responsible with children, just not money. Besides, she couldn't afford to pay a sitter for one kid, let alone two.

First, she had to get this debt straightened out, and then she'd focus on getting that job. Surely, there was something in town she could do. At this point, she wasn't going to be picky.

Smoothing her hands down her green sundress, she pulled in a deep breath. Her nerves weren't about to abate, so she rang the bell and stepped back…waiting to enter the enemy's lair.

This place was so huge, it was almost intimidating. A wooden bridge arched slightly over a creek that ran in front of the house between the drive and the entrance.

The man literally sat in his castle, complete with moat, waiting on the town peons to enter his kingdom. Oh, how she wished someone would knock him down a peg or two. She had an unhealthy dose of anger stored up with Colt Elliott's name written all over it.

She wasn't even getting into the anger she had toward her father for putting her in this position to begin with. All he'd told her is that Colt had fronted the money and the loan was paid off. Now they owed Colt, not the bank. She made sure her father got that in writing from Colt and Neil had said he did sign a paper and it had been notarized. So, at least her father had been smart enough not to just do things the old-fashioned way with a handshake and a promise. Because Annabelle didn't trust Colt Elliott. Not one iota.

The double doors swung open and an elderly man stood before her. Annabelle thought the Elliott boys' father had passed some years ago, so she wasn't sure who this man was.

"Come in, Ms. Carter. Mr. Elliott is expecting you."

She stepped over the threshold and nearly gasped. If she'd thought the outside was spectacular, the inside was breathtaking.

The entryway allowed her to see all the way up to the

third story. An open walkway on both floors connected each side of the house, allowing anyone upstairs to see the entire foyer.

Annabelle was getting a vibe that Colt liked to look down on people, to belittle them. Well, he may have pushed her father around, but he was about to deal with a whole new game player. She wanted to know precisely why he'd extended his hand of generosity to her family. Nobody did something like this just to play nice.

"I'm Charlie." The older gentleman closed the door and tipped his head down in greeting. "If you'll follow me, I'll take you to Mr. Elliott."

Annabelle continued taking in all the beauty of this home, and tried not to let jealousy take over. The Elliotts existed on a whole other level than her family ever had, especially now that they had nothing. But Annabelle wasn't about to let life run her over. She'd had enough and Colt Elliott was about to get the brunt of her frustrations.

The calming trickle of water drew her attention as she passed by a sunken living area. Who the hell had a waterfall wall in their home? Oh, right. The people who counted their billions as a hobby.

Annabelle forced her frustrations aside and continued on behind Charlie. There was a bigger issue at hand. She wasn't going to spend her time assessing how this family lived so lavishly when everything had been robbed from hers. Everyone created their own destiny; unfortunately, she was the victim of her father's.

No more. Annabelle had a vision for her future and it certainly didn't involve giving up her childhood home. Once she got to the bottom of this ordeal, she could start on rebuilding her life. Because she wasn't just worried about herself anymore, there were two sweet babies to consider.

Charlie led her through a maze and she wondered if

she'd ever find her way out once this meeting was over. Finally, he stopped in front of an oversize arched doorway. He tapped his knuckles on the door before easing it open.

"Sir, Ms. Carter is here."

Nerves gathered heavily in her belly as she smoothed her sundress down one last time. She didn't care what her emotions were, and there were plenty, but she had to keep them hidden. Someone like Colt Elliott would home in on any weakness and use it to his advantage. Clearly, or she wouldn't be here trying to get her house back from the man who'd snatched it from her father during one of his worst moments.

Charlie eased the door open and stepped back with a nod before disappearing back down the labyrinth of hallways.

Shoulders back, ready to battle the enemy, Annabelle stepped into the spacious office complete with a wall of windows overlooking back acreage. The second she shifted her focus to the other end of the room, she stilled. Her heart clenched, breath caught in her throat.

"You," she gritted through her teeth. If it wasn't Shirtless Stable Boy himself.

Colt had been right. She was just as stunning as he remembered. He wondered if he'd still feel the same way once he'd had time to process the events of earlier. But now that Annabelle Carter was in his home, he took another moment to appreciate the entire package.

That vibrant red hair, wide green eyes, simple makeup and a green dress that she probably thought practical…he found it tempting. How long would it take to undo each of those tiny buttons down the front?

"You lied," she accused him, not moving any farther into the room.

Colt rose from behind the antique desk that had be-

longed to his father, and his father before him. He circled
it and came to lean against the front. Crossing his ankles,
he rested his hands on either side of his hips and shrugged.
He always appreciated a good sparring opponent.

"I didn't lie," he amended. "I told you Mr. Elliott was
busy when you asked. And I was. I had just finished ex-
ercising my stallion and needed to get him brushed and
fed. I wasn't getting a manicure or stealing puppies. I save
those fun events for Saturdays."

Her expressive green eyes narrowed as she slowly made
her way across the room. Oh, she was going to be so fun.
He didn't miss the way she took her time in assessing
him, as well. Let her look. If all went as planned, she'd
have plenty of opportunities to do more than caress him
with her eyes.

"What is it you wanted to see me about?" he asked,
ready to hear what she thought she could do to rectify this
situation. He had a plan of his own to throw at her.

"I hardly recognize you with your shirt on."

So, Ms. Annabelle had claws. He liked that in a woman,
preferably when she clawed at his back, but verbally would
do…for now.

Colt couldn't hide his smile. She was definitely going
to be more of a joy to deal with than Neil Carter.

"If you're requesting I take it off, I'm happy to oblige."

She crossed her arms over her chest, doing nothing to
deter him from appreciating her lush shape. "The only
thing you can oblige me with is discussing the terms of
this contract you have with my father."

"Not my first choice during a meeting with a beautiful woman." Colt stood straight up, ready to get down to
business. Obviously, they would have to get this out of the
way first. "The arrangement is simple, as I'm sure he told
you. He has six payments left on the property. I paid off
his loan and now he owes me. I'm not charging interest

like the bank, so the payments are actually cheaper than he was used to. He came to me for help, and—"

"How kind of you," she stated drily.

Colt shrugged with a smile. "I thought so."

Annabelle sucked in a deep breath and dropped her hands to her sides. Stepping forward, she came within a couple feet of Colt, enough for him to see the variation of green in her eyes. Definitely eyes a man could get lost in. Not him, but some other man. Colt only did physical relationships, nothing more.

"You'll be dealing with me from now on."

Oh, he sure as hell hoped so.

"I will take over the payments, but I need you to give me a few weeks to get on my feet. I have no job, since I came back to Stone River sooner than I'd expected," she went on, a flash of sadness flickering in her eyes. "Our savings are…well, that's none of your concern. But I already called a few places this afternoon and I'm sure I'll have a job shortly."

She couldn't be playing any better into his scheme. Before he could present her with his brilliant plan, she held up her hand.

"If you can give me two weeks off initially, I'll make sure you get interest as a sign of good faith." Annabelle's lips thinned. She was furious with her old man, as she should be. "I have plans for my home, so believe me, I don't want to drag this out any longer than necessary."

Colt admired her determination. Hell, he knew all about setting sights on a goal and going straight for it. Hadn't he lived his entire life by such ideals?

The dude ranch dream he shared with his father was just the final piece of his life he needed to click into place.

There had been setbacks along the way. Colt hadn't expected his father to slip into dementia and require around-the-clock care. Colt hadn't planned on breaking his back and shattering his hip bone while rebuilding the barn after a tornado ripped through town last year. His brothers had instantly reminded him there was no need to lift a hammer, they hired their work done.

But Colt loved manual labor. He loved this farm and he wasn't about to let anyone, even his sexy neighbor, stand in the way of him taking it to the next level.

"Here's the deal." He took one step forward, closing the gap between them. Head tilted up, her eyes locked on to his. "You will make the payment on time, as was agreed by your father. One late payment and the land will permanently be mine."

It would be in the end anyway, but if a payment was missed, at least Colt would have his property sooner.

Those green eyes narrowed. "I had no idea about this deal until last night when I returned home. I've been back less than twenty-four hours. I need some time to make job arrangements before the payment is due next week. Surely you're not that coldhearted."

Part of him felt sorry for her, but he was about to extend the proverbial olive branch…whether or not she chose to accept it was on her. Either way, he would be the real winner at the end of the day.

"Not at all." He offered a smile that he knew had brought women to their knees…literally. "I have a position for you right here at Pebblebrook."

Silence settled between them as he waited on her response. They both knew he held the upper hand, but she could make this entire encounter much easier on herself.

The muscles in her jaw clenched as she glared at him. Damn if her sass and grit weren't the sexiest things he'd seen in a long time.

Agreement or not, this woman would be in his bed. Visions of that crimson red hair spread all around his navy sheets flooded his mind. But seduction would have to wait, at least until she wasn't shooting daggers at him.

"I don't even want to know the position you think I'm qualified for."

Colt laughed, realizing he'd felt more alive being the target of her snarky attitude than he had in a long time. "I like you."

"Well, right now, I hate you."

He shrugged. "You're the yin to my yang. Sounds like we're going to get along perfectly in the stables."

"Stables?" she repeated, with a quirk of a brow.

"I'm short a stable hand and you need a job. You can start tomorrow and I'll use your wages toward the payments."

Annabelle pulled in a breath and shook her head. "I can't work long hours. I have another commitment and I need a job that offers some flexibility."

He leaned forward, pleased when her eyes flared. "The way I see it, you don't really have a choice. So, if this other obligation is going to get in the way, I suggest you give it up now."

For a split second Colt was convinced she was going to cry. He didn't like being played and he figured she'd try to get his sympathy by weeping. But when she blinked and glanced away, Colt realized she was simply trying to control herself.

Yeah, Annabelle was quite a strong woman to come here and face her father's problem. Colt despised the man for putting his child in such a position. Everyone had their breaking point and Colt figured she'd dealt with her father's addiction for far too long.

The strength she projected was quite the turn-on. Too bad all this business got in the way of him getting her into his bedroom. Soon, he vowed.

"Whatever this other commitment is, you're going to have to let it go."

She shoved her hair behind her shoulders and turned her attention back to him. "I can't. I will work here, but you have to understand there are times I will have to adjust my schedule. I can give you a few hours at a time."

Colt considered her ultimatum. He wasn't one to give in to demands, but he had to admit, he liked what he saw with his new neighbor. Someone with that much grit would be a fun way to break up his days. Besides, remaining somewhat on her good side would only aid in his seduction plan.

"Fine. I'll pick you up at seven tomorrow morning," he informed her.

Annabelle laughed. "I can drive myself."

"If you hit another section of my fence, I'll have to take the repairs out of your check and you're indebted to me already. The transportation is nonnegotiable."

When she let out an extremely unladylike growl, Colt forced himself not to crack a smile. Not even a little one. He may hang out with cowboys all day and make business deals all other waking hours, but he knew how to treat a woman. His father had instilled manners in him—somewhat—and Colt wasn't about to laugh in her face. But he couldn't resist the fence jab or the scheme to get a few minutes of alone time with her each day.

"Fine," she gritted out between her teeth. "I'll be ready."

When she turned to leave, he couldn't help but take in the fine sway of her skirt and imagine what lay beneath.

"Oh, one more thing." He waited until she stopped, throwing a glance over her shoulder. "Be sure to wear old clothes. We tend to get dirty."

Her eyes flared before narrowing. "Did I mention that I hate you right now?"

"It will pass," he informed her with a smile. "See you first thing in the morning."

Three

"You don't have to do this, honey."

Annabelle pulled in a deep breath and attempted to count backward from ten. She moved off the last step and met her father's worried gaze.

Neil Carter stood next to the front door, his hair messed from more than just sleeping. She hadn't expected her father to be waiting on her so early, but that's the type of man he was. Neil may be a professional gambler, losing pretty much all he'd worked for and all he'd provided, but he loved his family. He'd been the rock when her mother passed while Annabelle and her sister had been in grade school—well, until it all became too much and he turned to gambling. But he hurt, too, and Annabelle knew he was devastated after Trish's death only weeks ago. They both were. But for now, she could only deal with one crisis at a time.

The mourning would have to come later, at least for her…because she had to get over the betrayal first and she truly didn't even know if that was possible.

"I do have to do this, dad." Now was not the time to get into her arrangement with Colt, not when her ride was due any minute. "You left me no choice since we have no other way to pay."

Her father had lost his job at the factory one county over when he couldn't make it to work on time. He'd been embarrassed to tell her, but now that she was back, there was no way to hide anything. She needed to be aware of every ugly truth so she could make things right.

Her father raked a hand down his face and stared up at the ceiling. "I'm sorry, baby girl."

Wasn't he always sorry after the fact? This time, though, she had to put her life on hold and dig them both out of this hell. She didn't know what he would've done had she not come home.

"I can't do this right now, Dad. Between you and Colt, I'm pretty stuck. But we'll get through this."

"I'll talk to him," her father vowed, his gaze seeking her once more. "I can make this work, Belle. I can stop gambling. I'll get another job and help out. I know you and—"

"No." She held up a hand, not ready for him to take this conversation in another direction or make promises he couldn't keep. "We're going to be fine. I'll still do everything I'd planned to, it's just going to be on a different timeline."

As in, years away. The family life, the bed-and-breakfast...those plans would have to wait.

The doorbell rang and Annabelle jerked her attention to the old oak door. Her father turned, but Annabelle stepped forward to cut him off.

"I'll get it." Closing the space between them, she put her hand on her dad's shoulder. "Maybe you shouldn't be in here right now."

"But—"

"No. You and I will talk, but not now and you're not talking to Colt. You've done enough."

Her father cringed, but she refused to feel guilty. This was a mess—a mess he'd gotten them into. Perhaps he needed a dose of reality.

Finally, her father nodded and headed toward the steps. Annabelle waited until he was gone before she pulled in a breath and opened the front door.

Colt stood on her porch with his black hat in hand, as if he were there to ask her on a date. Damn that man. As if his Southern charm and manners would make her not loathe him on sight.

But he was a sight to behold. A black T-shirt stretched across his broad shoulders and those well-worn jeans fit in all the right places. She'd never seen a finer cowboy. If she were to pass Colt on the street, she'd never guess him to be a billionaire rancher who swooped in and stole properties while trying to charm the panties off unsuspecting women. There was no way he didn't have his own agenda with her family's land, and regarding this little matter of him giving her a ride. If that wasn't the worst use of a euphemism, she didn't know what was.

Colt raked his eyes over her and she forced herself not to fidget. Someone like Colt probably had eye candy for every night of the week, one on each arm. No doubt leggy blondes with big hair and big boobs, hanging on his every word. They probably wore booty shorts and cowgirl boots, too.

"I see you dressed for the day."

She'd found her oldest jeans and a simple tank. Any girl from Texas had a great pair of worn boots, so she'd thrown those on and pulled her hair into a ponytail. No makeup, no fuss. She was there to save her home, not get marks for her grooming.

Behind her, Annabelle heard the familiar sounds she'd grown to love over the past few months. Before she could turn or say a word, Colt's gaze widened and she knew exactly what he saw.

Not that she wanted him to have any part of her personal life, but she was pleased to render him speechless for a bit. Maybe Colt Elliott could be shaken and knocked down a peg.

"And who are these pretty girls?" he asked, still keeping his eyes over her shoulder.

Annabelle smiled. "Emily and Lucy. My twins."

Colt was rarely at a loss for words, but seeing Neil hold two mini versions of Annabelle was quite shocking. She hadn't mentioned having a baby—or babies. Now he understood why she needed a flexible work schedule…and he felt like a complete jerk.

Twins were definitely a handful. He should know, considering his mother always said that about him and his brother Beau. Colt wondered how Annabelle thought she could work and manage two infants back at home, but—

No. He wasn't going to get involved. Business and seduction were the only items on his agenda.

But could he still seduce her? Was she taken? There hadn't been a ring on her finger and she'd never said anything about having a husband…not that he'd asked her any such thing.

Annabelle turned, crossed the foyer and kissed each girl on the cheek. Instantly, one of the girls reached for Annabelle, but she shook her head.

"I'll be home soon. I love you both."

As she came back to him, one baby started to fuss, which somehow triggered the other one to start whimpering. Annabelle kept walking until she was out the door. With his hands full of unhappy infants, Neil held on to Colt's gaze, but Colt didn't feel a bit guilty. That man had done some major damage to his family…damage Colt hoped Annabelle never found out about. He'd lost their home and that was bad enough. But there was more and it was certainly not Colt's place to share.

He closed the door behind him, settled his hat back

on his head and turned to Annabelle. She swiped at her cheeks, as if he didn't notice the tear tracks.

Guilt punched him in the chest.

"Where's the truck?" she asked, obviously not wanting to address her emotions.

Fine. He wasn't one to get in touch with his emotions, either. Just another area he realized they may be more alike than he'd care to admit. They both clearly had a love for their family and were determined to get what they wanted.

But only one of them would be the winner in the end... and he never lost.

Colt stepped off the porch, making mental notes to expand its width and put in a stone walkway when the place was officially his. He needed to stay focused on the goal. While this house had good bones and was fine for everyday living, Colt wanted it to be up to the standards of his ranch. If they were going to merge the properties and open it to the public, all homes had to be similar in upgrades.

Colt nodded toward the side of the house. "I didn't bring my car."

Walking ahead of him, Annabelle rounded the house and stopped. "You've got to be kidding me?"

Colt shook his head. "She needed a walk, so we're taking him."

Annabelle stood next to Lightning and glared his way. "I'm not riding with you."

Glancing around, he held his arms out, palms up. "I don't see another horse. Do you have one?"

Her lips thinned. He knew damn well she had no animals. Her father had sold them all.

"I seriously hate you," she murmured.

Yeah, he got that. But Colt also saw how she looked at him. She may hate his actions, but she appreciated him as a man and he was more than fine with that. Keeping things physical would assure that everything stayed simple.

When he stepped forward to help her up, she shot him a stare that could've frozen hell over. He held up his hands to signal that he was backing off.

Hands on her hips, Annabelle stared at the horse as if weighing her options. She had none really.

"I'll just drive," she told him.

"That wasn't part of our deal. Get on the horse."

Her hand went to the reins. "Do you ever ask people nicely?"

"I can be very nice, Annabelle." He stepped closer. His hand covered hers as her eyes widened. "Get on the horse or I'll be forced to assist you like the gentleman my father raised."

She pulled her hand from beneath his and let out a mock laugh, hoisting herself up onto the horse. "I haven't met your brothers, but you are certainly no gentleman."

Colt slid his foot through the stirrup and settled in right behind Annabelle. Her backside was nestled between his thighs and he was starting to question his own motives. He'd wanted this alone time. He'd purposely made this stipulation so he could use these moments to seduce her. The concept of riding the horse developed after the deal had been made.

Colt had no idea he'd lose grip on his power. He never thought she'd be the one seducing him…and she didn't even have a clue.

The last woman he'd let have control over his emotions had left him mentally scarred and jaded. Colt pushed aside thoughts of his ex and reached around Annabelle to grab the reins. Her entire body tensed.

"Relax." He snapped the straps lightly, sending Lightning into motion. "We're just going next door."

Which would take several minutes because of the expansive fields between their properties, and he had every intention of taking the scenic route.

"Why are you heading toward the back of the property?" she asked.

Strands from her ponytail blew in the breeze, tickling the side of his neck. Images of that hair spread all over him assaulted his mind. The floral scent from her shampoo or soap assaulted his senses. She shouldn't smell like heaven, shouldn't have the ability to affect him without saying a word.

"You've only seen this land from your side," he explained. "I'm going to familiarize you with Pebblebrook."

"I thought I was just going to be in the barns cleaning horse sh—"

"Oh, you will," he laughed. She truly despised him, yet there was a fine line between lust and hate. He'd wear her down. "There will be times you'll accompany me in the fields and you need to know the area. With five thousand acres, it's easy to get turned around. But you'll be working directly with me every day."

Her shoulders slumped. The movement was slight, but being this close, he was attuned to every aspect of her.

"And what happens at the end?" Her voice was so low, almost defeated. "You're just going to give the property back and play hero for saving the day?"

"I'm not a hero." Her body rocked back and forth against his as he murmured into her ear. There was no way he was going to answer that question outright. "I do have motives, but we don't have to talk about that right now."

Annabelle jerked around. "I knew you weren't doing any of this out of the kindness of your black heart."

Facing the open fields once again, she asked, "So why this game with my father?"

"I'm not a complete bastard, Annabelle." Though some would say otherwise. "I'm giving your father a chance to redeem himself. I don't think he can, but everyone deserves a second chance."

"You weren't expecting me to come home."

"A minor glitch, but a pleasant surprise," he replied as he neared the fence line separating the two properties.

"This isn't a game, Colt." She glanced back over her shoulder, her deep green eyes piercing his. "You're playing with our lives, my dreams."

His father had dreams as well, and Colt was going to see them through no matter what sultry beauty stood in his way. Business first, seduction second—and nothing else mattered.

"I'm fully aware of the stakes," he informed her. "I have a vision, too."

"To toy with people's lives and count your money?"

He couldn't blame her for being angry. He'd feel the same if he were in her position. But he'd never let himself get into this predicament. His land was his life. From the time he was a toddler with his first set of boots and shiny belt buckle, he knew ranching was the only future he wanted. His brothers all set out in different paths, but Colt wanted to stay right here. And yes, money was a nice byproduct of the lifestyle he loved so much.

All the Elliott boys had grown up with a rather lavish lifestyle. They were all doing what they loved, but they'd also been handed a handsome inheritance when their grandfather passed away. Still, regardless of their last name, they worked hard and played hard.

"You aren't the only one with goals," he stated as he steered Lighting toward his brother's house, settled in the back of the property. "That log home back there is Nolan's."

She may not care about his family, but she was going to be working for him and he took his ranch very seriously. At the end of the day, regardless of the fact he wanted her physically, she would have to do the job he hired her for.

When she remained silent, he kept going. "He's the

oldest. He'll help occasionally, but he's a surgeon so his time is limited."

"He sounds nice."

Colt agreed, even though her comment was a jab at him. "I have another brother, Hayes. He's in the army."

"Wow. Two brothers who give back and help others, then you who steal. We haven't even discussed your movie star brother."

Colt swallowed. "My twin, Beau. He rarely comes home. Ranch life was never for him."

Beau and Colt never saw eye to eye on most things, but they had a special bond. Colt loved Beau, even though he wished he would've stuck around. Apparently fame was more important than family.

"Sounds like they made wiser life decisions."

Colt had developed thick skin over the years. He couldn't be in the ranching industry and not toughen up. But he wasn't about to sit there and have her question his integrity or his purpose.

"My grandfather built the first house on Pebblebrook, the one Hayes lives in when he's home. Then he passed this land down to my father who ended up building the house I live in. We all work hard, Annabelle. We do what we love, we make good money, and that's nothing to be sorry for."

Once again, those green eyes turned to him. "No, you have plenty of other things to be sorry for."

Perhaps he did. Maybe he was no better than her father who'd put her in this position. Colt didn't want to expose his reasons for paying the loan. The fact she knew he had a motive was enough for now. A wise businessman never showed his entire hand from the get-go.

Annabelle hated him, that was definitely no secret. But he wasn't backing down. Not on the land and certainly not on the woman.

Four

Annabelle absolutely loathed being on this horse with Colt. Well, her body enjoyed the ride, but that physical reaction didn't mean a thing. So what if his body fit perfectly against hers? So what if his voice tickled her ear and sent shivers through her? She could handle that. She had bigger issues to deal with than her body's unwanted reaction.

Colt seemed like such a normal guy in some ways. When he discussed his family there was such love, such adoration. The love and adoration she had for her own family had been shattered, broken, and she was left to pick up the shards and attempt to piece them back together.

The twins were the one bright spot in all of this chaos. They were precious, innocent, and Annabelle intended to keep them protected from the worries she faced. They would have a stable family life, maybe not the traditional family she longed for, but what was traditional these days?

Circling back to her more lustful thoughts, Annabelle couldn't ignore the tingle each time his body rocked against hers. That broad, strong chest would brush her back, his muscular forearms aligning with hers. His tanned skin to her pale. They were completely opposite in every way imaginable.

Colt Elliott was a gorgeous man, there was no denying that fact. He was also arrogant, frustrating, and the bane of her existence.

"I'm sorry to hear about your sister." Colt's words broke through her thoughts, and he actually sounded sincere. "I know you don't want to hear it from me, but losing a family member is hard."

Harder when there was betrayal involved.

She didn't want his pity or his kind words. She couldn't afford to accept that there may be a nice bone in his body. "I'm more concerned with my father and how he will handle the loss."

"That's why you came back?"

Annabelle swallowed. "One of the reasons. My fiancé and I had plans, but…"

She was so not getting into this with him. She didn't want to talk about how her entire life had blown up in her face over the past few months. The only bright spots were Emily and Lucy, and everything Annabelle did from here on out was for those sweet angels.

"I didn't realize you were engaged."

Pain pierced her heart, but not necessarily because she thought he'd been the one. Looking back now she realized she wasn't in love with him so much as the idea of being in love. She wanted to be a wife and mother, come back to Stone River and open her bed-and-breakfast.

She'd always wondered about fulfilling her mother's dream, but over the past year, she'd decided to just go for it. Yet now she was stuck in an arrangement with Colt, who, despite massive personality flaws, had more sex appeal than should be legal. Annabelle had to get her life back on track. She couldn't handle this lack of control and uncertainty.

"My fiancé is no longer in the picture."

Even with the bright morning sun beating down on

them, she shivered. The pain, the loss, the trust she'd once had in people she loved was all too much. This topic wasn't bearable.

"How many acres did you say you have?"

"Just over five thousand. There are three homes, mine, Nolan's, and Hayes's, for when he's stateside. We have seven ponds and eight barns."

Pebblebrook was like a city in itself. Annabelle would be lying if she didn't admit that she was jealous. Not that she wanted a large spread like this, she'd be so content with getting her bed-and-breakfast up and running. Still, she was envious that Colt had known exactly what he'd wanted, apparently from the time he was a kid, and had accomplished it all. Granted, the majority had been handed to him, but Colt had stepped up as part of the new generation to lead the ranch to the next level and beyond.

Anger bubbled within her. He had it all and he still wanted more. She wasn't about to go down without a fight. The bed-and-breakfast, her childhood home, was all she had to make something of her life and to secure a stable future for Emily and Lucy. So whatever he had in his head about her land, he could think again.

"Do you plan on taking me back and forth several times a day?" she asked, glancing back at him.

She hated looking over her shoulder because each time she did, she saw that sexy scruff along his jawline and those striking blue eyes. Not to mention the movement pressed her lower half deeper into the V of his thighs. It was like this man was created to drive her out of her ever-loving mind.

And she couldn't forget the fact she'd seen him sans shirt. Like that was an image she'd ever forget. Colt Elliott had embedded himself in her deepest fantasies...not that he would ever know.

"If I'm not around, I will have Ryan or Josh take you. They are my most trusted employees."

"It's a ride home, Colt."

His bright blue eyes zeroed in on hers, then dropped to her lips for the briefest of seconds. "They're both married."

"Just because they're married doesn't mean they're committed," she countered, hating the bitterness in her tone. "And I can take care of myself. I'm working for you, I'm not a little sister you need to watch over."

A corner of his mouth kicked up in a naughty grin that had her toes curling in her boots. "Considering my thoughts, it's best we aren't related in any way."

Annabelle jerked back around, her heart beating double time in her chest. "You aren't going to flirt with me, Colt. I'm here to make sure those payments are made on time and I get to keep my house. So whatever it is you're thinking, keep it to yourself."

"But you'd enjoy every one of my thoughts," he whispered in her ear.

The brush of his lips along her cheek sent tremors racing through her. How could she hate him and be so turned on at the same time? This man stood in the way of her only chance at a stable future.

No, her father had stood in the way, Colt was just an extra hurdle she had to jump. She really didn't want to be one of those bitter, scorned women, but every man in her life had let her down. Why the hell would she expect any different from her new employer?

Besides, he was just trying to throw her off her game. And, damn it, it was working. She had to be sharper from here on out…and he needed to keep his shirt on.

"Let's just stick to business," she suggested as they neared a massive two-story barn.

She forced herself not to gape at the large stone archway that led into the tunnel where the horses were kept.

The wide planked sides were weathered, but in that deliberate, expensive way. A smaller door up top no doubt led to the hayloft.

Annabelle couldn't help but wonder how many women Colt and his sexy, Southern charms had seduced up into that romantic space. She vowed not to be one of them. She wasn't naive. She knew he looked at her with interest, but she and her fiancé hadn't even consummated their relationship, and she sure as hell wasn't going to let Colt Elliott charm her into bed.

"These are the stables for our older horses. We have two mares and three stallions housed here. Ryan tends to oversee this group."

A man in a fitted plaid shirt stepped through the doorway, leading a gorgeous black stallion by the reins.

Colt steered Lightning toward the barn. As they neared, the forty-something man turned toward them.

"Ryan, this is Annabelle Carter," Colt said. "She's going to be working with me for the foreseeable future."

"Ma'am." Ryan nodded with the tip of his hat. "Pleasure to meet you. Colt, the engineer called earlier and needs you to call when you get a chance."

"I'll do it this afternoon," Colt replied.

Every time he spoke, the rumble in his chest vibrated against her back. There was something entirely too intimate about this situation. The way she fit so perfectly between his thighs, the way her body heated that had nothing to do with the sun, the way he looked at her mouth like he wanted to devour her.

And she knew without a doubt he'd methodically planned this mode of transportation and made it nonnegotiable just so he could annoy her further. Added to that, he must be well respected because his employee didn't bat an eye at the sight of the new recruit and the way she'd arrived on the scene.

"Also, Monte from the feed store called and our truck-load will arrive around two this afternoon."

"We'll unload it in the barn on the west side. Make sure to tell Josh. We need all hands for that."

Ryan nodded once again and tugged on the reins of his horse. "Nice to meet you, ma'am."

He climbed onto the stallion and headed around the side of the barn.

"He seems nice. It's strange how the two of you get along."

"You're hurting my feelings, Belle."

She cringed. "Don't call me that."

"What do you prefer? Annabelle suits you, but it's a mouthful. Besides, I want my own name for you."

"Ms. Carter would work fine. Or, you don't have to refer to me at all."

That low chuckle sent even more tremors through her, causing her body to respond in ways she did not want where Colt was concerned.

"Oh, come on now, Belle. That's no way to start your first workday."

Fisting her hands on the horn of the smooth saddle, Annabelle forced herself to take calm, deep breaths. "I offered to get a different job, I'd prefer a different job, actually. I just needed some time to start getting a paycheck."

"I can give you time, but then you'd lose your land."

"Isn't that your ultimate goal anyway? To see my father and me fail? I'm not naive, Colt. I figure you want our property for something."

"I don't like to see anyone fail," he corrected as he led them toward the front of the property. "But if I'm going to be in a fight, I want it to be fair so my victory is that much sweeter."

A fight. She had to remember that's exactly what this was with him. She was fighting for her life, her future.

All she'd wanted was to take her meager savings and start minor renovations on her house to bring it up to par for her dream.

But then life had intervened. Her sister and fiancé were taken away, Annabelle found herself an instant mother to twin babies, and her father had ultimately failed her when she'd needed him most.

She wasn't going to fail him, though. He was hurting. He'd lost his daughter, was trapped in his own hell with his addiction, and Annabelle would fight to the death if necessary to keep her family safe. She would make a home for Emily and Lucy, take back her land, and see the B and B come to fruition. Anything less was not an option.

Colt Elliott may have knocked her down a peg, but she was determined to fling him off his podium.

Colt's shoulders burned, his arms strained as he hoisted the last bag of feed onto the pile he and Ryan had created. Josh had been taking loads and dispersing them to other barns.

And Annabelle had been holding her own. Sweat had her little tank clinging to her back. Damp tendrils of hair had escaped her ponytail and were now plastered against her neck. She'd gone home for lunch and had returned just before the shipment had arrived. He'd been busy and asked Ryan to take her and bring her back…using the truck.

But there was no way he was missing an opportunity to deliver her back home. They'd worked hard and he was utterly exhausted. He could only imagine how she felt as someone who wasn't used to this type of work every day.

He had a walk-in shower with three rain heads and jetted sprays waiting on him. Not to mention a bottle of bourbon he'd just acquired from a special selection that had been aging in a barrel for decades. He loved his contacts in Kentucky.

Guilt nipped at his conscience. When Annabelle went home, she had two babies to take care of and he highly doubted she took any downtime for herself.

Annabelle continued stacking boxes from the pallets into the corner of the barn. She didn't once stop to look his way, didn't say a word, and didn't complain. She was already a better employee than the stable hand he'd fired last week…only she wasn't a regular employee. She was there under duress, against everything she wanted.

Part of him wanted to tell her to go, to let her father handle the mess he'd made, but he knew she wouldn't go for that. She was too proud, too loyal to her family. She'd lost her sister and her father had completely let her down. And from her tone when she'd briefly mentioned her fiancé, he'd let her down, too. Colt had to assume the man was the twins' father, but he honestly had no clue…and it wasn't his right to ask.

The more tidbits into her life he discovered and pieced together, the more admiration he had for her. "That's the last of it," Ryan stated.

Colt pulled his hat off, swiped his forehead with his arm and turned to Ryan. "Go ahead and take off. I'll finish up here."

"Want me to give her a lift on my way out?" Ryan asked, nodding toward Annabelle on the other end of the barn.

"I'll take care of her, as well."

Ryan eyed Colt and he knew what was coming.

"Don't say it."

Ryan merely shrugged. "Someone needs to. You're playing with fire."

Oh, he sure as hell hoped so. Was there any other way to play a game of seduction?

"I know what I'm doing."

Ryan's brows lifted. "Do you? Because your father

may have had a vision, but he wouldn't have put someone through this just to gain the land."

Colt jerked his work gloves off and shoved them into his back pocket. "Which is why she'll be with me. I won't let her do more than she's capable of."

"Did you know her hand was bleeding?" Ryan asked.

Colt jerked his attention toward her once again. "What?"

"When I walked by earlier, she was wiping her hand on her pants and I saw blood. She'd torn her work gloves."

Damn stubborn woman wouldn't ask for help no matter what.

"I got her another pair," Ryan went on. "But I have a gut feeling she'd fall over before she came to one of us for help."

That she would. Colt raked a hand over the back of his neck and nodded. "I'll make sure that doesn't happen again."

"That land is going to be yours regardless," Ryan added in a low whisper. "Why don't you just let her go?"

Reasons he couldn't even explain. When she'd shown up yesterday morning and literally busted through his ranch, he hadn't been able to take his eyes off her. He'd always gone after what he wanted—livestock, business deals, employees…women.

Annabelle Carter was a total game changer.

Colt kept his eyes on Annabelle as she stacked her last box. Guilt slammed into him when she pulled off her glove and examined her hand.

Without glancing at Ryan, Colt said, "See you in the morning."

His trusted worker wisely walked away. Colt moved across the cobblestone walkway, closing the distance between him and Annabelle.

"Why didn't you tell me you were hurt?"

She spun around, clearly startled. "I'm fine."

With a hand to her chest, she tipped that defiant chin. Damn if he didn't want to kiss her. That fire in her eyes dared him to come closer, so Colt took a step forward until they were toe to toe. He'd never backed down from a challenge and Annabelle was one fight he was enjoying…except for her injury.

Colt gently curled his fingers around her wrist and pulled her hand out so he could examine it. She had a nasty blister that had been worked too hard.

"I have a first aid kit in the office."

When he met her eyes, he was surprised anger didn't look back at him. If anything, he saw desire. Interesting… and useful. Passion left people weak and he'd definitely home in on that.

Annabelle blinked, as if she realized she'd been caught staring at him. Pulling her hand back, she held it against her chest once again.

"I'll take care of it when I get home. I need to start dinner."

"The hell you say?" He hadn't meant to shout, but was she kidding? "You've worked all day."

Annabelle let out a humorless laugh. "Well, Colt, in the real world people work, make their own meals and tend to their families. We all can't live the life of luxury and sit back, living the dream."

Is that how she saw him? He'd worked his ass off taking over this ranch when his father had fallen ill. He'd poured more blood, sweat and tears into this land than any male in the Elliott family. Being the youngest, he always felt the need to prove himself, especially against his brothers. How the hell could he compete with a surgeon, a war hero and a Hollywood star? He was a damn rancher. A billionaire, but still a man who wore dusty boots, a worn hat that had been his father's, and holey jeans.

"You can take two minutes and let me clean that wound up."

When she stifled a yawn with her good hand, he muttered a curse and stomped off to get the first aid kit. Why did she have to be so stubborn and why did he have to find her even more attractive because of it?

By the time he came back, she'd taken a seat on one of the heavy wooden benches between the stone stalls. Her lids were lower and she seemed to have finally run out of steam. Perfect. Then she wouldn't be able to argue with him.

"You work harder than nearly any man I know," he told her, opening the kit.

"Does that mean I get a raise?" she asked, leaning her head against the wall behind her.

Colt laughed as he placed her hand in his palm. He swiped around the perimeter of the cut with an alcohol pad, careful not to get near the wound. He blew on her hand to dry the moisture. When she trembled, he glanced up to find her eyes on his. That shade of green never failed to kick him in the gut. She could pierce a man with that stare and have him wound in her web so fast, he'd have no idea he was caught until it was too late.

"I know you hate me, but you really shouldn't be fighting your father's battles."

A sad smile crossed her face. "Isn't that what family is all about? When one is weak, others stand up and take the lead. We're all we have left. My mother passed when Trish and I were younger. Now that Trish is gone…"

She shook her head and he wanted to know so much more. When he'd wanted a woman in the past, he'd never asked personal information. Backstory had no place in the bedroom. He had to remember that here because he could so easily let this niggle of guilt guide his emotions.

He had a goal. He had a vision he would see to the end,

to honor his father, to prove to his brothers he wasn't just playing cowboy and to prove to himself he could do it. The dude ranch was only one more business deal away… he just had to get past this fiery vixen to make that vision a reality.

Five

"What the hell, Colt?"

Nolan slammed the office door, jerking Colt's attention from his empty tumbler. He was going to need another round because he'd been waiting on his oldest brother to show up and let him know exactly what his thoughts were on Annabelle.

Gripping the glass, Colt met his brother's angry gaze. "All right, get it out of your system."

"Did you think to ask my opinion—"

"Not once."

Nolan crossed the room and flattened his palms on the glossy desk. "You have Neil Carter's daughter working here for what purpose?"

"He owes me money. She confronted me and said she was taking over the payments."

"So you put her to work like some pack mule?" Nolan shouted. "Do you think Dad would want this?"

Slowly, Colt came to his feet. He refused to sit there and let his brother talk down to him. "Dad left the control of this ranch to me because I understand his vision and I'm the one who's busted my ass my entire life to stay true to it."

"Don't throw that in my face," Nolan countered.

Colt shrugged. "Simply stating a fact. I don't tell you how to do surgeries."

The muscles in Nolan's jaw ticked. Colt wasn't trying to be a jerk, but he wasn't going to be reprimanded or have his decisions second-guessed. He'd done enough doubting of his own actions…something he never did with business.

"You want this dude ranch so damn bad, but you're going about this the wrong way."

Colt grabbed his glass and headed to the bar in the corner. His hip irritated him a bit more today, but that was expected on days he worked harder. It was just one more area where he refused to give in and let life get him down.

"We need that property and Neil was about to lose it to the bank. If I hadn't stepped in, someone else would've. Besides, it's all over now and perfectly legal."

Nolan turned, crossed his arms over his chest and nodded. "I agree that someone else would've gone after that land. It's your actions afterward that I don't understand."

Colt had gone over this in his own head, as well. "At first I wanted Neil to learn a lesson and actually work for something. Then when Annabelle showed up, hell… I couldn't resist."

He didn't look up at his brother, didn't want to see disappointment staring back. Colt had his reasons for his actions and he wasn't going to be deterred by anyone…not even his oldest brother.

"I don't want to see you hurt again," Nolan stated as he crossed the room to stand before the bar. He rested his palms on the etched edge. "Dad would be proud of how smooth this place is running and the growth since he's been in the assisted living facility. You don't have to prove anything at this point."

Colt grunted as he poured two fingers of amber liquid. "I started this for him, but now it's also for me. I want that dude ranch. I want people from all over the world to know Pebblebrook is the greatest ranch, the best getaway money can buy. I want to share all of this work our family has done and if I happen to have a little fun along the way, then so be it."

Colt held out a glass and Nolan shook his head. "I'm on call." He took a seat on the bar stool, lacing his hands together. "This is the first girl you've mentioned at all since Layla."

Colt took a hearty sip. "I'm not looking to settle down. And Layla has nothing to do with now. There's only one thing I'm focused on and that's making the dude ranch happen. Annabelle is working here to pay off the debt. If she misses one payment or can't come up with the entire sum at the end of the time frame, then it's completely mine. But it's mine in the end anyway. They just have to pay off their original debt. Neil paid no attention to the paperwork he signed."

Nolan stared for a minute before shaking his head. "You can handle this how you want, but I'm telling you it's a moral mistake."

With a shrug, Colt finished his glass and recapped the bottle. "I've made mistakes before. And, if Annabelle is a mistake, then she'll be the sexiest one I've ever made."

Layla had been his one and only serious relationship. He should've known it was too good to be true when she'd wanted to marry so soon after they'd started dating. Colt had thought she was interested in him and shared a passion for the farm. She'd shared a passion all right…for his bank account. She didn't care about the land, the animals, his vision. She cared about how she could keep up with the latest trends in clothes, vacations, cars. Colt had been completely blind and eager to give her anything she wanted.

When he'd had an accident and been laid up with broken bones post-surgery, he found out all too quickly just how little she cared about him. She'd told him she needed a break from their lifestyle and then jetted off to his vacation home in Aruba…with another guy. If Colt's cleaning service hadn't told him, the joke would still be on him.

While recovering from surgery, Colt broke off the relationship, kicked Layla and her stud out of his house and sold the place, deciding he didn't like the beach anyway. He needed nothing but his home in Texas. He loved to travel, but what did he need a second home for? His jet and his pilot would take him anywhere he wanted to go.

He was finished with romantic entanglements and refused to get sidetracked by such emotions as love. Hell, he hadn't even been in love with Layla. He'd wanted a family one day and he figured he and Layla were the best match. He still carried that goal of having a wife and children. There was nothing he wanted more than to raise another generation of Elliotts and keep the ranching tradition going. Family and loyalty were everything to him.

He'd let his libido guide him once before, but now he knew exactly what he was feeling. Everything inside him that flared to life around Annabelle was pure lust. He wanted her, he'd have her. End of story.

"Is this necessary?" Annabelle asked.

Colt held tight to the reins, his body aligning perfectly with hers. She hadn't just dreamed of his strength. When she'd woken in the middle of the night after a vivid, detailed dream regarding her new employer, she'd thought her imagination had just gotten the best of her.

But now she knew better. She'd tried to avoid his touch yesterday, but being on horseback with him made that impossible. Maybe it was time Annabelle renegotiated this whole pickup routine.

"It's a perfect day for a ride," he replied.

His low, soft tone was in direct contrast to the chaos

she felt inside. She wanted to continue hating him, and she would, but why did she have to be attracted to him at the same time? It truly made for some mixed up hormones and she couldn't keep eating her weight in doughnuts like she wanted to. Her favorite jeans were already snug as it was.

"I'd be fine to drive myself," she retorted, keeping her eyes on the bright horizon, as opposed to focusing on the proximity of his hands to her inner thighs. "Or Josh or Ryan can take over delivery duties."

"I'm a hands-on employer," he murmured against her ear. "You'll get used to it."

That was the problem. This was day two in her duties and she could honestly say she didn't hate this part. She wanted to hate it. She wanted to stomp her foot like a toddler and declare her independence by not getting on that horse with him.

But she was still a woman. Despite her jaded view on men and their loyalties, and ignoring the fact Colt had her in a tough position, she was a woman with basic desires. And her body felt exactly the way it should when a sexy man entered the scene: tingly, hot, achy.

"You're thinking awfully hard about something," he stated. "You tensed up on me."

"Just counting down the days until we're free of each other and I can go about my life with my house."

"You've still got quite a while. I wouldn't be making those plans just yet."

Annabelle shrugged. "I'm optimistic. I know I won't miss a payment and I have every reason to keep going, even if I want to give up."

She felt her hair shift aside seconds before his fingertips trailed across the back of her neck. Annabelle jerked to glance over her shoulder.

"What are you doing?"

His mouth was only inches from hers and completely

tempting, so she focused back on the fence line dividing the properties. It had to be a sign, a symbol of exactly how different they were and how she needed to compartmentalize their arrangement.

"Your hair tickled my face. Why didn't you put it in a ponytail?"

She held up her wrist. "I have my band here. I didn't get time before you arrived because Emily was sick last night and I was trying to get her sheets washed and put back on the crib so Dad could lay her down for a nap later."

Why had she told him all of that? He had no place in her personal life.

"You could've texted me to give you an extra five minutes."

"That would've made me late. You're not going to win that easily, Colt. Just forget I said anything," she quickly added. "I'm not looking for sympathy or special treatment. After this debt is paid, I'm going to pursue my dream."

"Care to share what that dream is?"

Annabelle bit the inside of her cheek and thought for a half second, but shook her head. "Nope. You've stolen enough from me. I won't give you my hopes, too."

"It's not your secrets I'm after, Anna."

Every part of her stilled. He wanted her, that was obvious. He wasn't even trying to pretend otherwise. But she wasn't about to comment on that.

"Don't call me Anna."

His soft chuckle had his entire body vibrating against hers. "I'm willing to call you anything, but you don't like any name I've chosen."

"Like I said before, maybe it would be best if you didn't address me at all, except for work purposes, and then you can call me Ms. Carter."

Colt pulled back on the reins, bringing Lightning to a stop at the edge of the property line. "And what about now, when we're alone and not working. What should I call you?"

Slowly, Annabelle turned her head slightly, knowing full well he'd eased forward and his face would be right there. And it was. Those lips mocked her, the edge of his hat bumped the top of her head, bright eyes stared back, daring her to answer the question.

"Maybe we shouldn't talk."

The instant his eyes flared, darting to her lips, she realized he took her comment as a challenge. He eased forward, his eyes locked on hers the entire time. Her mind told her to stop, but his eyes mocked her as if he knew she would. So she didn't.

His lips grazed hers and everything in her stilled. The slow caress of that mouth had her closing her eyes and forgetting who they were. For once, she was going to just take this moment of pleasure and ignore all the warning bells inside her head.

Colt eased her mouth open beneath his and Annabelle responded as if it were the most natural thing in the world. She wanted Colt's mouth on hers, she wanted him to…

No. This wasn't right. Annabelle pulled away, instantly feeling a chill from the loss of his touch.

"You can't possibly believe you're going to get anywhere with me," she stated, needing to get control back in her grasp. That kiss had only temporarily caught her off guard. Still, his body rubbed against hers, making her want things she'd never had.

"I tend to get what I want," he whispered. "And from the way you responded, I'd say we want the same thing."

She was out of her league with this one. He was charming, smart and devious. But she was determined not to succumb to his attempt at seduction. And that was exactly what he was doing, no doubt so she would lose focus and hand over her property. Not in this lifetime.

"Then I'd look elsewhere because this will never be yours."

"And you?" he asked, quirking a brow and smiling.

Anna reached around and palmed the side of his face. His jaw muscle ticked beneath her hand as she looked into his eyes.

"You won't get that lucky," she said sweetly, then patted his face before letting go. "Now get me to work."

When he didn't reach for the reins again, she lifted them, lightly tapping Lightning into motion again. Which she instantly discovered to be a mistake.

Colt's hands flattened against the tops of her denim-clad thighs. She refused to tense, refused to even comment on his actions. They'd already crossed a professional boundary, but it wasn't like this was a typical boss-employee relationship. Nothing here was normal. She had no idea how to react, what to say. All she knew was that Colt challenged her minute by minute and she had to stay on her toes and never let her guard down again.

She could still taste him, though, knew exactly how he felt, how gentle he'd been. She'd expected someone like Colt to go in full attack mode when trying to seduce a woman. It was like he knew her situation and catered specifically to her needs…her desires.

Surprisingly, he let her guide them straight to the barn. Annabelle figured his cockiness, as shown by him keeping his hands on her, overrode the need to be in control for now. But she wasn't under the illusion that he was relinquishing his power.

"What's on the agenda today?" she asked as she stopped in front of the barn.

Barn was such a generic, ridiculous term for such a structure. The interior of the barn alone rendered her speechless, she couldn't imagine what the other barns and homes on the property looked like inside.

He slid his hands over hers on the reins. "You and I will be going out and checking the fence lines around the property. I tend to have Josh and Ryan do that, but I'm giving your hands a break after yesterday."

The warmth from his touch, the way he literally enveloped her would be so easy to get caught up in if this were any other type of situation. But he was the main obstacle standing between her and her bed-and-breakfast, and the life she wanted for Emily and Lucy.

Annabelle worried Colt had something up his sleeve... something she wouldn't see coming until it was too late.

"I don't want special treatment. My hand is just fine." Sore, but she'd put some antibiotic ointment and a bandage on it. "Treat me like you would any other stable hand."

Colt grunted. "That's not going to happen."

He eased off the horse, then extended a hand to assist her. "I can get down myself."

As she slid off the side, firm hands gripped her waist. "A gentleman always helps a lady."

Annabelle turned in his arms and placed her hands on his chest. A very firm, solid, muscular chest. She pulled in a deep breath and forced herself to focus.

"If you're trying to seduce me, it won't work." But it could if she didn't keep giving herself mental pep talks. He had to keep those lips to himself, though. "And if you're trying to make this process more difficult, then don't waste your time. I'm not backing down and I'm not quitting. So, tell me where I'm working today and knock off the shenanigans."

He pursed his lips and she knew from that naughty twinkle in his bright eyes that he was holding back a laugh. With a tip of his hat, he took a step back.

"Then that goes both ways."

Shocked, Annabelle held a hand to her chest. "Excuse me?"

"No seducing me. I know, it will be tough to control yourself around me, but try. I'm not just here for my looks."

When he let go and offered a full smile, she smacked his shoulder. "Get out of my way, you arrogant jerk. I will not seduce you. I'm sure a number of women find you charming, but I am certainly not one of them."

Annabelle started to move, but he snaked an arm around her waist. Bringing his lips next to her cheek, he whispered, "You will be."

Before she could reply, he turned and headed into the barn. As if she weren't irritated enough, the man had the gall to start whistling. Annabelle gritted her teeth and fisted her hands at her sides.

Colt Elliott was not going to get under her skin. She would not find that arrogance attractive, nor would she allow herself to feel any more attraction to the sexy cowboy. She'd been burned too many times and if she didn't keep her guard up, she'd find herself hurt more than ever before.

Maybe it was time to give Colt a little dose of his own medicine.

Six

"I think Genesis will be the perfect mare for you to use while you're here."

Annabelle slid her hand down her new friend's velvety nose. Josh had pulled this mare from her stall when Annabelle came in to find Colt and give him a piece of her mind. But he was nowhere to be found. Probably off in some corner plotting on new ways to drive her out of her mind—and off her land—with that killer body of his. If he strutted in there with no shirt, she wasn't so sure she'd be able to resist.

Mercy, when had she gotten so pathetic and weak? An impressive collection of muscles only went so far…and she had too much in her life to get distracted.

"She's beautiful." Annabelle looked into the mare's deep brown eyes. "I miss riding."

When she'd been younger, she and her sister both had horses. Their father would take them riding nearly every day, especially during the time when their mother was ill. But then her mom had passed and soon her dad's gambling began, the debts piled up and the horses were sold. Their lives had crumbled so quickly, there wasn't even time to adjust.

She wanted to hate her father, she truly did. She hated the decisions he'd made, she hated his addiction, but she loved him and she wasn't about to give up.

"I believe you and Colt will be riding the perimeter today," Josh went on. "Looks like your face got a little pink from working outside yesterday."

Instinctively, Annabelle tapped a fingertip to her cheek. "Yeah, a little. I thought I had used enough sunscreen."

"I can get you a hat," Josh told her as he looped the reins around the horn. "We have plenty in the office."

"I've got one right here."

Annabelle turned at the sound of Colt's voice. He came sauntering up the stone walkway, hat in hand. That flutter in her chest had her cursing. How could she be strong when he made her want so much? She'd never been this drawn to a man physically. Even her fiancé hadn't given her that nervous flutter in her stomach.

Why did it have to be the one man she wanted to hate? And why did he have to do little things to make it seem as if he actually had redeeming qualities?

"Ryan is in the steer barn," Colt said to Josh. "There's a calf that isn't looking good. I called the vet, but I'd like if both of you were there. Take the radio with you and keep me informed."

"Sure thing." Josh glanced at Annabelle and nodded. "See you later."

She waited until they were alone before she turned her attention back to Colt. "Do you ever ask anyone politely or do you just enjoy ordering people around?"

"I have a busy schedule and those guys don't need coddling." Colt slapped the hat on her head. "If you have a problem with how I run my ranch, you're free to go at any time."

Annabelle adjusted the hat, narrowing her eyes. "You know I can't."

"Then stop trying to school me on manners. My guys and I get along just fine and run this place quite successfully."

Annabelle's phone vibrated inside her pocket. She pulled it out, glanced at the screen, then looked at Colt. "I have to take this."

She didn't wait for his reply as she swiped her finger over the screen. "Dad, this isn't a great time. Can I call you back in a bit?"

"I think Emily has a fever."

Annabelle pinched the bridge of her nose and willed herself to remain calm. She had no experience with sick babies. She was still getting used to being a guardian, but she would always put them first. Before the farm and before her father's addiction. She adored those babies, hated when she was away from them. They were a balm on her battered heart.

Annabelle could tell by the concern in her father's tone that she had to keep a level head, even if worry flooded her. Between the two of them, they were still figuring out their new normal.

"When I fed her around four this morning she was fine. Did you take her temperature?"

Boots shifted over stone behind her and Annabelle tried to block out the fact that Colt was no doubt clinging to her every word. Again, she didn't want him involved in her personal business any further.

Cooing in the background brought her back to reality. If Emily was getting sick, Annabelle didn't want the girls close together. The last thing anyone needed was two sick infants.

"I can't find a thermometer."

"Go into my room and look in the top nightstand drawer. I have one in there as well as some infant pain reliever. Take her temperature and call me right back."

She disconnected the call and turned back around. Colt's eyes studied her, as if he were waiting on her to open up about the call and her life. Not likely.

Colt took a step forward. "Do you need to go back home?"

"I'm fine." A little worried, but she'd never let him see it and this was none of his concern.

"Take Genesis and go check on Emily."

Before she could answer, her phone vibrated in her hand. "Dad," she quickly answered. "What was it?"

"It's 99.9."

Okay, not terrible. "Give her a dose of that medicine. Just measure it in the dropper. The dosage is on the back for her weight. Is she acting okay? How's Lucy?"

"Lucy is perfectly fine. Emily seems more tired than usual, but she's not cranky."

"That's good," Annabelle muttered. "Just keep me posted. Even if it's to say she's still fine, I want you to text me updates until I get back for lunch."

"All right. And, Belle," he added softly. "I'm sorry. For all of this."

Tears pricked her eyes. He was always sorry, and she truly believed for the moment that he was. Only time would tell if losing everything could really change a man. So far, since she'd been home, she hadn't seen any signs of his habits returning, but that didn't mean anything. He'd always managed to sneak some game, race or sporting event. He'd gamble on the color of the sky if that was an option. Neil Carter never turned down a bet.

"I'll be home in a few hours."

As she slid her phone in her pocket, Colt continued to study her. "Nolan is home this morning. Do you want me to send him over?"

"The doctor?" Annabelle asked. Part of her was touched that he offered, but she didn't want anything from Colt or his family...other than her house back. But, if Emily got worse, she wouldn't turn down at-home care...especially since she couldn't afford a doctor. "Emily will be fine."

Colt stared another minute before reaching up onto Genesis and pulling the reins down. "Then you have work to do."

Annabelle led the mare from the barn before mounting her. Why was Colt being so nice? The hat so her face wouldn't burn, the simple day so her hand wouldn't hurt, the offer to send his brother over to check on Emily...all of that showed there was a kindhearted man inside. But he still made no apologies for planning to take over her land or trying to seduce her.

When Colt came up beside her, she kept her eyes on the horizon. He'd opted to take Phantom out today instead of Lightning. All of his horses were gorgeous animals. Annabelle couldn't pick a favorite. They were all so well mannered, so loving.

Pebblebrook was a beautiful spread, there was no denying that. Colt was obviously passionate about ranching. She was curious about his limp, there had to be a story there, but he'd never mentioned it or acted like it hindered his work. And she couldn't help but wonder why he was still single. Not that she cared, but he was rather blatant with his advances toward her. Which reminded her, she could play that game, too.

"Lead the way, Boss."

He threw her a glance before getting Phantom into gear. Annabelle followed to the side, staying back just enough to appreciate the view—the land and the cowboy.

As he headed toward the fence that ran as far as the eye could see, Annabelle started thinking, remembering. There was a time she'd wondered what the other side of this fence held. She'd wondered about the family who lived here, the house they must love and the number of people who must work here to keep such a place running.

Her family's farm had been minute compared to this one, but she'd loved her animals, her childhood. She couldn't complain about the first ten years of her life.

"You're quiet back there, Belle." Colt cast a glance her way. "Plotting revenge?"

She tapped her heel into Genesis's side to come up even with Colt. "Don't call me that."

"Still waiting on you to give me something you'll answer to that doesn't sound like you're my grade school teacher."

"You'll be waiting awhile," she replied. "And I wasn't plotting revenge, not yet, anyway. I was just thinking about my own farm from when I was little."

"I didn't know you or your sister," Colt stated as he kept Phantom at a steady pace. "Our fathers knew each other, though."

"Really?" Annabelle asked. She shifted her hat to block the morning sun. "I wasn't aware of that. I don't recall Dad ever mentioning yours."

"No. He probably wouldn't have."

Confused, Annabelle slowed her horse, reached out to touch Colt's arm. "What's that supposed to mean?"

He brought Phantom to a stop and shook his head. "Exactly what I said. You were young, so I doubt your father would mention mine. That's all."

Annabelle had a gut feeling he was hiding something. Dread spread through her. Surely their fathers hadn't gambled together. People as successful as the Elliotts didn't get a ranch like this from betting their earnings away. Did her dad owe them, too?

She had to know. "Does my dad owe you all money? Aside from the house?" She glanced down to her tight grip on the reins.

Silence settled between them and Annabelle glanced at Colt from beneath the brim of her hat. He stared out into the pasture, his jaw muscles clenching.

"How much?" she whispered.

"There's no debt other than the house."

But he wouldn't look her in the eyes, so there was something. An old debt, at least a story, and he didn't want to tell her. Was he protecting her?

Damn it. She'd only been with him two days and already he showed her more good sides than bad. But the bad outweighed the good. Didn't it?

"I want to pay you for everything he owes," she went on, needing him to understand. "I'm sure you're not the only person he's indebted to—"

"There's nothing. Let it go."

His stern tone, so final and angry, had her stopping short. Something had happened, but if she wanted to know, she'd have to go to her father and confront him. She almost didn't want to find out the truth.

They rode for another hour, randomly stopping to check the fence. Colt would type notes into his phone and Annabelle tried not to think about how he seemed like such a genuine guy. He worked hard, he obviously didn't want to upset her earlier about her father, but he wasn't sincere. He was a business shark.

As if she could forget.

They approached one of the ponds and Annabelle spotted movement amidst the cattails. She steered Genesis away from Colt and made her way over. She squinted, trying to home in on where she saw something.

"What's up?" Colt trotted beside her. "Wait, I see it."

Annabelle pulled back on her reins, but before she could hop down, Colt was off his horse and carefully moving toward the edge of the pond. He limped slightly, favoring his left side, but she wasn't about to question him.

Colt squatted down, extending his hand and muttering something Annabelle couldn't decipher. She waited, then sucked in a breath when he came to his feet. The sight of Colt cradling the cutest, chocolate-colored puppy had Annabelle climbing off her horse.

"Is this your puppy?" she asked as she approached.

He stroked the top of the puppy's head. "I've never seen this little guy before. But it's not unusual for us to have strays on the farm. People drop them off at the end of our drive all the time. Pisses me off."

"Do you think there are others?" she asked.

Colt shook his head, still staring down to the pup. "I have no idea. I would assume they'd all be together, but we'll ride around this area and see. They could be anywhere. Damn it. I hate when people treat animals like this."

Oh, no. He could not be an animal lover, too. Her emotions were still raw, still so exposed that she couldn't afford to let any more of his kindness seep in.

"Will you keep him?"

Colt met her gaze. "Do you want him?"

She hadn't thought about having a dog, but she'd always had one growing up. Honestly, over the past several years, she'd missed animals. When she'd lived in an apartment in the city, she hadn't been able to have them. She'd worked in a bakery and was gone all hours.

As she stared at the poor pup shaking, her heart went out to him. She totally could relate to being scared of what would happen next.

"I'll take him if you don't want him."

Colt nodded. "Fair enough. If you think you can handle a puppy and babies. Otherwise, I'll keep him."

Annabelle had a feeling the puppy would be the easiest aspect of her life. And having an animal that could grow up with Emily and Lucy would be precious. Plus, it was another way for Annabelle to establish roots in her home—well, it would be her home once it was paid off.

She eyed him, purposely zeroing in on his mouth. "I can handle anything."

When his nostrils flared, Annabelle reached forward in an attempt to get the pup, but Colt twisted his body away. His gaze remained on hers as he cocked his head to the side to avoid bumping their hats.

"You know exactly what happens when you play with fire," he growled.

A tingling swept through her, but she shrugged. "I've been burned before, Colt. I'm immune."

He stepped closer, easing the puppy into her arms and deliberately brushing his forearms along her chest. "You've never dealt with someone like me. You may like it."

Oh, she had no doubt. If that kiss yesterday was any indicator, she knew full well just how much she'd like it. But then she'd have to live with the consequences and she wasn't ready for anything like that. She was a forever kind of girl. If he only knew what she'd gone through with her ex and just how inexperienced she truly was…

"I'm sure I'd disappoint," she stated simply. Not because she doubted herself, but she knew, given their age difference, that he was much more experienced. There was no way she'd be able to live up to his expectations… and someone as sexy and wealthy as Colt definitely would have high expectations for a woman.

The puppy snuggled against her chest and Colt ran a bare fingertip up her arm, smiling when she shivered.

"I'm sure we'd both be thoroughly satisfied."

Why did that sound like a promise and not just a hypothetical situation?

The radio in Colt's saddlebag screeched, breaking the tension. He stared another moment before turning to grab the handset.

Annabelle cradled the dog in one arm and hoisted herself up onto her horse with the other. She listened as Josh assured Colt that the calf was going to be just fine and the vet had done a thorough workup and left antibiotics.

When Annabelle grabbed the reins and started to turn her horse, Colt jerked his gaze to hers.

"I'll be back after lunch," she told him as she trotted away.

Okay, so she was running, just via horseback. But she couldn't get into any more sexually charged talks with that man. Besides the fact that she was probably the only twenty-four-year-old virgin in the world, she would not get swept into Colt Elliott's web of charm, deceit and sex appeal. He was probably just trying to keep her sidetracked and it could very well work. But she had a larger goal in mind than just cashing in her virginity for a night with a sexy cowboy.

She'd dated guys before her fiancé, but never felt a passionate desire to get intimate. Then when Matt came along and they'd gotten engaged, she'd wanted to wait until they were married. He'd been fine with that, telling her he wanted it to be special. That bald-faced lie had made her feel special. If only she'd known he'd found her sister the better option. So here was Annabelle, nearly a quarter of a century old and untouched. That was definitely not something to brag about, so she tended to keep that tidbit of information to herself.

But for a minute, okay maybe more, she wondered what it would be like to be taken by someone so experienced, so powerful.

Annabelle held the pup a little tighter as she rode home on Genesis. She hadn't asked to take the horse, but she couldn't stand the tension simmering between her and Colt another minute.

When he'd touched her just a moment ago, her entire

body had felt the zing…the same type she'd felt when he'd kissed her. What would happen if she gave in to those blatant advances and let him have his way?

If her entire future weren't hanging in the balance, she'd very likely find out.

Seven

"Your basket is ready."

Colt had just stepped into the kitchen to find Winnie, his cook and all-round awesome woman, patting the top of a picnic basket. He'd requested something extra for today and, as always, she'd delivered.

He circled the large granite island and kissed her on the cheek. "You're amazing, Winnie. I'm going to marry you one day."

She swatted him with her towel and laughed. "Get out of my kitchen, boy. It wasn't that long ago I spanked your bottom for stealing cookies before dinner."

Colt shot her a grin as he picked up the basket. "I still swipe your homemade cookies before dinner. I hope you put some in this basket."

"Of course I did."

She grunted as if he'd offended her. But Winnie Miller had been with this family for nearly forty years. Taking care of cowboys broke anyone of having thin skin.

"Mind telling me where you're taking that?" She raised a brow. "Maybe to see some lady friend?"

"Nothing so exciting," he replied as he headed toward the back patio doors.

"You're going to have to settle down and bring some babies in this house eventually," she called to his back. "Too many empty bedrooms."

Considering she had her own suite on the first floor, she knew exactly how many rooms sat empty now. With his father in the nursing home, the absolute best they could find, and his brothers gone, Colt was also aware of how lonely this house was. Winnie only stayed over on occasion, but she mostly went back to her cottage on the edge of town.

Deciding not to take Winnie's bait, Colt headed out the back doors and gripped the basket as he made his way across the concrete drive and stone path leading to the barn. Annabelle should be finishing up brushing the horses and then she'd be heading home for the day. He hadn't pressed her further when she came back after lunch. He knew he'd shaken her up with the sexual innuendos.

Part of him wanted to get a rise out of her, but there was something so sweet about her flirting, he was starting to wonder if he was out of his depth. Maybe she hadn't come up against real men before…men who wanted more from her than a nice, calm romp.

He could do slow. Clearly, by the pace he was setting to get Annabelle's property, he was a patient man when he wanted something.

He stopped short at the entrance to the barn. The sun was starting to set, casting an orange glow through the wide opening on the opposite end of the structure. Annabelle had lost her hat some time back, and her ponytail swayed against her back as she shifted with each brushstroke. Damp tendrils clung to her face. She never failed to shock him with her hard work. She didn't complain, never had a negative word—other than those directed straight at him and his character—and she seemed to care for these animals like they were her own.

But when she'd asked about her father owing money,

Colt had clammed up. The way dread had laced her tone, her facial features, he just hadn't had the heart to come clean.

If it were up to him, she'd never have to know. She was already hurting enough and he was going to take her land. He couldn't deliberately add to her heartbreak.

Colt took a step into the barn, and his boots scuffing against the stone pulled Annabelle's attention toward him. Brush in hand, she gestured toward the basket he carried.

"Bringing a picnic for the horses?" she asked, going back to finish stroking the mare.

"Actually, this is for you."

Annabelle froze, throwing him a side glance. "Nice try, Romeo. I'm not having a picnic with you."

He couldn't help but smile at her immediate rejection. Good to know. Not that he wanted to have dinner with her, he was thinking more along the lines of sheets, showers, and haylofts. Besides, sharing a meal was too intimate.

"I had Winnie make dinner for you and your dad."

He set the basket down on one of the benches between the stalls. Shoving his hands in his pockets, he narrowed the space between them.

"Winnie?" Annabelle asked as she tossed the brush back into the bucket. She turned, crossing her arms over her chest. "Is she part of your harem of women who bow at your every command?"

Colt burst out laughing. He couldn't help himself. Damn if Annabelle Carter wasn't a good time. He could almost be her friend if business and his hormones weren't in the way.

"Winnie is actually my cook, but she'll get a kick out of your guess."

Annabelle eyed the basket, then narrowed her eyes back on him. "Why did she do that? I can make my own dinner."

"You can," he agreed. "But you were exhausted when you left here yesterday and still had to go home and cook.

Then I heard you tell your dad you were up at four this morning to feed Emily and I'm sure you were up with Lucy, as well. No reason I can't make your situation a little easier."

He wasn't sure what reaction he expected her to have, but when she threw her arms in the air and turned to pace, he waited. If nothing else, the woman always kept him on his toes.

"You can't do things like this," she all but shouted as she whirled back around. "I'm trying to hate you, to remind myself that you're the enemy. But part of me wants to believe you're not a monster and when all is said and done, I won't get hurt."

Guilt slid through him, but he couldn't let it hinder his plans. He still had a goal. But damn it. Annabelle touched something in him that he couldn't identify and he had no clue how he could make the outcome less painful for her. There was no happy ending.

Still, she made it impossible not to like her. She made him want to go the extra mile to make her days easier and ignore the inevitable pain he would cause.

Life was so much easier when Colt was only dealing with Neil.

"But you do things like this and I don't know what angle you're working," she went on, her tone lowering as she seemed to be running out of steam. As she spoke, he advanced, step by slow step. "If you're trying to seduce me, I can tell you you're wasting your time. Even if I find you attractive, that doesn't matter. I can't—"

Colt gripped her shoulders, backing her up to the post between the stalls. "You find me attractive?"

Her lids closed as she blew out a breath. "That is all you would take away from what I said."

How could he not? He was going to take this minor victory and run with it. Not that he hadn't already guessed it, but to hear her admit her thoughts had his body tightening.

Colt knew he'd have to take advantage of every moment of her weakness if he wanted to penetrate that wall of defense she'd erected.

He leaned in closer as he flattened his palms on either side of her head. Her flush from the work she'd done, her musky scent, the way her chest rose and fell against his own, it would be so easy to turn this into something more right here and now. They were alone, there was nothing stopping him. And he knew Annabelle was his for the taking.

Colt shifted until his lips grazed across hers like a whisper. "A man could get used to hearing a beautiful woman give him compliments."

"Then maybe you should find a beautiful woman who wants to," she murmured.

He nipped at her bottom lip. "I've found her."

"Colt." Her hands came up to his chest.

The way his name came out on a breathy sigh had his entire body stirring to life. The fight she attempted to put up was weak. There was no conviction in her tone, no pressure from her hands to push him away.

How could he want someone so desperately? He had always been able to control his needs, but not with Annabelle. She challenged him in so many ways, and she was the one woman he really shouldn't want.

Still, seducing her was too sweet, too perfect.

Keeping one hand beside her face, he ran the other over her hip. His thumb slid beneath the hem of her tank. Her smooth skin beneath his touch was everything he'd been dreaming of…and he'd dreamt of her plenty last night.

"I want you."

"No, you want to control me."

"Only in bed."

Her eyes met his. "You're blunt."

"Honest," he corrected, going in to graze her lips once again.

"You have no idea what you're doing," she muttered, as if thinking out loud. "I'm not... Trust me when I say you don't want me."

He cupped her cheek with one hand, his other still at her hip. "Don't put yourself down. I know exactly what I want and I assure you, it's you."

"I'm not putting myself down or fishing for compliments. But you need to know that I'm..."

"What?" he urged.

Now she did push him away. "Not for you."

She picked up the basket, keeping her back to him. Shoulders hunched, she appeared to be defeated. How was that possible? His body was revved up and she seemed as if she'd just lost a battle. They could both win here if she'd just quit fighting the chemistry.

"Just take me home," she whispered. "I can't do this."

When he didn't make a move, she turned to face him, tears swimming in her eyes. "Please."

Whatever internal battle she waged with herself, Colt wanted no part of it. He'd wanted simple, he'd wanted sex. He still did.

Someone like Annabelle would take time to seduce, but he wasn't about to back down. She was needy, aching, just the same as him. He'd felt her heart beat against his chest, felt her arch into him slightly before she pushed him away.

It was only a matter of time before he unleashed that passion.

Annabelle's hands still shook as she unloaded the basket. *Get a grip.*

She tried to focus on the amazing food that Colt's cook had prepared. The fact he'd done this for her simply because he'd heard her discuss her hectic home life… Annabelle had no words to describe her emotions.

Of course, maybe she was speechless because her brain was totally fried after that heated encounter in the barn. Yet as hands-on and blatantly sexual as he'd been, he was a total gentleman on the ride home—in his truck. He'd also procured a bag of dog food for the new pup. Confusing, frustrating man. And she'd never wanted anyone more.

"What's all this?"

Her father stood in the doorway, holding Emily and patting her back.

"Dinner. Where is Lucy?"

"She's content chewing a doll head in the Pack 'n Play. I actually just fed her some apricots." He eased Emily into one of two high chairs. "Where on earth did you get all of that food?"

"Colt's cook made extra."

She didn't look up as she busied herself unwrapping everything. No way did she want to see her father's face. She already knew she'd have to answer questions.

"Colt's cook, huh? Sounds like you're getting friendly with him."

Friendly wasn't the correct term. But she truly didn't know what label to give this warped situation. She was caught in between the proverbial rock and a hard place, all the while getting completely turned on by her boss.

Of all the men she could feel a stirring for, why did Colt Elliott have to be the one? She hated her emotions, but the reality was, she felt more of a need, an ache for Colt than she ever did with Matt, and they'd been engaged.

In light of all that had happened, though, Annabelle was relieved she hadn't slept with Matt, that he'd respected her wishes to wait until they were married.

But if the scenario were different and she were engaged to Colt, she couldn't guarantee she'd wait.

"Belle?" Her father waved a hand in front of her face. "What the hell is going on? You bring home this food, you're daydreaming. Is that Elliott boy pressuring you?"

Boy? Not hardly. Colt was all man.

Annabelle circled the long farm-style table and crossed to the high chair. Emily's big green eyes met hers and Annabelle's heart melted. She loved her girls so much. Even though her sister had betrayed her in an unforgivable way, they'd still been family and these twins were all Annabelle had left.

She kissed Emily on her head, smoothing the red curls aside. "He's my temporary boss, Dad. Nothing more."

That wasn't a lie, not for lack of trying on Colt's part, but it was clearly a tidbit of information her father didn't need to know about. That kiss out in the field had to remain her secret…and her fantasy.

Emily clapped her hands together, then banged them on the tray. "How has her fever been today?"

"Just a little this morning, but otherwise it hasn't come back. She's played more this afternoon."

Annabelle went to the pantry and pulled out a jar of baby food. "Never worry about calling me. I want to know if there's any problem with her or you."

Neil grabbed two plates from the cupboard and started filling them with homemade fried chicken, mashed potatoes, and corn. The homemade rolls had Annabelle salivating. She'd hurried through her glamorous lunch of a turkey sandwich so she could get back to work. Ranching was the fastest way she'd ever known to burn calories.

"Where's the puppy?" she asked, glancing around the kitchen.

"I put him outside in the fenced area to run around for a bit. He's a cute little guy, but a handful when I'm alone with the two girls."

Annabelle couldn't feel guilty about that. The situation they were in was part his fault, part fate.

As far as the dog was concerned, she should come up with a name for him soon. She wished the girls were old enough to decide, but at six months, they were just making random sounds and squealing.

Annabelle pulled a wooden kitchen chair over to the high chair and scooped up a bite from the jar. Emily pressed her lips together and turned her head.

"If that's green beans, I tried those for lunch. She hates them. Though Lucy was quite a fan. They're total opposites, except for their looks."

Annabelle chased Emily's mouth around with the spoon. "Yeah, well, I'd like a chocolate cake for dinner, too, but we can't all have that. Come on, little one. Veggies are good."

As she wrestled bite after bite past Emily's lips, Annabelle went over in her head exactly how to approach her father about the debt to Colt's family. It was more than the house, she was positive. Colt, surprisingly, hadn't been willing to throw her dad under the bus. But she needed to know what she was up against. She didn't have time to try to piece all these snippets together for the full story.

Maybe being blunt was the best approach. "Did you gamble against Colt's father before all of this happened?"

"What?" he asked, his fork clanging against his plate.

Annabelle shifted in her seat to face him. "Before now, had you borrowed money or gambled against Colt's father?"

Neil Carter's face tightened, his lips thinned. "Is that what he told you?"

Attempting to distract herself from the ball of tension in her stomach, Annabelle scooped up another bite for Emily. "He didn't tell me anything. That's why I'm asking you."

"There's nothing for you to worry about." He aggressively cut into his chicken. "I don't like you working over there, Belle. You and I can move and start over. We don't have to stay here, you know."

Nearly everything she'd ever loved had been taken from her and as long as there was fight left in her and a chance this place could be hers again, she wouldn't back down.

"If you want to go, then go."

She knew he could never afford to live on his own. His addiction wouldn't allow it. He didn't have any savings, and everything she was bringing in would have to go to bills. There was no extra.

"We can find something inexpensive," he argued. "I know your mother had this dream, but she's gone and…"

"Well, I'm still here," she snapped. "I will see this through with or without your help."

Her father leaned back in his seat and raked a hand down his face. "Don't let them come between us. You've been over there for two days and your attitude has changed already."

Perhaps she had changed, but not because of Colt.

"I'm not the same person I was a month ago," she informed him. She scraped the bottom of the jar and fought to get the last bite into Emily's mouth. "Losing my sister and fiancé, then finding out they were having an affair pretty much destroyed me."

"I lost a daughter," he murmured. "I know how much it hurts."

Yes, he was hurting, too. But, they were both feeling different types of pain. He'd lost a child, Annabelle had lost her future. They were going to have to lean on each other to get through this nightmare or she'd never make it.

"I need you here," she told him. "I need you for Emily and Lucy so I can work. You need to get better for not just yourself, but for those babies who will look up to you one day. And I need you to work on making yourself the father I used to know because I can't do this without him."

Her voice caught on that last word. Tears clogged her throat as she blinked away moisture. Sometimes a girl just needed her dad.

"I'm trying."

Silence settled between them. Suddenly she wasn't in the mood to eat. She pulled Emily from the high chair and wiped her mouth with the bib before tugging it over her head. She dropped the dirty rag onto the tray.

"I'm going to give her a bath and then I'll come back for Lucy," Annabelle told her father. "If you can let the dog in and feed him, that would be great. I'll clean the kitchen later, after the girls are bathed."

"You're not eating?" he asked as she headed out of the room.

"I'm fine," she lied. But she didn't want to get into the mess inside her head. Especially not with her father.

Annabelle hugged Emily a bit tighter as she mounted the steps. "We're going to make it," she vowed. "You guys will have a stable home and never doubt my love. We're in this together."

All Annabelle had to do was make it through the next three months and she'd be free. She'd be able to push forward, take control of her life once and for all…and be rid of Colt Elliott.

Eight

"Hayes will be home next month."

Nolan laid the blanket across the horse he'd appropriately named Doc. Colt grabbed his own blanket and saddle and readied his stallion.

"I already asked Charlie to get the house ready and stock it before he arrives," Colt replied. "I'm sure he'll be ready to have some downtime to adjust to civilian life again."

Hayes had been in the service for the past fifteen years. He'd enlisted straight out of high school and now he was getting out for good. They'd thought he'd stay in a few more years and then retire, but Hayes wasn't the same man he used to be. He'd seen too much, things he'd never discuss, and there had been a haunted look in his eyes last time he'd been home.

Colt wasn't sure if Hayes would want anything to do with ranch life or if he'd like to explore other venues, but Colt would readily welcome him here for as long as he wanted to stay. Hayes had enough money that he'd never have to work a day in his life, but Colt intended to keep him a little busy so those demons didn't creep up and take control.

"Think Dad will remember him?" Colt asked.

Nolan hoisted the saddle across his stallion's back. "Depends on the day Hayes goes to see him. I stopped in earlier after my shift and he wasn't having the best day. He kept telling me to find Virginia because the dog had been hit by a car."

Virginia, their mother, had been gone for years. He still asked about her, still would question why she wasn't there. He may have dementia, but they had a love that would rival any fairy tale Colt had ever heard.

"That dog was killed when I was a baby," Nolan added. "So he's gone back pretty far. He thought I was Hank."

Hank had been their father's right-hand man at the stables, but he, too, had passed on. Their father was a prisoner in his own mind and he had no clue. All they could do was keep visiting, and hopefully he could grasp that he wasn't alone in his living hell.

"I'm going to see him tomorrow." Colt adjusted the saddle and patted Lightning's side before mounting him. "It's been a hectic couple of days."

When Annabelle had gone home an hour ago, Colt had been too keyed up to do anything. He'd just wanted to ride, but then Nolan had stopped in for some downtime.

"How's your new employee working out?" Nolan asked as he set off toward the back pasture.

Colt gripped the reins in one hand and tipped his hat down with the other. Who knew what truth his eyes would tell? He'd thought of little else since that kiss. Well, he'd thought of excuses to touch her again, because he was having a damn hard time *not* touching her.

"She's a hard worker. Josh and Ryan are impressed, too."

He rode parallel with Nolan, as they'd done so many times over the years. The inquisition was coming, Colt would bet the ranch on it.

"And you?" Nolan asked easily. "You're impressed."

He could still feel her tight body against his when he'd pressed her against the wall. Could still feel that warm breath brush across his cheek, his neck. She wasn't immune to their chemistry. She practically melted against him when they touched, and he couldn't wait until she was his.

"She doesn't complain about the heat or the work. She does her job and is prompt."

The sun, barely visible on the horizon now, cast an orange glow. The gorgeous summer nights never ceased to catch his breath. There was nothing more peaceful than a sunset on the ranch. There was nowhere else he'd rather spend his days than Pebblebrook.

"This is a hard life," Nolan said, giving Doc a gentle pat. "Think she'll be just as professional in three months?"

"She's determined to pay off her father's debt. She knows I want her land."

Nolan's disapproving sigh had Colt gritting his teeth. "Don't start," Colt warned.

"I didn't say a word. Sounds like the guilt is already getting to you."

That wasn't the only thing getting to him.

"I can't make decisions based on personal feelings, Nolan. This ranch is a business."

"Fair enough. So what are you going to do at the end of this, when the debt is paid?"

Colt rubbed the back of his neck. "I'm going to give them time to find another place."

"She's not going to be happy."

Colt pulled Lightning to a stop. "I'm not making friends. I'm pursuing a goal Dad had and I'm making sure it's carried out. How do you suggest I acquire the land? Because I asked multiple times to buy it."

Nolan eased to a standstill as well and glanced around

at the acreage stretching as far as the eye could see. "You know, I made a poor choice years ago that affected the rest of my life. I just don't want to see you doing something you regret."

Colt didn't need his oldest brother to spell out the mistake he'd made. Nolan had been in love, but when she'd pressured him to settle down, he'd gotten scared. Add an unexpected pregnancy and a miscarriage and Nolan hadn't been able to deal.

While Colt didn't know the entire story, he knew Nolan had never found that type of bond since. He flitted between the hospital and dates, occasionally working on the ranch when he could. But there was barely a weekend that Nolan didn't have someone on his arm…or in his bed. Of course, he never brought women back to Pebblebrook because that would be too personal.

"I'd regret if I let that land go," Colt stated simply. "I'm going to turn Pebblebrook into the greatest dude ranch the west has ever seen. I already have an engineer coming to draw up some plans for renovations on the house next door."

Nolan tugged his hat off and settled it onto the horn. "I wouldn't let Annabelle know that."

"She doesn't."

His brother's blue eyes bore into Colt. "You're starting to care for her. What are you going to do when you can't stop your feelings from getting involved with business?"

Colt snorted. "I want to take her to bed, if that's what you mean by 'care for her.' You should know something about meaningless sex."

Nolan nodded. "Touché."

"Besides, I want to settle down eventually. I definitely want kids to fill Pebblebrook with, but I want my dude ranch and my life in order first."

Laughing, Nolan shook his head. "There's no perfect

time to start a family and settle down. You need to do it when you find the one or you'll be left alone, trying to fill a void you caused."

Colt wasn't worried he'd fall for Annabelle. They wanted vastly different things and just because he ached to strip her down and have his way with her, didn't mean he was ready to monogram her initials on the plush towels in his master bath.

Tugging on his reins once more, Colt settled into an easy pace. "I've got a rancher from Oklahoma coming in two days to pick up forty head of cattle."

"Can't help you there. I'm on call for the next three days, starting tomorrow."

"Weren't you just on call?" Colt asked.

Nolan's horse jerked to the side before Nolan eased him back. "I was, but I picked up some extra shifts for a coworker. He's taking his wife on a surprise second honeymoon."

"You're going to work yourself to death."

Nolan cast a sideways glance. "I could say the same for you. But we're doing what we love, so it doesn't feel like work."

There was nothing else Colt had ever wanted to do. Nothing could pull him from Pebblebrook. He was anxious to have Hayes come back, and maybe he could help out for a bit until he decided fully what he wanted to do. Beau had been filming a movie in parts unknown for the past few months. Some action film where he would surely win the lady and save the day.

"Storms are coming in," Nolan stated, nodding toward the darkening skies.

Colt pulled on the reins. "We'll head back."

Colt couldn't recall the last time all four of them were together, but he was definitely going to call Beau and see if he could fly home for Hayes's homecoming. Maybe they could even all go visit their father. Better yet, maybe they could bring him to the ranch for a day.

Emotions threatened to overtake him at the idea of all of them there once again. Colt may be the youngest, but he had the most to prove. He wanted this property to thrive bigger and better than it ever had. He wanted his brothers to see just how hard he worked to make sure Pebblebrook remained the greatest ranch in Texas. And even though his father didn't always know what was going on in the world around him, Colt was going to honor him and personally see to it that his dude ranch came to fruition.

He'd set this dream in motion, so failing now would be a sure sign that he couldn't handle tough times. There was no way he'd let this scenario end without him getting the land and the house.

And letting Annabelle Carter appeal to his compassionate side was not an option. The only place he wanted her was in his bed.

"The truck?" Annabelle asked as she climbed into the cab. She set the basket from last night between them and reached for her seat belt. "Did I get a promotion?"

Colt dangled his wrist over the steering wheel and shot her a smile that shot straight to her heart. The instant response wasn't welcome, but she had no way of stopping it. At this point, all she could do was hang on for the ride.

"I need to run into town real quick and thought you'd enjoy a few minutes of air-conditioning before we hit it hard today."

Annabelle stretched her denim-covered legs out. "You're the boss."

"I do like how you keep saying that, sweets."

She let out a groan. "*Ms. Carter* still works fine."

Tipping his hat, he pinned her with his striking gaze.

"You've arched that sweet body against mine, you've kissed me, and you've imagined us as lovers. We're beyond formalities."

Annabelle's breath caught in her throat. She'd never met a man so blunt…and so dead-on with calling her out on her feelings. But she was a different woman than she was even a month ago and she wasn't about to be intimidated by Colt Elliott.

"That may be," she stated as she leaned closer, pleased when his eyes dropped to her lips. "But you've had the same thoughts, and you're no closer to getting me there than you were days ago."

Colt reached out, curling his fingers around the back of her neck. He captured her mouth, parting her lips, tangling his tongue with hers. The intensity of his touch, the urgency of the demanding kiss should have scared her, but Annabelle was too turned-on, too stunned at his actions to be frightened.

This was nothing like the sweet, delicate kiss he'd first given her. This was a toe-curling, body-tingling kiss like nothing she'd ever experienced before.

Annabelle fisted her hands in her lap, refusing to reach for him…but she wasn't going to deny she didn't want this to end.

Colt's grip on her neck softened as he trailed his fingers around to her jaw. Gently, he nipped at her lips before easing back. He stroked the pad of his thumb across her bottom lip and Annabelle couldn't stop her tongue from darting out and tasting him.

"I'd say we're one step closer," he murmured.

Annabelle was just digesting those words when he pulled back and reached over to start the truck. She had a snappy comeback, something snarky about his arrogance taking place of his ego, but when he extended his arm and waved, Annabelle cringed. She turned to see her father standing on the porch, cradling a girl on each hip, and from the look of his face, he'd witnessed everything.

Great. Nothing like having your father see you make out with the enemy. Just when she thought this situation couldn't get any worse.

Nine

At the end of the day Colt was still cursing himself for losing control with Annabelle earlier. Not that he regretted finally getting to taste those sweet lips again. No, he was more irritated with himself than the fact that he'd let her goad him. He did everything on his terms, his timeline.

The kicker had been looking up and seeing Neil on the porch, holding Emily and Lucy, that pup frolicking around his feet. Colt didn't mind that her father had seen them because he honestly didn't care what the old man thought. But he sure as hell didn't want an audience when his seduction of Annabelle was finally complete. He wanted to get her alone, to prove to her that they were indeed closer to intimacy. They'd been dancing around the subject for days and it was only a matter of time before they succumbed to what they both wanted. There was no way she could deny that, not after the way she kept responding to his kisses.

Colt had put Annabelle with Ryan today because he'd needed some time to think. When he was around her, he felt his control slipping by the second. He still had a ranch to run, and besides, he'd wanted to sneak away to visit his father.

Today had not been a good day for Grant Elliott. He hadn't recognized Colt at all. No matter what happened in Colt's life, nothing hurt more than looking into his father's blue eyes and seeing the blank stare, the confusion.

But his father had talked about a dude ranch. Colt had listened as his dad went on about all the things he'd incorporate onto the farm. The small cabins he'd build on the east side where the view of the pasture was breathtaking at sunset, the horses he'd bring in special for children who came to visit. He'd even mentioned having programs for physically handicapped riders who wanted to see what ranching was all about.

Colt knew his father was in there somewhere because he'd mentioned all of his original plans. Ranching had been so ingrained into the Elliott patriarch, that it was something Colt didn't think would ever be lost to this nightmare disease.

He had asked the nursing staff about the possibility of bringing his father home for one day when Hayes returned but, in the end, they decided to play it by ear. As much as Colt wanted his father at Pebblebrook, even for a short time, he would do whatever was best for his health.

Colt shut off the engine and grabbed his hat from the passenger seat. As he stepped from his truck, Colt headed toward the barn, but froze for a split second before taking off in a dead run. Annabelle lay on the ground just inside the structure, Ryan kneeling over her and patting the side of her face.

"What the hell happened?" Colt asked, skidding to a stop and dropping to his knees.

"She passed out, Boss."

Her color was off, perspiration dotted her forehead. He glanced at her body and noted that the white tank she'd worn was clinging to the dampness on her torso. He jerked his hat off and started to fan her.

"Get some water," Colt demanded, never taking his eyes off her pale face. He felt the pulse on her neck. Steady, thankfully, but he didn't like seeing her on the damn ground.

While Ryan rushed to the office, Colt eased his arms beneath her knees and her back. Carefully, he lifted her and stepped back to take a seat on a bench. Her lids fluttered as her head fell toward his chest. Ryan came back with a bottle of water and handed it to Colt.

"Want me to call Nolan?" Ryan asked.

Colt shook his head. "He's at the hospital. She's coming around."

Slowly, she turned her head, her brows dipping as if she was hurt. "What happened?" Colt asked again. "Were you in here when she fainted? Where's Josh?"

"Josh took off early because his daughter has some dance recital." Ryan pulled a handkerchief from his back pocket and wiped the back of his neck. "Ms. Carter and I had been out herding the cattle from the west field and we'd just gotten back. I walked around the side to turn the hoses on and when I came back in, she was all flushed. I asked if she felt all right, but she went down. I was fast enough to catch her before she hit her head, though. Scared ten years off my life."

Yeah, Colt was still trying to get his heart rate back under control after seeing her motionless on the ground.

"What else should I do?"

Colt shook his head and focused back on Annabelle. "I'd say she got overheated. It happens. Why don't you go ahead and tend to the horses and get them put away? I'll take care of her."

Ryan gave a clipped nod. "Yell if you need me."

Cradling her with one arm, Colt set the water bottle on the bench beside him and smoothed the stray, damp tendrils from her face. Her lids fluttered again and he silently pleaded for her to open them and give him hell for holding her.

He'd seen many cowboys go down due to heat and lack of hydration, but none of them had affected him like this. She'd worked herself to the point of exhaustion, and it was all his fault.

"Open those eyes, sweetness."

She fluttered once again. "You never ask nice," she murmured.

Relief spread through him as swiftly as a Texas storm in the spring.

Finally, those bright green eyes met his and for the first time in several minutes, he breathed a sigh of relief.

"Wh-what are you doing?" she asked, starting to ease up.

"Stay still." Damn it, he needed to hold her another minute. "You passed out."

One shaky hand came up to her forehead as she blinked in confusion. "I did? Where's Ryan? We were going to—"

"Forget it. He's outside tending to the horses and you're done for the day."

He helped her sit up, but kept a hold around her shoulders. Colt reached for the water bottle and brought it to her lips. "Drink."

She took the water from him and sipped, then swiped the bottle across her forehead. Condensation slid down the side of her face, down her neck, and disappeared into the scoop of her tank. He shouldn't be thinking how sexy she looked right now, but he couldn't help himself. He'd been away from her all day, then to come back and see this… his emotions were in overdrive.

"You have to take care of yourself," he stated, his tone much harsher than he'd intended.

With careful movements, she slid from his lap and set

the bottle down on the bench. "My welfare is none of your concern. I take care of myself just fine."

He came to his feet, going toe to toe with her. "Clearly not. And your welfare is my concern when it affects your work."

When she squared her shoulders, but rubbed her forehead as if her head ached, he felt like an ass. She was gearing up for a fight and he was just angry he hadn't been there to make sure she was fine.

"Damn it." He raked a hand down his face. "Get in the truck, I'll take you home."

"I'll ask Ryan."

Colt leaned forward, towering over her until she reached for his shoulders to stay upright. "When you need anything, I'll be the one to deliver it. Get. In. The. Truck."

Her eyes searched his face. "Something happened."

"Yeah, you passed out and scared the hell out of us."

She shook her head, her hands softened against him. "Something else. You're angry at me, but there's a sadness in your eyes I haven't seen before."

Colt hated how she homed directly in on the nugget inside him he tried so damn hard to keep hidden from the world. "Don't analyze me, sweetness. Unless you want to get into *your* secrets."

"I just thought…" She took a step away and swiped the back of her hand across her forehead. "Nothing. Forget I asked."

When she turned to head toward the truck, Colt grabbed her arm and hauled her side against his chest. "I had a bad day. That's all. It's nothing I want to talk about, but, thanks. I've never met anyone who knows what I'm feeling or thinking without me saying a word."

Those captivating eyes turned to him. "Maybe one broken heart recognizes another."

"Who broke your heart?" he whispered.

Her eyes went to his throat, as if she couldn't look directly at him. "Who hasn't?"

Those two words spoke volumes. She'd been broken, perhaps she still was, but she was a damn fighter. She stood before him ready to discuss what pained him when she was clearly just as shattered. But he wasn't asking, he couldn't. Getting involved on an emotional level was not an option. How many times did he have to remind himself of that?

Colt gripped her chin between his thumb and finger, tipping her head to capture her lips. Softly he caressed her mouth with his. His knees weakened the second she slid her hand over his forearm. The kiss was so innocent, definitely not the stepping-stone to sex he typically delivered. But this was the most relaxed he'd ever known her to be. Her body literally eased against his as she returned the passion so delicately.

"Maybe someday you'll trust me," he muttered against her lips.

Her hand tightened against him. "It's not my trust you're after."

Colt grazed her lips once again. "Maybe not, but if you trust me, then you'll be more likely to give me everything else I want from you."

Annabelle eased away as she blew out a sigh. "We both know that would be a terrible idea. I've still got months to go and we're already…"

"What are we? Because this could be so much better."

She glanced out the doorway. With the light breeze blowing in, strands from her ponytail danced around her shoulders. "I can't get involved with you, Colt. I already have to explain this morning's kiss to my father when I get home."

"You didn't go home for lunch?" he asked.

She shook her head. "I couldn't face him. After all that's happened—"

"Nothing has happened."

She turned her attention back to him. "Yet, right? You fully intend to keep this up until I give in."

Why answer such a rhetorical question? They both knew what was going on, they were adults. Colt wanted Annabelle and the feeling was mutual. He knew desire when it stared back at him.

"Come up to the house."

Those green eyes widened. "What?"

"For dinner. We'll talk." He held his hands out. "Nothing more. I swear."

Unless she wanted more, then who would he be to turn her down?

"I need to get home to the girls."

"Bring them."

What the hell was he saying? He never dated a woman with a baby, let alone twins. Never brought kids back to his home. But why shouldn't he now? It was no secret that he wanted Annabelle. Perhaps appealing to that side of her would make her come around.

Annabelle laughed. "Wow. You're letting your desperation show, Colt."

Yeah, maybe he was, but he wanted her trust, damn it. He was running out of patience. His body ached for her, responded to her when she merely cast a glance his way. He'd never felt this urgency toward one woman before.

"Give your dad the night off and bring your twins to the house. I know Winnie will have a feast prepared. She always does."

He could see her thinking, but refused to take no for an answer. "One dinner, darlin'. That's all. I think you could use a break."

"Fine," she sighed. "I'll bring Emily and Lucy in my own car and you will not touch me. Deal?"

Colt winked. "Sure thing, but what happens when you touch me?"

With an unladylike growl, she spun around and headed out the barn. "In your dreams."

"Every damn night," he muttered to her retreating back.

Ten

"You're not seriously going over there."

Annabelle slipped on her flip-flops and picked Emily up. "I'm only going for dinner. Anything I can do to stay on his good side and figure out his ulterior motive, I'll do it."

"I saw you doing it in his truck this morning."

The accusing tone, the knowing glare had guilt surging through Annabelle. She'd been home for nearly thirty minutes, long enough to change clothes and feed the girls, before he said anything. But she refused to allow him to turn this around on her.

"You're the reason I'm in this position," she countered, keeping her tone light since she held Emily.

"That's your excuse for kissing Colt Elliott?" Her father's silver brows drew in as he crossed his arms over his chest. "That man doesn't care about you, Belle. People like the Elliotts only care about money."

She swallowed back the hurt. Someday a man would be interested in her for no other reason than the fact that he liked, or even loved her. She'd been used and discarded too many times to care right now, though. Kissing Colt had been a pleasure, and she was going to steal those moments when she could. She was smart enough to know Colt wanted her in bed. And she couldn't deny she'd been fantasizing about it.

"Leave the girls here," her father stated.

Annabelle shook her head. She needed them as the buffer. "We'll be fine. Besides, I don't get to see them much."

"At least leave Emily since she's still been fussing."

"I'll take Lucy," she stated. She had to drive home to Colt that she wasn't the type to play around. She had a family she needed to look out for.

Finally, her father nodded. "I'm going to need some cash."

"What for?"

She'd taken over all finances, cutting him off since she'd been back. Until he proved himself to be addiction free, it was the only way for them to get his debt paid off in time.

"I'll go to the grocery while you're gone. We're low on diapers and we could use some milk and eggs."

Annabelle did the quick math in her head. Holding Emily on her hip, she crossed to her purse hanging by the front door. She pulled out a few bills and handed them to her father.

"Just put the change back in my purse," she told him. "I shouldn't be too long."

Before he could make another argument as to why she shouldn't go, Annabelle grabbed the diaper bag and her keys and headed out the door. Once she got to Pebblebrook, she pulled in to the large, circular drive near the front door. She'd only been in his office, so she had to admit she was curious about what the rest of the house looked like. Did any other rooms have that spectacular waterfall?

Annabelle unfastened Lucy from her car seat and headed up the wide stone steps. The small creek running in front of the home soothed her nerves with the trickling effect. She knew coming here was just another tactic of

Colt's to sway her into his bed. Little did he know nobody had been able to accomplish that in the past and she had a strong resolve built up. Well, she couldn't deny it was slipping, but she could hold out longer than him.

And she was pretty confident she was driving him insane. He wanted her and he was getting desperate. A thrill of power shot through her.

When the wide door swung open just as she hit the top step, Annabelle was a little surprised to see Colt in the entryway.

"I figured one of your minions would answer the door."

He held a hand over his heart and stepped aside for her to enter. "I'm crushed you think so little of me."

"You think enough of yourself for both of us," she countered as she stepped over the threshold.

The house was just as gorgeous as she remembered. Breathtaking. So far out of her league, she was afraid to take a step any farther. But she took her time in glancing around, taking it all in.

"Just one of the girls?" he asked.

Annabelle nodded. "This is Lucy. Emily stayed with my dad. I won't know how to act with just one. I'm always taking care of them both at the same time."

"Let me have the bag." Colt eased the diaper bag off her shoulder and set it on the accent table next to an enormous vase containing a spray of bright flowers. "Follow me. Winnie did indeed make a feast and she was thrilled to have someone enjoy it other than me."

"Where is she?"

"Oh, she's probably heading home," he replied as he led her down the wide hallway toward the back of the house. "She went to her suite earlier, but she's not staying."

Her suite. Of course. What chef didn't have their own suite?

Annabelle held on tight to Lucy, who had finally laid

her head down on Annabelle's shoulder. It had been a long day for everyone.

"How are you feeling?" Colt asked, stepping into the massive kitchen.

"I'm fine." Even if she weren't, she wouldn't admit it. She was still mortified she'd passed out earlier. But, the moment she'd woken up, she'd seen that worry on Colt's face. That was definitely something he couldn't fake.

Annabelle tried not to gawk, but she couldn't help herself. The massive center island dominated the kitchen. It featured a small sink and a second gas stove as well as an overhang stretching across the length of the island. There were even bar stools made from antique saddles.

Massive dishes of food had been set out: cornbread, potatoes, smoked sausages with peppers, and a pie. Apple. Her favorite. The spread on the island had her mouth watering.

"I should've worn my bigger jeans." Her stomach growled and she cringed. "And I shouldn't have skipped lunch."

His bright eyes narrowed. "No, you shouldn't have. You know how hard ranch work is and you need to take care of yourself."

Annabelle nodded. "It won't happen again. Believe me." Lucy let out a deep sigh. "I'm pretty sure she's fallen asleep."

Annabelle turned so the baby faced Colt. "Is she?"

"Oh, yeah. She's out."

Grabbing a plate off the edge of the bar, Annabelle started dishing up potatoes with one hand.

"I'll get your damn plate."

She eyed him. "No language around the baby."

Tipping his head, he pursed his lips. "She's already talking?"

"Well, no, but I don't want *damn* to be her first word, either."

"Fair enough, sweetness."

Rolling her eyes, she set her plate down and glared at him. "You've got to stop with the tacky pet names. I'm sure you've used those names on a number of other women, but I'm not falling for your charms."

"You think I'm charming?" That sidelong grin had her body instantly responding. "And I've never used *sweetness* on anyone else. Maybe that can be your name."

Slowly easing Lucy to her other side, Annabelle snorted. "I'd rather you not call me that, especially when we're working."

He put a piece of cornbread on the side of her plate and turned to face her, pinning her with that direct baby-blue gaze. "And when we're not working?"

She would not stand there and flirt with him. She had to cut that off before it could get started because she was losing ground. Her willpower was cracking and she couldn't afford to have it completely crumble.

Breaking his stare, Annabelle turned away. She headed toward the long, farm-style table in front of the floor-to-ceiling windows looking out onto the pool. Of course there was a pool house off to the side. She could only imagine what that looked like inside.

"Good evening." Annabelle jerked toward the doorway to see a beaming elderly woman. "I'm Winnie. I won't get in the way, I just wanted to introduce myself and tell you how amazing that cinnamon bread you sent back was."

Annabelle ignored the way Colt's gaze widened. "You're welcome. I love to bake and wanted to thank you for the dinner. I guess I should be thanking you for two."

She waved a hand. "It's no trouble at all. I'm happy to have someone else to cook for. I'd love for you to share that recipe, if you don't mind."

"I don't mind a bit," Annabelle replied with a smile.

"You made bread?" Colt finally asked as he poured two glasses of sweet tea.

"It was in the basket she sent back," Winnie stated.

"I had no idea or I would've dug into it." Colt crossed the kitchen and set Annabelle's plate and tea on the table. "This looks delicious, as always, Winnie. Did you eat?"

"I did." Her eyes zeroed in on Emily. "And who is this precious baby?"

"My daughter, Lucy." That still felt so strange to say. There were so many emotions tied to the fact the twins were legally hers. Emotions she'd not fully faced. "She and her twin, Lucy, are six months old."

"Oh, my. Two precious angels. Well, she's a doll with that red, curly hair. I can see she looks like you," Winnie stated with a confident nod and grin.

Of course they looked alike. Annabelle and her sister both shared the same skin tone, red hair, green eyes.

Winnie's gaze darted between Annabelle and Colt before she took a step toward him. "I thought about going to see your father, unless I'm needed here."

Annabelle took a seat at the table. The bench seating made for nice family-style dining, but she had a feeling Colt didn't host too many family gatherings. She didn't know the story behind his father, and he hadn't offered to give her details, so she tried not to pay attention to the conversation behind her.

She stabbed a potato with her fork and took a bite. In such a short time, she'd gotten used to doing things with one hand while holding Lucy or Emily with the other.

"We're good here," Colt replied. "Maybe, uh, why don't you take Dad some pie. Apple was his favorite. I don't know…"

This was the first time Annabelle had ever heard Colt even remotely sound unsure. And there was that sadness again. Colt may be a big, powerful rancher, but there was no masking the pain he obviously felt now.

"I'll take some," Winnie stated. "Let me just get that and I'll be out of your way."

Annabelle took a drink of her sweet tea and patted Lucy's back. She hated being caught in the midst of what was obviously a family moment. If anyone understood not wanting outsiders involved in a private affair, it was her.

"It was lovely to meet you."

Annabelle turned slightly, waving to Winnie. "You, too. And thanks for this wonderful meal."

"I hope you'll come back."

Before Annabelle could even reply, Winnie walked away with her container. Colt scooped hearty portions onto his plate and Annabelle stared at him, wondering what to say.

"Don't ask."

His firm command had her straightening in her seat. "I wasn't. I honestly don't know what to say. I don't know why I'm here."

Crossing the room, he set his plate down right next to hers and settled down onto the bench. "You're here because I'm tired of eating alone and I enjoy your company. You're here so you can see that you can trust me. And you're here so I can feed you."

When Annabelle reached for her fork, Colt covered her hand. Her eyes met his and he took the fork from her. When he scooped up a bite and held it in front of her lips, she froze.

"What are you doing?"

His mouth twisted into a half grin and Annabelle's heart kicked into a higher gear. "Making sure you're taken care of."

Annabelle took the bite he offered. Whatever Winnie had done to those potatoes was amazing, but it was difficult for Annabelle to concentrate with Colt sitting this close. His thigh rubbed against hers on the bench and it was all she could do not to touch it.

He fed her several more times, never taking his eyes off her as she closed her lips over the fork. Finally, she couldn't take it anymore.

"I can finish," she told him. "I'm used to holding her and eating at the same time."

"I'm getting to you."

"Yes." Why deny the truth? "Which is why I can't keep doing this."

Silence settled around them, save for the occasional clatter of their utensils against the plates. Annabelle only ate a little before she eased her legs around and came to her feet. She grabbed her plate and took it to the counter. She held on to Lucy and closed her eyes, willing some semblance of self-control to come back.

Coming here was a bad idea. She honestly didn't know what she wanted. Well, she knew, but she couldn't even go there. She had too much to worry about with her home, her father, learning about how to care for two babies. No wonder she was thinking of throwing every bit of common sense aside and letting Colt seduce her. She knew full well she'd enjoy it, that was never in question. The issue was what happened afterward? How would she work for him and try to keep the various aspects of their relationship compartmentalized?

Lucy started fussing and wiggling around. Rocking back and forth, Annabelle patted her back.

"You're really good with her."

Annabelle glanced up to see Colt standing on the other side of the island. "It's a learning process."

Wasn't that an understatement?

"What happened with the father?"

Colt's question took her completely off guard. Annabelle froze. "He's not in the picture."

"You said that, but I assume since you were engaged and now you're left alone with two babies, he wasn't man enough for the job."

Considering the father of this child and her fiancé were two different people, this could get tricky. But, she also wasn't about to get into the ordeal. She didn't intend to get too personal with Colt, and she didn't want him to look at her with pity, so there was no need to let him in on the truth behind the twins.

"The girls' father signed over all rights." That much was true. Trish had gone to him when she'd discovered she was pregnant, but he wasn't ready to be a daddy. "We're fine, though."

Because Annabelle wouldn't let them be anything but fine.

"I can't imagine any man not wanting to be with his children," Colt added, crossing his arms over his broad chest as he stared down at Lucy. "And if he was engaged to you, why would he just throw all of that away?"

"Stop," she murmured. "This isn't…I can't get into this."

Colt eased around the island and came to stand directly in front her. His eyes locked on to hers. "I'm trying to gain your trust, Annabelle. I want you to trust me when I take you to my bed."

"You're not taking me to bed," she insisted, though nerves in her stomach danced wildly at the thought.

"I am," he countered. "But I want to make sure it's my face you see, my name you say when you're there."

"Considering I've never said anyone else's name, that won't be a problem."

She hadn't meant to just blurt that out, but seeing the shock on his face was worth it.

"What?" he asked, shock lacing that single word.

She'd come this far. Might as well let him know what he was dealing with. Maybe he'd back off and get that ridiculous idea out of his head.

"I'm a virgin."

Eleven

Very little in Colt's life shocked him. He'd traveled all over the globe, dealt with a variety of people and liked to believe he could think on his feet. But nothing prepared him for the confusing statement Annabelle had just dropped between them.

"How the hell is that even possible?" he asked. "I know the girls aren't adopted. They look just like you."

Annabelle patted the sleeping baby and nodded. "No, they're not adopted. My sister was their mother."

Her sister. The one who passed away.

Colt attempted to make things clear in his head, but he was at a loss. How the hell did he respond to that? She was clearly out of her depth with so much, having life throw things at her she wasn't ready for—motherhood...sex.

And he was an ass for being so forward, so blatant.

Well, he was a jerk for other things as well, but that was business.

In his defense, how the hell was he supposed to know she was so inexperienced? She had babies, for crying out loud, and the way she'd flirted, kissed...

"I don't know what to say."

Annabelle held his gaze as she rested her cheek against

the sleeping baby's head. "There's nothing to say. You needed to know what you were up against. Clearly, I'm not swayed by easy charms and sexy men. So, you'd probably be better off moving on to a woman who will actually give in to your advances."

Colt would've laughed had her statement held any conviction or had she not melted against him when they'd kissed. Annabelle was already giving in to his every advance, whether she wanted to admit it or not.

"You think because you're inexperienced that I'll move on?" he asked, taking a step closer until his chest brushed the arm she held Lucy with. "Baby, if anything, I want you more. To know I can be the one to show you everything, I've never been more turned on."

"Don't call me *baby*," she whispered.

"When I get you into my bed, I'll call you your name and you'll damn well love every second of it."

She jerked back. "You're not seriously still interested in me. You just want the challenge."

"It's true I've never backed away from a challenge," he assured her. "But I want you, sweetness. I've wanted you from the moment you plowed into my fence. And you want me, too, or you wouldn't have stared at my bare chest so long that day."

Her eyes narrowed. "If I weren't holding Lucy, I'd smack you."

Colt believed she probably would. He couldn't help but laugh as he leaned close to her ear. "Save that energy."

"You're impossible." Annabelle took a step back, then shifted Lucy in her arms. "I'm going home. Tell Winnie thanks for dinner and I'll get her that recipe."

"Why didn't you tell me you like to cook?" he asked, the thought of her leaving suddenly unbearable.

"I never said I liked to cook," she retorted.

He leaned against the edge of the counter, feigning calm and giving her a bit more breathing room.

"You didn't have to," he stated. "You baked bread and brought it back. Someone who hates cooking wouldn't have done that."

Annabelle bit her bottom lip as if she were contemplating letting him into her personal life any further. She'd already dropped a bomb. What did it matter at this point?

"I actually love to bake," she told him. "Bread is my weakness. My mother always baked bread. Our house always smelled amazing. I guess I just want to keep up that tradition, and hopefully pass it down to the girls one day."

The importance of family traditions. That was definitely something he understood, something his father had instilled into each of his children.

"The girls are lucky to have you," Colt told her. "I'm sorry about your sister."

He'd already apologized, but knowing more about the situation gave him another tug on his conscience. Damn it.

"I don't want to talk about her."

There was something in Annabelle's tone that had him cocking his head and studying her. The sadness was there, but something else, too, something almost bitter or resentful.

"Do you want to lay her on the sofa?" he suggested. "We can talk while she rests."

"You just want to talk? Don't you think we've exhausted all the topics for the night? Unless you'd like to ask about my father's gambling. Better yet, why don't we talk about your father or why you have a limp."

The limp he could discuss, but he didn't want to talk about his father. He missed the man his father once was, and discussing him, given his current mental state, wasn't Colt's idea of a good time.

"Your father is a gambler and mine has dementia. That

sums up that topic." He pulled in a deep breath. "As for the limp, when a tornado ripped through Stone River last year, our main barn was torn up. I was helping to rebuild it when I fell off a ladder, shattering my hip bone and breaking my back. I'm still getting back to normal...if that's even possible."

Before she could offer pity, which he did not want, Colt opted to throw the focus back on her. He glanced down toward her half-empty plate. "You didn't eat enough."

Annabelle shrugged. "I haven't had much of an appetite lately."

"Which is why you passed out."

"You're not going to let that go, are you?"

Colt shook his head. "Not until I see you're taking care of yourself properly."

Annabelle wrapped both arms around Lucy as she turned and headed toward the patio off the kitchen. Colt followed, pleased she'd given up on the idea of just flat out leaving. For reasons he didn't want to examine too closely, he wanted her there, in his home. Annabelle took a seat on the sofa and laid Lucy down beside her. After making a wall with throw pillows, Annabelle settled against the cushion and tipped her head back.

"It feels so good to sit and do nothing."

Colt remained in the doorway, leaning against the frame. She looked so peaceful. Surprisingly, having Annabelle and Lucy there didn't feel awkward. The women he dated didn't have children, but Lucy was so damn adorable, it was impossible not to be lighter, happier in her presence. Both girls were precious and obviously so loved by Annabelle. She'd clearly do anything to keep them from harm.

But as Colt studied Annabelle, something shifted inside him. She was making him feel, she was making him want and that wasn't going to work. He didn't want to start thinking of her beyond business or the bedroom.

Maybe having her there wasn't the best idea. He still wanted her, that wouldn't go away until he'd gotten her out of his system. But he'd learned more about her, quite a bit, and she made him want to take care of her. She made it nearly impossible not to admire her acts of selflessness.

Annabelle Carter was one of the most amazing people he'd ever met.

And she'd just let out a most unladylike snore.

Colt stepped down onto the enclosed patio and stood over her. Her mouth was softer when she slept, her light lashes fanned out over her cheeks, her chest rose and fell so lightly, so steadily. She'd worn herself completely out.

Lucy whimpered and Colt's gaze jerked to the baby who was starting to wake up. Fear gripped him. He didn't want to wake Annabelle and he didn't want Lucy to start crying.

When Lucy started squirming even more, her eyes opened and she whimpered once again.

Colt instantly lifted her from the sofa. Throw pillows slid to the floor as he hurried from the room. Annabelle needed sleep, probably more than she needed to eat. But what the hell did he know about babies? Fussy babies at that.

As he headed through the kitchen and to the front of the house toward the diaper bag, Colt figured he was about to find out.

Annabelle woke with a start. She glanced around the large room surrounded by windows and filled with indoor plants. Then she recalled she was at Colt's house.

Her focus shifted to the sofa cushion beside her where Lucy had been. The pillow barrier had fallen to the floor.

Pushing her hair away from her face, Annabelle came to her feet and smoothed her shirt back into place. She had no clue how long she'd been out. The last thing she remembered was sitting down for a second and Colt leaning against the door frame. She'd wanted just a moment to relax before heading home.

After dropping the bomb about her personal life, she figured he'd be done with her, but apparently not. He said he wanted company, that he enjoyed talking with her. And she had to admit, as much as she hated owing him money, she enjoyed their talks, as well. Who was she kidding? She enjoyed more than their talks. She enjoyed the way her body tingled when he entered the room. Enjoyed the way his slightest touch fired up her every nerve ending. She only wished they'd gotten to know each other under different circumstances.

But this was the hand she was dealt. Unfortunately, she had no idea what card to lay down next.

Annabelle stepped up into the kitchen. Colt wasn't around. She headed through the wide hallway, not having a clue where he'd be. She wasn't worried, she knew Colt had a handle on Lucy or he would've woken her up. At least, she hoped that's what he would've done.

A wave of embarrassment swept over her. She'd obviously been even more exhausted than she'd first thought.

Glancing at a large wall clock at the end of the hallway, Annabelle realized she'd probably been asleep nearly an hour. She knew it had gotten later because the sun was setting, based on the pink and orange glow streaming in through the windows.

"Colt," she called out. She heard absolutely nothing as she peeked in various doors and headed down another hall.

When Annabelle stepped into the spacious living room, she stood in awe of an entire wall of bookshelves. The amount of cookbooks she could fill those with made her baker's heart speed up.

But she'd never be filling those shelves with anything. Pebblebrook wasn't her house. She'd do well to cling to the home she had.

As her eyes swept over the room, she stilled when her gaze landed on the set of patio doors leading out to the side yard. With the sun setting, the magical glow stretching across the horizon and cattle like little black dots in the distance, Annabelle's breath caught in her throat.

Colt stood beneath an old oak tree. He was cradling Lucy in one strong arm and feeding her a bottle. Annabelle had never witnessed a sexier sight than this man holding the child that had become her own.

Tears pricked her eyes as she gripped the handle of the patio door. She wanted to take in this moment, pretend that it wasn't fleeting. What would it be like if this were her home? If Colt wanted her for more than sex, more than her land?

He'd be an amazing father. Obviously he'd taken Lucy so Annabelle could sleep. How could that act of kindness not make her look at him a different way? How could she not find herself even more attracted to him?

But she was realistic. In just a few months, she'd have her debt paid off and he'd have no use for her. If she slept with him, well, she didn't know what would happen because she'd never been in that situation before. She obviously wasn't a casual-sex person, but nearly every part of her wanted to know what being with Colt would be like. She had a pretty good imagination.

Pulling in a deep breath and praying for strength where that man was concerned, Annabelle opened the patio door and stepped outside. When she started making her way across the yard, Colt turned and met her gaze. His smile nearly had her knees buckling. That man could do so much without ever laying a hand on her.

"I'm sorry I fell asleep on you," she told him as she drew closer.

"I won't take it personally." He glanced back down at Lucy who patted the side of her bottle with her chubby hand. "It got a little hairy when I was trying to hold her and read the directions on the formula can. I'm thankful you already had water in the bottle, so I hope I did everything right."

Annabelle stepped closer, catching Lucy's eyes. The instant their eyes locked, the infant smiled, milk streaming down the side of her mouth.

"Oops." Annabelle laughed as she reached for the baby and the bottle. "She tends to get sidetracked easily."

Colt swiped the dribble of milk from his forearm and shrugged. "I work with farm animals. I'm not afraid of a little formula on my arm."

Annabelle took over feeding Lucy. She loved looking down into those green eyes. Loved seeing her sister's reflection. For the past twenty-four years, Trish had been Annabelle's best friend. At some point, she'd have to forgive her sister for her betrayal, but she wasn't quite there yet. It was too fresh, too soon.

But raising her babies was easing the pain, it was bridging that gap even though her sister wasn't there. Annabelle knew in time, she'd forgive Trish, because there was no way to care for those babies and still hold ill feelings.

"My sister and my fiancé were killed in a car accident."

She didn't know why she just blurted that out. Maybe she thought it would be therapeutic to get her feelings out in the open.

"They were seeing each other behind my back." Okay, that didn't make her feel any better at all. If anything, now she felt like a fool. "I didn't know they were involved until the day of the accident. We got into an argument. My sister was crying, Matt was trying to justify their actions. Then they left and that was the last time I saw either of them."

Colt took a step toward her, but Annabelle kept her gaze on sweet Lucy. She didn't want to look up and see pity in Colt's eyes.

"Annabelle…"

She smiled. "Now you use my name?"

"I'm sorry," he said, not a trace of humor in his voice. "I had no idea about this. I just knew your sister had passed away."

"It's crazy. For so long, I looked up to her, wanted to be like her. She was a wonderful mother to Emily and Lucy. I couldn't wait to get married and start my own family."

She'd have to wait a little longer for that. She had plenty of other things to get straightened out in her life first.

"After the wedding, I planned to come back here and get my business off the ground."

"What business?"

Annabelle shook her head, meeting Colt's worried gaze. "It's nothing."

He reached out, curling his hand around her shoulder. "It's something important enough to bring you back home."

It was everything. The dream her mother had had, the affection she'd had in her voice when she'd talk about opening the B and B, the people that would hopefully fill it and enjoy the beauty that Stone River had to offer.

"Tell me."

The command was delivered so softly, she knew he cared or he wouldn't pursue the issue.

"A bed-and-breakfast," she murmured, looking back down at Lucy. With the bottle nearly empty, Annabelle pulled it from Lucy's puckered lips and eased the baby upright. "It was a goal my mother had before she passed. She taught me how to bake, telling me that's what would be the heart of our business. People who came to stay with us would want good food. I couldn't wait to grow up and help her run the place. After she passed, I was nervous to do it all alone. But this past year, I got engaged and thought it was time to just go for it."

Holding Lucy on her hip, Annabelle looked out to the

horizon and forced her emotions down. She didn't want to break here, not in front of Colt.

"Over the past few months, these setbacks nearly destroyed me. But I know my mom wouldn't want me to give up, so I'm not. I'm doing all of this for her."

That last word came out broken as tears clogged her throat. Apparently she wasn't as strong as she thought.

"I don't know what to say," he murmured, squeezing her shoulder.

Annabelle turned her attention back to him. "There's nothing to say. Life sometimes has other plans for us. If I gave up each time I had a stumbling block, I would've thrown in the towel a long time ago."

Colt's bright blue eyes studied her and Annabelle wanted to know what was going through his mind. Did he see her as weak because she couldn't hold on to the life she'd wanted? Did he think she was pathetic because she had no real vision at the moment? Her life was in chaos and there was no clear picture in sight.

"You're one of the most remarkable people I've ever known," he stated.

Lucy tugged on Annabelle's hair and pulled some into her mouth. Annabelle eased the strands from the baby's clutches and pushed them behind her shoulders.

"Then you don't know too many people," she laughed.

Colt's hand trailed up to cup the side of her face. "I know people all over the world. None of them has half the tenacity for life that you do."

Such a compliment coming from Colt Elliott warmed her…as if she needed to be warmed in any more areas where he was concerned.

He leaned in, and Annabelle knew he was going to kiss her. She shifted Lucy slightly on her hip and tipped her head to meet Colt's lips. The gentle way he swept his mouth across hers while stroking his thumb along her jawline…yeah, that man was powerful without being force-ful. He made her want things. Things that she would never have with him.

When he eased back, Annabelle knew she needed to go. If she stayed any longer, she'd start getting delusions that this life could be hers, that she could live on a sprawling ranch like Pebblebrook. That a man like Colt could fall in love with her. This wasn't a fairy tale. This was real life and she was crawling day after day to get hers back.

"I need to go," she stated, licking her lips to taste him once more. "Thanks for dinner."

He dropped his hand and stepped back. "I'm sure Winnie would love for you to come back again."

"And you?" She couldn't resist asking. "Would you love for me to come back again?"

Heat filled his eyes as he stared at her mouth. "I think you already know the answer to that."

Yeah, she did. And Annabelle knew if she came back for dinner, she would not be bringing a baby.

Twelve

Annabelle rifled through her purse before work the next morning. She needed a pen to jot down that recipe for Winnie, but she couldn't find one.

She also couldn't find the fifty dollar bill she'd had in there yesterday. She'd given her father some money for the store, and he'd put the change back like she'd told him to. She hated immediately thinking he took the cash, but she knew full well she didn't use it. Where had she been besides the barn, Colt's house and her house?

Dread filled her stomach.

Annabelle sank on the edge of her bed. She was going to have to confront him. She'd not only looked in her purse that had been on her bed, she'd looked all around the bed, beneath the bed, thinking maybe it had fallen out.

She should've known better than to leave cash around, but she'd sincerely hoped he was trying to be a better man, be the father she'd asked him to be.

Annabelle didn't know if she wanted to cry or throw her hands in the air and give up.

She grabbed her phone from the nightstand and texted Colt to tell him there had been an emergency and she'd drive herself over a little bit later. Shoving her phone in the pocket of her jeans, she cast a glance at Emily and Lucy, still sleeping in their cribs against the far wall. Both girls tended to wake once a night to eat and since they'd both gotten up at four and were wide-awake until six, they now opted to sleep in. Of course they fell asleep right when she needed to get ready to go to the farm.

The scent of coffee filtered up from the first floor—a sure sign her father was awake. She took a few minutes to compose herself before she went into full attack mode.

Pulling in a breath, Annabelle went downstairs and into the kitchen. Her father had his back to her as he poured himself a mug of coffee.

"Did you take money from my purse?"

His shoulders stiffened. "You gave me money for the store. I put the change back like you said."

The fact that he evaded her question told her everything she needed to know. Her heart sank—and her hopes weren't far behind.

"What was it this time, Dad? A ball game? A horse race? Online poker?"

Neil Carter dropped his head between his shoulders. "I'll pay you back. I know that investment will return—"

"It's not an investment, Dad," she all but yelled. "We have no extra money. I'm not only paying off this house, I'm trying to raise two babies now. When will you be a responsible adult? When will you see that this habit of yours is destroying us? Because it doesn't matter how much I want you to change, you have to want it, too."

Could he not see that this wasn't just about him or her anymore? Emily and Lucy needed them—they had no other family. No matter what happened with the farm, with the gambling, Annabelle vowed to hold strong. She would not fail those babies. She loved them like they were her own, and she wanted to honor her sister's memory, despite what had gone down in those final days.

Her father set the mug on the counter and turned to face her. "I do, Belle. It's just going to take time."

The subtle tap on her front door had Annabelle cringing. Colt. No doubt he'd shown up even though she told him she'd be late.

"Time is something we don't have," she whispered before turning away.

"Belle," he called after her.

"I have to go to work," she stated without looking back as she headed to the front door. "Someone has to hold this family together."

Considering she only had a few ones in her purse, she wasn't even bothering to take it. He could have her last dollar. What did it matter at this point? The money for the house wasn't even going through her hands. Colt was keeping her wages, so at least that was something. But she didn't have any extra and she knew she'd have to go to the store soon. Not to mention the bills would be coming due. Apparently, her father had no respect for such necessities as water and electricity.

Annabelle jerked the door open, causing Colt to jump back. She stormed past him, ignoring his questioning gaze. The sooner she got to the ranch, the sooner she could work out her frustrations.

"Hold up, sweetheart."

She whirled around on Colt. "Not today. Do not start with the pet names. I'm not in the mood."

The black hat shaded half of his face, but those eyes still managed to pierce her. "Care to tell me why you look like you want to kill someone?"

Annabelle closed her eyes and blew out a breath. "Not really. Just…get me out of here."

Colt opened his mouth to say something, but finally nodded. Annabelle turned and mounted Lightning before Colt got on behind her.

The instant his arms came around to grab the reins, Annabelle leaned back against his chest. She didn't care if this made her weak.

"Not a word," she muttered. "I just need this for a second."

"Lean on me all you want."

With a flick of his wrists, he set Lightning into a soft trot. Annabelle fought back tears. If her father didn't get his act together, she didn't know what they'd do. She couldn't pay off this house and keep them afloat if he was pilfering money. Annabelle had already hidden her mother's emerald ring. If her father found that, she hated to admit that he'd probably hock it.

"I was going to drive in a few minutes late," she told him after a bit.

"When you said emergency, I was afraid something was wrong with one of the girls. You didn't specify, so I went ahead and came anyway."

"I'm a mess, Colt. I'm more of a hindrance than help at this point."

He grasped the reins in one hand and wrapped his free arm around her waist, hugging her into his body. "Why this negativity? That's not like you."

"Just a morning dose of reality. And I haven't even had my coffee, yet."

She started to ease up when his arm tightened. "You're fine right here, darlin'."

"What did I tell you about the names?" she asked, the fight gone from her voice as she settled back against him.

"I think my nicknames are growing on you."

She couldn't help but smile. "Don't get too cocky."

They rode another moment in silence and her heart sank when they approached the barn. She could've kept riding, pretended nothing was going on in the world. For just a little bit she wanted to imagine her problems, her father's problems, weren't gnawing at her heels as she tried to outrun them.

"Something happen with your father?" Colt asked softly.

Annabelle sat up, mostly because if Josh or Ryan were in the barns, she didn't want them to see her nestled against their boss. Although she figured they knew something was up. It wasn't normal for a man to pick up a woman on horseback for work.

Funny how she'd not only gotten used to it, she actually looked forward to their rides.

"I'd rather not get into it," she stated as she focused on the stone building ahead. "What do you have planned today?"

"Something you've never done before," he promised. "You up for a ride on Genesis?"

"Sure. Anytime I get to ride is great."

Colt brought Lightning to a stop and dismounted before reaching a hand out to assist Annabelle. She let the touch linger. She'd take all the Colt she could get today.

"I left without grabbing a hat."

Colt patted Lightning as he looped his reins around the post outside the barn. "You won't need one today."

Confused, Annabelle blinked and crossed her arms over her tank. "I won't?"

"Nope. Go get Genesis ready. I'll meet you back here. I need to give some final orders to Ryan and Josh before we take off."

The man was intriguing, and she had a feeling that's exactly how he wanted to be seen. He wanted to keep her on her toes. Another reason she needed to be ready at all times for whatever he threw her way.

Colt didn't recall being nervous about anything in his life. He'd been angry and frustrated when Layla had left, he'd been hurt when his father slipped into a tragic state of mind and he'd been worried each time his brother Hayes was deployed. Even when his twin brother, Beau, had a movie opening in LA, Colt didn't have a bundle of nerves dancing in his stomach.

But today he was a mess. He was going to take Annabelle to a portion of the property that was rarely seen unless you specifically ventured back there. It was behind Hayes's house, stretching along the riverbank that ran on the edge of their property.

It was the most peaceful spot on the ranch. After Annabelle opened up emotionally at their dinner last night, he wanted to just relax with her. Forget the fact they were boss and employee. He wanted her to trust him.

Stupid of him really, considering his intentions hadn't changed one bit. But there was a part of him that wanted her to talk to him, to tell him her fears, her needs…her desires.

When he'd been in the yard feeding Lucy, Colt had been smacked in the face with a dose of reality. He did want a family, that wasn't news to him, but he wanted it sooner rather than later. Maybe his life didn't have to be in perfect order before he found someone to settle down with.

And he certainly wasn't saying he wanted Annabelle and the twins as his family. That would never work even if he'd had those thoughts. But holding Lucy just had him thinking and wondering if he could have it all and throw out the timeline he'd given himself.

Pushing his thoughts aside, he pulled out his phone and shot off a group text to Josh and Ryan. The edging around the landscaping needed trimming and the vet was due this afternoon to check on the steers once again. A fairly simple day, but Colt knew that not every day on the ranch could be predictable. Even if you had plans, sometimes livestock and Mother Nature had other ideas.

Just as he shoved his phone back into his pocket, Annabelle stepped out of the barn. Leading Genesis, she focused that bright green gaze on him. The punch of lust each time she looked at him never lessened. And to know she was untouched only made him ache for her even more.

How had someone so sexy, so damn passionate, gone all this time without giving herself to a man? More important, what type of man had been with her and not been able to pull out that desire? She practically dissolved in a puddle at his feet when he touched her, and he wasn't too proud to admit the feeling was mutual. She did something to him, something that made him want to possess her in a primal way.

"Where to, boss?"

He loved when she called him that. As if she surrendered to his power and fully accepted that he was in charge.

"Mount up and follow me."

He hated that he wouldn't reap the benefits of riding behind her, but she had no idea this little place even existed and he had to be the one to lead the way.

Colt pushed himself back up onto Lightning and set off to the east side of the land.

He called over his shoulder, "It will take us some time to get there, but I promise it will be worth the wait."

"No problem. I'm enjoying the view."

Colt sent her a wink. If she was going to flirt so blatantly, he sure as hell was going to return the gesture. He figured she was doing anything to forget what happened this morning with her father. Whatever had gone on, it must have been something major for her to be so angry when he'd picked her up. She seemed to want to stay mum about it so Colt would have to draw his own conclusions.

He just hoped like hell Neil Carter wasn't gambling again. Not now. Now when Annabelle was literally busting her ass to save his.

After about fifteen minutes, they reached Hayes's

house. It would be good to have his brother home for good. Colt only prayed he managed to adjust to being back and settling into civilian life.

"This is the house your father grew up in?" Annabelle asked.

"My grandfather had it built when he started ranching." Colt pointed to the old oak tree to the side of the house. "That tire swing has seen many years and every Elliott kid. It's just a neat location the way it's tucked between the river and the brook."

This house could tell stories. Colt figured one day Hayes would tear it down to rebuild, and Colt couldn't blame him, but he hoped he'd keep it and just put his home on another section of the ranch.

"I love this house."

Annabelle's wistful tone had him smiling. She appreciated the finer things, and he didn't mean expensive. She saw the beauty in everything. His ex, on the other hand, had had a taste for pricey, designer clothing, flashy cars, trips all over. He didn't mind pampering the woman in his life, but he expected he'd be her top priority…not his bank account.

"We can stop here." Colt made sure the horses were in the shade beneath one of the large oaks before looping the reins around the hooks. "We'll walk to the place I want to show you."

When he looked back, Annabelle was staring down at him, her head tilted in question. Colt crossed the distance between them and extended his hand.

"Trust me."

The two words were so simple, yet so complex, considering their relationship. She shouldn't trust him. She should hate him with every ounce of her being. He wished things were different, he wished she'd never come back into the picture because taking things from Neil didn't bother Colt's conscience one bit. But knowing he was going to take the land that was the foundation for Annabelle's dream…that twisted something inside of him that he didn't want to face.

Part of him couldn't help but wonder what his father would think. His dad had been determined to make this dude ranch a reality, but he was also a family man first.

Damn it. Colt couldn't think like that. He and Annabelle couldn't be more even if that's what he wanted. Once she discovered the truth, she'd hate him.

Annabelle slid her leg over the side of the horse and Colt gripped her waist to help her down. He stepped closer behind her, aligning their bodies perfectly.

"Is this why you brought me out here alone?" she asked, turning her face just enough for him see her half-grin.

"I've never brought a woman to my brother's house for sex." That much was completely true. "What I have to show you is in the back."

Without asking, he took her hand in his and led her around the side of the house.

"Oh, my word," she gasped. "It's beautiful."

The river curved around the property as if framing it with crystal clear water. An old stone outbuilding sat right on the riverbank at the edge of the property. The original stone wall ran along the edge of the property line.

"It's peaceful. I figured you could use some of that in your life."

Annabelle turned to face him fully, still holding on to his hand. "How do you know when I need anything? Dinner, a nap, a quiet place to relax. I'm going to get fired for not working if you keep this up."

He'd never fire her. And he wasn't sure he wanted to let her go at the end of this three-month period, either. She was a hard worker. Granted, she had her home as motivation, but he was going to hate to lose her.

And not just for the business. Cutting her out of his life would hurt and he'd have to learn to cope with the mess he'd made.

As Annabelle glanced back out onto the water, a strand of hair blew across her bottom lip, and before Colt could think better of it, he swiped it away. His fingertip grazed her mouth, sending a jolt of desire through him.

Her eyes swept back around and met his. "You did bring me out here to seduce me," she murmured.

Colt slipped his hand along her jawline, threading his fingers through her hair. "I didn't. But you've been seducing me since the moment you ran into my fence."

"I don't know what to do."

That whispered admission was the green light he'd been waiting for, the one he hadn't seen coming. But he sure as hell wasn't going to give her time to change her mind.

"Listen to your body," he told her, stepping into her. "What's your body telling you right now?"

A small smile spread across her lips. "That I want your shirt off again."

Colt laughed. "I can deal with that."

He tugged the shirt from his jeans and unbuttoned it, keeping his eyes on hers the entire time. Once he dropped it to the ground, he propped his hands on his hips. The approving once-over she gave him had him ready to rip off the black tank she wore. It was only fair.

"I've never known a man to look so hot in just a hat, jeans, and boots."

He didn't know what to say to that, so he slid his fingertips up her bare arms. "How slow do we need to take this?" he asked. "Because I don't want you scared and you deserve to get full enjoyment."

She shivered beneath his touch. "I'm enjoying this pretty well right now."

Oh, she was going to be so damn fun. His body trembled with need. He wanted this woman more than anyone he'd ever been with. He didn't know if it was the thrill of being her first or just the fact that this was Annabelle. Probably both. But he wasn't going to waste time in his head analyzing his every thought.

He had a woman to strip.

"Just…tell me if I do something wrong. Okay?"

Colt stilled. There was a hesitation to her voice that he didn't like.

"Are you sure about this?" he asked. "Because I don't want you to feel pressured. You have to want this as much as I do or we're done."

She reached down, tugged on the hem of her tank, and flung the garment over her head. Standing before him in a plain white bra and jeans with her hair around her shoulders, Colt had never seen a sexier sight.

"I'm nervous, but I know what I want," she told him. "So do what you want to me and I'll tell you if it's too much. Deal?"

Do what he wanted? Oh, hell yes, that was a deal.

Unable to wait another second, Colt slid his hands around the dip in her waist and tugged her until she was flush against his chest. Finally. Skin to skin. She was all curves and all his.

Colt captured her mouth and willed himself to slow down. He had an ache for this woman and he couldn't go into this like she'd been his every fantasy for days. He had to take his time, to make sure she got as much pleasure as he could possibly give.

Thirteen

Annabelle had never been so nervous and anxious at the same time. Colt's mouth magically moved over hers. There was an urgency in his kiss, yet she could tell he was restraining himself.

She eased her mouth from his and framed his face. "I'm not fragile. Don't hold back."

His eyes held hers for the briefest of moments before he picked her up. She couldn't help the squeal that escaped her. Instinct had her looping her hands behind his neck and wondering if he was shooting for romance.

This wasn't romance, though. This was nothing more than her finally giving in to a need she'd had for some time and it had never been stronger than with Colt Elliott.

For once, she was going to take exactly what she wanted, when she wanted it. Consequences be damned.

Colt carried her behind the house, his gait a bit off.

"Put me down," she told him.

"In a minute."

"You're limping."

He stopped, holding her so securely against him, and turned his focus to her eyes, her lips. "Sweetness, let me do this right."

Part of her wondered how many times he called other lovers by these names. He'd claimed none, but Colt was a natural charmer. Still, there was something that blossomed inside her at the idea that he only used those terms for her.

Annabelle closed her eyes and rested her head against his shoulder. What was she thinking? This wasn't the pivotal moment that would lead to a happily-ever-after for them.

Colt made her feel sexy and he wanted her. It was all that simple and that wonderful.

He started off again until he came to the riverbank. When he set her down, he nipped at her lips as if he couldn't get enough. Her chest rubbed against his and she couldn't help but arch against him.

"Wait right here," he muttered against her mouth.

He darted back around the house and Annabelle felt rather foolish standing there with her jeans, boots and bra. She waited a minute, wondering where he went, when he finally came back carrying the blanket that had been beneath her horse's saddle.

She couldn't help but laugh. "I figure you didn't plan this or you would've had something already set up."

"I really didn't plan this," he laughed. With a swift jerk, he fanned the blanket out over the ground. "But I'm damn sure not going to let this moment go."

When he turned back and raked his eyes over her, Annabelle had never felt such a jolt in her life. He may as well have touched her with his hands, his mouth. Anticipation curled deep in her stomach.

"Maybe you could help me undress, that would help." She went for the snap on her jeans. "Or maybe we should just—"

"No." Colt closed the space between them and eased her hands aside. "This belongs to me."

"Me, or getting me naked?"

He jerked the snap open, keeping his gaze on hers. "Everything."

Just as she processed his words, he reached behind her and flicked her bra open. Nerves fell away. Colt's intense stare, his passion and need, they all combined to make her forget she should be nervous. Ache replaced her anxiety and she wanted more.

Annabelle toed her boots off and watched as Colt reached for his belt buckle.

"Wait," she told him. "Shouldn't I get to return the favor?"

He shook his head with a laugh. "Honey, if you touch me right now, this will go faster than either of us wants."

"Maybe I'm ready for fast."

Where had that breathy voice come from? Was she seriously that girl? That flirty vixen? Apparently, with Colt she was another person, but this felt so right.

He slid his thumbs inside the waistband of her jeans. As his rough fingertips grazed her skin, Annabelle trembled. Colt jerked her pants down, pulling her panties with them.

When he dropped to his knees and removed the rest of her clothes, Annabelle pulled in a breath and willed herself to remain calm. She certainly didn't want to make a complete fool of herself right now. Between the ache and the nerves, she wasn't sure what to do, what to say.

But when she stood before him naked and Colt remained on his knees, sampling her with his heavy-lidded gaze, Annabelle knew for a fact that she held the control. He was giving her the reins, so to speak.

She dropped to her knees in front of him and curled her hands around his shoulders. "Touch me," she whispered.

Colt cursed his shaky hands. He finally had Annabelle naked before him and he was nervous. He'd never been nervous with a woman before, not even when he was a virgin. He'd always been about pleasuring his partner, being in control.

But with Annabelle, something was different. Something he didn't want to think about. He only wanted Annabelle, right here, right now.

Colt captured her mouth beneath his as he lowered her back to the blanket. Extending his arms to the ground, he caught himself before he could fully put his weight on her. Wrapping her slender arms around his neck, she threaded her fingers through his hair.

Colt pulled back, glancing down at the beauty laid out before him. He came back to his feet and quickly shed the rest of his clothes and boots. Annabelle's eyes roamed over his bare body. That passion he saw in her eyes only amped up his ache for her.

Despite the fact she told him to do anything, Colt had to have some semblance of self-control. He'd never taken an inexperienced woman before.

With her hair fanned out all around her, Annabelle reached for him. Colt grabbed his pants, pulled a condom from his wallet and covered himself. He dropped between her knees, took her hands in his, and stretched her arms above her head. She arched at the adjustment and it was all Colt could do not to devour her.

"You're driving me crazy," she stated through gritted teeth.

"At least I'm not alone," he muttered.

He used his knees to shove her legs wider. His free hand trailed up her inner thigh, instantly causing her to tremble beneath his touch. When he found her center, Annabelle's eyes drifted shut as she let out a moan.

Yes. That's exactly the response he wanted. Her hips tilted, urging him for more. He leaned down, placing his mouth on her stomach and trailing his lips up to her breasts. Her hands jerked beneath his grip as if she wanted loose from her restraints.

"Not so fast," he murmured against her heated skin. "I'm not done and you can't touch me just yet."

"I need…"

"I need," he agreed. "Too much."

So much, that he wasn't about to reveal everything on his mind. Hell, he wasn't even sure what he was thinking because he was trying *not* to think it.

When Colt removed his hand from between her legs, she let out a whimper. She was so ready and he…damn if he wasn't eager to show her what she'd been missing. He wanted to freeze that moment. To lock away this second of her staring up at him with such desire. He'd never felt so wanted before. Definitely not with…

No. He wasn't bringing any other woman into the picture, not even in his mind. Annabelle was perfection. She was his.

Everything else in the outside world didn't exist for him. Not the farm, not the potential dude ranch, not his brothers or even his father. There was nothing, no one but Annabelle.

Releasing her wrists, he placed both of his hands on either side of her face as he settled between her thighs.

"Tell me you're okay with this." Because if she wasn't completely on board, he'd stop. It would kill him, but she called the shots here. "You want me to keep going?"

"Don't even think of leaving me like this," she panted. "Finish what you started."

Music to his ears. Slowly, Colt joined their bodies. He kept his eyes on hers, waiting for a sign that she needed him to stop.

But her eyes merely widened as she bit her lower lip. Her hips jerked up to meet his and a low, sexy groan escaped her. Colt gritted his teeth. The agony of not claiming her the way his body needed to was excruciating. He wanted to gather her up and have her wrap those long, lean legs around his waist as he made her his.

Next time, he vowed. Because there would be a next time.

Annabelle lifted her knees on either side of him as she rocked her hips. "I told you not to hold back."

"I'm hurting you."

Her eyes held his as a smile danced around her mouth. "You're torturing me. I need this. I need you. Now move."

Colt nipped at her lips. "Whatever you say, sweetness."

"Don't—"

He crushed his mouth against hers as her arms looped around his neck. Colt quickened the pace, finally. He relished the sting of her fingertips on his skin. He wanted her to feel, to make him feel. They came together perfectly and she was certainly holding her own.

"Wrap your legs around me," he demanded against her lips. "Now."

As she circled his waist, locking her ankles behind his back, Colt pumped faster. Her little pants and whimpers spurred him on as she matched his rhythm.

"Colt."

"Right here, baby."

Her taut body beneath his trembled, then tightened. She tipped her head back and closed her eyes.

"Look at me," he commanded.

When that green gaze came back to his, Colt tried not to get lost in the depths there. Tried not to see exactly what was staring back at him, because it was definitely more than just sex. There were feelings. Feelings that he sure as hell didn't want to see.

Colt leaned down to run his lips along the side of her neck, across her chest. She cried out his name as her body stilled, her nails biting deeper into his shoulders.

Thrusting again, Colt shattered right along with her. This was exactly what he wanted, what he could control. All the feelings and emotions had no place here.

As her tremors ceased, Colt gathered her close, inhaling her jasmine scent. As much as his instincts told him to flee, he wasn't that big of a jerk. This was her time—he couldn't help if everything he saw in her eyes scared the hell out of him.

He prayed she didn't have some crazy notion that this meant anything more than just sex. He couldn't let her believe they had a future. Acting on their attraction had been inevitable, but he hadn't said anything up front about not getting involved. He had plans, damn it, and they didn't include getting wrapped up in those expressive green eyes.

But there was still that part deep inside him that could want more…with her.

Colt eased to the side, pulling her in his arms. He wasn't one to cuddle, but again, he wasn't about to be a jerk. He just needed to relax and consider his next step.

And that nugget of emotion circling his conscience could shut the hell up.

Fourteen

Colt was already having regrets.

Even though he hadn't said a word, he didn't need to. Annabelle lay against his chest, feeling his heart beat beneath her cheek and Colt was miles away—mentally at least.

His entire body was rigid and she knew he didn't want to be there. Didn't want to be holding her. The pity snuggle was not working for her and she refused to ever be made a fool of by a man again.

Annabelle sat up, causing Colt's arm to fall away. She smoothed her hair back from her face and attempted to radiate confidence she didn't feel. When it came to intimacy, she had zero experience, but her body was still humming… while he was silently stewing beside her.

If he was having regrets or doubts about what had happened, that was on him. Not her problem.

Coming to her feet, Annabelle purposely didn't look back at him. Bad enough she was walking around the riverbank retrieving her clothes, she didn't want to see guilt in his eyes.

What a fool. How could she think a man like Colt Elliott would actually want to be with someone like her?

He'd known exactly how to touch her, what to say, and just how forceful to be.

She'd relished every single moment.

Annabelle jerked her panties on, then wrestled back into her bra. Clutching her jeans to her chest, she whirled around to see him sitting up on the blanket watching her.

"If you're sorry this happened, just keep it to yourself."

Not a care in the world that he was as naked as the day he was born, Colt lifted a knee and propped an arm across it. "I'm not sorry this happened."

"Did I do something wrong?" she asked, heat flooding her cheeks. "Because you're not exactly giving off a vibe like you had a good time."

Like a panther, he rose and stalked toward her. "I had a good time, darlin'. I just didn't want you to get the impression that this meant more than what it was."

It took a second for his words to sink in, but when they did, rage boiled within her.

"Are you kidding me?" she asked, swatting her hand on his bare chest. "You think you show me a good time by the river on your family's property and I'm going to be head over heels in love with you? You do have quite the ego, Colt. I'm not going to start planning our wedding, so relax."

She hated to admit, even to herself, that she could see herself falling for him. She hadn't gotten there, yet, but it could happen. Still, the fact that he was afraid of it happening pissed her off. Like he was some gift to women because of his magical penis.

"Listen, if you have a problem, don't put it on me," she stated, still holding on to her jeans like a shield. "This wasn't what I expected when I left the house this morning, but it definitely got my mind off my problems."

"That's it?" he asked, one brow quirking. "You're glad I

could help you push aside your problems for a while? Don't downplay the joys of your first experience."

Strike one to that ego.

"The sex was great. Is that what you want to hear?"

He wrapped an arm around her waist and hauled her body to his. With his free hand he jerked her jeans away and flung them aside. That cool power and confident strength was too damn sexy.

"That's exactly what I want to hear."

Oh, that low tone could get her aroused in less than a second. And he knew it, too.

"We're going to do this again." He slid his mouth back and forth over hers as he spoke. "Whenever I can get you alone again, you'll be mine."

She had to grip his biceps to hold herself upright. "What makes you think I want to do this again?"

Colt eased his hand between them and palmed one of her breasts. His thumb raked back and forth over her thin bra. "Because I can have you squirming and panting in no time. And because we're not done with each other."

The moment was getting too intense and she needed to regain her composure. She patted the side of his cheek. "I'll let you have sex with me again, but if you go and fall in love, don't say I didn't warn you. I'm quite a catch."

The muscle in his jaw ticked as his eyes dropped to her mouth. She had no clue what was going through his head, but he clearly didn't like the idea of love. Well, that made two of them.

They dressed quietly and found their shirts around the front of the house by the horses. Colt threw her blanket back on Genesis before adjusting the saddle back in place.

As they rode back, all the issues awaiting her flooded her mind. If only life were as perfect as it had been moments ago on the riverbank. Annabelle couldn't even enjoy the euphoria because of the crap storm life had thrown her way.

Since her father was clearly gambling again, she had no idea how she was going to make everything work. He'd ring up more debts, and she'd have to bail him out. That was the cycle and she could only be stretched so thin. She knew gambling, as with any addiction, was a difficult habit to break. But she'd truly hoped losing a daughter and having to borrow money from the neighbor to pay off the mortgage would've slapped some sense into him.

Apparently not.

Annabelle's first priority was making sure Colt got every penny owed to him. She couldn't be her father's keeper and worry about his actions. "Once I get the house paid off, do you think I could continue to work for you until I find something else?"

Putting her pride aside was a bitter pill to swallow. The timing of her question was beyond tacky, but she had no shame at this point. She'd slept with her boss…what was the protocol?

"There's always work to be done on the ranch," he replied easily. "But I figured you'd want to take some time off to be with your girls."

Her girls. Yeah, they were hers. She'd come to think of them as her own and obviously Colt saw that, as well. And sure, in an ideal world where she wasn't broke she could take time off to spend with her family, but these weren't exactly typical circumstances.

"I've got too many bills to take time off."

Silence settled between them before he spoke up again. "Your father is gambling again, isn't he?"

Instantly, tears clogged her throat. She didn't want the world to know her father couldn't keep it together for his family. She despised that he was seen as weak and she resented having to clean up his messes. But the reality was, he had an addiction and she couldn't heal him.

"He took some money from my purse," she muttered, hating how saying those words made her heart ache—hating even more that she had to face the cold reality. "We argued about it this morning."

Great. She'd shared her body with him and now she felt it necessary to open her heart. She didn't want Colt, or anyone else, to know the details of her father's downfall.

She stole a glance at him, noticing his white-knuckled grip on the reins, the firm set of his jaw.

"Anyway, I've just got more on my plate than I'd hoped for," she went on. "But don't keep me at Pebblebrook out of pity. I'd rather be broke. Besides, I'm sure there are several places in town that are hiring. I worked at an upscale bakery before, so if I could do something along those lines, that would be—"

"You'll stay on at Pebblebrook as long as you want."

His low, commanding tone silenced her. Okay, then. At least that was something. It wasn't the position she dreamed of, but it paid and Colt understood her need to be near Emily and Lucy. If she could just get her bearings and keep her head above water, maybe she'd see the light at the end of the tunnel.

And maybe she'd quit thinking in cheesy clichés, as well.

"Tell me about your brothers," she threw out there. With all the intensity of the day, Annabelle needed normal. Just a simple conversation.

"I know their professions, but why don't they want to be cowboys like you?"

She kept her eyes on the horizon. Pasture as far as the eye could see. In the distance, the tip of the main barn near Colt's house guided their direction.

"Nolan loves the ranch," Colt stated. "He's swamped

with the hospital and he's always taking on more shifts. But he helps where he can."

"You have to be pretty proud of what all of your brothers have accomplished. And I'm sure they're proud of you for keeping all of this running so flawlessly. It's the greatest ranch I've ever seen."

Colt laughed. "I am proud, but it wasn't that long ago you were bashing me and praising them for being nicer and giving back to society."

A sliver of guilt spiraled through her. But, in her defense, that was before she'd developed feelings for Colt.

Oh, no. She was falling for her boss. Was *boss* even the correct term? Landlord? Virginity taker?

Regardless of the label, Annabelle's emotions were calling the shots and now she'd gone and slept with the man. But she wouldn't have been intimate with him if she didn't care for him. And she was starting to care. A lot.

"I think what you've done here at Pebblebrook is amazing."

His thigh brushed against hers as they rode side by side. "I can't take the credit for something my grandfather started and my father carried on."

"No, but you can take credit for keeping up the tradition and loving this land and these animals like they deserve."

She squinted against the sun and tried not to let that random touch throw her off. It was rather difficult to ride back to work like he hadn't just removed her wall of defense and changed her life. No matter what happened at the end of their agreement, or how long she stayed on at Pebblebrook, Colt Elliott would always be her first lover.

"If I owned this land, I'd never want to leave," she added. "It's so peaceful, so perfect."

"That's why I'm here," he told her. "I travel to get away, but I'm always eager to come back home."

As they neared the barn, Annabelle wondered how she

was going to be productive when her body still tingled. He'd blatantly told her that their encounter was not a one-time thing. Fine by her because she was more than ready to have that strong body pressed to hers again. When she'd pictured her first experience she'd been married, in a bed, wearing some sexy lingerie she'd purchased for just that occasion.

Instead, she'd been deliciously ravaged on a riverbank before her first cup of coffee.

"I like that smile on your face."

Colt's statement pulled her from her thoughts, and made her realize she had indeed been smiling.

"Makes me think you and I are both having the same thoughts," he added.

"I'm sure we are," she agreed with a slight laugh. "But right now I need to work so I can pay off the rest of my house. So, what are we getting into today?"

Colt's expression sobered. "Actually, I need to run an errand. I'm going to have you take it fairly easy today and clean out the stalls. I'll have Ryan pull down the extra hay from the loft."

"I can do that." How weak did he think she was? "I'm here to work, Colt. Stop coddling me."

He slowed Lightning down, so she pulled Genesis to a stop. When he tipped his hat up and flashed those killer baby blues her way, Annabelle's heart rate skyrocketed.

Is this how it would be each time he looked at her, now that they'd been intimate?

"I'm not coddling you, sweetness." He reached across and placed his hand high upon her thigh. "I don't want you worn-out because I have plans for you later."

Oh. That promise had her heart in her throat, her body responding. Yes, she was slowly falling for him when she had sworn she wouldn't. Sex clearly had messed with her mind.

"I won't be worn-out," she told him. "I'm sure Ryan has plenty to do without babysitting me and doing part of my job. I've got it covered."

A naughty smile crept over him. "If you're too tired, I guess I'll just get to do all the touching."

"Oh, I won't be that tired, cowboy."

And apparently sex made her a little saucier, too. Who knew?

Fifteen

Once Colt left Annabelle to take care of their horses and get to work, he sent a text to Ryan and Josh to check in on her throughout the day. She wouldn't appreciate it, but too damn bad. He couldn't worry about her and concentrate on this last-minute issue at the same time.

Colt drove a short distance from Pebblebrook and willed himself to calm down. He gripped the wheel, his knuckles turning white. There was too much anger, too much rage and guilt. That last one was on him, but the first two were on another man in Annabelle's life and Colt refused to sit back and watch her have to deal with more pain.

He glanced at the place that would soon be his and the guilt intensified. No, that was the sex talking. He was just feeling the aftershocks of having Annabelle wrapped all around him. He couldn't let those sultry eyes and passion-filled kisses deter him from reaching his goal. He would make sure she had a home, something nice and perfect for her business. But this one was perfect for this business he wanted.

Colt's anger still hadn't eased by the time he pulled up near the porch, but he would keep his head on straight, because Annabelle and her girls were the victims here.

Damn it. There was no way not to hurt Annabelle. But he could make the pain less intense.

He rang the doorbell and took a step back. After a minute, Neil Carter opened the old oak door, with the puppy right at his feet. He didn't offer to open the screen—as if that thin partition would keep Colt from business he had with the old man.

"We need to talk," Colt stated.

"Then talk."

He was going to be difficult. Colt didn't know why he thought this would be a simple trip. How could someone as sweet as Annabelle come from someone as cold and self-centered as Neil?

And there went that flare-up of guilt once again. Because Colt knew full well that he was self-centered…otherwise he wouldn't be so dead set on owning this property.

"I'm going to pay off your gambling debts," Colt announced. "Give me the names and contact information. And if I hear of you gambling anymore after that, I'll personally make sure Annabelle knows every last detail of how many times you've borrowed from my family over the years."

Neil crossed his arms over his chest, but before he could utter a word, one of the babies' cries sounded through the house. Neil turned from the door and marched away, the loyal pup on his heels. Colt wasted no time in letting himself inside. With his hand behind him, he caught the screen door before it could slam shut. The anxious puppy turned back around and ran toward Colt, sliding along the hardwood floors and bumping into the toe of his boot.

Colt reached down and petted the little guy and wondered if Annabelle had come up with a name yet. He'd ask her later, but right now, he had some unpleasant business to take care of.

Like any gentleman, Colt removed his hat and hung it

on the peg by the door, and then he proceeded to follow
the cries into the living room. He walked slowly, careful
not to trip or step on the bouncing dog.

Neil picked up one of the girls from some portable
pen—Colt believed they were called Pack 'n Plays. They'd
both been laying in their side-by-side, chewing on matching pink teethers.

Colt couldn't tell which twin Neil was holding, but he
looked closely and thought it might be Lucy. One of them
had thicker hair, but that was the only difference he'd noticed. Both girls were like mini-versions of Annabelle.

Lucy continued to whimper, but when she spotted Colt,
she reached her arms toward him.

Okay. That was extremely unexpected. He'd held her the
other night and fed her, but he didn't realize she'd already
know who he was. Neil tossed a glance over his shoulder,
reluctant to hand the baby over.

Colt stepped forward and took Lucy from Neil's arms.
Her crying ceased as she sniffed and stared at his hair. He
figured it was a sweaty mess between his morning activity on the riverbank and riding with his hat on.

"I see you've made an impression on my granddaughter,
as well," Neil stated, clearly irritated. "And I don't need
you or anyone else to take care of my debts."

"No?" Colt retorted, throwing Neil a sidelong glance.
"Because as I see it, your daughter is busting her butt to
pay off this house because you couldn't. And when my
portion is paid back, she has to continue to work like a
dog because she's still trying to save you and now raise
twins on top of that."

Colt kept his tone somewhat light because he didn't
want to scare the baby. One of her pudgy hands patted
the side of his face and Colt couldn't help but smile at
her. Those green eyes were going to bring a man to his
knees one day.

"I don't need an Elliott taking care of my family," Neil growled. "And whatever you think you're doing with my daughter, she's smarter than to fall for your charms."

Colt wisely kept his opinion on that topic to himself.

"If you would man up, nobody would have to take care of your family."

Colt patted Lucy's back when she laid her head on his shoulder. The innocence of this child humbled him. One day he'd have a baby of his own, raise children on his ranch, and have a wife who shared his passion for the farm. A vision of Annabelle sprang to mind but he quickly vanquished it.

"So far, Annabelle is the only one working toward securing a future for all of you."

Neil's eyes narrowed. "What did she tell you?"

Oh, he wasn't throwing her under the bus. Hell, no. He was there to protect her from all angles…well, except his own agenda. That he couldn't help.

"She didn't have to tell me anything," Colt replied. "I can see how exhausted she is when she comes to the ranch. She gives it her all and then comes here to take care of you guys. There's only so much a person can take before they break and I won't see that happen to her."

"Is that so?" Neil crossed his arms over his chest and shifted his stance. "Why the sudden interest in my Belle? I won't have her hurt."

Something Neil should've thought of before he made the bargain with the Carter ranch and then signed documents he didn't fully read.

"You ever tell her about the jewelry?" Colt threw out.

"No," Neil ground out. "And you don't need to, either. That time has passed. I'm not proud of what I did."

"Passed?" Colt repeated. "You're telling me that you have completely stopped gambling? With no help at all?"

"How do you know I haven't had help?"

Colt merely raised his brows. Lucy's sweet breath tickled the side of his neck. From the steady rhythm, he'd guess she'd fallen asleep. What was it like to be so trusting and innocent?

Annabelle was exactly the same way. She'd trusted the wrong people: her father, her sister, her fiancé… Colt.

"Did you come here to berate me or just rub it in my face that you've gotten close with my daughter and granddaughters?"

"I came here so you'd realize what you have. You lost one daughter and your other one is here, ready to do anything to make her family work. Is that not enough for you to want to be a better man?"

Neil's lips thinned as he continued to glare at Colt. He didn't care if Neil was pissed, Colt was pretty much boiling since Annabelle had told him her father took money from her purse. Clearly, Neil had an illness, but Annabelle shouldn't have to endure the same struggle. She was trying to restore her life, yet she couldn't even move forward for worry over her father and his ongoing issues.

Damn it. He hadn't planned on getting personally involved. That plan obviously went to hell. Between that kick-ass attitude layered over vulnerability and her loyalty to her family, how could Colt ignore the tug of emotions Annabelle brought to life? But he couldn't allow those emotions to cloud his judgment.

His father had big plans, plans that Colt was to carry out. Colt always made good on his promises. With his father in the nursing facility, there was no way in hell Colt would let him down. Still, that niggle of doubt kept creeping up on him lately. Grant Elliott had always prided himself on being a family man first and foremost. Colt wanted that family life, but he couldn't sacrifice his promise to his father…could he?

If he'd met Annabelle under different circumstances,

gotten to know her, date her...but he hadn't. There was nothing but sex between them and when she found out about the legal documents, that would be gone. Even so, Colt would make sure she was taken care of.

Neil closed the distance between them and eased Lucy from Colt's arms. Lucy was indeed fast asleep, while Emily remained fully entertained across the room. Neil cradled Lucy against his chest and stared down at her.

"I'm doing what I can," he murmured. "And after this debt is paid, we won't need your help anymore."

Colt wasn't about to argue. He'd made his point and if Neil didn't want help, then so be it. But that didn't mean Colt wouldn't look out for Annabelle and her babies.

He let himself out the door and climbed back into his truck. He was on borrowed time where Annabelle was concerned. He couldn't go against his family and decades of wishes. Maybe on some level, she would understand that.

Regardless, he wanted her again. He wanted to see her, to touch her. He had a feeling today's workday might just be cut short.

Annabelle swiped the sweat from her forehead with the back of her arm. Ranch life was no joke. No wonder Colt had muscles like that of a calendar model. He'd earned each and every taut bulge.

Finally, the stalls were clean. As if anything in this immaculate barn was ever dirty. Still, she took pride in her position, in the animals. They were such beautiful creatures and deserved to be treated as such.

As she pushed the broom down the stone walkway between the stalls, familiar arms banded around her waist. Instantly she found herself hauled back against a broad chest.

"Sir, I'm working here and there are other employees that could see us."

"Those employees are nowhere near this side of the property and your boss sent me to find you," Colt whispered in her ear. "He said it's time for you to call it a day and meet him at the main house."

Annabelle dropped the broom and turned in his arms. "It's only two o'clock."

Colt shrugged. "Boss's orders, ma'am."

He stepped back and winced slightly. Annabelle reached for him, but he held his hands out.

"It's nothing," he assured her. "I've been riding more than usual and not soaking at the end of the day like I should."

"And you talk about me taking care of myself?"

"Touché."

"Seriously, I need to work. I've only put in about four hours today."

Colt shot her that side grin that never failed to curl her toes. Stupid charming man. Why did she have to be so easily swayed by a dashing smile and a sexy body? Hadn't she learned her lesson the first time a hot guy showed her attention? She'd ended up with his ring on her finger. That incident left her scarred, hollow. But Colt was different. He was loyal to those he cared for.

Never in her life would she have thought that she'd be half in love with an Elliott. Who knows, after this debt was paid off…maybe they could date and see where things went. She wasn't going anywhere and he obviously wasn't, either.

"This will count as a full day's work. You've earned it."

Annabelle reached down to pick up the broom and leaned against it. "Let's say I come up to your house."

"Which you will."

She bit the inside of her cheek to keep from smiling at his confidence, which made him too damn irresistible for his own good. "Let's say that I do. What about Winnie and Charlie? Where are they?"

Colt shrugged. "I'm not positive. I imagine Winnie is in the kitchen preparing some feast for the guys. Charlie is actually out at a ranch in Calhoun County because we're hoping to do some business with them. I sent him because his daughter knows the family there."

Annabelle weighed her options. If her tingly body would shut up, she'd be able to think a little clearer.

"So what do you tell Winnie when I come up to the house and…"

"To my bedroom?" he asked, quirking a dark brow beneath his black hat. "She'd probably throw a party, but to save your reputation, I can sneak you in the back door. She'll never know you're there."

He made things sound so simple, so perfectly tempting. Colt Elliott's bedroom was only a "yes" away and she stood here contemplating her move. What woman did that?

A woman who'd been burned and was falling in love.

Just that morning she'd made some grand speech on the riverbank, naked as a jaybird, about how she wasn't going to fall for him and he had nothing to worry about.

Liar, liar. It had only been a few hours and she'd analyzed their situation to death. He wanted her land, she wanted him. That pretty much summed up their crazy status in a nice, neat, jam-packed package.

"If you have to think that hard, maybe I didn't do my job earlier today."

Oh, he'd done his job…if his job was to make her fantasize about him all day and watch the opening of the barn for that familiar silhouette. Every time an animal shifted or she heard something, she'd jerked her gaze to that wide-open bay. It was rather schoolgirlish how quickly she'd become infatuated.

Was it the sex? She truly didn't think so. She'd been

turned on and intrigued by him since day one, when he'd been nothing but a shirtless stranger.

"Maybe you should show me again just as a reminder," she said, pleased when his bright eyes darkened with arousal.

Good. She wanted to affect him the way he did her. She hoped he thought of her today when they were apart. And, no, she didn't care if that was naive. She had to be honest with herself, if no one else.

"Where did you go today?" she asked.

Colt lifted one broad shoulder. "My day wasn't near as important as my afternoon is about to be."

Sixteen

Colt didn't bring women back to his home, and he sure as hell didn't sneak them through the back door and into his bedroom. The entire third floor made up his domain. He had a balcony off the front and back so he could see the acreage which had been handed down to him...which had been entrusted to him.

So the fact that Annabelle now stood staring out through the back double doors had Colt stilling in the middle of his suite. That long, red hair spiraled down her back. She typically kept it up, but sometime between their morning activities and now, she'd let it all down. He preferred it down, preferred it between his fingers and sliding over his skin.

"I don't know how you ever leave this room in the mornings. I bet the sunrises are amazing."

It was on the tip of his tongue to invite her to see it sometime, but that would require a commitment he couldn't make. Still, he could see it. Annabelle in one of his T-shirts and nothing else, standing just like she was now after a night of lovemaking. He was certain it was an image he would return to long after he revealed the truth and she cut him out of her life for good. Why was that thought becoming more and more agonizing?

Annabelle spun around, her hair dancing about her bare shoulders. She did amazing things to tank tops.

"I should warn you that I've been in horse stalls all day." She wrinkled her nose and damn if it wasn't the most adorable thing he'd ever seen. "I'm not sure what you got into, but you still seem fairly clean, like your deodorant is still working."

Colt laughed. He did that more with her than he had in years. She was unaware of her appeal, she spoke her mind and she was a hard worker. How could a man not find that charming and sexy?

"You're in luck," he told her as he crossed the room. "I happen to love the smell of my ranch."

She rolled her eyes. "You're really a terrible liar."

Actually, he thought he was a stellar one...which was where that guilt kept creeping in from.

He took her hands in his and squeezed, pulling her against his chest. "You're also in luck that I have a shower built for twenty with jetted sprays and three rain heads."

She raised her brows. "A shower? You mean...you're going to shower in the middle of the day?"

"With you," he added, with a smile as her mouth fell open and her eyes widened. "You need to clean up and I need the heat on my hip. It's a win-win."

"I've never...I mean, that just seems so intimate and..." She narrowed her eyes. "Are you laughing?"

Colt pursed his lips and shook his head. "Not at all."

"Terrible liar," she muttered.

"Then maybe I should use my mouth for more important things."

Before he could ease forward, she took a step back and let go of his hands. "Seriously, Colt. I'm not feeling very attractive right now."

Heat speared him. "You spent the day working on my

ranch, tending to my animals. That's the sexiest thing I've seen in a long time."

She tipped her head to the side, her eyes softening. "You take so much pride in this place. It shows."

"It's my life," he stated simply.

When a sadness swept over her features, Colt wasn't having any part of that. Not here, not now, when he wanted her with a need he couldn't even identify.

Reaching behind his back, he jerked his T-shirt up and over his head. There. That's what he wanted to see. Annabelle's eyes locked on his bare torso. Needing to keep her in the moment, he went for his belt buckle.

"If you really want out of those smelly clothes, you could remove them," he suggested.

Her hands shook as she reached for the hem of her tank. Even after this morning she was nervous, or maybe in spite of it. Colt figured she knew exactly what to expect now and fear was getting to her.

Damn it. That was worse than seeing her slip into unhappiness about her current life situation.

"Tell me what you want, sweetheart." He toed off his worn boots and shucked his jeans and boxer briefs. "I'm here for you."

Annabelle finished undressing until she was standing before him just as bare as he was. "I want to see this promised shower that will fulfill my every need."

Colt reached out, snaking an arm around her to pull her into his body. "That would be my job. You have a need, I'll be the one meeting it."

"You might want me to rinse off before you join me," she stated, placing her hands on his shoulders.

Colt turned her toward his bathroom and smacked her rear end. "I'll be the one to wash you, darlin'. Now let's go."

* * *

Annabelle's jaw dropped. "This should have another name besides something so simple as a shower."

The walk-in area could indeed hold twenty, she was positive. His bathroom was the size of her entire living room. The all-glass shower with glass tile floor was something from a magazine, as was the rest of his home. How was she ever going to just move on like none of this ever happened?

Colt stepped inside and turned on all the various sprayers. Good grief. Who thought up such necessities? And this was a necessity. She'd give up nearly anything to have a shower like this one.

Annabelle followed him inside and instantly groaned at the glorious heat spraying her from all angles.

"Okay, now I know for sure I'd never leave this room if I lived here. The shower, the view. If I could get food delivered, this would be my very own domain."

"Winnie would be more than happy to—"

She whirled around, shoving her wet hair back from her face. "Winnie will not know I was here in the middle of the day."

Colt laughed as he reached for her. "I'm a bit sore, so you may have to take the lead."

Wrapping her arms around his waist, Annabelle was surprised how easy this felt. How right.

But it wasn't right, was it? He wanted her land, she wanted to fulfill her mother's dream. So they were at a standstill.

"Tell me what to do," she murmured, focusing on the here and now.

Colt grazed his lips along her jawline and up to her ear. "Listen to what your body wants. I guarantee it will match what mine is telling me."

She went up onto her toes to kiss him. Curling her

fingers around his shoulders, she backed him toward the bench running along the back wall. His mouth devoured hers and it was all she could do not to climb all over him.

Everything between them had escalated at an alarming speed, but she couldn't stop...didn't want to stop. Colt had becoming a craving and she wasn't going to deprive herself. She deserved happiness, even if it was only temporary.

Annabelle eased her mouth away and pushed on Colt's shoulders, silently urging him to have a seat. As he sat, he raked his hands down her sides, grazing her breasts as he went.

She stepped back out of his reach and glanced around. She spotted the soap and shampoo on the built-in shelf on the adjacent wall. An idea sparked and then fully engulfed her mind. She was going to be daring and seductive, she hoped. If she could drive him out of his mind half as much as he had done to her, this afternoon shower session would be a success.

Annabelle grabbed the shampoo and squirted some into her hand. As she lathered her hair, she made sure to get a good arch in her back, thrusting her chest in Colt's direction...and she was pretty sure she'd heard a groan escape him.

Tipping her head back, she rinsed the shampoo away, suds gliding down her body. She shot him a wink and a smile as she went back for the soap. With no washcloth in sight, she squeezed some soap into her hands and lathered them up before sliding it over her arms, her legs, her torso.

Each slow stroke was like torture. She wanted his hands on her, but the way he was squirming on that bench, his piercing gaze locked on her every move, Annabelle knew it was only a matter of time before he snapped.

Anticipation flooded her.

"Enough."

Colt's harsh demand had Annabelle jerking around to

face him fully. His body was tight, shoulders squared, jaw set, and those eyes held hers as if he'd reached out and touched her.

"Come here."

Water hit her from all around as she made her way back across the shower. Annabelle came to stand between his legs, and his hands instantly gripped her waist.

"I think you're clean enough for what I have in mind."

Arousal spiraled low in her belly.

"I didn't bring any protection in here with me," he told her. "But I've never gone without and I guarantee I'm clean."

Even though she'd been a virgin up until this morning, she'd been on birth control since she was twenty.

"I'm safe," she assured him.

His eyes darkened as he raked them over her bare chest, her torso, between her thighs. As his gaze traveled back up, she shivered and braced her hands on his shoulders. Colt urged her forward and she placed her knees on either side of his hips.

"I want nothing between us," he muttered.

Slowly, Annabelle joined their bodies. At the onslaught of sensations, her head fell back. Colt reached around, gripping her wet hair and pulling just enough. Her body went into action as she couldn't stay still another second.

As he tugged on her hair, his mouth closed over one breast and Annabelle didn't know how long she could hold out. The sprays hit her from the back, the side, and Colt's hands and mouth were assaulting her in the most delicious ways.

"That's it," he urged.

Apparently he knew her body better than she did because she instantly tightened around him as pleasure tore through her.

Colt flattened his palms against her back, captured her

mouth and crushed her entire body against him as if he wanted to completely absorb her. The tip of his tongue parted her lips, and everything inside Annabelle exploded. Colt stiffened beneath her as he tore his mouth away and rested his forehead to hers. His fingertips dug into her back as his own release consumed him.

Moments later, when the trembling had ceased and the water continued to caress them, Annabelle kept her eyes closed. She didn't want to face reality. She didn't want Colt to look in her eyes because of what he'd see. She'd fallen for him. Completely. She had no idea how she would continue to work for him and keep this secret.

But she had no choice. They were on opposite ends of life's spectrum and he'd made it clear that this was nothing more than sex. Too bad her heart didn't get that memo.

Seventeen

"I was engaged before." Colt laid that declaration between them as they dressed after the shower. "You're the only other woman I've ever had in this house."

Annabelle squeezed her hair into a plush towel, but her eyes remained on his. "I didn't think you were a monk, Colt. Besides, this is just physical, right? I don't need to know your history."

Wearing only his jeans, Colt crossed the spacious bathroom until he stood before her. He pulled the towel from her hands, grasped her hair, and proceeded to rub the dripping ends of crimson.

"I believe we both know this escalated into more than just sex." As much as he didn't want it to, and as much as these damn emotions complicated everything, there was no denying the fact that Annabelle had gotten to him. "I don't know what to call it, or if we even need a label, but I like being with you even outside the bedroom."

"Like on a riverbank?" she asked, a half smile curving over her swollen lips.

Tossing the towel aside, he curled his fingers around the back of her neck and brought his forehead to hers. "Everywhere. I like you in my barns, on my horses, the

way you look at my land. I just, I don't know how to explain it all."

Annabelle looped her arms around his neck. "I've only
really known you for less than a week," she stated. "I
knew Matt for a year, was engaged to him, but I never
felt like this."

His ego, which she'd claimed was inflated, grew even
more at her words. Warmth spread through him, knowing that there was a strong undercurrent of emotions running through her, as well. But how the hell did he go about
this without totally screwing everything up? How did he
keep the land and the woman once all was said and done?

Maybe she never had to know about the documents.
Perhaps now that their connection was growing deeper,
he could use that momentum.

This was crazy. One of the most reckless decisions he'd
ever made, but in order to have it all, it was his only option.

Colt framed her face, tipping her head up so he could
see those gorgeous green eyes. "Move in with me."

Her chest pressed against his as she pulled in a gasp.
That unpainted mouth dropped into a perfect O. He wasn't
going to give her a chance to turn him down.

"You can take your time finding a job you like or keep
working at Pebblebrook," he went on. "I don't care. But I
want you here in my house, in my bed."

"But…but I have six-month-old twins," she muttered,
as if thinking aloud of reasons she shouldn't agree.

"I didn't expect you to come alone. There's even plenty
of room for your dad if he wants to join us. I have eight
bedrooms on the second floor. The master is plenty large
enough for cribs."

What was he saying? Was he really willing to play
house to ensure that her land remained his and she would
never know what he'd done?

Yes. And in his defense, some of his motives were completely selfish, but he truly wanted to spare Annabelle any more hurt. She'd been through so much, too much, and all at the hands of people she'd trusted.

And she trusted him with the most important aspect of her life. No way could he betray her now. Seeing her in pain, knowing he'd caused it, would be like a knife to his heart.

She closed her eyes and blew out a sigh. "Colt, this is all so much to take in. I don't trust my feelings right now."

Colt took her hand, placed it over his bare chest and flattened it with his own. "You feel me, feel us. I'm not asking for anything more than you to live here and give this a shot."

"I'm adjusting from so much," she whispered, tears pricking her eyes. "I lost my sister, a man I thought I trusted. My finances are a joke and I'm learning how to be a mom."

"All the more reason for you to come here. Finances will never be an issue." Colt would make it his personal mission to keep her father out of trouble. "And Winnie would be happy to help you care for the girls. In fact, she'd love it."

"And you?" she asked, her eyes hopeful.

"I've always wanted a family and kids." That was absolutely true. He just never thought they'd land in his path like this. "This place was made for children."

"You want kids of your own?" she asked, then shook her head. "That was a silly question. You asked me to move in, not bear your children."

An image of her pregnant with his baby ripped something open in him. Yeah, he did want children and if he had them with Annabelle, he knew they'd be strong-willed, independent kids who could take on the ranch in the years to come.

Was he…no. He wasn't falling in love. Was he?

He'd vowed to keep deeper emotions separate, but that

simply wasn't possible anymore. Still, she couldn't find out about the paperwork her father signed. Colt refused to be the one to destroy her life once again.

"I don't want to get hurt."

She blinked back her tears, and Colt knew in that moment, he'd do anything to keep her safe.

And he also knew then that he had fallen for her. How had this happened? Within days he'd gone on such a roller coaster ride of emotions with her, Colt didn't know when his control had started to slip.

Perhaps all of his power transferred over to her the moment she plowed into the fence and stared at him as if she wanted to mount him right in his driveway. Because from the start, Annabelle had held the proverbial reins. She'd pulled him into her world and he knew now that he wanted to stay.

"If you need to think about it, that's fine," he told her, knowing someone like Annabelle didn't make rash decisions. "I'm not going anywhere."

"I need to pay off my father's debt," she told him. "How would we work that out? I mean, I'd feel a little weird paying you and sleeping in your bed. Assuming that's where you'd want me."

Colt wrapped his arms around her waist, filling his hands with her backside. "My bed is the only option for you."

When she went up onto her toes and covered his lips with her own, Colt knew she'd already made her decision. She may not have voiced it yet, but she would.

He would have everything he wanted and nobody had to get hurt. A burst of relief spread through him as he captured her lips, but a shrill ring from the bedroom broke the moment.

Annabelle pulled away and rushed in to answer the call. Colt grabbed his shirt and pulled it over his head.

"I'll be right there."

He noticed Annabelle's worried tone as she slid the cell into her pocket. "I have to go," she told him.

"What's wrong? Is it the girls?"

She shook her head, glancing around the room for her boots. Pulling one from beneath the bed skirt and one from the other side of the bed, she hopped on one foot then the other to pull them on.

"Dad didn't say. He just said he needed me home right now."

Fear pushed through him as he grabbed his own phone from his dresser and followed her out of the bedroom. They hurried out the back door of the house, just the same way they'd come in. Silence accompanied them as he drove her back home in his truck.

Colt had barely pulled to a stop in front of her porch when he recognized the silver SUV in the drive. His heart sank.

"Annabelle, wait."

But she was already out of his truck and running toward the door. That future he'd just secured only moments ago in his bedroom was about to blow up in his face.

And that vow to keep Annabelle from getting hurt by his actions? Well, he was getting a front row seat to an epic debacle and there wasn't a damn thing he could do about it.

"What's wrong?" Annabelle asked the second she stepped through the front door. "Where are the babies?"

She took in so much at once. Her father stood in the middle of the foyer with a stranger. The puppy was bouncing between everyone like he'd just found new friends.

"I just laid them down for a nap," her father replied. "It seems this engineer was hired by Colt to do some work on the house."

"I'm only here to take a quick look around," the stranger

replied as he turned his attention toward her. "My name is Sam Stevens. I work for the Elliott family. They gave me this address and I just came to do a quick survey. I wasn't aware people were living here."

Confusion settled deep as she tried to grasp what was happening. And all of this was on the coattails of Colt asking her to move in with him.

Annabelle crossed her arms over her chest and addressed Sam. "What exactly did Colt ask you to do here?"

The engineer had a clipboard in his hand and held it up for her to see a long list of items. "Various renovations. But I can come back at a better time."

"We don't need you to come back," Neil chimed in.

"I'll take care of this."

Annabelle turned to see Colt standing in the doorway. She was still perplexed at why this man was here, but the guilt written on Colt's face painted a clearer picture.

"Sorry, Mr. Elliott." Sam tapped the clipboard against his side, drawing the puppy over to his feet. "When we talked the other day, I figured you were ready to move forward with this project so I wanted to come out and get your estimate—"

Colt held up a hand, cutting the man off. "I appreciate your work. But for now, let me handle this. I'll be in touch."

Annabelle watched as the engineer nodded obediently, then sent her and her father an apologetic smile. Once he was gone, her father scooped up the rambunctious pup.

"Let me put him out back and then I want to know what the hell you're doing, Elliott."

Annabelle watched her father walk away, not wanting to glance back to Colt. She didn't want to know the truth, didn't want her fears to come to life. Surely he wasn't the monster she was imagining right at that moment.

"Darlin'," he began.

She held up a hand. "No. Don't start that. Tell me what that man was doing in *my* house."

The muscle in his jaw ticked as he raked a hand over the back of his neck. His hair was still damp from their shower, as was hers. She jerked the band from her wrist and pulled her hair back into a loose bun. Only a short time ago she was in his arms, coming apart, and then he was opening up to her about his feelings, his hopes for a future with her.

And now he stood before her a total stranger.

"Sam works for me."

"We got that," her father said, coming back to stand next to Annabelle. "What the hell was he doing here on your orders?"

Annabelle watched as Colt waged a war with himself. Her stomach tightened as she leaned against the banister on the staircase for support. She met his gaze from across the foyer. "The truth, Colt."

"I was going to have some work done on the house to get it up to the standards I needed."

A piece of her heart broke, fell at her feet and shattered.

"Because?" she asked, thick emotions welling up in her throat.

"Because this house is going to be part of my dude ranch."

"The hell you say?" Her father was on the verge of exploding. "I paid off my loan to the bank and this house is mine."

Colt cleared his throat, his chest puffed out as he drew in a breath. "Actually, the house and the land belong to me."

"What?" Annabelle gasped. "How is that possible? I've worked myself to death for the payments coming due."

Honestly, she didn't want to know the answer. He'd deceived her. He'd lied to her face, made a joke of her and she'd given him her virginity. How naive could she be?

Baby cries echoed over the baby monitor in the living room. She'd come to tell them apart and this was definitely Emily. Annabelle turned toward the steps, but her father held up a hand.

"I'll go." He threw a glance to Colt before turning back to her. "See what this mess is all about."

Once they were alone again, Annabelle sank onto the steps. The fight was leaving her. She'd been hit so hard, so often lately, she wasn't sure she could keep standing for the final knockout.

"Just tell me," she stated as she wrapped her arms around her knees.

"I want to explain why—"

"No." Annabelle held up her hand. "I don't care about the why. That part is obvious. You're a selfish bastard, only looking out for your family, your precious land and not caring who you hurt in the process."

"Yes. That was the case at first. But then you came into the picture."

Annabelle laughed. "Seriously? That's the route you're going to take for the defense? You were dead set on having my childhood home, but then you saw me and the error of your ways shone bright. Am I close?"

Suddenly she felt like fighting. The burst of anger surged her to her feet. It felt good, and kept the hurt at bay. "So let's hear it. How do you own this? Because when you gave Dad the money, he paid the bank. Now we owe you and he signed a paper with you… Oh, no. What did he sign?"

Any minute she'd wake from this nightmare.

Colt took a step toward her, but she held out both hands. Emily's cries echoed once again over the monitor, along with her father's soothing words. This house meant everything to her and she wasn't about to let Colt take it away. Surely there was something she could do.

"When he asked for the money to pay off the loan, I offered to buy the place for more than market value, all cash. He turned me down. So when I gave him the money to pay off the loan, I had everything put in writing. My attorney drew up a document stating the amount due back and how it should be split into payments."

Annabelle shook her head. "Wait. Why would Dad come to you for the money anyway? I've wondered that from the beginning."

When he hesitated and glanced away, she threw her arm in the air. "Oh, come on. It's a little late to protect me now, isn't it? You've taken everything from me, just say it."

Colt dropped his head between his shoulders and stared down at his worn boots. "That's not the first time I've loaned him money."

She couldn't have heard him right. "What?"

"He's borrowed before," Colt stated, bringing his bright gaze up to hers.

"And…has he paid you back?" she whispered.

Colt shook his head. "That's how I knew I could have this place. He was so desperate for the money, he didn't read what he signed. It states that after the debt is paid back to me, I will be the sole owner of your property, the house, and all outbuildings."

The wind literally was knocked out of her as if he'd punched her in the gut. She reached out, placing a hand on the newel post, and looked out the window toward the large oak tree in the front yard.

How could this day be so bright and sunny when inside her heart was black and stormy? There was nothing left. She literally had nothing but a gambling father and two babies depending on her.

"Annabelle."

"Don't say my name. Don't talk to me and don't ever touch me again." She jerked and took a step backward.

"You made a fool of me. You used me on your ranch, worked me like one of your minions, purposely seduced me and made me feel...I hate you for that most of all."

Dampness tickled her cheeks, and she swiped the backs of her hands across her face. "Get out. Get the hell out so I can figure out what to do now."

The harsh reality slapped her in the face. "I can't order you out of your own house, can I? Damn it. Can you at least give us a few days to find someplace to go? We need to pack...and my mother's things are in the attic...her dishes, where will I store all of that?"

She was thinking out loud, muttering really, because she certainly wasn't talking to the devil disguised as a cowboy.

"You can stay here," he told her. "I wasn't going to just kick you out. I will buy you someplace to stay. You can pick it out."

Tears flooded down her cheeks and she didn't even care at this point. Pride be damned. She had nothing left to lose.

"I don't want a thing from you," she growled. "I don't ever want to see your face again. I don't want to hear your name. We'll be out by Friday. Tell your precious engineer he can return then."

He continued to stare at her, and she had to be hallucinating because she could've sworn she saw pain in his eyes. But men with cold hearts and no souls didn't hurt.

"Everything that happened between us was real," he told her. "I have feelings for you and I wanted you to move in so we could try—"

"So I wouldn't find out what a lying jerk you are?" she asked, another realization hitting her square in the chest. "My eyes are wide-open now. You only wanted me at Pebblebrook so I wouldn't learn the truth. But you got your wires crossed with one of your minions, exposing you for the worthless man you are."

Why did looking at him hurt so badly? Those blue eyes

that had captivated her for days, held her when they made love…

No. They hadn't made love. They'd acted on their attraction and used each other for sex. Nothing more. No matter how much she thought she'd been in love with him.

"I care for you," he told her, and his tone might have been convincing had she not known the truth. "I want you happy, I want to help your family. Let me find you another house."

A humorless laugh escaped her. "I'd think you of all people would understand the importance of family tradition and loyalty. I don't want another place and I most definitely don't want you paying for it. I'd live on the street before I took a dollar from you."

It may come to that. But she'd figure something out. An inexpensive apartment in town could always serve as backup.

"Annabelle—"

"Leave, Colt. You've got the house, the land. That's what you wanted, right?" She bit down on her quivering lip and swallowed. "You have everything now."

His eyes misted. "Not everything."

Then he was gone, leaving Annabelle to sink back to the steps. After all the fighting, all the hurdles she'd jumped, she had been defeated by a man she'd fallen for in a whirlwind affair.

Her broken heart would have to wait. Right now, she had a house to pack and a future to try to piece back together…a future without any dream coming true.

Eighteen

Colt slammed his office door and cursed the moment he'd decided to back Neil Carter into a corner.

The land was his. The debt wasn't fully paid, but the end result was inevitable since Neil signed the papers. For years Colt had dreamed of this moment. He'd waited for the day when he could tell his father that they had secured the land next door and were ready to move forward with Pebblebrook Dude Ranch. The extra home and barns would be useful space. Added to that, the other property carved into the corner of Pebblebrook and now their ranch would be complete.

But instead of texting his brothers the news or rushing to the nursing home to tell his father, Colt went straight to his bar and poured himself a tumbler of bourbon. He downed it, welcoming the familiar burn.

Getting drunk wouldn't solve a thing. It sure as hell wouldn't turn back the clock and give him the chance to handle this whole ordeal differently.

But he truly didn't know what he'd change. He wanted the land, that was obvious. Hurting Annabelle was never part of the deal. She'd come to him broken, ready to slay any dragon in her way to save her family. He'd admired her from day one and had instantly set out on claiming her.

Well, he'd done that, as well. So now what? He had the land, he'd slept with Annabelle, and now she held his heart. How the hell did he get himself into this mess and how could he work his way back out without doing more damage?

Damn it. He hadn't expected emotions to botch up the triumph of his success.

His office door jerked open and Colt barely raised his gaze to his brother in the doorway.

"Not in the mood," Colt growled as he poured another round. Nothing like toasting your failures with yourself and having your oldest brother, the miracle surgeon, as a witness.

"I saw you tear in here like your world just ended." Nolan didn't take the not-so-subtle hint that Colt wanted to be alone. He crossed the office and stopped on the other side of the bar. "I assume this has to do with Annabelle."

Colt tipped back the glass and closed his eyes before slamming the empty tumbler back onto the mahogany bar top.

"The land is ours and the engineer will be moving forward with drawing up some plans and getting us an estimate."

Nolan braced his hands against the grooved edge of the bar and leaned forward. "Which is what you've always wanted, so I'm assuming Annabelle knows that she no longer has a home."

"She knows everything."

Well, not everything. There was one more thing he could do for her that might lessen her pain. She'd still hate him, he couldn't change that, but he owed her.

"You care for her." Nolan let out a low whistle. "I didn't see that coming. But I can tell you from experience, if you want to be with her, fight. No matter what you've done, you can't let her go."

Colt shook his head. "She doesn't ever want to see me or talk to me again. Those were her parting words."

"And you're just giving up? You fought for years for this property, but when you find a woman you care for you opt to drink and will the pain away?"

Wasn't that what any cowboy did?

"She deserves for you to grovel, to show her that she means more than this dream of yours," Nolan went on. "But only if she does mean more. I could be reading you all wrong, but you look like hell."

Colt had never second-guessed a business decision he'd made. Confidence was key to maintaining a successful ranch. But right now, he wanted this pain to go away. And he knew if he was hurting this much, that Annabelle was miserable. She was still trying to pick up the pieces of her shattered life and all he'd done was throw more shards into the mix.

"There's no fixing this," Colt stated, pushing away from the bar. "I can make the process a little easier, but she doesn't want my help. I offered to buy her another house."

Nolan laughed and raked a hand through his dark hair. "You don't get women at all, man. She doesn't want another house. She wants the one she grew up in. We don't need that property to grow, Colt. We have five thousand acres. Use some of the east side to build cabins. You want the girl, go get her. If you're content with simply keeping the property, stay here and drink your day away."

Nolan started back toward the door before stopping and glancing over his shoulder. "Don't make the same mistake I did."

Colt knew Annabelle didn't want to see him. He needed to give her time before he approached her again and explained his side, and maybe then she'd understand.

But if he wanted to nudge her in the right direction, then he needed to take something to her, something that rightfully belonged to her.

There was no denying the truth any longer…he loved Annabelle. In a short time, she'd captured his heart. Oh, she'd fought the attraction, but he'd pursued her and he wasn't sorry. How could he be? She was the greatest thing that had happened to him and he'd destroyed their chance at happiness before it could even get started.

He had to prove to her that he wasn't an unfeeling jerk.

Colt headed to his master suite to retrieve the box he'd had hidden for nearly two years. Doing the right thing at this point was rather moot, but he couldn't let Annabelle believe he was the monster she claimed.

"I'm sorry, Belle."

If she only had a dollar for every time her father had said those words just this evening alone…

Annabelle cradled a sleepy Emily and swayed back and forth on the porch. "There's nothing we can do now. We wouldn't have the money to fight that document anyway. But I am going to demand to see it. I know Colt wouldn't have allowed for any loopholes, but I won't take his word for it."

From the start, she'd known he had an agenda, but she'd thought most of it was getting her into bed. She had a clue he wanted her land, but she never dreamed he already owned it.

She heated all over again when she thought of how foolish she was, how much of a laughingstock she must've been each time she showed up for so-called work at the ranch.

From here on out, she was focusing on her girls. Annabelle needed to go out first thing in the morning and find a job, and then she'd look into housing.

The thought of packing up the only place she'd ever

wanted to be hurt almost as much as Colt's betrayal. Just his name in her mind had her heart aching.

"We'll get through this," she told her father. "But when I say no gambling, I mean it. This can't go on. I don't care if it's one dollar or one hundred. No more."

He stood up from the swing, sending it rocking on its own in the breeze. "I'm going to do everything I can. I know we need to do this together. I'm trying."

"I know." He was always trying, but this time he had to stick to a plan and now that she was back, maybe she could watch him more closely. "Go on to bed," she told him. "I'll come in later. I just want to hold her a while longer and enjoy the silence and the fresh air."

She wanted to sit on this porch swing with Emily and Lucy, just like her mother used to do with Annabelle and her sister. Leaving the memories behind would be the hardest part. Seeing the inside of this home bare would quite possibly break her.

"I can take Emily in and lay her down if you'd like. It's rather late."

Annabelle nodded. "I know, but she can sleep in my arms. She calms me, gives me peace. I guess I'll have that time to spend with my babies after all until I find another job."

Considering the hell she'd been through, Annabelle needed peace. She needed to focus on her family, on piecing the broken hearts back together.

"We're going to rebuild our lives," he told her. "With your mother and Trish gone…"

His voice caught and it was all Annabelle could do to hold it together. Her father never broke down in front of her.

"Now that they're gone," he said on a shaky breath. "You are all I have. You and those sweet girls. I want to be a better man for you guys and I want you to know I'm going to help by getting a job. We'll do this together."

She truly hoped so because she wasn't sure she could do it alone. "I love you, Dad."

He crossed to her, kissed the top of her head, and headed inside. Annabelle patted Emily through the cotton sleeper and made her way to the swing. Wherever she ended up, Annabelle vowed to own a porch with a swing. It may not be this porch, it may not be this swing, but it was a tradition she could take with her.

Tears slid down her cheeks as she pushed off the porch with her toes to set the swing in motion again. Emily clutched onto Annabelle's T-shirt as she drifted off to sleep. Trish's precious babies were counting on her to provide protection, stability, a future, and she planned to deliver.

So much had happened today and Annabelle was still trying to wrap her mind around the fact that she was still in love with a man who had hurt her so deeply, she didn't know if she'd ever recover.

But he'd told her all along that family was everything to him. He hadn't been lying.

He'd cradled her in his arms after making love and told her his father's ultimate goal when he'd been in charge. Now Colt was pushing forward with those plans no matter who was run over in the process. A part of her knew where he was coming from, realized the importance of clinging to a parent's dream.

Still, it didn't cancel out what he'd done. He'd stolen her home. From the moment she met him, he knew exactly what the outcome of this situation would be and he chose to play with her life anyway. Those actions were unforgivable.

Headlights swept up her driveway and Annabelle came

to her feet, tightening her hold on Emily and pulling her into her chest.

Colt's truck came to a stop and Annabelle braced herself. If he was coming to beg for forgiveness, he could take his shiny, expensive vehicle and get the hell off her...

It was his land. He had every right to be there.

The soft glow from the porch cast enough light for her to see that he was carrying a box. As he drew closer, she recognized that box. Her mother's.

Annabelle went to the edge of the porch and met his eyes when he stopped at the base of the steps.

"I'm not staying," he told her. "I just thought this should be returned to you."

There was no holding back the tears, making it difficult to juggle a sleeping baby while swiping at her eyes with the back of her hand.

"Why do you have my mother's jewelry box?"

Colt held the box between his hands, his attention never wavering from her. "Because your father needed money. He knew there wasn't anyone around who could afford to buy this, so he came to me."

She'd known her father had sold the jewelry, but she hadn't known to whom and she never dreamed she'd get it back.

"Is it all in there?" she dared ask.

"Every piece," he confirmed. "I had no use for it. I always figured if Neil got straightened out, he may want this back. But you deserve it."

She didn't know what to say. He could've kept this box and she never would've known. Clearly, her father wasn't going to say anything.

Annabelle stepped aside. "Can you set it on the table over there?" she asked.

Colt stepped up onto the porch and placed the box on the side table next to a rocking chair and potted fern. The breeze kicked up, bringing Colt's familiar woodsy scent with it. The same scent she'd been up close and personal with in his shower earlier.

When he turned back around and locked his eyes on hers, Annabelle froze. "Don't," she whispered.

"I know you hate me. I know you think I'm the worst person you've ever met."

In the pale glow, those blue eyes glistened with unshed tears. She didn't want to believe he had a heart. She didn't want him to have feelings. He'd done all this to himself, to her and her family.

"But everything that happened with us was real. I didn't want it to be," he added. "I wanted to keep things business and physical. You showed me there was so much more. I know you don't believe me, but I had to tell you that I'm not the man you think. I'm just a guy who put his father's wishes above all else. I'm a guy who wanted to prove himself to those people he loved most."

Colt pursed his lips, but Annabelle didn't miss the way his chin quivered. Her heart ached for him, but again, she hadn't done any of this. All of his pain was self-inflicted.

"And in the end, I hurt the woman I'd fallen in love with."

Annabelle had barely processed the words when he turned and walked off the porch. That limp, a little more prominent this evening, only reminded her that he was human. That he made mistakes, he wasn't perfect. But he'd hurt her and now he just wanted to turn her world on its side once again with those words?

She clutched Emily and turned, going down the steps.

"You can't drop that bomb so conveniently and then just leave," she called.

"Too late. But there's little I can do to make you believe me," he told her as he opened the truck door. "I just want you to know…"

He shook his head and glanced toward the starry sky before looking back at her. "I just want you to know that those moments I spent alone with you were some of the best of my life."

Colt hopped into the cab of his truck and backed away, not looking in her direction again. Emily slept through the entire encounter and Annabelle envied her for it.

Colt had brought back her mother's box, the box Annabelle remembered playing with as a little girl. Oh, there were plenty of real pieces in there, but her mom had also kept costume jewelry, too.

Annabelle sat in the rocker beside the box and nestled Emily into the crook of her arm. With her free hand, Annabelle lifted the lid and was instantly swept back in time. The emerald earrings that matched the ring Annabelle had were safely in their divider.

All of the other familiar pieces were there, too. Memories of her mother wearing each one came rushing back.

Closing her eyes, she rested her head against the back of the rocker and longed for answers. What was she supposed to do? How could she move on when it would be so easy to give up?

And how did she process Colt's announcement that he'd fallen for her? That wasn't fair. She wanted to continue hating him, but he'd sounded sincere. Those tears he blinked away were certainly not fake, but how could he feel that way about her and still treat her like he had?

Unless…

Annabelle needed to think. She needed to clear her head and dissect all that had transpired in the past few months. She couldn't just do what her heart told her to because there was no way she was following that advice anymore.

She had to be smart about this and make the best decisions for her and the twins. And that started with marching over to Pebblebrook first thing in the morning.

Nineteen

Hard work made a man forget, or at least that's what he'd told himself when he came to the barn at five that morning.

Colt had intentions of working until his muscles burned and he temporarily forgot how much his heart ached. He'd only meant to take that box to Annabelle last night, but then he'd seen her holding Emily and his mouth just opened, pouring emotions out.

And in that moment his future became so clear. Family, above all else, was the most important thing in life. His father had never put anything above his family…not even business. The Elliotts were all successful because they'd put integrity and loyalty first.

Annabelle may still hate him, but he wasn't giving up. He may have been determined to get her farm, but that was nothing compared to the motive he had to get her back. She was…everything. She was absolutely everything he'd ever wanted and he hadn't even known it.

Colt had texted Ryan and Josh, telling them to start work on the west side near Hayes's house. Not only did Colt want that place perfect for his brother's return in a few weeks, but he wanted the guys away because he was not in the mood for chitchat.

He'd taken Lightning out first thing and tried to clear his mind, but all he kept seeing was the hurt on Annabelle's face when she realized he'd lied to her. He'd not only lied, he'd stolen the one thing she'd held dear to her heart since she was a child.

As soon as he'd come back from his ride, Colt had gone straight into his office in the barn and fired off an email. He may never get Annabelle back, but he sure as hell wasn't about to continue the process of taking her home.

Guilt had gnawed at him into the wee hours. But there was so much more. That moment on Annabelle's porch last night had turned the final click on his heart, proving that he didn't only love her, he loved the image of her and those babies being his, living on Pebblebrook.

He loved her more than he'd thought possible and had completely crushed her.

All his own doing and his brother tried to tell him. Hell, his employees had, too.

But Colt had been stubborn. Now he'd have to do damage control. His father wouldn't have approved of Colt letting the woman go only to have the expansion. His father would be disappointed in how Colt had handled everything. But that wasn't the only reason Colt decided to fight for what he wanted.

A car door slamming caught his attention as he tossed another bale of hay from one side of the loft toward the opening near the ladder.

Stepping over hay, he crossed to the small hinged door and swung it open wide. Glancing down, he saw the most beautiful sight: Annabelle in a pair of fitted jeans, a green tank that matched her eyes and her boots. She pulled a stroller out of the trunk and slammed the lid. Then she opened the back door and removed Emily and Lucy from their car seats.

He watched as she strapped them into the stroller and

then looked around the open area. She was there to see him, but why? Had his words affected her last night? Was she willing to hear him out and maybe start over?

He hadn't had a chance to rehearse his speech in his head. He wasn't ready to face her when his emotions were so raw and vulnerable. But there was nothing more he wanted than to believe she came there to forgive him.

He was asking too much, he knew, but he still wasn't ready to give up. Maybe spouting off his profession of love last night had been wrong, but if it got her thinking, he wasn't sorry he'd exposed his weaker side.

"Up here," he called.

Annabelle jumped, a hand over her heart as she glanced toward him. Her eyes landed on his bare chest. "Oh, um… I need to talk to you."

"I'll come down."

He didn't bother to grab his shirt from the hayloft. It had been hot as Hades up there so he'd shed it early. As Colt climbed down the ladder, he didn't care that he was playing dirty by going at her half-dressed. He'd do anything to remind her of just how good they were together.

"I want to see that document my father signed."

He'd barely put his boot on the ground when she came up the walkway pushing the twins. The girls were bright eyed today and Lucy was chewing on some stuffed cowboy doll. The sight of those expressive green eyes clutched his heart.

He focused back on Annabelle. "I have the print copy in my office at the house."

She nodded. "Then let's go there."

"We can go into my office here and I can pull up the document in email format that I sent to my attorney."

She kept trying to look him in the eye, but she failed. Every few seconds her focus shifted down to his bare chest.

"That's fine. I want to know what I'm dealing with and if there's any way to get out of it."

"The document is binding, darlin'."

"Do not even start with that," she told him, her eyes now locked on his. "I want to know something and I want you to answer honestly."

He crossed his arms and nodded. "I have nothing else to hide."

She gripped the handles of the stroller and tipped her head. "When you asked me to move in with you, was that because you wanted me or because you were trying to cover your tracks so I wouldn't find out about the property? I assume you were hoping I'd fall madly in love with you and we'd just merge and live happily ever after. Am I right?"

Colt swallowed. "Yes."

When she lowered her lids over those mesmerizing green eyes, Colt felt as if the day had dimmed. Her light was gone and he'd put it out. He had to explain himself and then she could decide what to do.

"I asked you to move in because I was serious about wanting to try for something deeper with you." He took a step closer. "I asked because if you fell in love with me and we did this whole happily-ever-after, then you'd never have to know what your father or I did." Another step brought him toe to toe with her. "But I wanted to spare you the pain, I wanted you to start a new life without the heartache. The last thing I ever wanted was to hurt you."

She opened her eyes, tilting her head so she could meet his gaze. "You didn't want to hurt me? What did you think would happen? Did you seriously think I'd never find out about this form my father signed?"

Colt watched as Emily turned the toy over again, then put it back in her mouth. "After I started falling for you, I did what I could to keep you safe. I wanted to protect you.

I was trying to find a way to keep my father's wishes and hold on to you at the same time. What I didn't realize was that my father would rather see me happy and settled than to have the extra land for the dude ranch."

"How can I believe you?" she whispered.

She was breaking down. Now all he had to do was catch her.

"Because this place is better with you. Because my life is brighter with you here. I've always wanted a family and the moment I held Lucy out in the yard, I started falling. I had a weak spot for you, and getting to know your girls more only made the trio even more appealing. I want you all here, Annabelle."

She'd left her hair down today. The soft curls lay over her shoulders and he remembered the deep shade of red her hair turned when wet. He'd give anything to have her back in his shower again, in his bed, in his life.

"I messed up," he went on. "I'll freely admit that I should've been honest with you from the moment you came, but I didn't know you and I only wanted to fulfill my father's wishes...I guess the same as you did with your mother."

Annabelle's soft smile clenched his heart. "That bed-and-breakfast was her only goal."

"Then you can do it," he told her. "Take your house and do whatever you want with it."

Her brows drew in. "What?"

"I emailed my attorney this morning regarding the legal agreement. It will be reversed and the land will remain in your name."

Emily started fussing and threw her toy on the ground. Colt picked up the cowboy as Annabelle came around to lift the baby from the stroller. With Emily on her hip, Annabelle turned to face him once again.

"Why?" she asked simply.

Colt shrugged and held the toy up to Emily. "Because it's yours. I only want you and if I can't have you, then I sure as hell don't want to take your home."

There was an emptiness inside him that had existed since he left her house last night. He needed it filled, but only Annabelle had that power.

"You're just giving it back?"

Emily reached a hand toward him and instinct had him taking her into his arms. At least he still had one of them on his side. Lucy remained silent in the stroller and stared up at him as if assessing her own opinion.

"I'm giving it back with access to my engineer and contractor. You have an unlimited budget to do the bed-and-breakfast like you want."

Annabelle's eyes instantly filled. "Colt...but, what about your dude ranch?"

This was the tricky part. "I'm hoping I can still open it. I'm hoping we can do this together. That land can stay in your name, you can have complete control over what happens with your house, but there is something I want to merge."

Her eyes widened.

"I want you to have my name. Marry me, sweetness. Not for the land, or the house. I want your happiness and I hope that means you'll be with me and give me a second chance."

"You're serious?" she asked, blinking back tears.

"I've never been more so."

A shaky hand covered her mouth as she shook her head. Hope stilled inside him. He wanted it to grow, he wanted some sign that she was giving in.

"I want to," she whispered behind her hand. "I'm so scared."

Emily laid her head on his shoulder. Colt reached out

and wrapped an arm around Annabelle's waist, hauling her against his side.

"I'm terrified," he admitted. "This is insane for both of us, but I know what I want."

With a watery smile, she reached up and cupped the side of his face.

"The land stays in my name. I'll move in with you and let's see how things go."

Relief swept through him as he hugged her tighter against his side. "That's more than I deserve. There's one more thing."

"What's that?"

"I'd like to pay to have your father get some help. He can't do it alone."

Now she burst into tears. "You're going to take on so much with me. You must be serious if you're on board for all my baggage."

He nipped at her lips. "I'm more than on board, sweetness. I want you here more than I've ever wanted anything."

Lucy started fussing and Annabelle reached down to unfasten her. Once the baby was on Annabelle's hip, she instantly calmed.

Colt wrapped his arms around the family he'd finally found.

Annabelle smiled. "I have the perfect name you can call me."

Colt laughed. "What's that?"

"Yours."

Epilogue

Nolan hadn't had the best night at the hospital. This was the time of day when he couldn't go straight home to bed, he needed to ride to unwind.

Just as he rounded the corner to the main barn, he came up short.

Colt had his arms wrapped around Annabelle and her girls. Apparently he'd come to his senses and gone after the family he wanted.

Nolan swallowed and stepped back, so as not to be seen. He was happy for his younger brother. Nolan always figured Colt would be the first to settle down. He was a little jealous, though. Nolan would be lying to himself if he didn't admit that he wanted a family of his own. He was tired of coming home to an empty house. When he'd built it, he'd had every intention of filling it with a wife, with children.

But he'd let that dream go. Years ago, he'd let go of the only woman he'd ever wanted. He'd hoped he'd move on and someone would come along and fill the void in his life.

As Nolan headed back to his SUV, he realized that there was only one woman he would ever care for.

Pepper Manning. He'd let her go without a fight. They'd

been through hell together, but when it came to the time she needed him most, he hadn't been there. He'd messed up, but that was something he'd had to live with because there was no way to erase the past.

Living with that heartache was a battle he'd always face. He devoted his life to saving others, but he hadn't been able to save the one person he loved from heartache.

So, yeah, Nolan was jealous that his brother had found love, found a family. Because if Nolan had it to do over, he'd never let Pepper go.

But there were no second chances…right?

* * * * *

CLAIMING HIS ONE-NIGHT BABY

MICHELLE SMART

For Adam xxx

CHAPTER ONE

JAW CLENCHED, HIS heart pounding an irregular beat in his chest, Matteo Manaserro watched the coffin being lowered into the consecrated ground of Castello Miniato's private cemetery.

Surrounding the open earth stood hundreds of Pieta Pellegrini's loved ones, friends, family, colleagues, even some heads of state, with their security details standing back at a discreet distance, all there to say a final good-bye to a man who had been respected the world over for his philanthropic endeavours.

Vanessa Pellegrini, Pieta's mother, who had buried her husband, Fabio, in the adjoining plot only a year ago, stepped forward, supported by her daughter Francesca. Both women clutched red roses. Francesca turned around to extend a hand to Natasha, Pieta's widow, who was staring blankly at the wooden box like an ashen-faced statue. The breeze that had filled the early-autumn air had dropped, magnifying the statue effect. Not a single strand of her tumbling honey-blonde hair moved.

She lifted her dry eyes and blinked, the motion seeming to clear her thoughts as she grabbed Francesca's hand and joined the sobbing women.

Together, the three Pellegrini women threw their roses onto the coffin.

Matteo forced stale air from his lungs and focused his attention anywhere but on the widow.

This was a day to say goodbye, to mourn and then celebrate a man who deserved to be mourned and celebrated. This was not a day to stare at the widow and think how beautiful she looked even in grief. Or think how badly he wanted to take hold of her shoulders and…

Daniele, Pieta's brother, shifted beside him. It was their turn.

Goodbye, Pieta, my cousin, my friend. Thank you for everything. I will miss you.

Once the immediate family—in which Matteo was included—had thrown their roses on the coffin, it was time for the other mourners to follow suit.

Striving to keep his features neutral, he watched his parents step forward to pay their last respects to their nephew. They didn't look at him, their son, but he knew his father sensed him watching.

Matteo hadn't exchanged a word with them since he'd legally changed his surname five years ago in the weeks that had followed the death of his own brother.

So much death.

So many funerals.

So much grief.

Too much pain.

When the burial was over and the priest led the mourners into the *castello* for the wake, Matteo hung back to visit a grave on the next row.

The marble headstone had a simple etching.

Roberto Pellegrini
Beloved son

No mention of him being a beloved brother.

Generations of Pellegrinis and their descendants were buried here, going back six centuries. At twenty-eight, Roberto was the youngest to have been buried in fifty years.

Matteo crouched down and touched the headstone. 'Hello, Roberto. Sorry I haven't visited you in a while. I've been busy.' He laughed harshly. In the five years since his brother's death he'd visited the grave only a handful of times. Not a day passed when he didn't think of him. Not an hour passed when he didn't feel the loss.

'Listen to me justifying myself. Again. You know I hate to see you here. I love you and I miss you. I just wanted you to know that.'

Blinking back moistness from his eyes, his heart aching, his head pounding, Matteo dragged himself to the *castello* to join the others.

A huge bar had been set up in the state room for the wake. Matteo had booked himself into a hotel in Pisa for the next couple of days but figured one small glass of bourbon wouldn't put him over the limit. His hotel room had a fully stocked minibar for him to drink dry when he got there. He would stay as long as was decent then leave.

He'd taken only a sip of his drink when Francesca appeared at his side.

He embraced her tightly. 'How are you holding up?' He'd been thirteen when his uncle Fabio and his wife, Vanessa, had taken him into their home. Francesca had been a baby. He'd been there when she'd taken her first steps, been in the audience for her first school music recital—she'd murdered the trumpet—and had beamed with the pride of a big brother only a few months ago at her graduation.

She shrugged and rubbed his arm. 'I need you to come with me. There's something we need to discuss.'

Following her up a cold corridor—the ancient *castello* needed a fortune's worth of modernisation—they entered Fabio Pellegrini's old office, which, from the musty smell, hadn't been used since the motor neurone disease that eventually killed him had really taken its hold on him.

A moment later Daniele appeared at the door with Natasha right behind him.

Startled blue eyes found his and quickly looked away as Francesca closed the door and indicated they should all sit round the oval table.

Matteo inhaled deeply and swore to himself.

This was the last thing he needed, to be stuck in close confines with *her*, the woman who had played him like a violin, letting him believe she had genuine feelings for him and could see a future for them, when all along she'd been playing his cousin too.

It seemed she had been with him every minute of that day, always in the periphery of his vision even when he'd blinked her away. Now she sat opposite him, close enough that if he were to reach over the table he would be able to stroke her deceitful face.

She shouldn't be wearing black. She should be wearing scarlet.

He despised that she was still the most beautiful woman he'd ever seen and that the years had only added to it.

He studied the vivid blue eyes that looked everywhere but at him. He studied the classically oval face with its creamy complexion, usually golden but today ashen, searching for flaws. Her nose was slightly too long, her lips too wide, but instead of being imperfections they added character to the face he'd once dreamed of waking up to.

And now?

Now he despised the very air she breathed.

'To summarise, I'll take care of the legal side, Daniele takes care of the construction and Matteo takes care of the medical side. What about you, Natasha? Do you want to handle publicity for it?'

Francesca's words penetrated Natasha's ears but it took a couple of beats longer for her brain to decipher them.

She'd struggled to pay attention throughout the meeting Francesca had called, the outbursts of temper between Daniele and Francesca being the only thing that had kept her even vaguely alert.

'I can do that,' she whispered, swallowing back the hysteria clamouring in her stomach.

Ignore Matteo and keep it together, she told herself in desperation.

God, she didn't know anything about publicity.

She knew Francesca thought she was doing the right thing, inviting her to this meeting of siblings—and the Pellegrinis considered their cousin Matteo to be a sibling—and that Francesca assumed she would want to be involved.

Any decent, loving widow would want to be involved in building a memorial to their beloved husband.

And she *did* want to be involved. For all his terrible failings as a husband, Pieta had been a true, dedicated humanitarian. He'd formed his own foundation a decade ago to build in areas hit by natural disasters; schools, homes, hospitals, whatever was needed. The Caribbean island of Caballeros had been hit by the worst hurricane on record the week before he'd died, wrecking the majority of the island's medical facilities. Pieta had immediately known he would build a hospital there but before his own plans for it had fully formed his own tragedy had struck and he'd been killed in a helicopter crash.

He deserved to have this memorial. The suffering people of Caballeros deserved to benefit from the hospital Francesca would steamroller into building for them.

So Natasha had striven to pay attention, not wanting to let down the loving Pellegrini siblings who'd been a part of her life for as long as she could remember, since her father and Fabio had been old school friends. She'd never had siblings of her own and as soon as it had been announced she'd be marrying into the family the closeness had grown, even during the six long years of their engagement.

If only Matteo weren't there she'd have been better able to concentrate.

There had not been one occasion in his presence in the past seven years where she hadn't felt the weight of his animosity. Polite and amiable enough that no one could see the depths of his loathing, whenever their eyes met it was akin to being stared at by Lucifer, her soul scorched by the burn of the hatred firing from green eyes that had once looked at her with only tenderness.

She could feel it now, digging into her skin like needles.

How could Francesca and Daniele not feel it too? How did it not infuse the whole atmosphere?

A part of her understood why he despised her as he did and, God knew, she'd tried to apologise for it, but it had been seven years. So much had changed in that time. She'd changed. He'd changed too, turning his back on the reconstructive surgery he'd worked so hard to specialise in and instead going the vanity surgery route. With his twenty-eight clinics worldwide and the patent on a skincare range he'd personally developed that actually worked in reducing scars and the signs of aging, he'd gone from being a dedicated professional surgeon to an entrepreneur who fitted surgery in when he had the time. Matteo had amassed a fortune that rivalled the entire Pellegrini estate and Pieta's personally accrued wealth put together.

He'd even changed his surname.

He'd become famous with it. Tall with dark good looks, olive skin, strong jaw and black curly hair that he'd recently had cropped short, it had been inevitable. 'Dr Dishy' the tabloids called him. It seemed she could barely pass a newsagent or log on to the internet without seeing his seductive face blazing out at her, normally with some identikit lingerie model or other draped on his arm.

Today his usual arrogance had deserted him. Even with the laser burn of his loathing infecting her, she could feel his anguish.

Pieta had been more than a cousin and surrogate sibling. He'd been Matteo's closest friend.

Her heart wanted to weep for him.

Her heart wanted to weep for all of them.

Matteo pulled his car up by the kerb and turned off the engine. The grand town house he'd parked opposite from stood in darkness.

Slumping forward over the wheel, he closed his eyes.

What was he even doing here?

He should be in his hotel room, drinking the minibar dry. He'd made that arrangement assuming Natasha would be staying in the *castello* with the rest of the family. He hadn't slept under the same roof as her since she'd accepted Pieta's proposal.

But she hadn't stayed. A couple of hours after their meeting to discuss the memorial for Pieta she had made the rounds to embrace everyone goodbye. Everyone except him. By unspoken agreement—unspoken because he hadn't exchanged more than a handful of words with her in seven years—he'd kept a great enough physical distance between them that no one would notice they failed to say goodbye to each other.

He put his head back and breathed deeply, willing his heart to stop this irregular rhythm.

What the hell was wrong with him? Why was it today of all days that he couldn't shake her from his mind? Why today, when he was mourning his best friend and cousin, had the old memories returned to haunt him?

He could see it so vividly, leaving his room in the *castello* to head outside to join the rest of his family in the marquee for his aunt and uncle's thirtieth wedding anniversary party. Natasha had left the room she'd been sharing with Francesca just a short way up the corridor from his at the same time. His heart had skipped to see her and he'd been ecstatic to see the necklace he'd sent for her eighteenth birthday there around her slender neck. He'd been disappointed not to make it to England for her party but he'd been a resident doctor at a hospital in Florida close to where he'd been to medical school. An emergency had cropped up at the end of his shift, a major car crash with multiple casualties that had resulted in all hands on deck. By the time they'd patched up the last casualty he'd missed his flight.

He'd been taking things slowly with her, waiting for her to turn eighteen before making a physical move. And then, in that cold *castello* corridor, Natasha in an electric-blue dress, the epitome of a chic, elegant woman, he'd realised he didn't have to back off any more.

All the letters and late-night calls they'd been exchanging for months, the dreams and hopes for the future they'd shared, had all been leading to this, this moment, this time. It was time for their future to begin right then and he'd fingered that necklace before taking her face in his hands and kissing her for the very first time.

It had been the sweetest, headiest kiss he'd ever experienced in his then twenty-eight years, interrupted only by Francesca steamrolling from her room and clattering up the corridor to join them. If she'd been three seconds earlier she would have found them together.

Three seconds.

What would she have done, he wondered, if she had caught them in that clinch?

Because only two hours later Pieta had got to his feet and, in front of the three hundred guests, had asked Natasha to marry him. And she'd said yes.

Matteo rubbed his eyes as if the motion could rub the memories away.

He shouldn't be thinking of all this now.

Why had he even come here, to the house she had shared with Pieta?

A light came on upstairs.

Had she just woken? Or had she been in the darkness all this time?

And was Francesca right to be worried about her?

Francesca had cornered him as he'd been making his own escape from the wake and asked him to keep an eye on Natasha while she, Francesca, was in Caballeros. She was worried about her, said she'd become a lost, mute ghost.

Although Natasha and Pieta had only been married for a year, they'd been together for seven years. She might be a gold-digging, heartless bitch but surely in that time she must have developed some feelings for him.

He'd wanted her feelings for Pieta to be genuine, for his cousin's sake. But how could they have been when she'd been seeing them both behind each other's backs?

Other than the few social family occasions he'd been unable to get out of, he'd cut her out of his life completely. He'd blocked her number, deleted every email and text message they'd exchanged and burned all her old-fashioned handwritten letters. The times he'd felt obliged to be in her presence he'd perfected the art of subtly blanking her in a way that didn't draw attention to anyone but *her*.

He should have just said no to Francesca. Lied and said he was returning home to Miami earlier than planned.

Instead he'd nodded curtly and promised to drop round if he had five minutes over the next couple of days.

So why had he driven here when he'd left the *castello* fully intending to drive straight to the hotel?

Natasha pushed Pieta's study door open and swallowed hard before stepping into it. After a moment she switched the light on. After going from room to room in complete darkness, in the house that had been her home for a year, her eyes took a few moments to adjust to the brightness.

She didn't know what she was looking for or what she was doing. She didn't know anything. She was lost. Alone.

She'd stayed at the wake as long as had been decently possible but all the consolation from the other mourners had become too much. Seeing Matteo everywhere she'd looked had been just as hard. Harder. Her mother pulling her to one side to ask if there was a chance she could be pregnant had been the final straw.

She'd had to get out before she'd screamed the *castello* down and her tongue ran away with itself before she could pull it back.

The rest of the Pellegrinis were staying at the *castello* and with sympathetic but concerned eyes had accepted her explanation that she wanted to be on her own.

At her insistence, the household staff had all stayed at the wake.

This was the first time she'd been alone in the house since she'd received the terrible news.

Feeling like an intruder in the room that had been her husband's domain, she cast her gaze over the walls thick with the books he'd read. A stack of files he'd brought home to work on, either from his law firm or the foundation he'd been so proud of, lay on his desk. Next to it sat the thick leather-bound tome on Stanley and Livingstone she'd bought him for his recent birthday. A bookmark poked out a third of the way through it.

Her throat closing tightly, she picked the book up and hugged it to her chest then with a wail that seemed to come from nowhere sank to the floor and sobbed for the man who had lied to her and everyone else for years, but who had done so much good in the world.

Pieta would never finish this book. He would never see the hospital his siblings would build in his memory. He would never take delivery of the new car he'd ordered only the day before he'd died.

He would never have the chance to tell his family the truth about who he'd really been.

'Oh, Pieta,' she whispered between the tears. 'Wherever you are, I hope you're finally at peace with your-self.'

The sound of the doorbell rang out.

She rolled into a ball and covered her ears.

The caller was insistent, pressing the doorbell inter-mittently until she could ignore it no longer. Wiping the tears away, she dragged herself up from the study floor and went down the stairs, clinging to the bannister for support, mentally preparing what she would say to get rid of her unexpected visitor.

Please don't be my parents. Don't be my parents. Don't be my parents.

Bracing herself, she unlocked the door and opened it a crack to peer through.

Certain she must be hallucinating, she pulled the door wider.

Her heart seemed to stop then kick back to life with a roar.

Matteo stood there, shining like an apparition under the brilliance of the moon.

He'd removed his black tie, his white shirt open at the throat, bleakness in his eyes, his jaw clenched, breath-ing heavily.

Their eyes met.

Neither of them spoke.

Something erupted in her chest, gripping her so tightly her lungs closed.

Time came to a standstill.

There they stood for the longest time, speaking only with their eyes. She read a hundred things in his; varia-tions of pain, misery, anger and something else, some-thing she hadn't seen since the beat before he'd taken her into his arms for the only kiss they had ever shared seven years ago.

This was the first time she'd seen him alone since that kiss.

She would never forget the look in his eyes from across the marquee when she had said yes to Pieta's proposal only two hours later. That would be with her until the day she died. The regret at all that had been lost would live in her for ever.

Her foot moved of its own accord as she took the step to him and placed her palm on his warm cheek.

He didn't react. Not the flicker of a muscle.

Matteo stared into eyes puffy from crying but that shone at him, almost pleading.

All the words he'd prepared melted away.

He couldn't even remember getting out of his car.

Her trembling hand felt so gentle on his cheek, her warmth penetrating his skin, and all he could do was drink in the face he'd once dreamed of waking up to.

A force too powerful to fight took hold of him, like a fist grabbing his insides and squeezing tightly.

Suddenly he couldn't remember why he hated her. All thoughts had evaporated. All he could see was her, Natasha, the woman he had taken one look at nearly eight years ago and known his life would never be the same again.

CHAPTER TWO

THE WORLD AROUND them blocked itself out and, without a word being said, Matteo crossed the threshold, kicked the door shut behind him and lifted her into his arms.

Their eyes locked together. Her fingers burrowed in the nape of his neck and he carried her up the stairs and into a bedroom. There he laid her on the bed and, his heart hammering in his throat, closed his eyes and brought his lips to hers.

Her taste…

When she parted her lips and his tongue swept into her mouth, the sweet, intoxicating taste he'd never forgotten filled him and from that moment he was lost.

In a frenzy of hands and heady kisses, they stripped each other's clothes off, items thrown without thought, a desperation to be naked and for their bodies to be flush together. Then he speared her hair with his fingers and crushed her mouth to his, teeth and tongues clashing as if they were trying to peel the other's skin and climb inside.

There were no thoughts, no words, only this potent madness that had them both in its grip.

He cupped her small perfect breasts then took them into his mouth, her moan of pleasure soaking right into his bloodstream. He ran his hands over her smooth belly and followed it with his tongue before going lower to inhale her musky heat.

He devoured her, not an inch of her creamy skin with the texture of silk left untouched or without his kiss.

Never had he experienced anything like this, this combustible, primal need to taste her, mark her, to imprint himself into her.

To worship her.

Natasha was adrift in a world she'd never been to before, Matteo her anchor, and she clung to him as if he were all that was left to hold onto, dragging her fingers through his hair, touching every bit of smooth skin she could reach with her needy hands. Every touch seared her, every kiss scorched.

His kiss from seven years ago had flicked something on inside her, a heat that had briefly smouldered before the direction of her life had extinguished it. Now he'd switched it back on and it engulfed her, flames licking every part of her, heat burning deep inside her, an ache so acute she didn't know where the pleasure ended and the pain began. She could cry with the wonder of it all. All those years of living without this…

And it wasn't enough. She needed more. She needed everything.

As if sensing her thoughts, Matteo snaked his tongue back up her stomach and over her breasts, climbing higher to find her mouth and kiss her with such passion that it sucked the air from her lungs.

His hand found her thigh and pushed it out while she moved the other and wrapped her legs around him.

His erection brushed her folds and she gasped for breath at the weight and hardness of it then gasped again when he pushed his way inside her.

There was no pain, there was too much heat and fire

racing through her for that, just a slight discomfort as her body adjusted to this dizzying newness.

And then there was a moment of stillness from Matteo, a pause in the frenzy.

Suddenly terrified he'd sensed or felt something wrong, she grabbed the back of his head and kissed him deeply, hungrily.

And then she forgot to worry, forgot about everything but this moment, this time, and welcomed his lovemaking, the feel of him inside her, the pleasure taking over, taking her higher and higher until the pulsations burst through her and rippled into every part of her being.

As she absorbed these beautiful sensations with wonder, Matteo's movements quickened, his lips found hers and with a long moan into her mouth, he shuddered before collapsing on her.

For a long time they simply lay there, still saying nothing, the only sound their ragged breaths and the beats of their hearts echoing together through their tightly fused bodies.

Then, as the sensations subsided and the heat that had engulfed them cooled, something else took its place.

Horror.

She heard Matteo swallow into her neck, then his weight shifted and he rolled off her, swung his legs over the bed, and swore, first in his native Italian and then in English.

Coldness chilled her skin.

It was just as well she was lying down for if she'd been on her feet she was certain her legs would have given way beneath her.

What had they just *done*?

How had it happened?

She couldn't explain it. She doubted he could either.

Feeling very much that she could be sick, she stared up at the ceiling and tried to get air into her tight lungs. If she could get her vocal cords to unfreeze she might very well swear too.

After a few deep breaths to steady himself, Matteo got to his feet and went in search of his discarded clothing.

He needed to get out of this house. Right now.

He found his shirt under her dress. One of his socks was rolled in a nest with her bra.

Nausea swirled violently inside him.

What had they just done?

Why the hell had he got out of his damned car? Why hadn't he driven off?

He pulled on his black trousers, not bothering to do the button up, then shrugged his shirt on, not caring it was inside out.

His other sock had rolled half under the small dressing table that had only a thin glass of dried flowers on it. That this was clearly a guest room was the only mercy he could take from this.

Stuffing his socks into his jacket pocket, he slid his feet into his brogues and strode to the door. Just as he was about to make his escape a thought hit him like a hammer to the brain.

His hands clenched into fists as recriminations at his complete and utter stupidity raged through him, every curse he knew hollering in his head.

Slowly he turned around to look at her.

She hadn't moved an inch since he'd rolled off her, her hands gripping the bedsheets, her eyes fixed on the ceiling. But then, as if feeling the weight of his gaze upon her, she turned her face towards him and wide, terrified eyes met his.

That one look confirmed everything.

It didn't need to be said.

Natasha knew as surely as he did that the madness that had taken them had been total.

They had failed to use protection.

And he knew as surely as she did that Natasha wasn't on the Pill. Pieta himself had told him they were trying for a baby.

A thousand emotions punching through him, he left without a single word exchanged between them, strode quickly across the street and into his car.

Only when he was alone in it did the roar of rage that had built in his chest come out and he slammed his fists onto the steering wheel, thumping it with all the force he could muster, then gripped his head in his hands and dug his fingers tightly into his skull.

Another twenty minutes passed before he felt even vaguely calm enough to drive away.

He didn't look at the house again.

Two weeks later

It was taking everything Natasha had not to bite her fingernails. It was taking even more not to open one of the bottles of Prosecco that had been in the fridge since Pieta's funeral. She hadn't drunk any alcohol since the wake. If she started drinking she feared she would never stop.

Francesca was due any minute to go through the plans for the hospital they were going to build in Pieta's memory. To no one's surprise it had taken her sister-in-law only one week to buy the site and get the necessary permissions to develop on it. Her sister-in-law was possibly the most determined person Natasha knew and she wished she had an ounce of her drive and a fraction of her tenacity.

For herself, she seemed to have lost whatever drive she'd ever had. She felt so tired, like she could sleep for a lifetime.

Where this lethargy had come from she didn't know, had to assume it was one of those stages of grief she'd been told to expect. Everyone was an expert on grief, it seemed. Everyone was watching her, waiting for her to crumble under the weight of it.

And despite everything, she *was* grieving, but not for the reasons everyone thought. Her grief was not for the future she had lost, but the seven years she and Matteo had both wasted.

Mixed in with it all was that awful sick feeling in her belly whenever she remembered how the night of the funeral had ended.

God, she didn't want to think about that but no matter how hard she tried to block the memories, they was always there with her.

The bell rang out.

She blew a long puff of air from her lungs and tried to compose herself while the housekeeper let Francesca in.

Footsteps sounded through the huge ground floor of the house Natasha had shared with Pieta and then Francesca entered the study with her brother, Daniele. It was the figure who appeared behind her brother-in-law that almost shattered the poise Natasha had forced on herself.

As was the custom with her Italian in-laws, exuberant kisses and tight embraces were exchanged with whispered platitudes and words of comfort. Then it was time to greet Matteo.

Bracing herself, she placed a hand loosely on his shoulder, felt his hand rest lightly on her hip as they leaned in together to go through the motions of something neither could forgo without arousing suspicion. When the stubble on his warm jaw scratched her cheek she was hit by the vivid memory of that same cheek scratching her inner thigh and had to squeeze her eyes tightly shut to block the image, something she *must* forget.

But she could smell his skin and the scent of his cologne. Smell him. Feel the strength of his body, the curls of his dark hair between her fingers...

It had been a terrible mistake, something neither of them had needed to vocalise.

She didn't know it was possible for someone to hate themselves as much as she hated herself. She owed Pieta absolutely nothing, she knew that, but...

She just couldn't believe it had happened. Couldn't believe she had lost all control of herself, couldn't work out how it had happened or why.

It was as if some madness had taken hold of them both.

For one hour she had left behind the girl who had done everything she could to please her parents to the point of abandoning the life she'd so desperately wanted, and had found the hidden woman who had never been allowed to exist.

Protection had been the last thing on either of their minds.

They'd been stupid and so, so reckless.

Francesca hadn't said she would be bringing her brother and cousin with her. It hadn't occurred to Natasha to ask. Daniele and Matteo both ran enormously successful businesses that took them all over the world. She'd assumed their input for the hospital—especially Matteo's—would come at a later date.

But then she looked properly at Francesca and understood why Daniele at least had stuck around in Pisa. Her sister-in-law looked more bereft than she had at Pieta's funeral. More than bereft. Like the light that had always shone brightly inside her had been extinguished. Daniele would never leave his sister in this state.

And Francesca looked closely at Natasha in turn. 'Are you okay? You look pale.'

She gave a rueful shrug. None of them could pretend they were okay. 'I'm just tired.'

'You're holding your back. Does it hurt?'

'A little.'

The housekeeper brought in a tray of coffee and biscotti, which distracted them all from Natasha's health. They sat around the large dining table onto which Francesca placed a stack of files.

Natasha couldn't even remember what the meeting was for. Matteo being under the same roof as her had turned her brain into a colander.

Why had he come? Was it to punish her?

Every time she'd seen him over the past seven years had been a punishment she'd accepted. She'd let him kiss her and then hours later had agreed to marry someone else, in front of him, in front of everyone. Not just someone else, but his cousin and closest friend. She'd let the moment when she should have told him about Pieta slip by in the haze of his kiss.

Would things have been different if she'd told him, either then or in the weeks beforehand when Pieta's intentions had suddenly become clear? Or would the outcome have been the same?

She'd called and left dozens of messages but Matteo had never answered and he'd never responded. He'd cut her off as effectively as he'd wielded his scalpel.

If things had been different, though, would her life have been any happier? She'd long stopped believing that. Matteo wasn't the man she'd thought him to be. He wasn't a man any woman with an ounce of sanity would consider spending her life with unless she was a masochist. It wasn't just a love of wealth he'd developed since the days she'd fancied herself in love with him; he'd developed a hedonistic streak to match it. No man who had a new woman on his arm every week could ever be content to settle down with only one.

Daniele took control of the meeting, explaining where they were with the project and how he and Matteo were planning a trip to Caballeros in the next couple of weeks. It was hoped construction would begin soon after.

'That quick?' Natasha found the energy to ask.

'It's Caballeros, not Europe,' Daniele answered with a shrug. 'Bureaucracy doesn't exist there in the way we know it.'

'Have you had any publicity ideas?' Francesca asked, reminding Natasha of the role she'd agreed to take in the project.

'I'm sorry, but no.' She stared at the polished surface of the table in her shame. All she'd done these past two weeks was drift. 'I'll get thinking and send you some ideas over the next few days.' She rubbed her temples, hoping she wasn't promising something she would fail to see through. The more publicity they had for it the more donations they would receive, the more donations they received the more staff they could employ.

Dull thuds pounded behind her eyes. As Pieta's next of kin this was her responsibility. Everything concerning her husband's foundation now rested on her shoulders and so far she'd abdicated all responsibility for it.

She would abdicate that responsibility for ever if it was in her power.

At some point soon she would have to think things through clearly but right now her head was so full yet so loose that she could hardly decide what she wanted to eat for her breakfast never mind make decisions that carried real importance.

She couldn't carry on like this. She didn't know if it was shock at Pieta's death or what had happened with Matteo that had her like this but she had to get a grip on herself.

There was a whole new future out there waiting for her and sooner or later she needed to figure out what she wanted from it. So far, all she knew with any real certainty was that she would spend it alone. She would never remarry. She would never allow anyone, not a man, not her parents, to have control over her again.

Francesca raised a weary shoulder. 'There's no rush. The end of the week will be fine.'

Eventually the ordeal was over. Chairs were scraped back as her family by marriage rose to leave. Following suit, Natasha rose too but as she stood, a wave of dizziness crashed over her and she grabbed hold of the table for support.

Francesca, who'd been sitting next to her, was the first to spot something amiss and took hold of her wrist. 'Are you okay?'

Natasha nodded, although she felt far from okay. 'I'm just tired. I should probably eat something.'

Francesca studied her a while longer before letting her go. 'You know where I am if you need me.'

Considering that Francesca looked as bad as Natasha felt, the suggestion was laughable, but it had come from her sister-in-law's kind heart so she would never laugh at her even if she had the energy.

Burning under Matteo's equally close scrutiny, she found she could only breathe normally when the front door closed behind them.

Needing to be alone, she sent the housekeeper out to do some errands and sent silent thanks to Pieta for agreeing with her request that their other staff not live in. How sad was it that she had to request such things, like a child asking a favour from a parent?

Everything about her marriage had been sad. Its ending was the least of it. She'd had no autonomy over any of it.

Now the dizziness had passed she realised she was famished. She'd felt a little nauseous when she'd woken and had skipped breakfast, which had saved her the worry of deciding what to eat, and had managed to forget to have any lunch.

Opening the fridge, she tried to think what she fancied to eat. The housekeeper had stocked up for her and there was choice. Too much choice. After much dithering she took a fresh block of cheese out, then found the biscuits to go with it.

Her stomach was growling by the time she unwrapped the cellophane from the cheese but when she took the knife to it, the smell it emitted turned the growl into a gurgle that flipped over violently.

She chucked the entire block of cheese into the bin then clutched her stomach with one hand and her mouth with the other, breathing deeply, willing the nausea away.

It had only just passed when the doorbell rang.

She stood frozen, hesitant over whether she should open it. Her house had been like Piccadilly Circus for the past two weeks and all she wanted was to be on her own.

It rang again.

What if it was her mother-in-law? Vanessa had been a frequent visitor since Natasha and Pieta had married, and had visited or called daily since his death. Whatever Natasha was going through was nothing compared to what Vanessa was living with.

And yet, even though she continued to tell herself it was bound to be her adorable mother-in-law at the door, she found she couldn't draw the least bit of surprise to find Matteo there instead.

'What do you want?' she asked, tightening her hold on the door frame. There was no audience for them to pretend cordiality.

'I want you to take this.' He held up a long, thin rectangular box.

It was a pregnancy test.

CHAPTER THREE

THE PALE FACE that had opened the door to Matteo turned whiter. 'I'm not pregnant.'

'Take the test and prove it. I'm not going anywhere until you do.'

Her gaze darted over his shoulder.

'Expecting someone?' he asked curtly. 'Another lover, perhaps?'

Her lips tightened but she held her ground. 'Vanessa likes to drop in.'

'The grieving mother checking up on the grieving widow? How charming.' It sickened him that his aunt—like the rest of the Pellegrinis—all thought the sun rose and set with Natasha. It had been Francesca's worry and compassion towards the young widow that had set the wheels in motion for the events that had led him here today. 'If you don't want her to find me here and have to explain why I have this with me, I suggest you let me in.'

A long exhalation of breath and then she stepped aside.

For the second time that day he entered Pieta's home with the same curdle of self-loathing as when he'd entered it the first time. Revulsion. At her. At himself. At what they'd done.

Until Pieta had died Matteo had been in this house

only once, when Natasha had been in England, visiting her parents.

'Have you had a period since...?' He couldn't bring himself to finish the question.

Colour stained her white face at the intimacy of what he'd asked. 'No,' she whispered.

'When are you due?'

Her throat moved before she answered. 'A couple of days ago. But I've never been regular. It doesn't mean anything.'

'You're tired. You have a backache. You used the bathroom three times during our two-hour meeting.' He ticked her symptoms off his fingers dispassionately, although his head was pounding again. They'd made love at her most fertile time. 'My flight back to Miami leaves in three hours. Take the test. If it's negative I can leave Pisa and we can both forget anything happened between us.'

Neither of them said what would happen if the test proved positive.

He held the box out to her. She stared at it blankly for a moment before snatching it out of his hand and leaving the reception room they were still standing in. Her footsteps trod up the stairs, a door shut.

Alone, Matteo took himself to the day room and sat on the sofa, cradling his head in his hands while he waited. In the adjoining room was a bar where he and Pieta had had a drink together. The temptation to help himself to a drink now was strong but not strong enough to overcome his revulsion. He'd already helped himself to his best friend and cousin's wife. He wasn't going to add to his list of crimes by helping himself to Pieta's alcohol.

He'd read the instructions himself. The test took three minutes to produce an answer.

He checked his watch. Natasha had been upstairs for ten minutes.

The seconds ticked past like minutes, the minutes like hours. All he had to occupy his mind were the furnishings the man who'd been like a brother to him had chosen. He couldn't see any sign of Natasha's influence in the decoration.

She'd once wanted to be an interior designer. He remembered her telling him that during a phone conversation held when he'd returned home after an eighteen-hour shift.

Matteo had thought he could never hate himself more than he had when he'd been ten and his dereliction of duty had ruined his little brother's life. The loathing he felt for what he'd done with Natasha matched it, an ugly rancid feeling that lived in his guts. The loathing he felt for Natasha matched it too. Damn her, but she'd been Pieta's wife. Hours after burying her husband she'd thrown herself into his arms and he...

Damn him, he'd let her.

He wished he could erase the memories of that night but every moment was imprinted in him. He'd woken that morning with the vivid feeling of entering her for the first time and the certainty that something had been wrong. It was a feeling that nagged at him more, growing stronger as time passed.

He rubbed the nape of his neck and cursed his fallible memory.

Natasha had been no virgin. She'd been married, for heaven's sake, and had been trying for a baby with her husband.

Another five minutes passed before he heard movement.

She appeared in the doorway.

One look at her face told him the answer.

'There's got to be some mistake,' Natasha croaked, clinging onto the door frame for support. 'I need to do another test.'

She'd stared at the positive sign for so long her eyes had gone as blurry as the cold mist swimming in her head.

For two weeks she'd refused to believe it could happen. She'd refused to even contemplate it.

They had been reckless beyond belief but surely, *surely* nature wouldn't punish them further for it? Surely the guilt and self-loathing they both had to live with was punishment enough?

Eyes of cold green steel stared back at her. It was a long time before he spoke.

'That test is the most accurate one on the market. If it's showing as positive then you are pregnant. So that leaves only one issue to be resolved and that's determining who the father is.'

Afraid she was going to faint, she sank onto the floor and cuddled her knees.

'When did you and Pieta last...?' The distaste that laced his voice as he failed to complete his sentence sent a wave of heat through her cold head.

For the first time in her life she didn't know what to say or do. Whenever life had posed her with a dilemma the answer had always been clear. Do what her parents wanted. It was why she'd married Pieta.

But now her parents were the least of her considerations.

'Do I take your silence to mean that you and Pieta were active until his death?'

How could she answer that? She *couldn't*.

'If your last period was a month ago then it stands to reason you and I were together when you were at your most fertile. However, all women's cycles differ to a certain degree so if you and Pieta were intimate until his death there's a good chance he could be the father. Who else is in line?'

Her head spinning at the medical knowledge that meant he had a much better understanding of how her body worked than she did, she didn't understand what he meant. 'What?'

'Don't pretend you don't know what I mean. Who else have you had sex with in the past month?'

She recoiled. 'That's offensive.'

His laughter crackled between them like a bullet. 'Don't get me wrong, you're playing the grieving widow admirably but you were like a dog on heat with me so it stands to reason there have been others.'

A dog on heat?

She covered her ears, digging her nails into her skull.

A dog on heat?

How had he not *known*? And him a doctor?

There had been a moment, when he'd first entered her, that he'd stilled, but it had only been a moment, and then she had kissed him again, as desperate for him to continue what they'd started as she had been terrified he would figure out the truth.

'I'm waiting for an answer.' His curt voice cut through her thoughts. 'How many others?'

She remembered a time so long ago when his rich voice, the Italian accent faint behind the impeccable English, had always softened around her. She guessed that's what happened when you created a business re-puted to be worth billions out of nothing, your basic humanity was thrown in the gutter along with your principles.

'No one.' She raised her head to look him square in the eye. 'There has been no one else.'

He stared back for the longest time before nodding and getting to his feet. 'A scan will pinpoint the date of conception to a degree of accuracy so we can use that to determine who the likely father is.'

His cutting tone sliced through her.

Then the thought of a scan, of seeing the little one growing inside her...

Suddenly it hit her that she was pregnant.

She was going to be a mother.

Placing a hand to her belly, she blurred out Matteo's bitter face and imagined the life growing inside her.

Hello, my little one, she said silently to it, overwhelming joy spreading through every part of her.

She'd wanted a child for so long. After everything that had gone on with Pieta she had thought it would be a long and torturous road to get there if it ever happened and if she'd ever decided to take the road he'd wanted to conceive one. But it had happened as if by magic.

She was going to have a baby.

'How can you be smiling at such a time?' Matteo said acidly. 'Is this amusing to you?'

The smile she hadn't even known she was wearing fell but as it fell her spine straightened.

Whatever the future held for her, even if it was only humiliation, she had her little seed to think about. She couldn't fall into despair. She would be strong. She would be a mother.

'I'm pregnant,' she said, eyeballing him. 'You cannot know how long I have wanted this so, yes, I will smile and rejoice at my child's conception because it is a miracle.'

His jaw clenched, Matteo eyed her back with mirrored loathing. 'You intend to keep it, then?'

Of all the stuff he'd thrown at her, this was by far the cruellest. 'How can you ask such a thing?'

He breached the distance between them and placed a hand round the nape of her neck. Bringing his face close to hers as if examining her, he said with icy quiet, 'Because I know you, Natasha. You're selfish. You think only of yourself and what advances you.'

Stunned into silence at his closeness, at the warmth of his skin on hers, the fingers almost absently stroking her neck, memories of their one time together crashing through her, Natasha had to blink to get her brain back in gear. Breathing heavily, not taking her eyes from his, she raised her arm to find the hand laid so casually on her and dug her nails in as hard as she could as she shoved it away.

Raising herself to her full height, which was almost a foot shorter than his six-feet-plus frame, she said as icily as she could through the tremors in her voice, 'You don't know me at all. If you did you wouldn't have to ask if I wanted to keep it. I will do more than keep it. I will raise it and I will love it.'

Once she had longed for this.

If her eighteen-year-old self had been told that in seven years she would be carrying Matteo's child she would have danced for miles with joy.

But she couldn't tell him that. He wouldn't believe her if she did.

He rubbed the flesh of his hand where she'd stabbed him with her nails.

'I hope for your child's sake that your words aren't as

worthless as they usually are but time will tell on that. I've a friend who runs a clinic near mine in Florence with the newest, most accurate scans. I'll take you there. She'll be able to pinpoint the date of conception to at least determine if I'm in the frame as father. Her discretion will be guaranteed and I think one thing we can be in agreement on is the need for discretion.'

Natasha forced herself to breathe.

Everything was happening so quickly. She couldn't let him railroad her but likewise she had to do what was best for her and her baby and until she'd decided what she was going to do, she needed all the discretion she could get.

Oh, God, the implications were too awful to think about.

How many lives were going to be ruined when the truth came out?

The worst of it was she would never be able to tell the full truth. No one could know.

Like Matteo couldn't know that she already knew of an excellent clinic, this one in Paris, where discretion was also guaranteed.

And he couldn't know that he was the only man in the frame for the father of her baby.

Fighting back another bout of dizziness, she nodded sharply. She had to keep it together. 'When?'

'In a fortnight. The baby's heartbeat should be detectable by then.'

'So soon?' She'd known for twenty minutes that she was pregnant and he was saying her baby's heart was already forming? That was just mind-blowing.

He nodded grimly. 'Pregnancy is taken from the date of your last period so in a fortnight you will be classed as six weeks pregnant. Only the scan will be able to give us a reasonably accurate conception date.'

'And I'll be able to hear the heartbeat?'

'We both will.' His face a tight mask, he headed for the door. 'I'll be in touch.'

Only when she heard the door close did she sink onto the sofa and hang her head between her knees.

Soon she would be hanging it in shame.

All the people who were going to be hurt, Vanessa, Francesca... Ever since she'd married Pieta she would catch them looking at her belly, knew they were searching for the signs of swelling, the signs of life growing inside her. Since he'd died the stares had become more obvious. She knew how badly they wished she was carrying Pieta's child. Francesca was already suspicious.

She sat back and rubbed her temples.

She didn't have a clue how to handle this. Whatever she did, everyone would be hurt. Hopes were going to be raised then not just dashed but crushed. Then there was the Pellegrini estate itself...

This was too much.

Overwhelmed by the jumble of thoughts raging through her head, Natasha burst into tears.

It had to be like this, she told herself, hugging her belly, the urge to protect her little seed already strong, even if only from her tears.

The real unvarnished truth would destroy every single one of them, Matteo included.

Better to take it on the chin and have the world, including her own parents, think her a slut than for that to happen. She could hardly bear to think of the disdain and disappointment in their eyes when they learned she was pregnant and that Pieta wasn't the father.

Marrying Pieta was the only thing she'd done in her

twenty-five years that had pleased them. It had given them the opportunity to brag to the world that the great Pieta Pellegrini was their son-in-law and it was an opportunity they never let pass by.

Natasha dried her eyes and blew out a long breath.

All the tears in the world wouldn't change things. She was going to be a mother and that meant she had to be strong for her child's sake.

And all the tears in the world didn't change the fact that it was better for the world to think her a slut than for everyone to know that Matteo was the only candidate for father of her baby.

The world could never know that she had been a virgin until the night she'd buried her husband.

The clinic Matteo had booked them into was tucked away in a beautiful medieval building in the heart of Florence. To the unwitting passer-by it could be home to any of the numerous museums and galleries the city was famed for.

The interior was a total contrast. No one entering could doubt they were in a state-of-the-art medical facility.

The cool receptionist made a call and moments later Julianna, the clinic's director, stepped out of a door to greet them.

Matteo had met Julianna, a tall, rangy woman in her midforties, a number of times at conferences. They welcomed each other like old friends, exchanging kisses along with their greetings.

Then he introduced her to Natasha and they were taken through to the pristine scanning room where everything was set up for them.

'Are you happy for Dr Manaserro to stay in the room while we do this?' Julianna asked Natasha in English.

Her eyes darted to him with an inflection of surprise before she shrugged her slim shoulders. He doubted she'd ever heard him addressed by that title before.

'You will be a little exposed,' Julianna warned.

Another shrug. 'He can stay if he wants,' she answered tonelessly.

Matteo experienced a pang of guilt that was as unwelcome as it was unexpected.

Today was the first time he'd seen Natasha in two weeks. In the intervening period, other than arranging this scan, he'd done his best to forget her and the pregnancy.

The chances of him being the father were extremely slim, he'd reasoned. Even if the scan confirmed that he could be, he still knew it wasn't likely. They'd only been intimate the once whereas Natasha and Pieta must have…

His guts twisted violently as he thought of all the times they must have been together over the years. Pieta and Natasha had been actively trying for a baby. Pieta had told him that the last time he'd seen him.

And she was happy to be pregnant. She'd called it a miracle. Was that because of her longing for a child or because she was happy that a part of Pieta might be living inside her? Surely she must have felt *some* affection for her husband, whatever her actions the night of his funeral?

Surely she wouldn't have reacted like that if she'd thought there was any chance *he* might be the father?

Dio, he shouldn't be thinking like this. It felt too rancid inside him.

Since she'd accepted Pieta's proposal hours after

their one kiss, he'd pushed Natasha out of his mind, never thinking of her, never thinking of her and Pieta together. Only when he'd been in her presence had his loathing of her come out of the compartment in his head he'd put her in, and on those occasions he'd learned to hide it by ignoring her wherever possible. He'd moved on very quickly and in any case Pieta was too good a friend and too close a cousin for Matteo to let a woman come between them.

Pieta hadn't known Matteo and Natasha had been building a long-distance closeness which, looking back, had been strange as he and Pieta had often swapped stories about women. At the time it had felt too…special to be spoken of, which with hindsight had been comical. He must have been caught in a bout of sentimentality and had made sure never to have such ludicrous thoughts again.

If it was indeed Pieta's child then he too would celebrate to know a part of his best friend lived on, even if the mother the child had to live on through was a deceitful bitch.

It *had* to be Pieta's. The alternative…

It would destroy everything.

So he'd left her alone and fought the urge to call every five minutes and make sure she was eating and sleeping properly.

Looking at her now, he didn't think she'd had a square meal since he'd last seen her.

'Okay, Natasha, you are looking at this as a dating scan, I believe?' Julianna said.

She nodded.

'Have you seen a doctor or a midwife yet?'

She shook her head.

'Are you thinking of having the child here or in England?'

Her eyes darted to him again.

Julianna smiled reassuringly. 'It's okay, there are no right or wrong answers.'

'I haven't thought that far ahead,' she whispered.

'You have plenty of time to decide but you should be monitored. The obstetrician we employ here is the best in Florence or I can recommend a female for you if that would suit you better?'

Matteo, feeling perspiration break out on his back, had to bite his tongue to stop himself from cutting in. Now they were here, the ultrasound screen switched on, he wanted to get this over with.

But that appeared to be the end of the questioning.

'Are you ready to do this?'

'Yes.' It was the most animation he'd heard in Natasha's voice since she'd opened the door to him earlier.

'Lie down and lift your top and lower your skirt to your hips so your stomach is exposed.'

Matteo trained his eyes on the screen.

When Natasha was ready, Julianna tucked tissue around her lowered skirt and took her seat.

Even though he wasn't looking directly at her, he saw Natasha flinch when the cold gel was applied to her stomach.

Julianna then picked up the probe and pressed it over the gel. As she worked, all three of their gazes were fixed on the screen.

'There it is!' she said in delight. 'See, Natasha? There is your baby.'

Natasha craned her neck forward, trying hard to see what was there. 'Where?'

'There.' Julianna put a finger to the screen. 'See?'

Natasha really didn't know what she'd been expecting to see—a fully formed miniature baby this soon into the pregnancy was too wild even for her imagination—but had hoped it would be more than a blob. But then Julianna pressed some keys on the keyboard on her desk and the blob came into sharper focus. It was still a blob but there was something more defined about it that got her already racing heart ready to burst out of her.

'Do you want to hear the heartbeat?'

A moment later the most beautiful sound she'd ever heard echoed through the room.

She didn't dare look at Matteo. If there was anything other than joy on his face it would taint this special moment for ever.

So she continued to look at her little walnut now frozen on the screen and listen to its healthy heart beating while Julianna did whatever she was doing on her computer until her eyes blurred and the beats were no longer distinguishable.

Eventually Julianna pushed her chair back and wiped Natasha's belly clean with another, softer tissue.

'I would say that so far everything is looking good and healthy.'

'So far?'

The older woman smiled. 'I am a medical practitioner. We never talk in absolutes. What I can say with all honesty is that right now your child is developing well and you should be happy with that. As for when it's due…' She gave a date at the end of June.

Natasha closed her eyes. When she had searched the internet and put in the date of conception, every site she had visited had given this same due date within its narrow parameters.

CHAPTER FOUR

NATASHA HAD TO wait until they were back in his car before she had an inkling of what Matteo was thinking.

'This changes everything,' he said after a long period of silence.

'Not really,' she refuted quietly. 'You already knew it could be yours.'

'I know, I was praying that it wasn't,' he spat.

She dug her nails into the palms of her hands. She'd had two weeks to prepare for this moment, researching everything she could about pregnancy whilst hiding any nausea or backache from her steady stream of visitors.

If she hadn't been in such shock at the test coming up positive—who could expect to fall pregnant on their very first time of making love?—she would have been able think much more quickly on her feet and not put Matteo through the turmoil he must have been in over the past fortnight. When he'd asked when she'd last been intimate with Pieta her brain had been too frazzled to think of a straight-up lie. How badly she'd wanted to tell him the truth and spare him all the uncertainty.

The truth would shatter him. The truth would shatter everyone.

It had to be this way. As hard and as painful as it was, it was the lesser of two evils.

If there was a hell she would surely be sent to it for all the lies of omission she'd had to tell and would continue having to tell.

'Do you have any idea of the nightmare you've pulled me into?' he said scathingly, driving them out of the city and into the Tuscan hills.

'The nightmare *I've* pulled you into?' she retorted, raising her voice. 'As far as I recall, you were there too. I accept I behaved badly but you behaved badly too so don't you dare place all the blame on me.'

He changed gear with so much force she thought the gearstick would snap.

His jaw clenched, he drove them on in silence.

As a rule, Natasha loved Tuscany. She loved the glimpses of vineyards and olive groves, the old hidden monasteries that would suddenly spring into view, some old and decrepit, others renovated, beautiful whatever their states. Today the scenery passed her by without notice. Not until they entered a town they hadn't travelled through on their way to Florence did she realise he was taking a different route back.

Her heart sinking, she knew where he was taking her.

Sure enough, soon she caught her first view of Castello Miniato, centrepiece of the Pellegrini estate Pieta had inherited in its entirety when his father had died just weeks after their wedding. The estate he'd married her for.

Matteo pulled the car to a stop outside the fortressed wall surrounding the *castello*.

'What do you see?' he asked her roughly.

'Is this a trick question?'

'No.'

'The *castello*.'

She'd married Pieta in these grounds—thankfully

not in the *castello*'s chapel as that would have made their marriage even more of a mockery—with a heart that had felt dead. She'd seen the expectation on her mother's face and the silent nod of encouragement to put her best foot forward. She'd felt the pressure of her father's fingers digging into her upper arm, had thought of the vast amounts of money Pieta had given her parents during their long engagement and had dragged her feet towards him.

Pieta had been waiting under the floral arch. His expression had been neutral. It could have been anyone walking towards him.

She wished she'd had the courage to turn on her heel and run.

The *castello* she'd adored for so long, the castle that had fired her young imagination with thoughts of knights and maidens, had been the main reason Pieta had married her. They'd spent only a handful of nights there but she had grown to detest it, a manifestation of the trapped desperation she'd found herself in.

'Why are we here?'

'To remind you of what you married into. The inheritance of this estate is on hold until there is no longer any possibility you're carrying Pieta's child. But it's more than that—they're all waiting to see if you're carrying a part of *him* in you. They're all hoping for it, Vanessa, Daniele and Francesca, and now you are pregnant but it is medically impossible for it to be his, so I am going to ask you this one more time and I want you to think very carefully before giving me your answer. How many other men did you sleep with in the days before and after you and I slept together?'

Blood heating with loathing and humiliation, Natasha forced herself to meet his baleful glare. 'None.'

'You are sure about that? There was no one three days either side of when we were together? This is important, Natasha.'

'I know very well how important it is and I am telling you there was no one. You're the father.'

A low sigh escaped from him as he bowed his head over the steering wheel.

The hard reality of their situation crystallised in him. For two weeks Matteo had been able to tell himself it was too remote a chance for him to be the father. Natasha's vehement denial of there being anyone else held the ring of truth in it.

'I'm going to want a DNA test done when the child's born,' he muttered, thinking aloud, 'if only for my own peace of mind.'

She laughed derisively.

The anger he'd been holding onto spilled over. 'Do you have any idea of the destruction this is going to cause? This isn't just your life, it's mine too. Vanessa took me in when I was thirteen years old and treated me as if I were her own son rather than her husband's nephew. Daniele and Francesca treated me like a brother. This is going to cost me my family so you can be damned sure I want concrete certainty about the paternity if I'm going to lose everyone I love because of it.'

'Stop this right now,' she said tightly. 'I know how much you love them—I love them too, but you *are* the father and no amount of burying your head in the sand can change that.'

His lungs had closed so tightly he had to force air into them.

His phone vibrated. Taking advantage of the distraction, he pulled it from his jacket pocket.

It was an email from Julianna. Attached was a picture of the scan and a brief message asking him to forward it to Natasha.

He opened the attachment and, staring at the tiny life so small the resolution of the attachment struggled to distinguish it in any great detail, he felt a little of his anger deflate.

All the arguing and recriminations in the world didn't change the one undisputable fact that Natasha was pregnant and...

And he was the father.

Something flickered inside him, a bloom that expanded into his chest, up his throat, seeping into his brain, filling him with an emotion he'd never felt before because the emotion had never existed in him before.

He was going to be a father.

How could he deny it?

He couldn't.

Dio, he was going to be a father.

It was his child growing in her belly, no one else's.

It was time to accept responsibility for this because the other undisputable fact was that their child was innocent and deserved all the protection it could get from both its parents and also because Natasha was right. Burying his head would cause more pain to Vanessa and his cousins in the long term.

'We won't be able to keep this a secret for long,' he said, thinking aloud. 'The pregnancy is going to be noticeable soon. People—Vanessa and the family—will assume it's Pieta's. Their hopes will be raised.'

'They're going to be so hurt.' He heard the catch in her voice. 'They're going to hate me.'

'They're going to hate us both, but we can protect them from the worst of it.'

'How?'

'Come to Miami with me. I'm flying to Caballeros with Daniele tomorrow. We should only be there for a couple of days. When I get back I'll take you home with me. We can say you need a break from everything. In a month or so we can tell them you're pregnant with my child. It'll be easier for them to accept we turned to each other for comfort and that a relationship grew naturally than to accept the truth of the child's conception.'

'You want us to lie?'

'No, I do not want us to lie. I despise dishonesty but what's the alternative? Do you want to return to your parents in England and—'

'No.' Her rebuttal was emphatic.

'Then coming with me is the only answer. If you stay in Pisa, and Vanessa and the others think there is even a chance you are carrying Pieta's...' To build their hopes up only to cut them away would be too cruel. 'We need to show a united front starting from *now*.'

'So you do accept the baby's yours?'

'Yes. I accept it's mine and I will acknowledge it as mine. Come with me and I will protect you both, and we will have a small chance of making the pain of what's to come a little less in the family who have shown both of us nothing but love and acceptance. They have suffered enough.'

She rested her head against the window and closed her eyes. He hated that even looking as if she hadn't slept in a month she was still the most beautiful woman he'd ever laid eyes on.

Eventually she nodded. 'Okay,' she said in her soft, clear English voice. 'I'll come to Miami with you. But only for a while. We can fake a burgeoning relationship, I can get pregnant, and then we can split up.'

'We stay together until it's born.'

Her eyes flew open to stare at him with incredulity. 'That's seven and a half months away.'

'This is your first pregnancy. You need my support.' He remembered his early hospital rotation in the ER when he'd been a junior resident. He'd dealt with numerous pregnant women admitted with complications, knew first-hand that pregnancy was unpredictable.

'Support? You were talking about a DNA test only a few minutes ago. If that's your idea of support, I'd much rather go it alone.'

'Damn it, Natasha, I'd convinced myself there was no way the child could be mine! I wanted it to be Pieta's, I didn't want it to be mine. I wanted to be able to wash my hands of the situation but I can't. I *do* accept it's my baby you're carrying but this isn't going to be easy. Not for either of us. I am not going to let you go through the pregnancy alone, so get that idea out of your head.'

'What happens when it's born?' she demanded to know. 'How much involvement will you want?'

'I don't know!' He thumped the steering wheel in his anger.

This could not be happening. Natasha was having his child. It was going to destroy everything and everyone. But he would not let it destroy his child.

He was going to be a father. He could feel the magnitude of it building inside him.

It had been many years since he'd even considered fatherhood. He'd wanted a wife and a family once, a long time ago when he'd met a woman who'd stolen the breath from his lungs with one look. Until that point he'd been so focused on his surgical career that relationships had passed him by, his affairs with the opposite sex short and on occasion sweet, but never interfering with his focus.

The Rawlings were old friends of his aunt and uncle

but the first time he'd personally met them had been during the Christmas period when he'd been in the third year of his residency in a Florida hospital. He'd left Italy at eighteen to study medicine there because it was one of the best medical schools in the world, but had still travelled back to Pisa whenever he could.

He'd arrived late on Christmas Eve, the annual party Vanessa and Fabio threw in their sprawling Pisa villa already well under way. He'd taken one look at the sophisticated, beautiful woman chatting in a group by the enormous Christmas tree and had been instantly enamoured. But then he'd learned that she was only seventeen and had backed right off.

Seventeen? He'd thought she must be at least in her midtwenties.

Being under the same roof meant he'd got to know her a little. What he'd learned had made him want to learn more. Shy on the surface, a little probing had revealed a keen intelligence, a dry sense of humour and a maturity well beyond her years.

He'd returned to America days later, unable to stop thinking about her.

When he'd returned to Italy for Easter, the Rawlings had again been in residence. This time the chemistry between them had been tangible. He'd left with her phone number and the memory of her making him promise to call as soon as he arrived back in Florida so she wouldn't worry about him arriving safely.

No one had ever worried about him arriving anywhere safely before and it had touched him deeply.

He made the call. It became the first of many. Soon it became a habit to call as soon as his shifts at the hospital were over. They emailed. They wrote. They texted. They lived in different continents but it was only a physical separation. He told her things about himself he'd never shared with anyone. He opened himself up and laid himself bare as he'd never done before.

He was content for them to build a relationship from afar, knowing it wouldn't be long until she came of age and they could be together properly. It was the same for her too, going as far as Natasha looking into universities stateside so they could be together.

Spending over a decade studying and working to achieve his goal of being a surgeon had taught him that nothing worthwhile came easily or could be rushed. To him, Natasha was worth waiting for. It was more than desire, it was a meeting of hearts and minds he could never have explained to anyone because he couldn't explain it to himself. She'd tapped into something in him that he hadn't known existed, a need to create a family of his own. And she'd seen something in him no one else had either. Something good. She knew about the childhood fire that had left his brother so severely disfigured that Roberto had become a recluse, yet had never judged him for his part in it. She'd defended him from himself.

Matteo had always known he would never operate on Roberto himself, even when he qualified as a reconstructive plastic surgeon. Never mind it being unethical, he'd barely coped in the waiting room whenever Roberto had endured the many surgeries and skin grafts he'd needed over the years. To be effective, surgeons needed detachment. He could never have been detached operating on his brother. So he'd researched new techniques and the best surgeons performing them while at the same time researching proven topical remedies for burn scars, determined to come up with something practical that would help his brother. Natasha had had no medical knowledge but had listened and encouraged him.

Discovering that he'd opened his heart and laid himself bare to a lie and that she'd been playing with him had hit him right in the gut. But he'd got over it. He'd hardened his heart against her and had soon considered himself to have had a lucky escape. Since then he'd been far too busy, first finishing his residency and qualifying as a surgeon and then building his businesses, to waste his time thinking about her. Thoughts of a family had been put on the back burner. Life was short and he intended to enjoy it and to hell with the woman who'd played him for a fool.

He didn't deny it had given him satisfaction to imagine her reading the media tales of his self-made wealth and know she would be kicking herself for choosing the wrong cousin.

The irony that she would be the mother of his child after all would be laughable if the situation itself wasn't so tragic.

Taking another long breath, he controlled his tone to say, 'No, I *do* know. I'm going to want full involvement. This is our child and we will raise it together.'

'Together?' Her blue eyes flashed. 'I'm happy for us to raise it as some kind of team but only because I know it's best for the baby, but don't get any ideas about me living with you after it's born or marriage or anything like that because I won't.'

'You have no worries on that score,' he shot back. 'You are the last woman I'd ever consider marrying.'

'Good,' she spat, 'because it will never happen.'

He sucked in a breath, trying to keep a lid on his temper. 'We will work out maintenance and custody arrangements that suit us both and works for our child, but that's a long way off. Right now the priority is for you and I to pretend to be a couple falling in love.'

Her disbelief turned into a bark of bitter laughter. 'You? In love? As if anyone in their right mind would believe that. You're pictured with a different woman every week.'

'I will do whatever is necessary to protect my family and if that means being celibate while we fake a relationship then that's a sacrifice I'm prepared to make. We have to make this convincing.'

His uncle and aunt had taken him in when he'd been at his lowest, when the tension between himself and his father had become a poisonous living being. Fabio and Vanessa had loved him and cared for him as if he'd been a child of their loins. He wouldn't be able to protect Vanessa from the horror of Natasha's pregnancy but he could at least spare her and his cousins the truth of its conception and spare their hopes from flaring that a part of Pieta still lived on through her.

'I'm prepared to make some sacrifices but what about you?' he asked, turning it back on her. 'Can you make people believe the grieving widow is capable of finding love again so soon after burying her beloved husband?'

Instead of displaying the vehement outrage he was sure would come at him, Natasha covered her forehead with her hand. 'Trust me, I am an expert at faking things.'

Natasha sat in the living room waiting for the doorbell to ring. Her bags were packed, her affairs in order, passport at the ready, everything done to uproot her life for the foreseeable future.

Matteo's solution, as much as it troubled her to think of living under his roof, was the best way forward. Really, it was the only way. Francesca's unexpected visit just fifteen minutes after Matteo had dropped her home after the scan had proved that.

Francesca had come to tell her in person that she was getting married. Even with her own troubles and the guilty ache in her heart evoked just by being with her sister-in-law, Natasha had been taken aback by the news. Francesca had had a life plan in which getting married had been relegated to occur at least a decade from now. She hadn't planned on falling in love, though, and although she'd tried to mute her happiness, her radiance shone as brightly as the enormous rock on her wedding finger.

Her understandable self-absorption had stopped Francesca scrutinising Natasha with her usual zeal and she had left without asking if she'd had any publicity ideas yet for the hospital in Caballeros or even checking her out for signs of physical change, for which Natasha had been thankful.

For the first time in her life she'd developed a decent pair of breasts. If these changes were already showing, what would come next? Francesca was training to be a lawyer; inquisitiveness came as naturally to her as breathing. Next time those prying eyes would notice.

Leaving Pisa was the best way forward. She couldn't go home to England. That was unthinkable. She dreaded her parents' reaction when they learned of the pregnancy and the identity of the father as much as she dreaded her in-laws' reactions.

Her parents had forced this marriage on her. They hadn't cared that she'd had feelings for another man, hopes and dreams for a future with him. They hadn't cared when Pieta had dragged their engagement out over six long years. They'd never asked if their marriage was a happy one. If she'd told them the truth about it, they wouldn't have cared. They wouldn't have cared that she'd been trapped with no way out and no means to leave him. There would have been no help from them.

When she'd called her father to inform him of Pieta's death, his first question once the platitudes had been done with was to ask if she could be pregnant. Her mother had asked the same thing at the funeral.

Not even her mother-in-law had been so insensitive to ask that and it was her son who'd died.

Her parents' hopes for a pregnancy had nothing to do with any longing for a grandchild. For them it was all about the money.

So, yes, Matteo's option was the only sensible one.

Sensible and right. Right for her baby.

For all his hostility and for all the fallout he would endure, he wasn't shirking his responsibility. After what had seemed like hopeful beginnings for them, they'd been on the fringes of each other's lives for almost eight years and had spent one incredible night together. They both bitterly regretted that night. They didn't know each other. They didn't trust each other. They needed to use this time to form some kind of relationship that would allow them to raise their child in the spirit of togetherness and not as enemies.

All of this felt rational. Sensible. She needed to put her best foot forward and do her best, as her mother always liked to say, as if she were the leader of some Girl Guide group taking charge on an exciting expedition rather than a mother doing what was best for her child.

Her parents had never done what was best for her; they had always done what was best for them.

She could not live like that any more.

She'd lived her entire life as a pawn to be used, first by her parents and then by her husband, never good enough as she was, never *being* enough as she was, just a sad sap of a girl with a desperation to please.

When her baby was born she would think and do only what was best for it and she would do it on her terms, no one else's. But until then…

Best foot forward and do her best, and don't think about what it would do to her emotionally living with Matteo under his roof. That should be the least of her worries, but when her pulses surged to hear the doorbell ring, she knew it had the potential to be the greatest of all the dangers.

CHAPTER FIVE

MATTEO'S JET, WITH *Manaserro* emblazoned in bold red lettering on its sides, was ready for boarding as soon as they'd been whisked through security. Take-off occurred within minutes.

After showing Natasha all the facilities, including the bedroom, which he said was for her use during the long flight, Matteo settled himself at his desk and turned his tablet on.

He raised his brows when she took the seat opposite. 'Don't you want to get some rest? You look tired.'

That she could not deny. The pregnancy hormones were making her exhausted but she'd been so wound up over the guilt of their plans and all the other things weighing on her conscience that she couldn't switch her brain off to sleep.

'Maybe later. Tell me how it went in Caballeros.'

He shrugged and put his tablet down. 'I can honestly say I've never been to such a dire country in my life.'

'That bad, was it?'

'Worse. Francesca's fiancé—' He suddenly interrupted himself. 'Did I tell you she spent one week there and fell for her bodyguard? They're getting married.'

Natasha nodded. 'Francesca told me.'

'Her fiancé is not a man to be messed with and the

hospital site itself is secure. He's got men permanently posted there for the duration of the construction process but the Caballeron government is corruption itself.'

That came as no surprise. Caballeros was infamous. Ranked the sixth most dangerous country in the world, drugs and crime were rife. Daniele had insisted Francesca, who'd been hell-bent on getting the hospital site approved as a memorial to Pieta, only travel there with heavy protection.

Thinking of Daniele made Natasha chew her bottom lip, the weight of her conscience pressing down extra hard.

'Did you tell Daniele about us?' she asked in a small voice.

He grimaced again and sighed heavily. 'I set the seed and told him you were going to fly out to Miami for a break. He didn't seem to be bothered by it.' Suddenly he slammed his fist down on the desk, real anger on his face. 'How do you do it?' he demanded.

'Do what?'

'*Lie*. Daniele trusts me. It didn't occur to him that I was feeding him a steaming pile of manure. How does it come so naturally to you?'

'It doesn't,' she said, stung. 'I *hate* lying. It's deceitful.'

'Stop the pretence. Lying comes as naturally to you as breathing—you told me yourself that you're a pro at faking things.'

She clenched her teeth together knowing she deserved that comeback. She *had* told him that. He couldn't know she'd been referring to her marriage and the mountain of lies it had been built on.

'It was your idea for us to play it like this,' she reminded him icily, 'and you can't tell me you haven't told a bagful of lies in your time.'

'Not in my personal life.'

'You lie in your professional life?'

'There isn't a physician alive who hasn't told a white lie.'

'And what do your lies consist of? *Yes, your nose is huge, let me shrink it for you and charge you a vast amount for it*?' she taunted. 'Although from what I've heard you're too busy swanning around the world building your empire to bother with the nitty-gritty of surgery itself.'

His green eyes turned icy cold. 'I don't swan around, whatever that means. I employ the best surgeons from the top medical schools in my clinics and we operate under a strict code of ethics. A doctor's first duty is to do no harm and I am insulted you would imply otherwise. I have never lied to a patient but in my residency days I did on occasion lie to a relative at the patient's request, like with the mother who wanted to spare her child from knowing the prognosis of the cancer eating at her brain until she thought the child was in the right place to handle it. Those lies were told to prevent further suffering.'

She stared at his tight, angry face. For the first time in seven years she saw a glimpse of the man he'd been before, the man who'd been passionate and driven about his work, a man she'd thought no longer existed.

'Why did you turn your back on it?' she asked, unable to hide her bewilderment.

'I didn't. I became an entrepreneur alongside it.'

'You were going to be a reconstructive surgeon. You took the most direct routes to it that you could find...'

'And I *am* a reconstructive surgeon. I perform enough

to keep my skills sharp, but the surgeons in my employ fix people who are unhappy with how they look. That's what I always set out to do.'

'No, you didn't. You wanted to fix people who were maimed and disfigured. You never said anything about opening your own clinics. The skin cream you wanted to develop was to help your brother…'

'My brother died,' he said, drumming his fingers on the desk, the glint of danger in his eyes.

'I know and I'm sorry.' She knew that when Matteo was ten and his brother Roberto eight, Roberto had been seriously injured in a fire that had left him with horrific internal and external scarring. It was a miracle he'd survived to live another twenty years. When she'd heard of his death she'd known Matteo would be devastated.

Poor Matteo. One minute he must have been on top of the world, qualifying as a surgeon after so many years of hard work, then only three months later, when he'd hardly had the time to taste his success, the brother he'd adored and had longed to make better had died.

She had wanted so badly to reach out to him but had known her words of condolence would not be wanted. They wouldn't be wanted now either.

Adopting a softer tone, she said, 'I just remember all the conversations we used to have. I remember the ideals you had back then.'

'Those?' he mocked. 'They were a young doctor trying to impress a beautiful woman with his humanity.'

Heat spread low inside her at the backhanded compliment. 'So you *are* a liar, then.'

His sensual lips pulled into a smile but the eyes didn't change, holding hers with that dangerous yet somehow seductive glint. 'Not lies. I merely chose to alter the path I was taking. That's the beauty of life—it's full of options, something I am sure you're familiar with. After all, you chose to marry Pieta, heir to the Pellegrini estate, rich in his own right, when there would have been other options available to you. And now you're a reasonably rich widow you will have a pool of men to choose from to make husband number two.' The smile became cruel. 'Or have you already got a man in mind, *bella*? A rich surgeon perhaps who can comfortably keep you in the lifestyle you've become accustomed to?'

Even his endearment of *bella* sounded like a mockery.

'I've already said I don't want to marry you,' she snapped. 'I don't want to marry anyone.'

'But, *bella*, I don't trust a word you say so why should I believe that? If you're secretly hoping my invitation to live with me during the pregnancy means I have some latent feelings for you, you're wrong. I admit that once I did have feelings but you killed them when you accepted Pieta's proposal and I realised you'd been toying with both of us. If I ever marry I would need to trust my wife. I would require some form of loyalty and faithfulness and we both know you're incapable of any of that.'

Natasha's stomach shredded under the weight of his malevolence but she refused to cower under it. 'You haven't lived my life; you know nothing about me. And how dare you speak of loyalty as if it's an attribute you own when you bedded your best friend's wife on the day of his funeral.'

The mocking glint disappeared. Matteo rose to his feet, towering over her, his face dark and menacing. 'That is something I will regret for the rest of my life. You're a gold-digger. You chose Pieta over me because he had money and back then I had little—you see, *bella*, I do know you. I know you come from a greedy, grasping family who spent my cousin's money as if it was going out of fashion and his death means the gravy train is over. You only inherit his personal wealth, substantial, I admit, but nothing compared to the income you enjoyed from the Pellegrini estate when he was alive. Was that why I came back in your favour now I'm so much more than an overworked doctor?'

Matteo watched the colour drain from her face as he spoke but felt no guilt. He only spoke the truth. Pieta had mentioned a number of times about helping Natasha's parents out. He'd described them as leeches.

'You came to *me*,' she hissed, rising too and leaning on the desk between them, blue eyes spitting brimstone. 'You're entitled to your opinions of me—I can't change them, I know that—but you're not entitled to your own facts. You turned up at *my* door, not the other way round. We were both there, we both know what happened just…happened. It wasn't planned and I will not have you twist things round so that you can absolve yourself of any blame. Our child's conception is on both of us so you can damn well stop putting it all on me.'

Matteo threw his head back and clenched his jaw before looking at her.

Dio, even in anger she was beautiful. All she wore was a pair of slim fitting jeans and a navy top that fell off the shoulder, and she still filled his loins with an inexplicable craving.

He wished he had the power to eradicate their night together from his memories.

It hadn't even been a whole night. Barely an hour.

The most explosive, fulfilling hour of his life.

It had been an eruption of desire so intense and all-consuming it should have burnt itself out there and then, not remain simmering in his blood.

Natasha had the potential to drive him out of his

mind. She was a Pandora from mythology, beautiful, beguiling, radiating innocence but inside full of deceit. Natasha had the jar in her hand that when opened was going to unleash hell on his earth.

But she was right that it wasn't fair for him to put all the blame on her.

Wasn't that exactly what his father had been doing for twenty-five years, blaming Matteo for the fire rather than accepting his own responsibility for it?

He would never be like his father.

He *had* gone to her. It had been he who'd kept his finger on the buzzer until she'd opened the door. Even now, with a month's distance from the event, he had no insight into his own motives. He still couldn't understand what had compelled him to get out of the car and cross the street to the house.

Whatever the underlying reason, it didn't change the outcome. They were having a baby together.

'You're right,' he said, sitting back down with a sigh. 'The guilt belongs to us both. I shouldn't put it all on you.'

Her stony glare didn't drop an inch.

He rubbed his forehead, trying to ease the pressure building in it. 'Look, the next seven, eight months are not going to be easy for either of us.'

'No, they're not,' she agreed, her voice a fraction calmer.

'Like it or not, our baby ties us together. I've seen first-hand how destructive warring parents can be. I saw it all the time during my residency, parents who could hardly stand to be in the same room as the other even when their child was seriously ill. I don't want our child to suffer because of us. For our baby's sake, I'm willing to try and look past what went on between us before and build some kind of relationship that isn't based on loathing.'

Her eyes flickered. 'Really? You can stop throwing the past back in my face?'

'I can try. I'm never going to trust you but for better or worse we're now always going to be involved in each other's lives. I'm prepared to try. What about you? Are you willing to try too?'

Her gaze didn't leave his but there was a discernible softening in her eyes, a slight crease forming in her brow as if she was thinking.

She stayed like that for a long time.

Then her lips pulled together and her throat moved before she nodded and whispered, 'Yes. I'm willing to try.'

He almost put out his hand to invite her to shake on their truce but stopped himself before his fingers had moved more than a fraction towards her.

It wasn't just his fingers that yearned towards her. It was all of him.

He cleared his throat. 'So now that's settled, would you like me to order you some food?'

She shook her head and looked away. All the fire that had spilled out of her just a short while ago had been dampened. Now she looked lost.

'I'm not hungry. I think I'll take you up on your earlier suggestion and get some rest.'

'Whatever you wish.'

She walked to his bedroom with a gait that was almost a shuffle. When she reached the door she looked at him again. Even with the distance now between them he could see the crease still in her brow and something that looked like pain in her eyes.

'I know you won't believe me but I never meant for

any of it to happen. I never meant to hurt you. I...' She swallowed and bit into her lip.

Something reached out from his chest and clenched around his throat. Suddenly feeling that he could choke, he waved a dismissive hand. 'You didn't hurt me.'

Natasha closed the door behind her and put one clammy palm to her chest, the other to her mouth and blinked back the hot tears that had filled her eyes.

Despite his denial she knew she'd hurt him all those years ago.

She'd hurt them both.

Drained, her head pounding, she pulled the shades down, removed her shoes and lay on Matteo's king-size bed.

Soon these erratic feelings swirling inside her would subside and she'd be able to breathe.

The soft sheets had a delicious freshly laundered scent to them she found comforting.

Matteo had slept in this bed before. Many times.

How many women had slept in it with him?

She squeezed her eyes shut.

She couldn't afford to allow herself to care. Matteo was the father of her child but he could never be anything more. That ship had sailed. Even if it hadn't, and even if she wasn't determined to grab her freedom and live her life free from anybody else's chains, Matteo would not be the one.

If she'd thought marriage to Pieta had been hard she could only imagine the hell Matteo would have put her through.

He thought a few months of celibacy was a *sacrifice*. God alone knew how many times he would have cheated on her if she'd married him. He went through women like most people went through their laundry.

He wasn't the man she'd believed him to be all those years ago. She'd thought him a man of integrity. She'd believed him when he'd said he wanted to be the world's foremost reconstructive surgeon. The life he'd chosen, however, was the antithesis of those early dreams.

No, he most definitely was not the man she'd believed him to be. And now she was fated to be tied to him for the rest of her life.

The first two weeks in Miami passed a lot more easily than Natasha expected. That she was given Matteo's guesthouse at the back of his waterfront home helped. She'd expected to be physically living under the same roof as him but instead had her own place complete with her own private swimming pool. She'd yet to venture any further into his home than the utility and kitchen. They rarely saw each other but when they did they were at great pains to be polite to each other.

So far, their *entente cordiale* was holding up.

Matteo worked long hours. His headquarters and the clinic he personally practised from were only a mile from his home on Biscayne Bay but he made frequent trips across America to his other clinics.

The only real time they had spent together had been a visit to an obstetrician friend of his, who had asked her a myriad of questions and examined her with such a gentle touch that she'd found herself reassured. Whether she had her baby here or in Pisa, she would be in excellent hands.

Pisa…

At some point in the near future they would return there. The plan was for Matteo to return to Caballeros with Daniele when the structure of the hospital was complete. They'd decided that would be the best time to confess the pregnancy.

She was thinking all this as she sat with her legs in the guesthouse pool, soaking up the last of the day's sun, soul music playing gently through the earphones, sipping on fresh orange juice brought to her unasked by a member of his friendly staff. So lost in her own world was she that she didn't hear any sign of another's presence until a shadow crossed over her.

Turning her head, she found Matteo standing over her.

She whipped the earphones out, sloshing juice over her hand in the process.

'Sorry if I frightened you,' he said wryly.

'I wasn't expecting you back yet.'

'I finished sooner than expected.' He'd gone to Los Angeles the day before, preparing to open a new store that would sell his magic creams; the two he already had there were bursting at the seams with clients desperate to hand their money over for the miracle of reducing their crow's feet.

She could still hardly believe that the topical lotion he'd been intent on developing all those years ago to reduce his brother's burn scars had turned into such a phenomenon.

Two years after she'd become engaged to Pieta, Matteo had finally qualified as a surgeon. At some point in those two years he'd found the successful formula because he'd launched the lotion as a skin moisturiser six months after qualifying, only months after Roberto's death. It hadn't just helped reduce burn scars but acne scars and wrinkles too. It had been a word-of-mouth sensation that had gone viral on social media within days. Initially selling online, he'd since cannily resisted the pleas from department stores worldwide to stock it, instead selling it from the medical clinics he'd opened at an alarmingly fast rate and then opening his own dedicated stores.

While she admired the drive and dedication it must have taken to make such a success of himself in such a relatively short time, she'd never forgotten the humble doctor he'd been who'd wanted only to help his brother and be the best surgeon he could be. In all their long talks he'd never once said anything about money being a motivating factor in his life's choices. Of all the choices he'd made since his brother's death—and it was obvious to her that Roberto's death had been the trigger behind the new life Matteo had pursued—this was the one she found the saddest.

From his jacket pocket he produced a paper napkin from a well-known coffee shop chain. Crouching at her side, he took the hand covered with spilt juice and wiped it.

Taken aback at the gesture, Natasha didn't have time to resist.

Her cheeks flaming, both at his unexpected touch and the realisation she was sitting before him in nothing but a one-piece swimsuit, she muttered, 'Thank you.'

'How have you been?' he asked, removing his shoes and rolling his trousers up to sit next to her, dipping his large feet in the warm water.

'Good, thanks.'

'No more dizzy spells?'

'None.'

He nodded. 'Sleeping okay?'

'Yes.' Surprisingly well.

'That's good. You will let me know if you have any concerns or worries?'

'I've already promised that at least ten times.' This had been something else she hadn't anticipated, that

Matteo would take such an active interest in the pregnancy. Although they had seen little of each other, he messaged her frequently to check that she was feeling all right and had his staff check on her regularly. The guesthouse was connected to the main house by an enclosed glass walkway and there were intercoms in every room that connected straight to his head of housekeeping, who lived in the staff house. Natasha had her privacy but in her time here she'd never felt lonely or abandoned. And that was something else that surprised her. In Pisa, she'd hated living with staff. She didn't find it at all intrusive coming from Matteo's staff, who were a lot more relaxed and upbeat than those Pieta had employed.

'I'm just reinforcing the message.'

'Consider it reinforced.'

Their eyes met, a brief moment of humour flickering between them before she turned her face away to stare at their feet in the water. She never doubted his concern was all for the health of their growing baby.

'The foundations for the hospital have been completed,' he said.

'Already? That was quick.'

'Bureaucracy doesn't exist in Caballeros. The San Pedro Governor is behind the project so it's all systems go. Daniele's been out there again. He's paying his staff triple time to work through the night.' Natasha remembered the agreement that had been made that Pieta's foundation would pay for the site and that Daniele would pay the construction costs and for his own staff to build it. It would be costing him a fortune.

'You've spoken to him?'

'A number of times. He expects the shell of the building to be done within a month. He wants me to go back with him then, before they start the finishing process and it's too late to make any changes I think are needed from a medical standpoint.'

Matteo leaned back on his arms and breathed in the air, trying to unknot the tension that had become a permanent thing in him and always tightened whenever they spoke of Daniele or the other members of his family.

'Has anything been said? About us?' she asked quietly.

'He asked how you were doing. Said Vanessa was missing you.'

She bowed her head and hunched her shoulders.

'She keeps messaging me,' she whispered then swallowed. A tear rolled down her cheek. She wiped it away with the back of her hand. 'I don't know how to respond. It's the same with Francesca. She's called me three times. I try and keep things light and non-specific but I feel so guilty. They've been so good to me and it's killing me to know I'm going to break their hearts.'

He dug his fingers into the grass, resisting the compulsion to put an arm around her. Natasha evoked feelings in him he couldn't begin to understand. She always had.

He had no control over his body's responses to her; even now he was having to fight his own head to tune out that she was wearing nothing but a pretty striped swimsuit and that before she'd hunched herself over he'd seen a glimpse of breasts that had swollen since he'd last seen her only three days before.

It was the need to resist temptation that had seen him travelling more than normal these past few weeks and working the hundred-hour weeks he'd not done since his residency days. Being with her was too much, a constant battle that veered between wanting to shout and shake her, and wanting to pull her close and make love to her again.

He'd promised to try and put the past behind them but, damn it, it was hard.

But he had made that promise and he knew that however hard it was for him, she would be suffering more. She was carrying their child.

Keeping a distance between them might be good for his state of mind but she was under a huge amount of stress. It might suit him better to cast her as an unfeeling cow but that was far from the truth. His clinics in Los Angeles had seen him cross paths with many actresses, good and bad. He could spot a phoney a mile off. Natasha's distress about the Pellegrinis' reaction to the pregnancy was genuine. He'd brought her to Miami in part to support her through this pregnancy. It was time he started holding up his side of their bargain.

'When was the last time you left this place?'

Startled blue eyes found his. 'What do you mean?'

'According to my staff you rarely go out.'

She managed a weak smile. 'Have you got them spying on me?'

'Not spying, more keeping an eye on you. You've got too much thinking time on your hands and it's making you worry about something neither of us has any control over. You need to keep busy, *bella*. We can start by going out for dinner. Have you any favourite foods you like?' As he asked the question he remembered a long ago conversation about her love for spicy food. He blinked the memory he hadn't thought of in nearly eight years away.

'I'll eat anything.'

He pulled his feet out of the water and stood up. 'I'll

have a think about a decent restaurant. Come over to the main house when you're ready.'

Then he picked up his shoes and walked barefoot into his home.

CHAPTER SIX

NERVES CHEWED NATASHA'S stomach as she walked up the marble steps and into Matteo's vast house. It was the first time she'd gone further than the room she knew was used as a utility but which looked like an art gallery, and one of the kitchens, which had the same feel to it. If one didn't know its purpose you could assume it was anything. The first time she'd gone in it the chef had casually mentioned it was the smallest of the kitchens. Turned out Matteo had three of them.

A member of staff appeared and with a smile took her through the house. As they walked, she gazed around in astonishment at the uniqueness and beauty of it all. The exterior was a work of sleek art in itself, with masses of glass and white stucco, but the interior… Everything flowed, the many staircases gave the illusion of floating…it was incredible, a work of art come to life. No wonder Daniele, the architectural brain behind it, had won awards for it. At the time of completion, a year ago, it had been valued as the most expensive property in the whole of Miami.

She was taken through to a vast room, the ceiling at least two storeys high and with an abundance of cream sofas and armchairs, easily enough to seat two dozen people with space to spare.

Left to her own devices, Natasha looked out at the spectacular view of the bay, the sky shades of pink under the setting sun. The room seemed to jut out and touch the bay itself.

She turned round and stared up at what appeared to be a floating balcony but which she quickly understood was a walkway that was part of the second floor. What new delights were there to discover up there?

A glass wall that reached all the way up to this strange yet beautiful indoor balcony soon revealed itself to be a cabinet but it was the huge canvas print beside it that really caught her attention and she walked over to examine it in more detail.

The print was a photograph of two beaming young boys, the elder no more than ten, the smaller one only a couple of years younger. They were sitting on a bench, arms wrapped around each other, their cheeks pressed together, identical curly black hair almost fused into one mass.

'Sorry to keep you waiting.' Matteo's rich tones vibrated through the room.

Natasha looked around but couldn't see him.

'Up here.'

Craning her neck, she found him peering down at her from the floating balcony. A wry smile of amusement on his face, he walked the length of the balcony then disappeared from view, reappearing moments later on the other side of the room.

He must have travelled down a staircase hidden from view.

He'd changed into a pair of crisp navy trousers and a light grey open-necked shirt, his tall elegant frame carrying it off with a panache that made her think of Christmas perfume adverts that always featured suave, gorgeous men and lithe beautiful women. It was the swirls of exposed hair coming through the shirt that had her heart pounding so hard. She remembered so vividly running her fingers through that hair…

Swallowing hard as he strode towards her, she turned her attention back to the print and pointed a trembling finger at the older child. 'Is that you?'

He stood beside her and looked at it.

Fresh cologne filled her senses.

'Yes. I was nine when that was taken.'

'And is the other boy your brother?' It was a silly question really as other than the size difference they could have passed for twins.

'Yes.'

There was a long stretch of silence between them.

'I really was very sorry to hear Roberto died,' she said quietly. 'I know how much you loved him.'

They'd briefly mentioned Roberto's death on Matteo's jet over, but the conversation had turned into a spew of bitterness from him that had stopped her saying anything more about it.

If Matteo had been nine in this picture, then the fire that had torn their lives apart must have happened within a year of it being taken.

She blinked back hot tears as she looked at the happy faces of a life gone by.

Many stories had swirled in the aftermath of Roberto's funeral, gossip and whispers between the family members about a spectacular row between Matteo and his father. Natasha knew the two men's relationship had been strained since the fire, knew Matteo thought his father blamed him for the fire, something that had always made her heart wrench and her blood boil.

She'd never learned what the row at the funeral had

been about but it had been serious enough for Matteo to legally change his surname within weeks. It could only have been intended as a snub to his parents—Manaserro was Vanessa Pellegrini's maiden name. He'd chosen the family name of his uncle's wife. As far as she was aware, Matteo and his parents hadn't spoken since.

As Matteo stood looking at the last happy picture ever taken of his brother, he knew Natasha was thinking of the fire. He'd told her about it himself during one of their many marathon phone calls. He'd told her everything, how he'd been only ten years old when his parents had gone out for lunch leaving him in charge of eight-year-old Roberto, how Roberto had stolen a box of matches from the kitchen and taken them to the barn at the back of their house without Matteo even noticing he'd left the house, and how Roberto had lit those matches one by one, seeing how long he could keep each flame going. It had been a hot day after a period of hot weeks without any rain. The barn had been a tinder box and Roberto had been lucky to escape with his life.

Matteo had escaped with nothing more than the nightmares of his brother's screams, which had sounded as if they'd been dredged from the bowels of hell itself, and his own screams when he'd heard his brother's and had raced out of the house to find him. The image of his brother's small body engulfed in flames haunted him. If the gardener hadn't acted so quickly to douse the flames, Roberto would have died right before his eyes.

Natasha was the only person he'd shared this with. He'd never even told Pieta the sheer horror of what Roberto had been through and what he'd seen.

He hadn't held anything back from her, not his father's complete withdrawal of affection towards him, his belief that his parents blamed him for the fire, the increasing arguments and cold hostility that had culminated in him leaving the family home at thirteen to live with his uncle's family, not the visits back home to see his brother that had only been undertaken when his father had been out, not the many surgical procedures Roberto had endured throughout the rest of his life and for which Matteo had always sat in a separate waiting room from his parents.

He'd trusted her. He'd trusted her with everything.

The worst of it was she'd consoled him. He'd thought she believed in him. Her soft voice had given him comfort.

Then she'd taken his trust and ripped it to shreds.

They stood before the picture for a few more moments in silence before Matteo sighed deeply. It had all happened such a long time ago but sometimes, like now, it might have happened only yesterday.

'Come on,' he said. 'Let's go and eat.'

He led her out to the secure docking bay at the side of his mansion where a gleaming yacht awaited them.

'Is this yours?' she asked with an inflection of surprise.

He nodded and waved a hand to greet the captain awaiting them on deck.

'I've never noticed it before.'

'Have you been round this side of the house?' he said drily.

'No,' she admitted.

'There's your answer.'

'Where are we going?'

He pointed to the island floating in the bay some distance before them. 'Key Biscayne. It's quicker and more pleasurable to sail there rather than drive. How are your sea legs?'

'I guess we're about to find out.'

Within minutes they were standing at the front of the yacht, leaning over the railing as they cut through the water, her blonde hair whipping behind her.

'You like it?' he asked.

She nodded, a wide grin forming, the first real flare of joy he'd seen on her beautiful face in such a long time that it pierced his chest to see it now.

He turned his gaze from her to look at the approaching Key Biscayne. 'Why haven't you explored any of Miami since you've been here?'

'I don't know my way around.'

'I told you when we got here that you only had to ask and a member of staff would be happy to drive you or accompany you anywhere you wanted to go. You're not my prisoner, *bella*.'

'I know I'm not.'

'Then why stay in all the time? Miami is one of the most vibrant cities in the world.'

She shrugged and put a hand to her face to shield herself from locks of thick hair falling into it. 'Where would I go?'

'I don't know. The beach? A café? One of the museums? Jungle Island? An art gallery? A nightclub—there's plenty of those.'

She gave a wry smile. 'I can just see pregnant old me dancing the night away in a sweaty nightclub.'

So could he. Vividly. That long honey-blonde hair swaying, that lithe body in the slim-fitting off-the-shoulder blue-and-white-striped dress she was wearing, moving to the music, wrapped around his...

He blinked the image away and took a breath to drive away the burst of heat in his loins.

'You're pregnant, not dead. There's plenty of exclusive clubs here you can go to that aren't the sweaty places you're thinking of.'

'On my own?'

'I'm not speaking literally. I'm just saying you should be making the most of being fit and able to do things while you can. In a few months you'll be waddling like a duck with a watermelon for a belly.'

'You make it sound so delightful. I look forward to waddling like a duck.'

He grinned at her dryness. He didn't think for a minute that Natasha would ever waddle. She had too much elegance.

It struck him then that he would be there to see the changes in her. He would watch her belly ripen and her breasts grow.

He would be there for all of it. Nothing on this earth would make him miss any of it.

He wondered what changes had already happened that weren't yet visible to his eye, what physical shifts Natasha could feel within her.

'Do you really want to spend the pregnancy stuck in my little patch of the earth?' he said in a teasing tone that belied the depth of his thoughts and the emotions shooting through him.

'It's hardly little.'

'You know what I mean.'

She sighed. 'Yes, I do know. There's lots of reasons but the main one is because I'm trying to save money.'

'You're short of cash?'

'If I spend it frivolously I will be. I have no job. I'm pregnant with no employment history so there's no realistic prospect of me getting one in the foreseeable future.'

'I know you won't inherit the *castello* and the rest of

the family estate but you're going to inherit Pieta's personal wealth.'

'I don't want it. It wouldn't be right.'

'Don't be ridiculous. You were his wife. It's yours by right.'

'I could accept that if I'd contributed to it in any way but I didn't. Everything he earned was his and it was all earned without any help from me.'

'You provided a home for him.'

She shook her head, her hair swishing gently around her shoulders. 'The house was his. The staff were his. The furnishings were his and to his taste. Everything was *his*.'

There was an undertone to her words that raised his antennae.

'You were together for seven years,' he said slowly, trying to figure out what that undertone could mean or why something in his gut told him to listen to it.

'But only married for one. We didn't live together until we married. I cannot in all good conscience take that money, especially not now that I'm having your baby. I could never live with myself.'

His incredulity deepened.

She'd married Pieta for his money. And now she was planning to walk away from it?

A dozen more questions formed but they'd arrived at the dock by the quayside restaurant he'd booked them into so had to wait until they were at their table before he could ask them and the next dozen that formed in quick succession.

They were shown to a table overlooking the waterfront, the distant Miami skyline lighting up like a silhouette under the rapidly darkening night sky.

'This place is so *glamorous*,' Natasha said when they

were seated, her eyes too busy darting around the eclectic restaurant to bother looking at the menu she'd been given. 'Have you eaten here before?'

'I brought my Miami staff here for our Christmas party.'

'Lucky staff. The last time I ate out was at a stuffy ambassador's residence.'

'Not glamorous?'

'If you like old-fashioned glamour.'

'You don't?' He thought of her house in Pisa. Pieta had been a collector of antiques, his tastes shining through every item on display. Now he thought about it properly, there had been nothing of the Natasha he had known all those years ago in that house. It was as if her personality had been subsumed by her husband's.

She hesitated before answering. 'Not particularly. I'm more of a modern girl. What do you recommend to eat?'

'The lobster's good.'

She pulled a face. 'Lobster's boring.'

'Really?'

'Too sweet.' She peered at the menu and pulled another face. 'What the heck are Peruvian potatoes?'

'Potatoes from Peru?' he suggested drily.

She met his eye and sniggered. 'Maybe they come wrapped in a llama.'

He grinned. 'You should try them.'

'I will. Seed-crusted halibut, Peruvian potatoes, wild mushrooms, sea beans and red pepper coulis. Perfect.'

Their food ordered, drinks set before them, Matteo settled back and watched Natasha continue her unabashed admiring of the restaurant's decor.

'You know what I don't understand?' he said.

'What?'

'Why you gave up your plans to be an interior designer.'

The amusement that had flared between them faded, to be replaced by wariness. 'It just never happened.'

'Why not? You still did the degree you wanted in it, didn't you?'

He could tell by the look in her eyes she was remembering how seriously she'd been considering moving to America to do her degree at the Art Institute of Tampa. She'd sent him the prospectus. He'd looked at places to live that were commutable for them both.

She gave a slight nod. 'I ended up doing a BA in Interior Architecture and Design.'

'In England?'

Matteo had tried never to discuss Natasha with anyone over the years and he'd limited his trips back to Europe as much as he could, but it had been impossible not to hear chatter about her. By accepting Pieta's proposal she'd been embraced into the bosom of the Pellegrini family. It had been natural for them to pass on information about Pieta's fiancée to him. They'd assumed he would be as interested as they were. Everyone had assumed that once she'd graduated, they would marry. It had taken another three years for that to happen, although Pieta had bought an apartment for her in Pisa, close to his sister's apartment.

Tales of her had rarely come from Pieta himself. If he ever had spoken of her it had usually been in practical terms, never romantic.

She nodded again.

'Why didn't you take it any further once you graduated? Didn't you enjoy it?'

She gave a wistful smile. 'I loved it. I like to think I was good at it.'

'So what stopped you pursuing a career? You were engaged to a well-known man with contacts all over the world. It would have been easy for you to build a client list.'

'I know.'

'So what stopped you?' he repeated. 'Was it just that you preferred being a lady of leisure?'

Something flickered in her eyes before they flitted away from his gaze.

'I'm not picking a fight here, I'm just trying to understand.' He tried to keep his voice reasonable but as he asked the question he could feel the old anger swelling inside.

This was an extension of their earlier conversation and Natasha's insistence that she wouldn't accept her rightful inheritance. She'd spoken with such sincerity that he had to remind himself to tread carefully. It would be too easy to take her words at face value.

He must not allow himself to forget how he'd fallen for her sincerity before.

Had she been telling the truth on his yacht? Or was she trying to paint herself in a favourable light with him? And if so, for what purpose?

He'd spent seven years telling himself he didn't give a fig for her but the truth was her betrayal had lived in his guts like poison; he could feel it now, uncoiling inside him, the memories of his misplaced faith and trust in her biting into him.

He leaned forward and lowered his voice, trying to read what emotion lay behind the blue eyes staring back at him. 'Why did you choose him over me, Natasha? I always thought it was the money. Was it that? Was it the money and the lifestyle?'

Her hands had balled into fists but there was no fight in her returning stare, just starkness.

His chest rising heavily, Matteo took a large drink of his wine and stared hard at the anguish on her face. He should have ordered something stronger. 'I need to know why. I want to put the past behind us but every time I think I have, something reminds me and it all kicks back in. You strung me along for months…'

Her head shook but her lips stayed stubbornly stuck together.

'Talk to me.' Realising his voice had risen, he strove to lower it again. 'Tell me, Natasha. Make me understand.'

'Look…' She relaxed her hands and took a gulp of her grape juice. Before she could say what she'd intended their meals were brought to the table and laid before them with a flourish.

Natasha looked at her artfully displayed dish and struggled to hold on.

In the space of a minute she'd completely lost her appetite.

Matteo seemed in no rush to eat his food either. He didn't touch his cutlery, just sat there, eyes fixed on her, waiting for her to speak and explain herself.

She couldn't blame him. This conversation had been a long time coming.

She took another drink of her juice. How she wished the grapes had been fermented into wine. It would make this easier.

'I know you don't believe this but everything you and I talked about and the plans we made, I meant it all.'

Natasha knew before the words had finished leaving her mouth that it was the wrong opening gambit.

His eyes narrowed dangerously. 'If you meant any

of it then why were you seeing Pieta at the same time? Did you decide to string us both along until you worked out which of us would make the better husband and give you the better lifestyle?'

'Do you want to hear my side or not?'

There was the slightest flare of his nostrils before he inclined his head.

'I didn't string you along for months. The first time Pieta showed any interest in me was at my eighteenth birthday party. I didn't even think he would turn up for it. I assumed a party like that would be beneath him.'

She'd been devastated when Matteo had called to say he'd missed his flight and wouldn't be able to make it. She'd known it wasn't his fault and that his job wasn't one he could drop—his job, back then, had been a case of life or death. So she'd put a brave face on her disappointment and instead turned her calendar over to the following month when they would both be in Pisa for his aunt and uncle's wedding anniversary party, and drew a tiny heart in the corner of that date.

His jaw clenched. 'You strung me along for that long?'

She shook her head. 'I thought he was being polite.'

'Polite?' Disbelief etched itself on his face.

'He was so much older than me...'

'Pieta is—was—the same age as me.'

Her heart twisted to see the pain that flashed over him at the utterance of his best friend's name.

'But I never felt the age gap with you. Pieta was so serious, he came across as older than his years. He took me to the theatre as a birthday present to see a political play. I hate politics. I didn't have the heart to tell him it was the most boring two hours of my life. Maybe if I'd told him the truth he would have seen me differently and things would have turned out differently too but I didn't and things took on a life of their own. He was in England on business and took me out to dinner a couple of times but I swear I didn't think they meant anything…'

'If they didn't mean anything then why didn't you tell me about them?'

'Because it was during the week you went to Washington for that conference. We hardly spoke that week, don't you remember?'

A pulse ticked in his jaw, his lips tightening.

'Pieta took me to these wonderfully grown-up restaurants and spoke about politics and his humanitarian work. I admit, I was overawed by it all. He was this great man making waves across the world for his philanthropy… I was in awe of him and he knew it, but I swear, I never thought of those dates as dates. The first I knew that he was seeing me in a romantic light was when he asked my father's permission to marry me that Friday, two weeks before his parents' anniversary party.'

'He asked your *father*?'

'That was Pieta all over, wasn't it?' She smiled sadly. 'He took his responsibilities very seriously. It wouldn't have occurred to him to ask me for my views first. He saw the awe on my face and interpreted it as infatuation.'

'And your father said yes?'

'Of course he did. He didn't even have to think about it. It was exactly what he wanted. Pieta was rich and connected and had royal blood in his veins. He was the dream son-in-law to brag about down at the golf club.'

'I can understand why your father would have been keen but that doesn't explain why you went along with it. You could have said no.'

'I did say no.' She squeezed her eyes shut as the memory of her parents' fury played vividly before her eyes. 'My parents knew I was serious about you…'

'Really?' he asked sardonically, finishing his wine.

'Yes! I lived with them, remember? They knew how I felt but they didn't care. They told me to keep my mouth shut about you or I would ruin everything. They told me it was my chance to make them proud after a lifetime of disappointment.'

The scorn in his eyes diminished a little. 'They said that?'

'That and a whole lot of other things too. You had ancient royal blood too but they looked at the wealth Pieta was accumulating, looked at the estate he would inherit and knew that if I married him all their money problems would be over. They were *terribly* in debt. Pieta must have made promises to them because within months of our engagement their debts were gone and he'd paid for them to have an extension put on the house.'

'You agreed to marry him for an extension?' Matteo had picked up his fork and was running his thumb backwards and forwards over the prongs.

'No! That came later. I went along with it because I didn't know what else to do. I wasn't stringing you along, don't you see that? I was playing for time until you got to Pisa for the party and I could tell you to your face what was happening because I couldn't think of a way out.'

'You should have told me as soon as he asked your father's permission.'

'I know that now but at the time I thought it would make things worse. How could I tell you over the phone when you were thousands of miles away that your best friend and cousin wanted to marry me? My head was all over the place. I was only eighteen. I wasn't some cosmopolitan woman with years of experience behind her. I was weak and spineless and I'd got myself backed into a corner I didn't know how to get out of. I wanted desperately to please my parents but at the same time I wanted to be with you. I was waiting for you to get there because I convinced myself you would think of a way out of the mess.'

Natasha took a deep breath and stared at her plate.

Matteo stabbed a roasted shallot with his fork but made no effort to eat it. His eyes were as hard as the tone of his voice. 'You did have the chance to tell me. You made no effort to tell me, remember? But you did let me kiss you.'

She closed her eyes, remembering how she'd taken one look at him in the *castello* and her heart had beaten so hard she'd hardly been able to breathe. After months of increasingly intimate correspondence and phone calls and only a quick snapshot of him on her phone to look at, seeing him in the flesh again…

And then he'd kissed her, their very first kiss—*her* very first kiss—and there had been no breath left to steal. And then Francesca had come barging down the corridor, breaking the moment.

What Natasha hadn't known then was that it had been her last chance to tell Matteo the truth.

CHAPTER SEVEN

NATASHA OPENED HER eyes and forced herself to meet Matteo's unblinking gaze. 'I'm sorry. I thought I'd be able to tell you later that night. I thought I had more time but it was too late. I have kicked myself so many times for not anticipating he would propose publicly like that but I swear I didn't know he was going to do it.'

'Why should I believe you?' he said, not an iota of softening in his stare.

She shrugged helplessly. 'I went to your room in the *castello* that night. I still hoped even then that it wasn't too late for us and that you'd be able to come up with some plan, but you'd gone. I called you but you'd blocked my number—you blocked it that very night. How would I know that if I hadn't tried to call you?'

He *had* blocked her number straight away, Matteo remembered. He'd said goodbye to his family, had managed to force his congratulations to Pieta, walked into the *castello*'s courtyard and into the waiting cab and had immediately blocked her every means of contacting him.

Could she be telling the truth?

'A part of me even hoped you would tell Pieta about us,' she whispered into the bleak silence that had developed between them.

'After he'd publicly proposed and you'd publicly accepted? I would never have humiliated him like that.' He laughed bitterly, his mind reeling from everything she'd confessed.

He looked in the blue eyes that held his. He read the pleading in them.

But what was she pleading for? Forgiveness? Or for him to believe her?

Right then he didn't know what the hell to think or believe.

'You were engaged for six years. You left your parents' home and went to university. You had *six years* to end things with him.'

'When I knew there was no way back with you I decided to stop fighting and just accept it. Accepting it meant pleasing my parents. I told you, back then I was weak and spineless.'

'And you're not now?'

'No.' He saw the defiance bloom in her. 'No. I learned to grow a spine. I had to. And I'm glad I did because it will make me a better mother.' She hung her head and rubbed her temples before looking back at him. 'Just, please, believe my feelings for you were genuine.'

His heart as full as he'd ever known it to be, he nodded slowly. 'Did Pieta ever suspect your feelings for him weren't?'

'Why do you assume his feelings were any more genuine than mine?' Natasha asked before she could stop herself.

'Because he always told me he would know the perfect woman to marry when he found her.'

She clamped down on a burst of her own bitter laughter at the notion. As if her husband had ever looked at her as perfect for anything but the façade he wanted the world to see and the estate he'd wanted to inherit. It didn't matter how hard she'd tried, she'd never been good enough for anyone, not her parents and certainly not her husband.

But she would be good enough for her child and she would do everything in her power to ensure her child never felt that he or she wasn't perfect exactly as they were. She wouldn't diminish them and make them think their best could never be good enough. She would celebrate what they could do and love them regardless of what they couldn't. In short, she would adopt parenting skills at the opposite end of the spectrum to her own parents.

She stared levelly at Matteo. 'I tried very hard to be the best fiancée and then wife that I could be. Do you really think he would have married me if he'd had any doubts?'

Before he could answer, their waitress came to their table and looked at their untouched plates with concern. 'Is everything all right with your food?'

Like a switch had been turned on, Matteo bestowed on her his dazzling smile. 'Everything's great, thanks.'

Smiling, she bustled away.

The interruption had been what they needed.

When Natasha looked at him again he sighed deeply, his eyes boring into her but without the animosity of before.

'We should eat before it gets cold,' he said, finally popping the shallot into his mouth, his tone leaving no doubt that, as far as he was concerned, the conversation was over.

He'd got the answers he was seeking. Whether he believed them or not, she had no control over.

What difference did it make now, in any case? Whatever their feelings had been for each other, it was in the past and it had to stay in the past.

Matteo knocked on the guesthouse door. A minute later Natasha opened it, dressed in a pair of red pyjama bottoms and a black vest. Her usually sleek hair had an unkempt look about it.

She greeted him with one of the smiles that always pierced him in so many different ways.

'I wasn't expecting to see you today,' she said, standing aside to let him in.

'I had a conference call with my clinic managers. We were done sooner than I thought we'd be. Have I woken you?' It was approaching midday.

'I was reading.' She held up the book in her hand. It was a pregnancy book the obstetrician had given her.

'I thought you'd already read that.'

She shrugged. 'No harm in reading it again and there isn't much else for me to do.'

'That's why I'm here.'

'Oh?'

'Have you eaten?'

'What is it with you and my eating habits?' she asked, the trace of a smile playing on her lips.

'I like to be sure you're taking care of yourself. Have you?'

'I had breakfast a couple of hours ago.'

'Then get dressed. I'm taking you out to lunch.'

There was a definite brightening in her eyes. 'Give me twenty minutes. I need to shower.'

He bit back the offer he wanted to make of joining her in it, instead taking a seat at the dining table, following her retreating figure with his eyes. The pyjama bottoms emphasised her bottom, showing its rounded peachy shape beautifully.

He closed his eyes and rubbed his temples.

Since their meal at Key Biscayne ten days ago things had changed between them. It had been a subtle shift but one he felt in his marrow.

He'd gone over her words from that night many times. As hard as it was to override seven years of conditioned loathing towards her, the more he thought about it the more he believed her.

What disturbed him was how much he *wanted* to believe her, and not just because she was carrying his child.

He looked at her now, seven years older, and saw all the things that had been missing before. She *had* been mature beyond her years but it was only now that he was with the fully grown-up Natasha that he realised her maturity back then hadn't been that of a rounded woman with life experience under her belt. She'd been a wide-eyed innocent, blooming as she'd embraced womanhood, excited for her future and what it held. She'd also been a people-pleaser. She'd been almost desperate to please, never giving contrary thoughts or opinions. He remembered how delighted he'd been to find someone so like-minded but now he realised she would have agreed with his tastes and likes whatever they had been.

They'd spent more time together these past ten days. She had no qualms about giving her opinion now and although her tastes did concur a great deal with his own, she never hesitated to voice her own thoughts when they disagreed.

He'd taken her out to dinner a handful of times and to the theatre to watch a musical adaptation of a popular film. She'd clapped along all the way through it. When he'd asked her opinion at the end she'd said that she'd loved it but had wanted to gag the leading lady for her annoying voice.

She was far more interesting now. And somehow more desirable for it, which he hadn't thought possible. He would gaze at her creamy skin and remember how it had felt beneath his fingers. He would look at the honey-blonde hair and remember how it had felt brushed against his shoulder. He would look in the blue eyes and remember the look in them when she'd come with him buried deep inside her.

And he would remember that slight resistance of her body when he'd first thrust inside her and how he'd felt a warning shoot through his head that had been drowned out by the passion of her kisses and the ardour of her response.

If he didn't know better, he would have said that resistance had been the natural resistance of a body unused to being made love to. Which wasn't possible.

But it still nagged at him, playing in his mind like a distant but nearing wind, and though they'd both made a concerted effort not to speak of Pieta or the past since that first meal out, it was there too, hanging between them like a basket of dead flowers.

Until he'd brought Natasha to Miami everything had been cut and dried. He knew who she was and what she'd done. He knew who he was and what he'd done.

Now he was discovering that all his certainties were whispers in that nearing wind and the only thing with any substance to it was his desire for her. It was with him all the time, a constant thickening of his blood, a constant charge in his skin.

When she reappeared thirty minutes later wearing a white summer dress with strappy sleeves and a pair of flat roman sandals, her hair damp around her shoulders, her perfume filling the room as vibrantly as she did just by her presence, he felt the air escape his lungs.

Dio, was there nothing this woman wore that didn't make him want to rip it off?

He got to his feet, keeping his loins under control by the skin of his teeth. 'Ready to go?'

'Where to?' she asked.

'Downtown.'

Natasha strapped herself into the small sports car Matteo had chosen to drive from his vast collection while he pressed the button to put the roof down. The engine started at the press of another button, music pumped out and then he was driving them out of his garage, out of his estate and through the wide open streets of the exclusive gated community he lived in. Soon the verdant verges thick with trees thinned, the large, mostly hidden homes became buildings that steadily increased in height, and the open road filled with traffic.

Downtown turned out to be a thriving metropolis full of character and colour and all kinds of scents. Her hair whipped around her face which with the sun shining down on them acted as an industrial hairdryer.

He drove them round the back of a gleaming skyscraper that looked over the harbour and into the underground car park, coming to a stop in a space with his name on it.

'Handy,' she commented. 'Are these your offices?'

He grinned. 'I need to pop in for a few minutes to sign some documents before we eat.'

There was an elevator a short walk from the parking space. Matteo punched a code and the doors pinged open. Inside, he pressed the button with the number thirty on it.

'Why did you use a code?' she asked.

'It's a security measure. If you don't know the access code the elevators won't work for you. This is an exclusive elevator for my staff and patients.'

They arrived at their floor before she'd even registered the elevator moving.

The medicinal smell hit her the moment the doors opened.

'Do you do surgery here?' she asked in surprise.

'Where did you think I would do it?'

'Not on the top of a skyscraper. I thought these were your administrative headquarters.'

'They're on the next two floors up.'

'But you run your clinic in a skyscraper?'

He laughed. 'Trust me, the facilities here are second to none.'

Three receptionists dressed in white clinical uniforms manned the immaculately clean room with the fabulous views of the ocean they stepped into. Matteo had a brief chat with them while Natasha stared around in wonder at the plush furnishings and tasteful artwork.

It was like being in a hospital that had amalgamated with a five-star hotel.

'I can give you a quick tour if you want?'

'As long as you're not going to give me the hard sell for a buttock enhancement or a new nose,' she jested.

The amusement that had played on his lips since the exhilarating drive over faded. It faded from his eyes too, his stare unfathomable. 'You're the last person who needs anything done.'

It was his tone. The starkness to it. It made her veins heat and her chest fill with a longing that made her yearn to reach out and touch him.

That was all she seemed to want to do. Touch him. And smell him.

She could almost believe he meant it. Almost. But she knew too well that something in her did need fixing. Why else had she never pleased her parents in anything she did? Why else would Pieta have chosen her? She'd been wrong for him in every sense possible but still it had been her he'd chosen to be his wife. It had been her he'd trapped into staying with him even after the truth had come out between them.

She didn't want to think about Pieta.

Since her talk with Matteo ten days ago things had been better between them. They'd both made a concerted effort to build bridges without saying so in words. Like so much between them, it wasn't something that needed saying.

What also didn't need to be said was the reigniting of the chemistry that had always been there, swirling between them but now gaining an intensity she was finding harder to resist.

Resist she must. There was too much danger in it. She'd been besotted by Matteo as a teenager but she wasn't a teenager any more. She was an adult with a little life growing inside her that needed her protection. Learning to find her own voice and not be afraid to speak it had been hard, finding her spine and the courage to stand up for herself harder. She couldn't afford to lose that.

She didn't want to be so vulnerable again. She *couldn't* be. Not for herself and especially not for her baby.

So she swallowed the emotions pushing through her chest and up her throat at the way Matteo was staring at her and forced her tone to be airy as she said, 'I thank you for the compliment but I've always fancied a new nose.'

'Your nose is perfect.'

'Hardly. How about new breasts? We could do a deal—buy one boob, get one free?'

His expression changed, a wryness spreading over his features, as if he too was pulling himself back. 'I think being pregnant has already done that for you.'

The strange almost melancholic moment broken, he led her down a wide corridor and briskly said, 'I can't show you everything as we have patients in residence and surgeries being performed, but I can show you enough so you get a good feel for what we do here. After all, it will be our child who will inherit it all one day.'

'I hadn't thought of it like that,' she said, startled.

'Once everything's out in the open with the family I'll get a new will drawn up.'

'Really? So soon?'

'Death has no favourites. It can strike anyone at any time.' She knew from the look he gave her that it wasn't the patients he'd dealt with during his residency years he was thinking of but Pieta. 'With us being unmarried I want the peace of mind to know that if anything happens to me, our child will automatically inherit without any protracted legal drama. You should get one done too. We should both do everything we can to protect our child.'

'Okay,' she agreed, knowing it made sense, unbelievably touched at what he planned.

He'd said since the scan that he accepted paternity but his talk about a DNA test, although said in the heat of the moment and soon disregarded, had put doubts in her mind. Only small doubts, but they'd been there, tapping away at her.

This simple deed put those doubts to rest and she could hardly credit the relief sweeping through her.

If this didn't prove he accepted paternity then nothing did.

He believed her.

'We'll have to think about guardians should anything happen to both of us,' he said.

'You have given this a lot of thought.'

'I'm not prepared to leave our child's future to chance.' He pulled a tablet out of his pocket and pressed away at it, saying, 'These are the private rooms the patients stay in post-op.' He put the tablet back in his pocket and opened a door halfway up. 'This one's empty.'

Natasha looked inside. It was like no hospital room she'd ever seen. This was a plush hotel room except more clinically clean.

'Any thoughts on guardians?' he asked, closing the door and leading them on to the end of the corridor. Matteo entered a code into a silver box by the end door. It swung open and they stepped into another corridor with a very different feel to the one they'd just been in. The thick carpets had been replaced with shiny hard flooring, the soft hues of the walls now brilliant white.

'I don't know. If I thought Francesca wasn't going to disown the pair of us, I'd say her.' She only just managed to stop her voice from cracking.

'She might surprise us.'

'Do you really think so?'

'No.'

She sighed. 'Nor do I. We'll have to see how things go and then decide. But definitely not my parents.'

The grimace he gave showed he felt exactly the same way. 'Do they know you're here?'

'No. I haven't spoken to them since the funeral. They know how to contact me if they want anything.'

He stopped walking abruptly. 'They haven't called you?'

'No. I'm sure they'll crawl out of the woodwork when they think Pieta's inheritance has been sorted. In fairness, I haven't called them either.'

His jaw clenched and he breathed heavily. 'Fairness be damned. You don't owe them anything.'

'I owe them my life,' she pointed out, her heart twisting to see the protective anger on his face. She wanted to stroke that face. She wanted to feel those firm lips on hers again. She wanted it so badly it was becoming like a drug.

Sometimes when they talked she would see more glimpses of the man she'd fallen for all those years ago. Her desire for him then had had such purity to it. Her desire had been innocent, a longing to be with him, to be held by him.

'Anyone can create a life,' he said, his voice low, his face edging towards hers. 'We've proved that. It's how you care for the life once you have it that shows the person you are.'

Almost hypnotised by the intensity in his eyes, she felt her face inching closer to his in turn, her lids becoming heavy, moisture filling her mouth as the electricity of anticipation danced over her skin.

There was no purity to her desire now. She'd lost her innocence long before she'd lost her virginity. Now her desire was a living thing inside her that fed on his presence, a battle she fought harder with every day that passed.

She wanted him. She craved him. She couldn't bear to fall into bed with him again and when it was over for him to roll over and swear at the horror of what they'd done. For her own sanity she needed to keep a lid on her feelings for him but it was becoming harder as each hour with him prised it off a little more.

Because what she needed to remember more than anything else was that they had no future together as anything other than parents of their child. She'd had one disastrous marriage and couldn't contemplate another relationship.

Matteo didn't want a relationship with her any more than she wanted one with him. That did nothing to stop the chemistry between them taking on its own life form. That did nothing to stop her lips parting and her eyes closing as the whisper of his breath played over her skin and his scent played in her senses...

A loud bang jerked her back to reality as the large swinging doors they'd almost reached were slammed open.

Natasha stepped back and swallowed hard, managing a wan smile at the two medics who strolled past them, greeting Matteo loudly as they passed.

He ran a hand through his dark cropped hair and stilled for a moment before going through the doors that had only just stopped swinging.

'This is our operating wing,' he said in a gruff voice, resuming the tour. He reached again for his tablet, which she realised through the daze their almost kiss had put her in had all the information he needed about what was happening at that very moment in his clinic delivered to his fingertips. 'We have operating theatres and recovery rooms, everything you'd expect from a normal, functioning hospital.' As he spoke, a nurse in full scrubs walked past talking on a phone and waved at them.

'We leave nothing to chance,' Matteo continued.

'Room seven's empty. You can look from the doorway but I must ask you not to go inside. No one's admitted without scrubs on.'

He opened a door for her.

Natasha peered inside and gaped. This was an honest-to-goodness operating theatre, just like those she'd seen on the television. Except bigger. And shinier.

'I need to sign some papers off in my office and then we'll go and eat. How do you like the idea of eating by the docks?'

She strove to match the casual tone he'd now adopted, to pretend that they hadn't nearly just locked lips. To pretend her mouth didn't still tingle and her limbs didn't feel weak with longing for him. 'As long as a seagull doesn't try and steal my chips.'

'You want chips?'

She was glad to think of something that didn't involve his hands running all over her body. 'Yes. A big bag of chips. And a big American club sandwich.'

'Then that is what you shall have.'

They were back in the reception area, heading up a different corridor. The door at the end had Matteo's name on it.

He unlocked it and she followed him inside.

Like the rest of the clinic, his office was scrupulously clean.

'Do you see clients in here?' she asked, looking around, keen to look anywhere but at him, not when her heart was still pounding beneath her ribs.

'Those that I take on personally, yes.'

'Do you perform many surgeries yourself?'

'Not as many as I used to do. The business has gotten so big it takes all my time. I make sure I do enough to keep my skills sharp.'

He sat behind his desk and pulled a stack of papers from a tray. 'This should only take me ten minutes. Help yourself to coffee—there's decaf if you want it.'

She could sense him avoiding her gaze as much as she was avoiding his.

'I'm good, thanks.'

Needing to keep her gaze away from him, Natasha passed the time by looking round his office, at the shelves crammed with medical texts, the walls lined with his qualification certificates. His certificate from medical school still bore the name Matteo Pellegrini.

She hesitated before asking something she knew had been a majorly important decision in his life. 'Why did you change your surname?'

CHAPTER EIGHT

From the corner of her eye Natasha saw the nib of Matteo's pen hover over a sheet before he pressed it down and signed it, then placed it on the fresh pile he was making. 'Because I no longer wished to be acknowledged as my father's son.'

'It got that bad?' Their relationship had never been the same since the childhood fire that had ruined both little boys' lives.

'Don't pretend you don't know, *bella*. I'm sure you were told all the details.'

'Are you talking about the argument you two had at your brother's funeral?'

He jerked a nod and signed another form.

Pieta had asked her to go to Roberto's funeral with him. It had been one of the only times she'd ever denied him anything he'd asked of her. She'd stood her ground doggedly, pointing out she'd never met Roberto and that seeing as it was going to be such a small, intimate funeral, it would be inappropriate for her to be there. Pieta hadn't wanted her there for support—he hadn't seen Roberto in years—he'd wanted her there for appearances' sake. Even back then she'd known that. Appearances be damned, she'd thought; she wouldn't put Matteo through it. He would have hated to see her there. It would have made a bad day even more difficult for him.

Thinking back on it, her refusal had been the moment she'd discovered that she did have a spine. She'd found it for Matteo's sake.

'I know you two had a blazing row and that you changed your surname two weeks later. I never knew what the argument was about but I assumed the two events were linked.'

'You assumed? You never asked Pieta?'

'I never asked about you, not to him or anyone. Any news I heard about you came about in general conversation.'

Slowly he turned his head to look at her, his green eyes narrowed.

She raised her shoulders and pulled her lips in before saying quietly, 'I had this fear that if I brought your name up, they'd be able to see through me.'

'What did you think they'd see?'

'The truth about our past.'

And the truth that my feelings for you ran deeper than anything I tried to feel for Pieta.

'Eventually it stopped mattering, but not speaking about you became a habit.'

He stared at her for a long time, so hard it was like he was trying to dig into her mind. Eventually he sighed and dragged a hand down his face. 'At the funeral my father said it should have been me he was burying, not Roberto.'

Her mouth dropped open, utter shock thumping her.

'Seriously? He said that to you?'

'*Sì.*'

'That's *outrageous*. My God, Matteo, I'm so sorry. It must have been the grief talking—he couldn't have meant it.' How could a father say such a thing to a child? Her parents had manipulated her and twisted her emotions to suit their own purposes but never had they wished her dead.

Something sharp clawed into her chest, overlong talons scraping through her heart, making it bleed to imagine what it must have been like for Matteo to bury the brother he loved with one breath and then in the next to hear his own father say he wished him dead.

How could someone be so cruel?

'He meant it. He never forgave me for the fire. I always knew in my heart that he blamed me for it and at the funeral he confirmed it.' Matteo could still hear his father's words in his ear and feel the spittle that had flown from his mouth as he'd delivered his hate-filled words.

They'd buried Roberto under blue skies and warm sunshine, the kind of glorious day his brother had loved for the first eight years of his life but had shunned for the last twenty. He'd hated people seeing the horrific burn scars that had covered his body. He'd refused to look in mirrors, would refuse to enter a room if it had reflective surfaces in it. He'd shunned everyone who wasn't immediate family, only leaving the house for medical purposes. He'd lost all his love for life and become a recluse.

Matteo had said goodbye to his brother, his heart bursting that Roberto's last journey should be so blessed with such glorious weather, grabbing hold of any sign of blessing he could to ease the pain racking him.

Then, as he'd turned from the graveside, his father had snatched hold of his arm and spilled his venom all over him.

'That's *rubbish*.' Natasha looked like she was about

to burst into tears, her face white, her eyes glistening. 'How could it be your fault?'

'I was in charge of him when it happened.'

'You were *ten years old*.'

Somehow Natasha's outrage and upset warmed the coldness that had filled his core as it always did when he remembered that dreadful day.

'I know how young I was and it took a long time for me to accept the blame wasn't mine. It didn't—doesn't—stop the guilt,' he told her slowly. 'Deep down I always knew my father blamed me too and that it was the root cause of our estrangement. I spent twenty years hoping for his forgiveness. I always hoped he would see what I was doing with medicine and be proud of me. I always dreamed of the day he would welcome me back into the fold.' The bitter laugh escaped his mouth again. 'I learned at Roberto's funeral that I would never get it.'

'But *why*? I don't understand. How can he blame you? You were a *child*.' Fat tears shone in her eyes.

Those tears were for him...

Inhaling deeply, he said, 'He left a wilful ten-year-old boy in charge of a wilful eight-year-old. My parents left their two children on their own so they could enjoy a nice long lunch with their friends. To forgive me means accepting his own responsibility for the fire. He lies to himself about it every single day. He's lied to himself now for twenty-five years. He would rather lose two sons than accept his own part of the blame, so if he wishes me dead then to hell with him. When he said what he did at the graveside...something in me snapped. Roberto was gone...there was nothing to keep me there any longer. My last link with my parents was gone. I decided that if I'm not his son and he wished me dead then he didn't deserve for me to have his name.'

'But what about your mother?' she asked with a bewildered shake of her head, her words low and ragged. 'Didn't it upset her when you changed your name?'

'My aunt Vanessa was more of a mother to me than mine ever was and she wasn't even blood. My mother was no better than my father. She allowed me to visit Roberto when my father was away on business but she never stood up for me or insisted, as was her right, that I be allowed back to live in the family home. I was her first born and she washed her hands of me just as he did. Like my father she dishonestly put the blame on me rather than accept her own part in it. So I chose my aunt's maiden name. It felt fitting.'

The tears poured down Natasha's face, her shoulders shaking. Then, so quickly he barely registered her move, she was by his side and taking his face in her trembling hands. She pressed her lips tightly to his, not as a kiss of passion but one that had a clinging desperation to it, her tears splashing onto his cheeks.

Before he could respond or react in any way, she broke away and punched his shoulder, fury now mingling with the distress. 'How could you give it all up?'

'What?' Her sudden turnaround of both conversation and mood had him reeling.

'Your dreams.' She wiped her face furiously but the tears kept coming. 'Your plans to do reconstructive surgery. You keep saying you didn't give it up and only changed career paths but you *did*. You gave up everything you'd worked for. I know you could never have helped your brother surgically but you wanted to help others in the same situation. You *did*. You were so driven and dedicated. It was never about the money for you.' She raised her hands and waved them, taking in the luxury furnishings and the spectacular view he enjoyed. 'It was never about *this*.'

He didn't know what cut through his skin the most, her scornful words or the distress behind them. Both stunned him as much as her tears. Somehow he managed to hold onto his rising temper. 'I wanted to be a surgeon—I *am* a surgeon.'

'A surgeon with his own Jetstream, a yacht and the most expensive property in Miami. You followed the money. Was it to prove a point to your father when being the most brilliant doctor in a generation wasn't enough? You would have been brilliant. I know you would. You had everything there and you threw it away for money.'

'I didn't throw anything away,' he snarled, getting to his feet and kicking his chair back. 'I paid my dues. You know how hard I worked to get through medical school and my residency. I spent over a decade working so hard that there were days I never saw sunlight. I never shirked in my duty, not even when I couldn't feel my feet from standing for so long or when I had to drink gallons of coffee just to keep my eyes open. Yes, I followed the money but so what? Only a fool wouldn't. I developed the lotion for Roberto but it was too bloody late for him. His scarred lungs gave up on him. *Everything* I did was for him but he died, so what was the point? What was the point in working every waking hour when I had nothing to show for it apart from certificates to hang on my wall?

'I saw an opportunity with the lotion to create a skincare range that worked, and I took it. I make no apologies for that. The money I made from it allowed me to open my own clinics, which made me even more money. I've worked my backside off for years so why shouldn't I be allowed to enjoy it? I'm richer than I ever dreamed possible and, yes, it gives me *immense* satisfaction to think of my father knowing of my wealth and not being able to claim any credit for it because I threw away the name he gave me.'

Stark silence fell between them.

Somehow during his vehement rebuttal they'd finished barely a foot apart, close enough for Matteo to see the exact shade of red slowly creeping up Natasha's neck and over her cheeks.

Her tears had dried up and now she simply stared at him with wide eyes that held his for the longest time before a flash of pain raced through them.

Her throat moved before she whispered, 'I'm sorry. I should never have said any of that. I don't know what got into me.'

'Never apologise for speaking the truth. It might hurt but lies are always, *always* worse.' He looked at the light smattering of freckles over the bridge of her nose and brought his face lower to hers, remembering the feel of her lips on his before the torrent had spewed from her.

He'd never known such passion before. He'd had a steady string of women in his life over the years, pleasant interludes in a busy life, a pretty face to be photographed with when he opened a new clinic and used the media for publicity...

Natasha was right that part of what had driven him had been to prove a point to his father. That *had* been conscious, striving to achieve the riches his father had never been able to find, but it was only at that moment he understood there had been another driving force propelling him forward too.

Her.

Every photo posed for knowing it would be all over the media had been taken with *her* image in his head.

She had been with him of every minute of every day, living in his subconscious, the woman who'd thrown away a future that could have been special for them to be with his richer cousin. And only now, years later, did he realise he no longer believed any of it.

He believed her. He believed right down in his soul that she'd spoken the truth when she'd explained how it had been for her. It had never been about the money for her.

'Seven years ago you kept the truth from me,' he said, running a thumb over her cheekbone, unable to tear his gaze from those beautiful blue eyes. 'If you'd found your voice before it was too late who knows how our lives would have turned out? Maybe we would have married each other. Maybe we would have naturally drifted apart. Neither of us can know.'

Leaning to rest the tip of his nose against hers, he continued, 'We're having a child together, *bella*. I might not have liked what you just said but you've found your voice and have learned how to use it, and you can't know how good that is. I spent too many years distrusting and hating you—I don't ever want to return to feeling like that. For better or worse we're going to be tied together by our child for the rest of our lives and the only way we're going to get through it is by always being honest with each other. We will argue and disagree but you must always speak the truth to me.'

Natasha fought to keep her feet grounded and her limbs from turning into fondue but it was a fight she was losing, Matteo's breath warm on her face, his thumb gently moving on her skin but scorching it, the heat from his body almost penetrating her clothes, heat crawling through her, pooling in her most intimate place.

His scent was right there too, filling every part of

her, and she wanted to bury her nose into his neck and inhale him.

She'd kissed him without any thought, a desperate compulsion to touch him and comfort him flooding her, and then the fury had struck from nowhere, all her private thoughts about the direction he'd taken his career in converging to realise he'd thrown it all away in the pursuit of riches.

And now she wanted to kiss him again.

As if he could sense the need inside her, he brought his mouth close to hers but not quite touching, the promise of a kiss.

'And now I will ask you something and I want complete honesty,' he whispered, the movement of his words making his lips dance against hers like a breath.

The fluttering of panic sifted into the compulsive desire. She hated lies too. She never wanted to tell another, especially not to him. But she had to keep her wits about her because there were things she just could not tell because no matter what he said about lies always being worse, sometimes it was the truth that could destroy a life.

But, God, how could she think properly when her head was turning into candyfloss at his mere touch?

His other hand trailed down her back and clasped her bottom to pull her flush to him. Her abdomen clenched to feel his erection pressing hard against her lower stomach. His lips moved lightly over hers, still tantalising her with the promise of his kiss. 'Do you want me to let you go?'

Her hands that she'd clenched into fists at her sides to stop from touching him back unfurled themselves and inched to his hips.

The hand stroking her cheek moved round her head

and speared her hair. 'Tell me.' His lips found her exposed neck and nipped gently at it. 'Do you want me to stop?'

'Matteo...' Finally, she found her voice.

'Yes, *bella*?'

'Don't stop.'

Her words were all the encouragement he needed. His mouth swept across her cheek to find her parted lips and then he was kissing her with such hunger she melted into him.

The fuse relit in an instant. Need burned bright within her, all the desire she'd been suppressing by the skin of her fingers bursting out of her. She wrapped her arms tightly around his waist, her hands reaching up to clasp onto his back as she kissed him back, her tongue darting into his mouth, dancing against his.

And he held her just as tightly. One hand buried in her hair, the other gripping her to him, devouring her as if her kisses were the air he needed to breathe.

When he broke it and let go of her she almost cried a protest but then he took her face in his hands and rubbed both thumbs across her cheekbones as he stared intently into her eyes. 'I'm not making love to you here.'

Love...?

Although she knew his words weren't meant in the terms of what love itself meant, something in her heart broke free regardless, taking all the air from her lungs.

Only when she'd found her breath did she whisper, 'Then take me home.'

The drive back to Matteo's home passed in a blur. What had been a relatively short journey into downtown seemed to halve, Matteo driving his powerful car to the limit, weaving in and out of the traffic, his jaw clenched, his focus very much on the road before them. Only his right hand, holding hers tightly on her lap as he navigated the roads, showed any awareness of her beside him.

When he pulled into the garage what felt like only minutes later, Natasha shook her head, amazed to find she could remember nothing about the drive. All she'd been able to focus on was their kiss, replaying it in her head, her lips still tingling, her body still experiencing the hard pressure of his body pressed against her as if he'd imprinted himself on her.

As soon as he stopped the car, Matteo leaned over and kissed her again, a deep, heady kiss that sent her head spinning all over again.

'*Dio*, *bella*, you're driving me out of my mind,' he muttered into her mouth before pulling away to get out of the car.

On legs that felt as if they were new born, Natasha stepped out too. He was by her side in an instant, taking her hand and leading her up the steps of the garage and into the empty house.

She'd never been upstairs and where before she'd wondered a lot about what she would find there, she now found she didn't care, not even when she followed him up the hidden staircase. All she could see at that moment was Matteo. She refused to think about anything else.

But then they stepped into his bedroom and she gasped at the beauty and simplicity of it. It was so *clean* but without being clinical, huge without being oppressive and bathed in light that softened the high walls and gave it such a romantic feel that she felt her belly melt all over again.

She looked at Matteo to find his gaze very much on her, his jaw clenched as it had been during the drive back.

Stepping to him, she reached up to palm his cheek and stare at the face she'd adored for so many years it seemed she'd gone to sleep with it in her mind every night for ever.

He breathed deeply before reaching out to gently brush a fallen lock of her hair away from her eyes.

It was at that moment she realised she'd never got over losing him.

The pain she'd felt when hearing of his father's rejection and wish for Matteo to have been the son that had died had cut as deep as if it had been personally directed at her. Whatever choices Matteo had made with his life since they'd dreamed of building a future together all those years ago, it didn't change that fundamentally he was the best man she'd ever known.

He was the father of her child and she couldn't have chosen a better man for it if she'd been given a list with a thousand names on it.

Was this love? she wondered, dazed at the notion. Or was it just hormones from the pregnancy and a strong case of lust? Whatever it was, the need inside her for him was too strong to even want to fight it any more, not when the green eyes staring back at her were molten with his own unmistakable desire.

And then he hooked an arm around her waist and pulled her flush against him and his hot mouth was back on hers and they were kissing as if they could feed from the other.

Their lovemaking the night they'd conceived their child had been born of a passion fuelled by pain and anger, an old longing that had been kept locked away, out of sight and mind, only to erupt with vengeance at the first opportunity.

This time, as Matteo lifted her into his strong arms to carry her to the bed, the flames had lit to burn as brightly as they had then but this time there was a sense of wonder and a complete sense of rightness.

In a melee of arms and legs, he laid her down, just as he had before but with a tenderness beneath the passion.

When he kissed her, it was with a slow, tempered hunger that was only broken when his hands found the hem of her dress and he pulled it up to take it off her, then smoothed her dislodged hair before kissing her again.

Raking her hands into his short curly hair, Natasha sighed as his lips trailed down her neck, shivered as they brushed over her collarbone.

He bent his head lower, reaching her sensitive breasts that were already much heavier than the last time they'd made love. Kissing each one over her lacy bra, he rested his chin between them and looked at her. 'You're beautiful, you know that, *bella*?'

She swallowed, not wanting to think of all the beautiful women she'd seen him photographed with over the years.

'I mean it.' There was an intensity in his eyes that matched the intensity in his voice. 'No one can hold a candle to you.'

Matteo saw the doubt flicker in her eyes and wondered what Natasha saw when she looked in the mirror. He remembered her jests earlier in his clinic, words said, he knew, to detract from the spell that had woven around them, but there had been something underlying it.

Did she really not see how beautiful she was? Did she really not know that just listening to her voice was enough for his loins to tighten?

Raising himself up, he climbed off the bed and stripped his shirt off and divested himself of the rest of his clothes, her eyes following his every movement.

Only when he was naked did he get back on the bed and trail his fingers from her neck all the way to the line of her knickers, delighting in the way she quivered at his touch.

There was such innocence in her responses that he found hard to get his head around. On the one hand her responses were ardent, her need and hunger for him as visible and as open as a man could wish for, but now, gazing at the almost naked form of the woman he'd dreamed about for years in the hazy daylight, he could believe he was the first man to have ever seen her like this.

Placing a hand behind her back, he lifted her so he could undo the pretty bra hiding her breasts from him. As the lacy material loosened to free her, she tilted her head back and sighed.

The first time they'd made love had been in the dark. Now he could see her perfectly and she was even more perfect than he had imagined. Had her nipples always been that dark or was that the pregnancy working its magic in her?

Dipping his head, he took one into his mouth, eliciting another sigh from her.

As he'd done the first time, he kissed every inch of her, but this time he took it slowly. He wanted to savour it, savour her, to learn everything about her that he could, to find the zones that provoked the loudest gasps and the sharpest digs of her nails into his skin. When he hooked a finger to the side of her knickers, she wriggled beneath him, helping him pull them down her thighs and legs before he threw them with the rest of their discarded clothes onto the floor.

The heat he found in her most feminine part blew his mind and when he brushed over the soft hair and rubbed a thumb over the centre of her pleasure, her eyes widened and a moan flew from her mouth. Keeping a steady pressure with his thumb, he slowly slid a finger into the damp heat. She moaned again and arched her back, her hair falling like a waterfall onto the pillow.

Dio, he had never known anything like this. He could make love to her for ever.

He kissed the softly rounded belly then kissed lower to replace his thumb with his tongue, inhaling the musky sweetness he would gladly bottle and keep on him always.

Her little sighs of pleasure deepened and she whispered his name. Before he could finish what he'd started she wriggled beneath him and sat up, pouncing on him so she straddled him, her arms locked around his neck and her hands cradling his scalp as she fused her lips to his with a hunger that sucked the air from him.

Then she touched and kissed him everywhere, just as he had done to her, his shoulders, his arms, his stomach, his thighs, his aching erection, her mouth leaving a trail of heat on his skin that fired his blood to a level he'd never imagined. And in the fever with which she so beautifully caressed him was a reverence, almost as if she were exploring him with wonder in her heart side by side with the passion that drove them both.

He felt his flesh could burst open to admit her into *his* heart.

Gripping her waist, he manoeuvred them both so she straddled his lap and her legs were wrapped around his waist.

Their lips locked together, he placed a hand flat on her back and laid her back gently, the tip of his burning arousal finding the place it so badly needed to be. Then he entered her, slowly, tenderly until he was burrowed deep inside her tight heat.

The sensations that enveloped him threatened to make him come in an instant and he had to grit his teeth to keep himself in check. Only when he was certain he had himself under control did he start moving.

But, *Dio*, every long thrust built the sensation up to unimaginable levels, every moan and pant from her lips, every scratch of her nails, all combined to make him lose himself in the rapture that was Natasha.

Only when the moans breathing into his mouth deepened and the hand holding onto his buttock gripped tightly and he felt her thicken around him did he finally let himself go with a groan that came from the very centre of his being, plunging so deeply into her that he no longer knew where he ended and she began.

When the explosive pulsations inside him had dulled to a gentle buzz he shifted his weight a little so as not to crush her.

Immediately her arms tightened around him and she raised her face to bury it in his neck.

'If you regret what we just did tell me now so I can prepare myself before I have to look at you again,' she whispered into his skin.

His chest contorting to remember how he'd reacted in the immediate aftermath of their first time together, he held her securely in his arms and rolled onto his back, taking her with him. 'No regrets,' he whispered back, stroking her hair.

How could he regret that? Something that special could never be looked on with regret.

Her small hand groped for his and squeezed and she nuzzled into his chest with a sigh. 'I don't regret it either.'

'Good.' He brought her hand to his lips to kiss it. 'No regrets.'

'No regrets,' she echoed.

CHAPTER NINE

THEY STAYED IN bed until the sun began its descent. They'd made love again and, just as she drifted off, he asked if she was hungry. The mention of hunger was enough to make Natasha's stomach growl and remind her that they'd skipped the lunch he'd promised her.

He laughed and got out of bed. What looked like an ordinary wall had turned out to be a walk-in wardrobe. He disappeared into it, reappearing with a pair of tan shorts on, leaned over to kiss her firmly and said he was going to call a chef from the staff quarters to make them something.

Happy to have a few minutes alone to relive every beautiful moment in her head, Natasha burrowed her face into his pillow seeking his scent.

Making love to Matteo the first time had been an explosion that had detonated itself. This time it had been...

It had been incredible. He'd been so passionate and yet so tender. There had been a connection between them she could never have put into words but it filled her heart with such hope.

But hopes of what? A future together? Him and her and baby makes three?

She grabbed his pillow and pulled it over her head.

One incredible afternoon in bed together did not

make a future. It just made complications and there were enough complications in her life for her to be getting on with.

That didn't stop her waiting impatiently for his return.

When twenty minutes passed without him coming back to the room, concern began to nibble at her. Fishing in the pile of discarded clothes for her dress, she slipped it over her head, intent on searching for him. But no sooner had she stepped out of the room than apprehension suddenly suffused her.

What if he'd left the bedroom and become filled with recriminations again? What if she'd been lying in his bed waiting for his return while he'd been overcome with angry remorse and was trying to think of a way to kick her out and back to the guesthouse?

What if she'd been lying on his bed feeling that she'd slipped into a blissful dream and he'd come to the conclusion that he'd slipped into a nightmare?

She found him in the vast living space she'd been so enamoured with in her first visit there. He was sitting at the table, his long legs stretched out before him, talking on his phone.

He gave an apologetic smile and held out a hand to her.

Her relief was almost dizzying.

It was also terrifying.

She let her fingers drift to touch his and took the seat beside him, her heart thumping madly, her palms suddenly clammy.

Making love like they had had changed everything.

His eyes fixed on her, he continued his conversation, his Italian too rapid-fire for her to keep up. She'd never mastered the language, another regret in her life. It had such a beautiful cadence to it and in the days when she and Matteo had been planning a future together, she'd imagined him teaching her his language.

It had never occurred to her to ask Pieta.

When the call was over, Matteo put his phone on the table. 'That was Daniele. He wants to go back to Caballeros with me at the end of next week.'

She closed her eyes. All the euphoria of their love-making, which even her panic about Matteo finding regrets hadn't been able to fully quash, left her. 'Next week? And we'll go to Pisa after?'

'Yes. Next Friday. I'll charter a plane for you and meet you there. It makes more sense than me flying back to Miami to collect you.'

Natasha felt the panic welling up in her and fought hard to stifle it. 'At least that gives us almost two weeks to prepare. Do you think he has any suspicions about us yet?'

Saying the word 'us' felt different from all the other times she'd said it. This time it felt real.

'Daniele takes things at face value so I doubt it.'

She mustered a smile. 'I never got to know him that well. Not like I did Francesca and Vanessa.'

'You're speaking of them in the past tense.'

She met his eyes. 'When they learn about us and the baby my relationship with them will be in the past.'

'Yes. And so will mine.' His admission was like a long, drawn out sigh but then he leaned forward in his chair and stroked her face, staring intently into her eyes. 'There's going to be a lot of pain but we will handle it together. You and me. I won't let them hurt you.'

'It's not me I'm worried about.'

'I know it isn't.' He brought his face close to hers. 'We'll get through this, okay?'

His lips brushed hers, a gentle, soothing caress that

loosened a little of the anguish looping inside her at what they faced and the destruction they were going to cause.

Matteo's words of comfort helped a little but did nothing to ease the guilt that cramped her at what he was going through or the guilt at what she was keeping from him.

A loud cough from the other side of the room broke the moment.

The youngest of Matteo's chefs walked in carrying a tray with two plates covered in silver lids on it.

'Thanks, Leon,' Matteo said. 'Sorry to impose on your night off.'

'No worries. I'll hang around in case you need anything else.'

'If I need anything I'll get it for myself. Take a couple of hundred from petty cash and take your girlfriend out.'

Leon's face lit up. 'You're sure?'

'Sure I'm sure. Pay for any cab on the staff account.'

Leon saluted and scarpered before Matteo could change his mind.

'That was generous of you,' Natasha said, finding she could smile again.

'He was prepared to give up his night off. He's the generous one. Now let's see what we have.' He leaned over the table and lifted the lid off her plate and then the lid off his own to reveal plates heaped with thick-cut English-style chips and thick club sandwiches that managed to be artfully presented.

'You remembered,' she said in delight.

'I'm like an elephant.' He winked. 'In more ways than one. And eating here rather than by the docks guarantees your chips won't be stolen by seagulls.'

She couldn't help but laugh.

'That's better,' he said approvingly before his features

became serious. 'I know it's going to be hard but there's no point in worrying about what's going to happen when we tell them. It's beyond our control. We'll deal with it when the time comes.'

Knowing he was right, she picked up her sandwich and bit into it. 'It's lovely,' she said when she'd swallowed the second bite down. And it *was* lovely. How could it not be? He employed world-class chefs who could make an ordinary sandwich taste as if it had been touched by magic. Everything he owned was the best.

A few minutes later Matteo had wolfed his plate clean and sat back lazily to watch her eat.

As if her eyes were magnets drawn to him, she was helpless to stop from staring back at him.

When she couldn't manage another bite she pushed her plate to one side and took a sip of the juice he'd poured for her.

'You've had enough?' he asked.

She nodded.

'Can I get you any dessert?'

'Can you cook?'

'No.' He grinned. 'I can get one of the local restaurants to deliver.'

She laughed. 'Honestly, I'm full.'

Just as he was about to lean in for another kiss, his phone vibrated across the shiny surface of the table.

Matteo debated ignoring it but knew he couldn't.

That's what came of having a business that spanned the globe, he thought ruefully, swiping to read the message that had come in. Your time was rarely your own.

Today had been an exception, one he felt he should make a regular thing. He rarely worked evenings but his days were always full.

'It's from Francesca,' he said, reading the message.

'She wants to know how I'm getting on with equipment and staffing levels for the hospital.' He rolled his eyes. 'I would have thought her new fiancé would have distracted her from ordering everyone around.'

Her answering grin showed she knew there was no malice behind his observation of his bossy cousin.

'How are you getting on with it?' As she asked, Natasha topped both their glasses up with more juice.

'I've ordered most of the equipment but I'm coming up short on the staff.' Matteo had promised to send his own medical staff to work there for a month to get the hospital up and running, giving them time to recruit permanent medical staff and train local Caballerons to do the auxiliary work.

'What are you going to do about it?'

'I don't know. I'm offering incentives but…'

'Nobody wants to work in such a dangerous country even if Aguadilla and the Dominican Republic are close enough to fly to,' she finished. She scrunched her nose and looked at him. 'Did you really expect it to be any different?'

'What do you mean?'

'You employ doctors and nurses who've turned their backs on healing patients. They're hardly humanitarian sorts.'

'My staff *are* healers,' he refuted. 'They're dedicated professionals.'

'They're professionals,' she conceded. 'But if they ever had ideals they've traded them for money. Your clinics are specifically tailored for the filthy rich. Your surgeons are some of the top earning professionals in the world.'

He hated that she was right. He hated that she must put him in the same bracket. He hated that she was right to.

Like him, the surgeons he employed had paid their dues in the long years of their residencies. Like him, they and the other clinicians he employed had gone into medicine for noble reasons.

She tilted her head and narrowed her eyes as if she was thinking. 'What kind of incentives are you offering? More money, like Daniele's done with his construction staff?'

'Yes. I offered to double their salaries.'

'Forget the money. You want to go for their egos.'

'What do you mean?'

Although she'd only minutes ago declared herself full, she helped herself to a cold chip from her half-empty plate. 'Tell them there will be lots of media at the opening of the hospital like there is when you open a new clinic, and that there's a good chance they'll be interviewed about it and that the world will laud them for their self-sacrifice and humanity. I bet they'll rip your arm off to go there if they think they could make the cover of a magazine off the back of it.'

He shook his head and bit back a laugh. 'I can't believe I didn't think of that.'

'So you think that *could* work to incentivise them?' She looked rather stunned, as if she hadn't thought her idea would pass muster.

'It's a great idea. I've got lots of contacts in the media; we should get in touch with them and get some interest going.'

'I can do that. I did promise Francesca I would take care of the publicity for it and until now I've barely thought about it.'

'I'll get a list together for you. I warn you, it's a long list so you might find it easier to work from my study.'

Her eyes widened. 'Really? You wouldn't mind me working in there?'

'Why should I? Most of my contacts are involved with the fashion and film industry side of the media so it's unlikely to interest them, but they should be able to give you other contacts to speak to about it.'

'Why are your contacts from the fashion and film world?'

'Because the people who come to my clinics and use my skincare range are generally people seeking to emulate what they see on the catwalk and the big screen, whether it's by buying a fifty-thousand-dollar handbag or making improvements to their skin.' He saw the flicker of distaste wrinkle her nose and added, 'That's not all we do, although I can appreciate why you would think it is. When I opened my first clinic I deliberately targeted that market, but the work we do, it's not all breast lifts and tummy tucks and people who want a new nose for cosmetic reasons. We also deal with cancer survivors; women who've had mastectomies and come to us because they know we'll reconstruct their breasts to look so natural that no one would know they weren't real, people who've lost half their noses because of a malignant mole...all sorts of people. It's not all vanity.

'But I do employ the best and I pay them accordingly and charge my clients accordingly for it. We've grown quickly and gained a reputation as the best for a reason—because we *are* the best at what we do. Yes, my staff have enormous egos but they earned them. They worked as hard as I did to become as skilled as they are now, and now they're reaping the rewards for all the dedication and commitment they gave for all those years.'

Her eyes never left his face while he explained the

facts of the situation, delivered because of a compulsion for her to understand.

When he was done a wry smile played on her lips. 'I'm sorry if I came across as judgemental.'

'Don't be,' he urged. He took her hand and kissed it. 'I meant what I said. Always be honest with me. Always tell me the truth. I don't know what's happening between us. I don't know if there ever will be an "us" in the real sense of the word but I know we owe it to ourselves and our child to explore it and see if it leads anywhere, but that can't happen unless we trust each other. I want to trust you, *bella*.'

'I trust *you*,' she admitted in a whisper, those vivid blue eyes huge. He thought he detected fear in them.

What did she have to be fearful about…?

'But what if it doesn't work?' she continued in that same low voice. 'What if the past—'

'Then we deal with it,' he said, cutting her off. 'The past is done. It's the future—our future, our baby's future—that matters. We can make a whole list of what-ifs but neither of us knows what the future holds.' He took a long breath, unable to believe he was having these thoughts and having this conversation with the woman he had so recently despised with every fibre of his being.

But he didn't hate her any more, and as he was the one demanding complete openness and honesty, he had to be honest with himself and admit that his feelings for her had consumed him since the day he'd first set eyes on her. One way or another, she had always been with him.

'Let's just take it a day at a time.'

'One day at a time?'

'One day at a time.'

Her answer was to shift onto his lap, wrap her arms around him and kiss him.

* * *

The most delicious swirling sensation was happening on Natasha's belly. It took a few moments to realise she wasn't in the middle of a dream.

Slowly she opened her eyes to find Matteo propped on an elbow looking at her and trailing his fingers over her naked stomach.

His lips curved into the sensual smile that made her heart skip before he leaned down to brush a kiss on her mouth.

'What time is it?' she asked sleepily. The sun was up but the light filtering into the bedroom was still hazy.

'Seven.'

'Shouldn't you be gone?' He had a full day of surgery booked in at his clinic and then he was flying to Los Angeles to conduct interviews for a new general manager for one of his stores in the morning. He'd promised to be back in time to take her out to dinner tomorrow night.

In the week since they'd become lovers it would be the first time she'd slept without him.

In four days he would fly to Caballeros.

In five days they would be facing the music.

'I should, yes.' He brushed another kiss to her lips. 'Something much more important caught my attention.'

'Oh?'

He circled one of her breasts with his forefinger. 'I was looking at the changes the pregnancy's made to your body.'

'And?' She was barely three months but the changes were there.

'And they're beautiful.'

'Will you still think that when I'm waddling like a duck and covered in stretch marks?' she asked, trying to make her voice jokey, not wanting to admit her fear that the coming changes would be enough to turn him off her.

He rolled on top of her, his erection pressed right at the apex of her thighs, and gazed deep into her eyes. 'Whatever changes the pregnancy makes will only make you more beautiful. Do you know why?'

She shook her head.

'Because every stretch mark and all the other things that come with it will be visible proof of the life you've nurtured. And I'll tell you something else…' He slid inside her and with a groan said into her ear, 'You'll still be the most beautiful woman in my eyes.'

CHAPTER TEN

NATASHA'S PHONE RANG and she dived into her bag, which she'd laid by her feet, glad of the distraction.

In twenty minutes Matteo would be leaving to fly to Caballeros. She read the message and bit her lip.

'Who's that from?' he asked, leaning over and helping himself to a slice of toast from the spread that had been laid out for their breakfast.

'My mother. She wants to know if I've heard from Pieta's lawyers.' She fired a quick message back.

'Is she after money?'

'Probably. They're going to have a fit when I tell them I'm not taking any of it.'

'Are you still set on that?'

'More than ever. I spoke to the lawyer in charge and told him I want it to go to the foundation.'

'When was that?'

'Yesterday when you were at work.' He'd gone to New York for a day-long business meeting. Instead of staying in his Manhattan apartment he'd flown the six-hour round trip to be home in time for bed. 'Sorry, it was an impulsive thing. I never got the chance to mention it to you.'

He shrugged. 'I'm not your keeper, *bella*. So you want all the inheritance to go to the foundation?'

'Every penny. When I think how much work it's been this week for us to drum up press interest and change your staff's minds about working there for a month it brings home how important a healthy bank balance is for the foundation.'

The day after they'd become lovers, Matteo had come home from work with a printout of all his media contacts. Natasha had snatched at it, delighted to have something she could get stuck into for the long periods of time she was alone.

As he'd promised, Matteo set her up in his office so she could work. He even gave her the password for his computer. At first she'd sat in the office feeling like an intruder, her mind fleeing back to the day she'd returned from her brief honeymoon, already knowing she'd made the biggest mistake of her life. Her new husband had turned to her and said his study was his private space and off limits to her. She'd known throughout their long engagement that Pieta craved his privacy but to be excluded from a room of the house she was now supposed to call a home had been yet another kick in the teeth. She hadn't suspected then that the worst kick was still to come.

Matteo never made her feel like a nuisance. He never made her feel that she was intruding in his space. Living with him felt natural.

With increasing confidence, she'd made the calls. As Matteo had suspected, a memorial hospital being built in one of the most dangerous countries in the world was not something that interested his glamorous contacts in the media. However, they'd been generous enough to point her in the direction of editors at the more high-brow end of the media and they *had* been receptive to the idea of covering the story, expressing enough of an interest that Matteo had been able to send a memo to his clinical staff worldwide telling them of the media presence that would be in Caballeros. As a result, over two dozen surgeons and nurses had signed up to spend a month there when the hospital opened. It wasn't as large a number as they'd hoped for, but it would be enough.

It felt good to know that whatever happened between them and the Pellegrinis, they would have played their part in the memorial for Pieta.

'You knew that already surely?'

'The only involvement I had with the foundation was attending the fundraisers and press events with Pieta.' She'd offered to become more involved. If she couldn't work then she'd wanted to be able to do something useful but Pieta had always resisted. His reluctance for her to work had extended to his foundation and she'd had to wait until they'd married to discover why he'd been so loath for her to have any involvement in the running of it other than as an adornment on his arm when he required.

She dropped her phone back in her bag and looked at Matteo. For the first time in her life she lived with someone who made no demands on her or tried to bend her to his will. For the first time in her life she lived with someone who treated her as an equal and a person in her own right. For the first time she lived with someone who wanted to please *her*.

That didn't stop her heart thumping as she braced herself to say, 'I wanted to ask you a favour.'

'Sure.'

'You don't even know what it is yet,' she chided.

'I don't need to know.' He stood behind her chair and put his arms around her waist. She leaned back into him, thinking how right this felt. How right they felt.

'Your guesthouse, can I do it up?'

He stilled. Clearly it was the last thing he'd expected her to ask.

'Please? It's a brilliant space but it's crying out for the interior to be pulled up to the same high standard as in here.'

'And you want to do that?'

'Yes. If you'll let me.'

'How much do you want me to pay you?'

'Nothing. But if you like the end result, you can recommend me to your friends.'

He moved away to take the seat next to her and poured himself a black coffee. 'You want to work?'

'Yes. I want to do what I always said I would do and build my own interior design business.'

'What's brought this on?'

'You sound surprised.'

He looked bemused. 'As far as I'm aware, you've never worked. I thought you liked being free.'

'Well, I don't.' She knew where that idea had come from. Pieta. It's what he'd always said to justify keeping her shackled to him financially. And she, stupidly desperate to please, had let him. 'I always wanted to earn my own money but it was never an option for me. Our baby's due in six months. That gives me time to make a decent go of things. If it turns out that I'm not any good at it then so be it, at least I will have tried.'

'Why was working never an option for you?'

'Pieta wanted me to be available whenever he needed me. A career wasn't compatible with that.'

The bemusement fell from his face, his eyes fixed on hers with that look that always made her feel he was trying to read her mind. Which he probably was.

Eventually, his lips pursed together, he nodded. 'You

are sure about this? You're ready to start building a career for yourself now?'

'Yes.'

'Then you have my support. Go ahead. Do the guesthouse up as you want.'

'That's it? No questions about what I want to do or if it fits in with your own vision for it?'

He shrugged. 'I got Daniele to design a guesthouse so I could have my privacy if I had guests stay. Other than that, I've no interest in it. I'll make you a signatory on one of my accounts so you can spend whatever you need on it and hire whatever tradespeople you need. Pay yourself a wage too. I've been thinking about setting you up with an allowance anyway...'

'I told you, I don't want to be paid for it and I certainly don't want an allowance from you.'

'Pieta gave you an allowance.'

'And it made me feel like a child being given pocket money in exchange for good behaviour.'

The longer she and Matteo were together, the closer they were becoming. There were times she simply ached to confide the truth to him. Matteo demanded honesty above everything else and knowing she was keeping something so fundamental about Pieta from him had settled like a permanent weight in her stomach. She had to keep reminding herself why it had to be like this when the doubts crowding in her head became too much. All she had to do was remember the devastation she'd felt when she'd learned the truth to stiffen her spine against confiding in him. However bad it had been for her, the truth would feel a thousand times worse for Matteo. He'd loved Pieta. They'd been as close as siblings.

But all this didn't mean she couldn't be honest about

the rest of her marriage. Matteo deserved that much from her.

'Before we married I lived in an apartment bought in his name that was never mine. I'm sick of feeling that I'm living on handouts. I'm living under your roof and eating your food—I haven't contributed a penny to anything since I've been here. Doing up the guesthouse for you is one small way that I can contribute and it also gives me the chance to cut my teeth on a project and see if the potential I was told I had at university is really there in me.'

Matteo swallowed back a boulder that had lodged in his throat.

Pieta hadn't wanted her to work. He'd given her an allowance that had made her feel like a child...

Pieta had been his cousin and his best friend but Matteo hadn't been blind to his faults. He'd been arrogant and aloof with an air of superiority born from being the eldest son of an old and noble family and knowing from the moment he could speak that one day it would all be his. But for all that, Matteo had always assumed Pieta would treat the woman he fell in love with like a princess.

He'd always been convinced Natasha's feelings for his cousin had been less than genuine, that it had been the money she'd been attracted to and not the man. It had made him furious to think of her playing with Pieta's emotions to her own advantage but had always assured himself that Pieta was a grown man. If Natasha didn't make his cousin happy he wouldn't be with her.

Now Matteo could see he'd got it all the wrong way round.

The question he should have been asking himself was

whether Pieta had ever made *her* happy. Had he ever made Natasha feel like a princess?

It stabbed at his chest to suspect that the answer was no.

Matteo got out of the car and gazed at the shell of the hospital, astounded at the difference since his last visit there.

Daniele stood beside him and grinned. 'What do you think?'

He shook his head. When he'd last been here the site had been cleared and ground workers had been digging the foundations. Now there stood a sprawling building, unmistakably a hospital, complete with roof and windows. 'Has Francesca seen it?'

'Not in the flesh. I've been sending her updates and pictures of every stage.'

As Daniele spoke a tall, handsome man built like a brick wall strode towards them. Felipe Lorenzi, the security specialist originally hired to keep Francesca safe in this mostly lawless country and now designated the task of keeping Daniele's construction workers and soon Matteo's medical staff safe. He was also the man who'd captured Francesca's heart and would shortly be marrying into the family.

With a pang, Matteo wondered if he would be invited to the wedding. Or would he be cast out of their lives as his parents had cast him out of theirs.

He looked at his watch. Natasha would be boarding her flight to Pisa. In a few hours he would get back on his jet and meet her there. Daniele was taking his own jet back to Pisa too and had already offered a bet over whose pilot could get them there first. His cousin was oblivious to the destruction that was going to be rained down on them all the next day.

But now was not the time to be thinking of that. He had the shell of a hospital to inspect and related issues to discuss. He'd stolen Pieta's wife. He would not ruin his memorial too.

Francesca Pellegrini yawned widely and shoved the box she'd been packing to one side. In two days she would be moving from Pisa to Rome, into the beautiful house her fiancé had bought for them to live in.

He didn't waste time, she thought with a smile. When Felipe wanted something to happen, he was prepared to move mountains to achieve it.

Deciding to take a break before packing anything else, she made herself a coffee and unlocked her phone. One of her guilty pleasures was reading online gossip sites. Unbeknownst to Daniele and Matteo, it was how she'd been able to keep track of their love lives over the years. She preferred for them to think she was all-knowing.

The top stories were about the latest Hollywood divorce, which, being a huge film buff, interested her greatly. Before she could tap on it for more salacious details, a story lower down the page caught her eye.

Her finger hovered over the link for a moment before she took a deep breath and clicked it.

There wasn't much in the way of text, the story mostly comprising photos. The subjects were at a beachside café eating ice cream. The man's face was directly in the frame and unmistakably Matteo. He was leaning forward to wipe ice cream from the mouth of the woman he was with, whose face was mostly hidden from the camera's lens. The second picture showed him leaning in to kiss the part he'd just wiped.

Her blood chilling, she enlarged the first picture, trying to see the woman more clearly, even though her thumping heart already knew who she was. She would recognise that honey-blonde hair anywhere.

The teardrop diamond earring twinkling under the bright Miami sun was the clincher. Natasha had worn those very same earrings at Pieta's funeral.

After staring at the pictures for so long her eyes began to sting and blur, Francesca snapped into action.

'Daniele?' she said when he answered his phone. 'I'm sending you a link. Prepare yourself. You're not going to like what you see.'

Only when Matteo was certain they'd inspected everything that could be inspected and discussed everything that could be discussed did he say they should call it a day.

As they were walking out of the hospital into the blazing Caballeron sun, Daniele paused to answer his phone.

'What?' he said, then took the phone from his ear and stared at it with a bemused expression. He looked at Felipe. 'Your fiancée is a complete drama queen.'

'Francesca?' Felipe asked, concern knotting his forehead.

'Do you have another fiancée?' Daniele jested. 'Oh, here's the mysterious link she thinks I need to prepare myself to look at.'

Watching Daniele open the link, a powerful sense of foreboding settled in Matteo's gut.

When he saw his cousin's eyes crease and dart to his face and then dart back to the screen in his hand, that foreboding deepened.

He just had time to register the darkest, ugliest expression he'd ever seen on Daniele's face before he was slammed into the wall.

Matteo had never been in a fight before but he kept himself fit and had reflexes that could put a boxer to shame. Pure survival instinct had him wrenching himself out of Daniele's stranglehold but the moment he was free, a flying fist connected with his cheek. He punched back, heard and felt the sound of crunching bone, pulled his elbow back to throw another but something as hard as granite attached itself like a vice to his wrist, rendering it immobile.

It was Felipe's hand.

Anyone else and Matteo would have been able to throw them off but Felipe was ex–Special Forces and knew how to use his body as both a weapon and a shield.

'What the hell are you two playing at?' he blazed before saying over his shoulder, 'If you take another step, Daniele, I will knock you out myself.'

But Daniele was already dusting himself down, staring at Matteo with pure loathing, seemingly oblivious to the blood pouring from his nose.

Breathing heavily, trying to get air into his winded lungs, Matteo stared back at the man who'd treated him like a brother, and heard himself say, 'She's having my baby.'

Daniele took a step back, his face contorted, then raised his hand. 'Don't say another word. Don't ever speak to me again. You are no cousin of mine. You're dead to me.'

In silence, Matteo and Felipe, who'd released his hold on him, watched Daniele stagger away and into the car that was supposed to take them all back to airport.

After too long a time had passed, Felipe said quietly, 'I'll get one of my men to collect us.'

'Thank you,' he muttered. 'You should go back to Pisa too. Francesca will need you.'

A meaty hand slapped him on the back in what he guessed was supposed to be a gesture of comfort before Felipe walked away to make the call.

Matteo knew he deserved no comfort and with another twist in his gut he remembered that at that moment Natasha was on a flight to Pisa, ignorant that the explosions they'd expected to deal with tomorrow had already detonated.

The jet Matteo had chartered for Natasha lacked the personal touch of his private jet but was still beautifully apportioned and the cabin crew were all brilliant people who couldn't do enough for her.

So soothing did she find the flight that after a good lunch shortly after take-off, she found her eyes getting heavy and went to sleep. After a four-hour nap she woke to find a dozen missed calls from Matteo but no message.

Cold dread coiled in her belly.

She called him back but reached his own voicemail and had to wait for an hour in nerve-shredding silence before her phone rang again.

'What's wrong?' she asked as soon as the phone was to her ear.

'They know about us.'

The line was terrible, the crackle of interference making it hard to hear. She put a finger to her other ear to try and drown out the background noise of her own flight. *'What?'*

'They know. The paparazzi took a shot of us when we went for lunch at Miami Beach.'

She whistled lowly and rocked forward, coldness filling her head.

They couldn't know. Not like this. Oh, this was awful.

'Natasha?'

'I'm still here.' A loud burst of interference crackled over the line. 'Matteo?'

'Listen to me,' he said, his voice raised, his tone clipped. 'Wait for me at the airport. Don't go anywhere. I'll be landing soon after you. Just wait.'

And then the line went dead.

Scrambling through her phone, a quick search found the pictures Matteo must have been talking about. The headline would have made her laugh if she didn't think she was going to be sick. 'Dr Dishy Serves Icy Treat to New Love.'

Her name wasn't mentioned, which was one small mercy, and her face was mostly hidden. But anyone who knew her well would recognise her. Her family. Pieta's family. They would all know it was her smiling mouth Matteo was wiping the ice cream from and her lips he was kissing.

She'd known that telling Pieta's family would be difficult, especially the part about the pregnancy. She'd known it would be even more difficult for them to hear it. The last thing she'd wanted them to think was that she and Matteo had embarked on a carefree affair with no consideration for the man they'd just buried. These pictures… It could only be worse if they'd been pictured dancing on Pieta's grave.

If there had ever been any hope of forgiveness these pictures had ended it.

Natasha had bitten her nails as a child, a habit finally broken by her mother smearing strong mustard over them. If she had still been biting them then by the time her plane landed she was certain there would be nothing left of them.

They landed in the early morning, the sun only just waking in the frigid cloudless sky.

Coming from the balmy heat of Miami, the dramatic change in temperature was a shock to her system and she was glad of Matteo's reminder to take something warm to change into for her arrival.

Once she'd cleared security she found a seat with a good view of all arrivals and waited.

An hour later he appeared.

Covering her mouth in horror, she got to her feet.

Impeccably dressed as always, in a dark grey suit covered with a lamb's wool overcoat, it didn't detract from his red cheekbone and puffy eye.

She went straight into his arms and held him tightly before tilting her head to look at him more closely. 'What happened?'

'Daniele.'

She closed her eyes and buried her head in his chest, felt his own arms wrap around her and hold her just as tight. 'I'm so sorry,' she whispered.

'So am I.' He rested his mouth on the top of her head, his warm breath swirling through her hair. 'Did you see the pictures?'

'Yes. I had no idea they were being taken.'

'Neither did I.'

'Your poor face.'

Unwrapping his arms from her, he took her face in his hands. 'It looks worse than it is. I think I've broken his nose.'

She turned her cheek to kiss his palm. 'Is he okay?'

'He will be.'

'What do we do now?'

'Now we go back to your house and get some sleep.'
That had always been the plan. Natasha needed to pack
the last of her stuff and deal with lawyers and all the
other things needed to make a clean break.

'Shall we still go and see them later?'

His face tightened. 'Francesca messaged me. They
don't want to see us.'

Her message had been emphatic, Matteo recalled,
his lungs tightening.

He'd known from the second Natasha had appeared
white-faced at the door with the pregnancy test in his
hand that he was going to lose his family but he hadn't
known how deeply the wound would cut...

He blinked, surprised at his own thoughts.

How had he known that when he'd managed to convince himself for two weeks that the chances of him
being the father were negligible?

*But you did know. You knew in your heart that you
were the father.*

Kissing her mouth, he rubbed his nose to hers. 'We're
both exhausted. Things will seem better once we've
slept.'

Just having Natasha back in his arms already soothed
a little of the pain.

CHAPTER ELEVEN

THE HOUSE HAD A COLD, unlived-in feeling that Matteo felt as soon as he closed the front door behind them.

Past the reception room, they went into the day room. The antique bureau in the corner was piled high with post.

'Are you okay?' he asked, rubbing Natasha's back. There had been visible apprehension on her face when they'd pulled up outside the house and now she seemed to have withdrawn into herself.

She looked at him and nodded, her smile rueful. 'It feels strange being back here.'

'Not what you expected?'

She rubbed her arms. 'It feels like I never lived here.' Then she blinked and seemingly snapped herself out of the melancholy. 'I'm going to make a hot chocolate before we go to bed. Do you want one?'

'Hot chocolate sounds good to me.'

She disappeared into the kitchen, leaving him to look around the gleamingly magnificent room. He recalled her saying once that everything here was Pieta's, remembered his own impression of the house that it had all seemed to match Pieta's personality.

There was nothing here of Natasha. His own house in Miami…it was like she'd imprinted herself into the walls. She fitted.

She didn't fit here. She didn't belong here.

This house was like a museum for antiquities.

He brushed his fingers over the surface of the bureau and as he wondered what century it was from, the postmark of the top envelope in the pile of post caught his eye.

Taking hold of it, he looked more closely, trying to comprehend why there should be a letter addressed to Mr and Mrs Pellegrini from Paris's leading fertility clinic. It was postmarked two days before Pieta's death, and from all the marks and stamps on it had been forwarded in recent weeks from Pieta's apartment in Paris.

'I hope you didn't want sugar added to yours,' she said, coming back into the room.

He spun round to find her carrying two steaming mugs, which she carefully placed on coasters on the antique coffee table.

'What's this?' he said.

'What's what?' She took the envelope from him, her hands stilling when she too noticed the postmark and the name of the clinic it had been sent from.

'Aren't you going to open it?'

She looked up at him, the colour draining from her face. There was definite apprehension in her eyes.

'Open the letter,' he commanded.

Still she didn't move, the apprehension now replaced with a hint of fear.

Snatching it from her hand, Matteo ripped the envelope open. Inside were two sheets of paper. He gave one sharp shake to unfurl them, and began to read.

He had to read them three times and even then it still didn't make sense.

'You were going to have fertility treatment?'

Her throat moved and her lips parted but no sound came out.

He held the first sheet up for her to see. 'This is a letter confirming an appointment in the New Year for you to begin fertility treatment and this…' he held the second sheet up '…is the confirmed price list. The letter also confirms that Pieta's sperm test results came back as normal.'

And still she didn't say anything, her eyes huge with an expression he recognised.

It had been the look she'd given him all that time ago when he'd asked the last time she and Pieta had been intimate together. It was the look she gave when she was trying to think of an answer when the truth should simply fall from her tongue.

He rubbed his hand over his head, trying to dull the thuds pounding in it. 'Why were you going the IVF route to conceive a child? This letter confirms Pieta's fertility and we both know you're fertile. You were only married for a year. Pieta himself told me you two only started trying after your wedding—that's too short a time to start thinking you might have fertility issues…'

He checked himself and blew a puff of air out. None of this made sense. None of it.

'Natasha, I need you to be honest with me. Why would a young married couple without any fertility issues like you and Pieta put yourselves through the quagmire that is IVF?'

Her features had clenched so tightly she looked as if she could snap.

'I can't tell you,' she whispered, her head shaking with increasing violence.

If she had simply turned around and said they had both been too impatient to try any longer without intervention he could have possibly accepted that. But she hadn't and her answer made his stomach lurch to his feet.

'If I mean anything to you, if our *child* means anything to you, then you *must*. I deserve to know the truth.'

The colour that had faded from her came back with a vengeance, staining her cheeks, but there was also a sudden calmness about her as if she'd decided to stop fighting the demons and confront them instead.

'If I tell you, you can't tell anyone.'

'What?'

'This is important. You have to promise me.'

A big warning light was flashing, telling him to drop it, telling him it wasn't too late to just stop this conversation and go to bed, that whatever had happened in her marriage to his cousin was none of his business.

But he couldn't listen to it. The nagging feeling about their marriage had become as loud as the siren playing and now, with the door to it prised open, all he needed was to push and the truth would be revealed.

'If that's what it takes to get the truth from you then, yes, I give you my word.'

She raised her chin and looked him square in the eyes. Then she cleared her throat and said, 'Pieta was gay.'

Matteo's first instinct was to laugh. It ripped out of him, echoing off the walls, and then soaked into the silence.

As if Pieta had been gay. It wasn't possible. He'd known him all his life, for thirty-five years. They'd been best friends, cousins, brothers... If Pieta had been gay then the moon really was made of cheese.

Natasha hadn't moved. There wasn't the hint of a smile on her face.

His laughter died as abruptly as it had begun.

'You're lying.'

'No,' she said softly, compassion in her eyes and in her voice. 'I'm not. I'm sorry but *he* lied. To all of you. He was gay.'

'I don't believe you,' he said flatly. 'I don't know why you would tell such lies but it's—'

'I'm not lying,' she cut in. 'We couldn't conceive naturally. He couldn't do it with me.'

It was the way her voice caught when she said, *he couldn't do it with me* and the bleakness in her eyes that made him wonder...

No. She couldn't be telling the truth. He would have known.

Feeling his legs could collapse beneath him, he sank onto the nearest armchair and rubbed again at his head. 'If—and I'm not saying I believe you—but *if* Pieta was gay, why didn't he tell anyone? Why the charade of pretending to be something he's not?'

While Matteo could feel the fabric of his life crumbling around him, Natasha seemed to grow stronger, compassion almost glowing out of her skin.

'Because he knew from before he could talk that he had to marry. It was drilled into him his entire life. It was in the terms of the trust for the Pellegrini estate. You know what it says and it's been the same for hundreds of years—the eldest son inherits but only if he's married. He could never admit who he was. He didn't admit it to himself until he was in his early twenties. He'd been groomed since birth to be the heir and it was a responsibility he took very seriously.'

'And you knew this?'

She shook her head and slumped onto the armchair close to his. 'Not until we got married. He wanted to wait until our wedding before we became physical with each other. I thought he was old-fashioned...'

'Wait, you had no intimacy until you were *married*? You were engaged for six years.'

'We kissed but nothing more.'

'And that didn't set alarm bells ringing?'

'It should have done but, to be honest, it was a relief.' She grimaced. 'He was a gorgeous man but I never felt proper attraction to him, not like I always felt for you. I always hoped that when it came to it, something would switch on inside me. Maybe it would have. I don't know. I was a virgin. I didn't know what I should be feeling…well, I had an idea, of course I did, but… In the end it didn't matter. He couldn't do it.' She inhaled and looked at the ceiling. 'It was painful and embarrassing for both of us but more so for him. I was the first failure in his life.'

Not once in the past seven years had Matteo allowed himself to imagine them in bed together. Now he felt he could easily vomit.

His cousin, his best friend, had lied to him for ever.

And she had lied too.

Dio, after everything they had been through, she'd been lying to him when she knew how important honesty was to him, when she knew how hard it had been for him to trust her again.

'Why didn't you tell me?' he asked roughly.

Her eyes found his, her expression unwavering. 'I was protecting you.'

Anger bubbled like lava so strongly in his veins that he couldn't even speak.

She'd been protecting him? That was the excuse she was going to use to negate her lies?

She took a cushion and pressed it protectively to her belly, as if trying to muffle their voices from their developing child's ears. 'I had to keep the truth about him to myself. I knew it would devastate you. You, his mother, his siblings…you all loved him. Francesca idolised him. How do you think they would feel if they knew the truth?'

'What, that he was nothing but a liar?'

'Exactly that, yes. He kept the most fundamental part of himself a secret. If they learned that now…can you imagine it? If they learned he had never trusted them enough to tell them the truth about himself? When I learned the truth it almost destroyed me. I gave everything up for him. You. A career. Even my own thoughts. Everything I'd believed about him, all my hopes for the future…all destroyed. How could I put them through that? How could I put *you* through that?'

Matteo concentrated on breathing, refusing to look at her deceitful face a moment longer.

How did that old saying go? Fool me once, shame on you; fool me twice, shame on me.

Well, Natasha had fooled him twice. The first time he could forgive himself for.

This time he should have known better.

'Answer me this,' he said, keeping his voice under control by a hair's breadth. 'If Pieta *destroyed* you, why didn't you leave him?'

'Where would I have gone? Back to my parents who'd manipulated me into the mess? I had nowhere to go, no money, no job. He'd seen to that. He'd even sold my apartment so I couldn't go back there. I'd been in Pieta's power and at his beck and call for so long that I couldn't see a way out.'

Natasha closed her eyes. The pain and anger vibrating from Matteo tore at her heart. To learn the man he'd regarded as a brother had been a manipulative bastard and a liar could not be an easy thing to accept. This was everything she'd been trying to protect him from.

'Why the hell did you agree to have a baby with him? Why agree to embark on something as physically painful as IVF for a man you hate?'

'He offered me a child in exchange for my freedom…'

'*What?* And you agreed to that?'

She could almost taste the disgust in his voice.

'No! Please, Matteo, I know you're upset…'

'Right now I am feeling many things but *upset* is not one of them.'

'I understand, I really do—I've been there. Why do you think I chose to keep it a secret? I didn't want to destroy your memories of him, especially when he's not here to justify or defend himself, but please, let me finish.'

'Go ahead. Finish your justification of how you would even *think* of bringing a baby into a relationship like that.'

'It took him months to make me even consider it. He made me many promises; that he would divorce me when the law allowed, that I would have primary custody, that he would buy a house for me and our baby to live in and put it in my name, all sorts of promises.'

'And you believed that after all the lies he'd already told you?' he sneered.

'Things changed between us. The truth being out in the open meant there was nothing left to hide. I knew I would never have another relationship—after what he'd done to me, how could I trust another man?—and I still wanted a baby, very much, so in the end I decided there could be no harm in going to the fertility clinic to discuss what it entailed. That was a week before he died.'

'So you *had* decided to go ahead with it.'

'No.' A wave of sadness flooded through her veins. 'When we got back to Pisa, he was so smug about it all. He took it to be a foregone conclusion that I'd agreed. I realised then that nothing had changed. He still thought he could manipulate me. I could never have trusted his promises.'

'How did he take it when you told him?'

'I never got the chance. The hurricane in Caballeros struck and he went into full-blown humanitarian mode, which for Pieta meant working around the clock with his foundation.' She looked at him, wishing he would meet her eyes. 'And I'm glad of it. I'm glad he died thinking we would have a baby together. I'm glad he died happy.'

With a sigh that could have been a groan, Matteo put his head back and closed his eyes, breathing heavily.

Sliding off the armchair, she knelt by him and put her hands on his thighs. His only reaction was to clench his jaw.

It hurt more than she could decipher to see the pain on his face.

Gently, wanting to take as much of the sting away as she could, she said, 'I know none of this is easy but he kept only one part of himself from you, nothing else. He was still a brilliant lawyer and humanitarian. He was still the man you played late-night poker with over a bottle of bourbon. He was still the man who supported you and was there for you when things became so intolerable in your home that you moved in with his family. Please, don't forget that. None of that was a lie.'

'Do *not* defend him to me.'

'I'm not.' She covered his hand that had clenched in a fist. 'He was a manipulative bastard but that doesn't take away the good things about him. It's not black and white. He was still human. In the end I came to feel sorry for him.'

His burst of laughter was guttural and bitter. 'He dangled you on a string for seven years and trapped you into a farce of a marriage and you felt sorry for him?'

'He trapped me, yes, but he was trapped too. He couldn't be with the man he loved. He'd trapped himself so tightly he could never be free to live his life as nature intended for him to live it.'

He moved his fist from under her hand and pressed his fingers into his forehead. 'I was your first, wasn't I?'

With a sigh she bowed her head. 'Yes.'

'A part of me knew that. I sensed it. I knew... I knew but I couldn't believe because I didn't see how it could be possible.' His fingers moved up to knead into his scalp, his knuckles white under the pressure. 'You let me believe he could be the father of our child.'

His eyes snapped open and met hers. There was a cold steeliness in them that sent shivers racing up her spine.

'I'm sorry,' she whispered.

"I'm sorry," he mimicked. Then, before she could blink, his face twisted and he leapt to his feet. In quick strides he was at the fireplace where a row of antique English pottery sat on display. Swiping his arm across it, he sent them all smashing to the floor.

'*Sorry* does not make things all right,' he snarled. 'You have had weeks, *months,* to tell me the truth.'

Ripping an old oil painting off the wall, he slammed it on the bureau so hard it split, then swiped it over the large pile of post, sending envelopes fluttering in all directions.

'I never lied to you...'

'You were covering his deceit!'

'No, that wasn't it at all,' she implored, getting to her

feet and holding onto the armchair to keep her shaking legs upright. She'd known he would react badly but it was still incredibly painful to witness his anguish. 'I wanted to tell you the truth, I really did, but I couldn't destroy your memories of him.'

'It's my memories of *you* that have been destroyed!' The lava in his veins erupting all over again, Matteo snatched a still full mug of hot chocolate and hurled it at the far wall. 'Everything we've shared has been a lie.'

'It hasn't,' she beseeched.

'You were a virgin! I have lived with the guilt of us making love on the night of his funeral, the guilt of you having my baby, the guilt of what our baby would do to my family... You have let me live with this guilt when you should have told me the truth after you'd done the pregnancy test...'

'I had a choice to make and I made the one I thought was right. I did what I thought was best...'

'You did what you thought was best for *you*, just as you've always done.'

'How can you *say* that? If I'd ever done what I thought was best for me I would have defied my parents and turned Pieta down. I would have married you.'

'Don't flatter yourself,' he scorned tightly. 'I would have seen through you before it ever got that far. You're a liar. You were a liar then and you're a liar now, but you're too clever to lie outright—you lie by omission because you're too spineless to tell the truth.'

She flinched as if he'd slapped her.

Matteo looked away, hating that his first instinct was to haul her into his arms and apologise.

How could he have been such a fool as to trust her again?

He took in the devastation he'd just wrought, the

shattered pottery and crockery littering the floor, along with the dozens and dozens of unopened letters, the cream wall now splattered with hot chocolate, and felt as winded as he had when Daniele had slammed him into the hospital wall.

He staggered back and propped himself against the bureau.

'You're right,' she said, speaking softly but standing tall, breaking the silence shrouding them. 'I've always been spineless. I've always thought there was something wrong with me. I've never been able to please my parents—I always failed them in some way. I couldn't even make a cup of tea correctly, it was always too strong or too milky. I loved to ride horses when I was young. I won a gymkhana when I was eleven and do you know what they said? Not congratulations like any other parent would have, but that my posture had been off. It was all those little things that wrecked my confidence.

'Pieta was this brilliant man and I was in utter awe of him, and once I'd committed to marrying him I deferred to his wishes, just as I'd always deferred to my parents.' I let him dictate everything because I wanted to please him like I always wanted to please them. He *did* keep me dangling on a string but I have to face the fact that I let him. Then I discovered he was gay...' She sucked in a breath, looking as if she could be sick. 'What did that say about me? A gay man who didn't feel even a twinge of desire for me chose to marry me.'

'He chose you because you were a virgin and would have no one to compare him to,' Matteo said flatly.

'Yes. I see that now. I believe that now because of you.' She swallowed and made a move towards him, then checked herself midstep. 'You are the only person in the whole world who has ever made me feel that I'm good enough exactly as I am. I never thought I could trust another man after what Pieta did to me but there you were, where you'd always been, in my heart. You encourage me. You listen to me. You respect my opinions. You make me feel I could be anything I want to be. You let me be *me*.'

A tiny choking sound came from her throat, a tear spilling out of her eye, but she didn't seem to notice. 'I wish now that I'd told you the truth about Pieta and our marriage when the test came up as positive but I truly did think I was doing the right thing. I wasn't lying by omission. I was protecting you because you loved Pieta and I loved you. I've always loved you. I just wish it hadn't taken me so long to see it. I wish I could go back in time and phone you or email or send a carrier pigeon asking for your help when Pieta first proposed. I wish I'd had the courage then that I have now to fix the mess for myself without thinking I needed your help. I regret so many things but that one is my biggest.'

Matteo's listened to her justification with a chest that steadily compacted on itself and solidified. Almost as if they had a will of their own, his feet moved towards her and his hand reached out to touch her cheek. He brushed the tear away and brought his face close to hers, looking deep into her eyes so she would see as well as hear his every word.

'I understand why you chose Pieta over me,' he said quietly. 'I can see that I should have known from the way you kissed me in the *castello* that night that your feelings for me were true. I should have fought for you. I shouldn't have blocked you and cut all communication between us. I accept the blame I bear for that. It's been hard getting over my distrust and loathing of you these past few months but I did get past it and I learned to trust you again.'

A flare of hope flashed in her returning stare but quickly dampened to trepidation, as if she could read his mind and knew what he was about to say.

He brushed his thumb over her mouth, knowing it would be the last time he ever touched her lips. 'And that was my greatest mistake. I should never have trusted you. I have been living with guilt since our first night together and you could have stopped it. You have let me believe so many lies when you know I cannot bear lies.

'The only thing I have ever asked of you is honesty. You know how much I hated myself for the lies we were going to tell about our child's conception…you were going to make *me* a liar when, if you'd only told me the truth, we could have found a better, more truthful way. When I think of everything we've shared and to think you were keeping this from me…it makes me sick to my stomach. You had so many opportunities to confide in me but you chose not to. You made me trust you again. You chose to let me live with the guilt and for me to keep believing the lies until I dragged the truth out of you.'

'I wanted to tell you but I couldn't,' she whispered.

'What you wanted doesn't mean anything. It's what you did that counts. Your actions. You say you love me but I have to tell you, *bella*, you could say the sky was blue and I'd have to go outside to check for myself. I will never believe another word that falls from your pretty lips. My instincts to cut all communication with you back when you accepted Pieta's proposal have been proven right. I was a fool to trust you again.'

More hot tears fell down her cheek and spilled onto his thumb.

'It had been playing in my mind to ask you to marry

me in the future but now I would rather marry the Medusa than spend another minute with you. The Medusa turned men into stone but you've turned my heart into it.'

'You don't mean that.' Her words were barely audible.

'Oh, but I do. The only contact I will ever want with you will be about our baby.' Dropping his hand from her face, unable to look at her another moment longer, he turned around and headed to the door.

He'd stepped outside—when had it become full daylight?—when she caught up with him and grabbed hold of his arm, forcing him round to face her.

'Don't tell me you're just going to walk away?' The tears that only moments ago had streamed like a waterfall down her face had been wiped away, although fresh tears still glistened.

They didn't spill, though.

'Were you not listening to me? Did I not explain myself clearly enough?'

'You explained yourself perfectly well but that doesn't mean you can just walk away. I've screwed up, I know I have, but we can get through this. What we have is too special to—'

'No, *bella*, what we *had* was special, but like your marriage it was a lie.'

'No, it wasn't and you can't pretend it was. I held back the truth about Pieta but I didn't lie to you. Everything we shared, you and me, that was real and you know it was. I love you and I know you have feelings for me too.' Another tear escaped but she didn't crumple. She kept her grip on his arm, her wet eyes boring at him. 'Please, Matteo, don't leave like this. Don't leave us.'

He had to force himself to remain unmoved. Natasha was the greatest liar he'd ever met. How could he believe anything she said or did again? 'Us?'

'We're having a baby...'

'You think I would leave our child?' he almost spat. 'Let me make this very clear, it's *you* I'm walking away from, not our baby. You should know better than anyone that I would never abandon my own child. I would never do what my parents did to me.'

'Then *stay*. Fight. I know you hate me right now but with a little time we *can* get through this. We're so good together. Our baby deserves to have both of us...'

'I agree.' Covering the hand holding his arm so tightly, he prised her fingers off, but before letting them go he brought his face down close to hers. 'And our baby *will* have both of us. But not together. I will never trust you again, and without that trust you and I have *nothing*.'

And then he let go of her fingers and walked down the steps to the path and to his waiting car.

'You let me go without a fight before, are you really going to do the same again?' she said, not shouting but with a timbre in her voice that made him pause.

He inhaled a breath and clicked his key fob.

'You say I'm spineless but you're the spineless one if you can walk away from something so special.'

He opened the door.

'Go, then.' Her voice had turned to steel with none of the softness his heart always melted for. 'But if you drive away now that's it for us. If you drive away now you can only come back for our child because I won't wait for you. If you're too spineless to stay and fight for us I will not put my life on hold for you. If you drive away then you and I are over for good.'

He got into the car and started the engine.

Numb to his core, he drove away. Before he turned out of her street, he looked in his rear-view mirror. The street was empty.

CHAPTER TWELVE

NATASHA SNATCHED UP her vibrating phone. When she saw it was her father, she didn't hesitate to decline the call. About to throw it back on the table, she stopped herself and took a deep breath.

She couldn't avoid her parents for ever. Between them they'd left over a dozen messages. If she didn't respond soon, they'd get a plane over to Pisa and turn up on her doorstep.

She spent a few minutes trying to get her brain to focus on what she needed to say and then composed a short message confirming that, yes, it was true she was pregnant and, yes, it was true the father of her child was Matteo Manaserro and not her late husband. No, she wouldn't be marrying Matteo. She signed off by confirming she would not be taking any monies from Pieta's estate.

Once the message was sent she breathed a sigh of relief.

Whatever she did next would be wrong in their eyes.

She'd spent twenty-five years trying to please them. Finally, she'd accepted she never would. And finally she found she no longer cared to try.

She wondered fleetingly if they would have the audacity to tap Matteo up for money. If they did she could well imagine the reception they would receive for their efforts.

Her phone vibrated again. This time it was one of the journalists she'd contacted about publicity for Pieta's memorial hospital in Caballeros. She declined the call, knowing she should just turn her phone off. The only people she wanted to hear from were the only ones who hadn't been in contact.

She wished they would, even if only to scream and shout at her. The silence was unbearable. Neither Vanessa nor Francesca would answer her calls. She'd gone to Vanessa's villa but had been turned away by the housekeeper.

Natasha's affair with Matteo was headline news in Italy. The great Pieta Pellegrini's widow falling straight into the arms of his equally rich and famous cousin was too juicy a story to ignore. Luck had finally been on her side—they'd only discovered her identity the day after she'd moved into a new house. Three weeks later she and her new home remained off the media's radar.

Two days after Matteo had driven out of her life, she'd walked the streets of Pisa looking for a job and a cheap place to live. She hadn't wanted to stay in Pieta's house a day longer than necessary. It was the focus she'd needed to carry on. She had a child to think about and refused to cry and wallow in self-pity. What kind of example would that set? No, the only way she could help her situation was by taking control of it and setting out as she meant to go on.

She'd found herself a job in a coffee shop within an hour. She hadn't had as much luck with a cheap home but that problem had resolved itself when she'd returned to the house to find a note pushed through the front door and a set of keys.

It had been from Matteo.

In the space of two days he'd bought a house for her

to live in. The note had made clear it was for their baby's benefit and not her own. When the baby was born he would put the deeds to it in its name. He'd also arranged regular maintenance payments effective immediately.

As much as her pride wanted to throw both the house and the maintenance back in his face, she'd resisted. Her baby deserved a decent place to live. Her new job would keep her going until the baby was born. She wouldn't spend a penny of the maintenance money on herself but her baby had a rich father and it wasn't fair to deprive it out of pride. She wouldn't take anything from him for her own benefit.

She'd hardened herself to him completely. If she was so disposable that he could walk away without a second thought, for a second time, then he didn't deserve her tears. That he visited her every night in her dreams was something she had no control over and something she refused to dwell on. It was safer that way. She needed to keep healthy, emotionally and physically, for her baby's sake. Their baby was their only reason for communication now, a few terse messages exchanged about appointments and scans and their baby's health. She knew she wouldn't see him again until the next scan in the new year. She stubbornly told herself that suited her fine.

But she couldn't harden herself to Vanessa and Francesca. Matteo had kept his promise and kept the truth about Pieta to himself so at least they'd been spared that truth.

Their reaction was nothing she hadn't prepared herself for but it still hurt. A small part of her had hoped they would forgive her. A large part of her still prayed they would.

She hoped they'd come to forgive Matteo too, then chided herself for thinking about him again.

And now, looking out onto the street from the dining room of the house paid for by his money and seeing Christmas lights twinkling from the houses across the road, knowing she was going to spend her first ever Christmas alone, she had to keep reminding herself why losing everyone she loved was for the best.

Matteo rummaged through the minibar of his hotel suite but couldn't find the brand of bourbon he preferred to drink.

About to put a call through to room service, he was interrupted by a knock on his door.

Wondering who the hell could be calling at this time of night, he walked the long length of the living area of his suite to the door. If the alcohol he'd consumed that night had done the job as well as he'd hoped, he'd be asleep by now.

He'd drunk steadily all night in the restaurant he'd taken his clinic staff in Florence to, their turn for him to grace their presence at their annual Christmas party. He'd seriously considered cancelling but knew it would result in a huge blow to morale. Tomorrow, Christmas Eve, he would fly to his apartment in New York and pretend to enjoy the festivities alone.

He couldn't even contemplate spending Christmas in Miami.

He was sick of travelling. He was sick of every place he visited reminding him in some way of Natasha, even countries that didn't have the slightest shred of a link with her. He was sick of the paparazzi following his every move.

From utilising the press shamelessly for publicity to promote his business, he now wanted to obliterate every journalist and paparazzo from the face of the earth.

He wished he'd been so lucky in obliterating Florence from the face of his schedule. Knowing Natasha was barely fifty miles away made it much harder to obliterate her from his mind. This was the city she'd had the scan in and he'd learned he really was going to be a father.

But he *had* already known it in his gut, his conscience insisted on reminding him. He'd known it from the second she'd appeared white-faced at the door with the positive pregnancy test in her hand, and had refused to acknowledge it for fear of what the truth would reveal.

He put his eye to the spy hole and stepped back in shock. Maybe the alcohol had worked better than he'd thought.

He took another look. No, there was his cousin Francesca and her fiancé, Felipe.

Apart from one phone call in which she had called him every name under the sun, Francesca had cut him out of her life, just as Vanessa and Daniele had done. Was this the moment his hot-headed cousin had talked her fiancé into beating him up?

Taking a deep breath first, he pulled the door open a couple of inches.

There were no kicks to batter the door in and neither was there any of the expected acrimony on her face. After a moment of awkward silence, she gave a tentative smile. 'Can we come in?'

He pulled the door open to admit them, bracing himself for a punch in the ribs. But as they stepped into his suite he saw the puffy redness of her eyes.

'What's happened?' he asked, concern immediately filling him.

Felipe shut the door behind them as Francesca said, 'Haven't you seen the news today?'

'I've been avoiding the media.' No papers, no magazines and no internet. He didn't need to read the world's opinion of him. None of it could be worse than his own opinion, which had been getting steadily worse, although he couldn't understand why.

Blinking back tears, she handed him a newspaper that had been tucked under her arm.

He took it from her. Before he opened it he knew what it was going to say.

His instincts were right.

Pieta's secret was a secret no more.

'I'll get us all a drink,' Felipe murmured, while Francesca flopped onto the nearest armchair and wiped away a tear.

'Is it true?' she asked him, her eyes pleading with him to deny it, to say that Alberto, Pieta's right hand man for his foundation, the man now purporting to have been his secret lover for over ten years, was a liar.

He dimly recalled Natasha saying Pieta hadn't been free to be with the man he loved. At the time his head had been reeling too much with the magnitude of everything else she'd said to take that in too.

Taking the seat opposite Francesca, wishing he wasn't about to confirm something that was going to break her heart, he nodded.

'How...?'

'Natasha told me.' Just saying her name hurt.

Francesca's face went white as Felipe appeared at her side. She snatched the glass of liquid from his hand and downed it without looking at it or asking what it was.

She pulled the face of a woman with a burning throat then blew out a long puff of air. 'Oh, my God. She knew. Poor Natasha.' She began to cry in earnest. 'Why didn't he tell us? How could he keep such a thing secret? Did he think we wouldn't love him any more? Or didn't he love us enough to tell us? Didn't he trust us?' Then she leaned into Felipe, who'd handed Matteo a measure of Scotch too before squashing himself onto the single armchair with her, and sobbed into his chest.

Felipe's steady gaze met his. *No lies*, his look said.

There would be no lies from his lips.

It suddenly struck him that his promise to Natasha meant he was now guilty of lies by omission too.

He would have kept that secret without making the promise.

If Alberto hadn't sold his story, he would have taken Pieta's secret to the grave, not for his sake but for Francesca and Vanessa's. Just as Natasha would have done.

Some hours later, when Francesca and Felipe had left, Matteo sat slumped in his hotel room's armchair and stared at the thick carpet.

He'd never been as mentally drained or as emotionally shattered in his life.

But it wasn't the talk of all the secrets and lies his head was full of, it was Natasha.

She'd been with him every minute since he'd left her but saying her name out loud seemed to have opened a sluice in his brain and now he found she was all he could think of. He couldn't rid himself of the urge to call her.

He'd had this urge before, when Roberto had died, a need to hear the soft calming voice that had always had the power to make him feel better. He'd gone into medicine to heal people but in Natasha he'd found the one person who could heal *him*.

He dragged a hand over his face and fought for breath.

He'd thought everything was so clear but it wasn't. He'd been swimming in the fog and now the fog was clearing and his entire life was flashing before him like a reel playing in his head. The happy early childhood ripped apart by the fire, the withdrawal of his parents' affection, the guilt over his brother that had only eased when he'd found the one special person in his life who fully believed in him and who he'd refused to fight for...

Why had that been?

On and on it ran; qualifying as a surgeon, his brother's shame at his scars and refusal to leave the house, his brother's death, his father's venomous words and hatred, changing his name to spite him, creating his empire, every hollow success, Pieta's death, his child's conception, everything forging together into a circle bound by the soft glow of the woman he'd let back into his heart, the woman who'd sucked up all the guilt and fixed all his broken parts without him even realising...

He thought of Pieta and Alberto having to hide and deny their love.

Even if Pieta had found the courage needed to be open and grab the happiness that could have been theirs, death had taken it away from them.

It hit him like a punch in the gut. What he'd done. What his pride and terrified heart had done.

He too had had a chance of happiness.

Natasha had bared her heart and her soul to him and instead of embracing it he'd stamped on it.

She hadn't turned his heart into stone, she'd opened it and moved in.

And he'd thrown it blindly in her face without a backward glance.

Natasha switched the light on in the dark kitchen and filled the kettle. Her early shift at the coffee shop started in an hour and she needed to wake up.

Only a few weeks into her job and already she loved

it. Right then, it was perfect for her. When the baby was born she intended to pursue interior design but for the time being this was just what she needed. It gave her the chance to be with people. She liked seeing shoppers pile into the shop laden with gifts for their loved ones. She liked the smiles, the little conversations conducted in her hesitant Italian, which over the last couple of weeks had suddenly improved by leaps and bounds. She liked the anonymity—if anyone recognised her from the press reports they would dismiss it as an uncanny likeness. She liked the constant smell of fresh coffee. She liked everything about it. She especially liked the reassurance that she wasn't alone in the world. That there *was* a world out there beyond her parents and the Pellegrinis. And Matteo...

Blinking his image away, she reached for a mug, then noticed her phone left on the counter overnight was flashing.

In amazement, she saw she had thirty-three missed calls, forty-nine text messages and over one hundred new emails.

What the heck was going on?

She scanned the missed calls first but there was no number she recognised. It was the same with the text messages until she came to one sent by Alberto.

What she read sent her reeling.

I'm sorry it had to be this way. I couldn't let them trash your reputation any longer. Forgive me for the pain I've caused you.

Gathering her hair together at the nape of her neck, Natasha struggled to control her breathing. She'd avoided all media since her name had been exposed but a quick scan of the internet told her what the apology was for.

She found she couldn't be surprised at what she read. Pieta had once drunkenly confessed to one great love in his life but had refused to name him.

It made sense of the pity she'd often detected in Alberto's eyes when he'd spoken to her through the years. It made sense of his weeping, 'I'm sorry,' when he'd clung to her as she'd said goodbye to him at the wake.

Oh, Alberto, what have you done?

Guilt at his and Pieta's treatment of her had led him to out himself and their relationship. Now the whole world knew.

Now Vanessa and Francesca must know too.

Her eyes fuzzy, her heart sad, she put the phone on the table. She didn't want to read any more. She didn't want to feel that if only she could bounce off the satellites that sent all these calls and messages she would find Matteo and he would make everything better.

Matteo had made his choice and he'd chosen to live without her.

And then the tears she'd blocked for over three weeks burst open again and she laid her head on the table and wept, crying for the love she'd lost, for the love her husband had never allowed to be free and open, and for all the hearts that were breaking.

It was the rap on the front door that cut through her tears.

She hadn't had a single visitor since she'd moved in.

CHAPTER THIRTEEN

APPREHENSION SLOWING HER DOWN, Natasha walked to the door, pulled the chains off then unlocked it and opened the door a crack.

And there he stood. Matteo. On her doorstep, a thin layer of snow falling onto his dark hair and long overcoat.

She pushed the door open wider.

For a long time, nothing was said.

All she could hear was the sound of her frantically beating heart. All her eyes could see was him, as beautifully handsome as he'd been when she'd last seen him. His eyes were bloodshot, though, she noticed. And he needed a shave.

She only just stopped her hand reaching out to touch his face.

Heat rising on her cheeks, the memory of how she'd once given in to the same impulse when he'd turned up at her door the night of their child's conception and then the fresher memory of how he'd cold-heartedly driven away all playing like a concerto in her head, she spun around and headed back to the kitchen.

'What do you want?' she asked, trying to keep her voice civil. However much she wanted to punch him in the face, she had to remember it was his child growing in her belly.

'To make sure you're okay. Have you seen the news?'

'Yes.' She sat herself at the table and looked at him, not inviting him to sit, making sure to keep her features stony and not betray the swirl of emotions rushing through her to see him again.

'Can I sit down?'

'If you want.'

He took the chair on the far side of the kitchen table to her and rubbed at his temples.

'Late night, was it?' she asked in as uninterested tone as she could muster.

'I haven't been to bed yet.'

'Been out partying?'

He sighed. 'No, I haven't been partying. Would you mind if I made myself a coffee?'

'Not at all.'

He pushed his chair back. 'Where is it?'

'I don't have any. I have decaffeinated tea or herbal tea. Knock yourself out.'

'You're not going to make this easy for me, are you?'

'Make what easy? Just tell me what you came here for then you can go on your merry way. There's a coffee shop round the corner you can get your caffeine fix from.'

Matteo had known this visit to Natasha's was going to be hard. After the way they'd parted he hadn't expected her to make things easy for him and he couldn't blame her for it.

She'd laid her heart bare for him and he'd walked away from her.

'I haven't been to bed because I've been up all night, talking to Francesca.'

'Francesca? You've seen her?'

He nodded.

The stoniness on her beautiful face softened a fraction. 'How is she? She knows?'

'She knows.' He closed his eyes. 'She's devastated, just as you said she'd be.'

'And Vanessa?'

'I haven't seen her yet but Francesca and Felipe came to me after they'd been with her.' He swallowed the bile that had lodged in his throat. 'She's in a bad way. They went back to her villa after they left me.'

'And Daniele?'

'I don't know about him. He could be with them too for all I know. I don't imagine he's in a better state than they are.'

She covered her face with her hands and pushed them up to brush through her hair. 'They must be going through hell.'

What could he say to that? Everything Natasha had predicted had come true. She'd known the truth would rip them apart and it had.

The man they'd loved and idolised all his life had not only lied about his sexuality but Alberto's exposé had revealed the truth about his marriage too. They knew their son and brother had married Natasha on a lie so he could inherit the estate he'd so badly wanted.

All their illusions had crumpled in the dust.

To his surprise, Matteo had found himself defending Pieta to Francesca. 'Remember how he was with you,' he'd told her gently. 'Remember the brother who was always there to give you advice and who encouraged you to fulfil your dreams when your parents were set on a different life for you. It isn't black and white. He was still a human and he still loved you.'

They had been so similar to the words Natasha had

used to try and comfort him with that he'd almost choked saying them.

Natasha had kept silent about the lie to protect those she loved when, in truth, she'd been the one hurt the most by it. Pieta had lied to his family but it was Natasha he had lied to and used and diminished for seven years without an ounce of conscience. Matteo could have forgiven him for not confiding the truth about his sexuality—with distance he even understood why Pieta had felt the need to hide it—but he could never forgive him for what he'd done to Natasha. He'd stolen her life.

And he, Matteo, had condemned her for it.

Moving from his seat, he knelt before her, only now taking in the soft white robe she was wearing. She looked different from the last time he'd seen her. Fuller. She looked like a woman on the cusp of blooming with pregnancy.

Whether she would let him be there to witness the dazzling changes soon to come was something he couldn't guess. This was no longer the Natasha who had lived her life wishing only to please the people she loved. That Natasha was still there but with a tougher shell. She'd grown a steely resolve that he couldn't help but admire even though he knew it would make convincing her to take him back that much harder.

But he had to try. He'd let her go twice without fighting for her and if he didn't try now he would spend the rest of his life hating himself and filled with bitter regret.

He took the stiff hand that was on the table and wrapped his fingers around it.

She stilled, her jaw clenching, then inhaled deeply. She didn't look at him.

'When Francesca asked me if it was true about Pieta, I wanted so badly to lie to her and spare her the pain. I should never have condemned you for wanting to spare me and the others that pain, not for a second. I have been living with the truth for barely a month and it's been like a noose around my neck. You've been living with it for so long I can hardly believe it didn't crack out of you sooner. I condemned you for what I considered were your lies of omission when all along you were doing what you always do and protecting the people you love. You have the kindest, purest heart I have ever known and when you told me you loved me I should have got down on my knees as I am right now and thanked God himself for giving you to me.'

Her face changed slightly. The eyes that met his glistened, her breaths deepening, but her mouth stayed tightly pinched closed.

'Do you know what date it is? It's Christmas Eve. Exactly eight years ago I saw you for the first time and something happened in me…it was like you sang to me. I fell in love with you before I'd even heard your voice…'

Now her throat moved and she tried to pull her hand away but he clasped it gently with his other hand too, forming an envelope around it.

'You've always believed in me,' he continued, knowing this was his one and only chance to make things right and that his entire future depended on his next words. 'You've always seen something good in me that no one else could see but I never allowed myself to believe it. It wasn't just my parents who couldn't forgive me for Roberto—I couldn't forgive myself. I knew in my head that the blame wasn't with me but my heart never accepted it, and in my heart I felt I didn't deserve happiness. It was easy to accept you chose Pieta over me when my own parents couldn't stand to be in a room with me, rather than trust in my heart and fight for you because, *bella*, the issue wasn't my trust in you but my trust in myself—can you understand that?

'If I had trusted my heart I would have fought for you but my demons wouldn't let me. There was a part of me that felt I didn't deserve the happiness I knew we would have together. I think I was waiting for you to prove yourself a liar this time round so I could justify to myself how right I was in cutting you off all those years ago because I was too blind to see and accept the truth, not about Pieta but about you and me.'

Her throat moved again and she inched her head forward a little. 'I don't want to hear any more,' she whispered. 'It's too late.'

His heart constricted. 'Maybe it is too late for us. I have to hope that it's not, but if it is then I will respect your decision but, please, let me finish what I came here to say. Let me have that and then I will leave.'

Her eyes closed and she inhaled deeply through her nose.

Sliding his hand around her neck, he pressed his forehead to hers and breathed in the scent of her warm skin. 'I knew something was wrong the night we first made love. I knew in my heart that I was your first but I refused to believe what every nerve and sense in my body was telling me. I was scared of what the truth would reveal, so you see, *bella*, I'm the one who's really guilty of lies by omission because I was too scared to confront what my heart had already told me was the truth.'

She was rigid in his arms.

His chest filling, he pressed his lips to her forehead. 'I'm sorry for hurting you. I'm sorry for every cruel word and deed. I'm sorry for abandoning you. I'm sorry for never fighting for you. I'm sorry for doubting you and for allowing my foolish pride and insecurities to blind me. I wish to God that I'd had the courage to believe in you as much as you believed and trusted in me and I wish I'd had the sense to admit my love for you before I threw it all away.' He found her lips and kissed them with the same clinging desperation she had kissed him with all that time ago in his office. He'd known then, in his heart, that she loved him but had been too blind and untrusting in himself to see it.

And now he had to accept that it was too late.

He breathed her scent in one last time. 'I love you, Natasha. Always know that. If you can never be mine again, know I will always be yours. I will wait for you, for ever if that's what it takes. My heart will always belong to you and the precious life you carry inside you.'

When he pulled away he found her eyes closed and her pale face taut.

He released his hold on her hands and gently stroked her cheek. 'Goodbye, *bella*.'

Natasha knew by the coldness that suddenly enveloped her that Matteo was walking away.

There was a lightness in her limbs and her head, a balloon filled with something undefinable expanding in her chest.

His words reverberated in her ears as his footsteps became more distant.

So many words. So much meaning behind them. So much love and tenderness and pain.

She opened her eyes.

Everything looked different. What had only minutes ago seemed dark was now filled with dazzling light, the surfaces of the kitchen units gleaming, the table she was sitting at shining.

And that dazzling brilliance was in her too.

She looked at the oven clock. She was going to be late

for work, late for the job that had given her her pride and self-worth…

Matteo had already given her those things. She'd proved she could make it on her own. One day she might even be happy. But it was this wonderful man who had loved her and broken her heart who completed her and she knew with utter clarity that if she didn't swallow her new-found pride any future happiness would be stained. The bright colours evoked by his words now would fade to sepia. He was the one who brought colour to her life.

The balloon in her chest, which had been steadily growing bigger and bigger while Matteo had finally opened his heart, suddenly exploded and flooded her with the warmth she had never hoped to feel again.

He *did* love her. And he did trust her.

And then her mouth opened and she was screaming out his name, laughing and crying all at the same time, her unsteady legs racing to catch him.

But he caught her, in the small hallway by the front door, capturing her in his strong arms and holding her so tightly her feet left the floor.

'Don't you dare go,' she said, before finding his mouth and smothering it and his entire face with kisses. 'Don't you dare, don't you dare.'

It was a long time until he put her back down. He took her face in his hands and kissed her, before staring into her eyes, bewilderment and hope ringing from his. 'You want me to stay?'

She smiled her first real smile in so, so long. 'Only if you promise to stay for ever.'

The bleakness that had been etched on his face lifted, wonder taking its place. 'If you'll have me, I will stay with you for ever.'

She covered the hand palming her cheek. 'I will always be yours. I love you. I will always love you.'

He kissed her again, a kiss that conveyed more meaning than any words could. Into her mouth, he said, 'And I will always love you.'

With one final deep kiss, he lifted her into his arms and carried her up to the bedroom, where he proceeded to show her exactly how deep his love for her ran.

EPILOGUE

NATASHA STOOD UNDER the glorious late-summer sun at
the entrance of the Pellegrini chapel at Castello Miniato
and waited for the music that would cue her entrance
to walk down the aisle. Holding tightly to her arm, as
proud as punch to be the one giving her away, stood her
brother-in-law Daniele, now the legal owner of the *castello* and who in approximately one hour would become
her cousin by marriage.

Behind her, flapping the train of Natasha's wedding
dress, was Francesca, taking her duties as chief brides-
maid with a little too much enthusiasm.

The music started and were it not for Francesca deliberately treading on the train to hold her back, Natasha
would have galloped down the aisle. As far as she was
concerned, she'd waited long enough to marry the man
she loved, a man whose greatness had only increased in
her eyes since he'd admitted his love for her. Matteo had
sold his chain of vanity clinics to a hedge fund manager
for an obscene amount of money.

When they returned from their honeymoon he would
be opening a new type of clinic in Miami, a specialist
hospital dedicated to performing surgery on the most
severely disfigured people, adults and children alike.
He would be funding the building and running costs

and staff wages himself. It would be the first of what he planned to be many such specialist hospitals. Natasha would be in charge of the interior design, her brief to make it as homely and comforting as a hospital could be.

Forcing herself to walk sedately, she put one foot in front of the other and beamed her way towards Matteo. By his side stood Felipe, his best man, who, naturally, didn't look once at her as his eyes were too busy fixing on his wife. The Lorenzis had beaten them down the aisle by four months.

She smiled at her parents, sitting in the second row, and wondered if they'd asked Matteo for more money yet. She couldn't find it in her heart to hate them. They might be contenders for worst parents in the world, but they were *her* worst parents in the world and she looked on them as an example of how not to parent her own child. As she and Matteo lived in Miami and her parents were perpetually skint despite the regular large deposits Matteo transferred into their account, she rarely saw them. It was no loss, just as Matteo no longer felt the loss of his own parents. They'd created such a tight family unit of their own they had no need to wish for things that could never be.

The squeals of a bored, grumpy baby mingled with the music. Vanessa, sitting in the front row rocking baby Lauren, smiled when Natasha met her eye and blew her a kiss before attempting to soothe the fractious child.

Natasha blew a kiss back and then aimed one at her two-month-old daughter. As if by a miracle, the kiss landed and Lauren quietened. Or maybe it was Vanessa's magic touch.

Slowly the family had pulled back together, drawing comfort and understanding from each other. Natasha and Matteo had been pulled back into the bosom of the Pellegrini family too, and Francesca and Felipe had been delighted to accept the honour of being Lauren's godparents and guardians.

And then she was at Matteo's side and they were exchanging their vows and sliding on the rings that would cement their love and declare to the world that they did belong to each other and that no one and nothing could ever tear them apart again.

* * * * *

LET'S TALK
Romance

For exclusive extracts, competitions
and special offers, find us online:

 facebook.com/millsandboon

@MillsandBoon

@MillsandBoonUK

Get in touch on 01413 063232

For all the latest titles coming soon, visit
millsandboon.co.uk/nextmonth

MILLS & BOON

THE HEART OF ROMANCE

A ROMANCE FOR EVERY READER

MODERN

Prepare to be swept off your feet by sophisticated, sexy and seductive heroes, in some of the world's most glamourous and romantic locations, where power and passion collide.

HISTORICAL

Escape with historical heroes from time gone by. Whether your passion is for wicked Regency Rakes, muscled Vikings or rugged Highlanders, awake the romance of the past.

MEDICAL

Set your pulse racing with dedicated, delectable doctors in the high-pressure world of medicine, where emotions run high and passion, comfort and love are the best medicine.

True Love

Celebrate true love with tender stories of heartfelt romance, from the rush of falling in love to the joy a new baby can bring, and a focus on the emotional heart of a relationship.

Desire

Indulge in secrets and scandal, intense drama and plenty of sizzling hot action with powerful and passionate heroes who have it all: wealth, status, good looks…everything but the right woman.

HEROES

Experience all the excitement of a gripping thriller, with an intense romance at its heart. Resourceful, true-to-life women and strong, fearless men face danger and desire - a killer combination!

To see which titles are coming soon, please visit

millsandboon.co.uk/nextmonth

JOIN US ON SOCIAL MEDIA!

Stay up to date with our latest releases, author news and gossip, special offers and discounts, and all the behind-the-scenes action from Mills & Boon...

 @millsandboon

 @millsandboonuk

 facebook.com/millsandboon

 @millsandboonuk

It might just be true love...

GET YOUR ROMANCE FIX!

Get the latest romance news,
exclusive author interviews, story
extracts and much more!

MILLS & BOON
True Love
Romance from the Heart

Celebrate true love with tender stories of heartfelt romance, from the rush of falling in love to the joy a new baby can bring, and a focus on the emotional heart of a relationship.

MILLS & BOON
Desire

Indulge in secrets and scandal, intense drama and plenty of sizzling hot action with powerful and passionate heroes who have it all: wealth, status, good looks…everything but the right woman.